Praise for #1 *New York Times* and *USA TODAY* bestselling author Linda Lael Miller

"Ms. Miller's unique way of tempering sensuality
with tenderness in her characters makes them
walk right off the pages and into your heart."
—*Rendezvous*

"Miller excels at creating extended-family
dynamics in an authentic Western small-town
setting and richly populating her stories with
animal as well as human characters."
—*Booklist*

"Miller is one of the finest American writers in
the genre."
—*RT Book Reviews*

Praise for bestselling author Donna Alward

"Great characters bring life to this beautifully
written story that explores trust,
friendship and hope."
—*RT Book Reviews* on
How a Cowboy Stole Her Heart

"Keep your hanky close, Donna Alward
works her storytelling magic to
tug at our heartstrings with
How a Cowboy Stole Her Heart."
—*Cataromance*

LINDA LAEL MILLER

The daughter of a town marshal, Linda Lael Miller is a #1 *New York Times* and *USA TODAY* bestselling author of more than one hundred historical and contemporary novels, most of which reflect her love of the West. Raised in Northport, Washington, the self-confessed barn goddess now lives in Spokane, Washington. Linda hit a career high in 2011 when all three of her Creed Cowboys books—*A Creed in Stone Creek, Creed's Honor* and *The Creed Legacy*—debuted at #1 on the *New York Times* bestseller list.

Linda has come a long way since leaving Washington to experience the world. "But growing up in that time and place has served me well," she allows. "And I'm happy to be back home." Dedicated to helping others, Linda personally finances her Linda Lael Miller Scholarships for Women, awarded annually to women seeking to improve their lot in life through education. More information about Linda, her novels and her scholarships is available at www.lindalaelmiller.com. She also loves to hear from readers by mail at P.O. Box 19461, Spokane, WA 99219.

DONNA ALWARD

A busy wife and mother of three (two daughters and the family dog), Donna Alward believes hers is the best job in the world: a combination of stay-at-home mom and romance novelist. She completed her arts degree in English literature in 1994, but it wasn't until 2001 that she penned her first full-length novel. In 2006, she sold her first manuscript, and now writes warm, emotional stories for the Harlequin Romance line.

In her new home office in Nova Scotia, Donna loves being back on the east coast of Canada after nearly twelve years in Alberta, where her career began, writing about cowboys and the West. Donna's debut Harlequin Romance novel, *Hired by the Cowboy*, was awarded the Booksellers Best Award in 2008 for Best Traditional Romance.

With the Atlantic Ocean only minutes from her doorstep, Donna has found a fresh take on life and promises even more great romances in the near future! She loves to hear from readers. You can contact her through her website, www.donnaalward.com, her My Space page, www.myspace.com/dalward, or through her publisher.

BESTSELLING AUTHOR COLLECTION

#1 *New York Times* and *USA TODAY* Bestselling Author

LINDA LAEL MILLER

There and Now

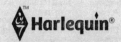

TORONTO NEW YORK LONDON
AMSTERDAM PARIS SYDNEY HAMBURG
STOCKHOLM ATHENS TOKYO MILAN MADRID
PRAGUE WARSAW BUDAPEST AUCKLAND

Recycling programs
for this product may
not exist in your area.

ISBN-13: 978-0-373-18056-1

THERE AND NOW

THERE AND NOW
Copyright © 1992 by Linda Lael Miller

MARRIAGE AT CIRCLE M
Copyright © 2007 by Donna Alward

This edition published by arrangement with Harlequin Books S.A.

For questions and comments about the quality of this book
please contact us at Customer_eCare@Harlequin.ca.

www.Harlequin.com

Printed in U.S.A.

CONTENTS

Dear Reader,

Welcome to the unpredictable world of time travel, one of my personal all-time favorite subjects to write *or* read about.

The idea for *There and Now* and *Here and Then,* the stories of Elisabeth and Jonathan and Elisabeth's cousin Rue and Farley—and their adventures in not just one world, but two—came to me in a memorable way. Long ago and faraway, my good friend Debbie Macomber and I were driving through the countryside, on our way to… somewhere. Truthfully, the destination eludes me, but it was probably a book signing. We were laughing and swapping stories (what we both do best) when we spotted this farmhouse, all alone in the middle of a field of some sort. It was your regulation farmhouse, ordinary in every way, except that there was a door in the second-floor wall— leading nowhere.

I turned to Debbie (I think she was driving) and said, "What if you opened that same door from the inside, and found yourself *in a room?* And not only that—what if it suddenly wasn't now anymore, but a hundred years ago?"

Well, since "what if" is the classic plotting question for writers, we were off and running. The result was *There and Now,* a story about a woman who opens a door just like that one, and finds herself in the Puget Sound area of another time. I hope you'll enjoy both Elisabeth's story and Rue's. I promise, their men are worth loving.

Also, be sure to visit my website, www.lindalaelmiller.com, for excerpts from upcoming books, contests, videos of very sexy cowboys and news of my annual Linda Lael Miller Scholarships for Women program, plus a daily blog.

Be well.

With love,

Linda Lael Miller

THERE AND NOW

#1 *New York Times* and *USA TODAY* Bestselling Author

Linda Lael Miller

Chapter 1

Elisabeth McCartney's flagging spirits lifted a little as she turned past the battered rural mailbox and saw the house again.

The white Victorian structure stood at the end of a long gravel driveway, flanked by apple trees in riotous pink-white blossom. A veranda stretched around the front and along one side, and wild rose bushes, budding scarlet and yellow, clambered up a trellis on the western wall.

Stopping her small SUV in front of the garage, Elisabeth sighed and let her tired aquamarine eyes wander over the porch, with its sagging floor and peeling paint. Less than two years before, Aunt Verity would have been standing on the step, waiting with smiles and hugs. And Elisabeth's favorite cousin, Rue, would have vaulted over the porch railing to greet her.

Elisabeth's eyes brimmed with involuntary tears. Aunt Verity was dead now, and Rue was God only knew where, probably risking life and limb for some red-hot news story. The divorce from Ian, final for just a month, was a trauma Elisabeth was going to have to get through on her own.

With a sniffle, she squared her shoulders and drew a deep breath to bolster her courage. She reached for her purse and got out of the car, pulling her suitcase after her. Elisabeth had gladly let Ian keep their ultramodern plastic-and-smoked-glass furniture. Her books, tapes and other personal belongings would be delivered later by a moving company.

She slung her purse strap over her shoulder and proceeded toward the porch, the high grass brushing against the knees of her jeans as she passed. At the door, with its inset of colorful stained glass, Elisabeth put down the suitcase and fumbled through her purse for the set of keys the real-estate agent had given her when she stopped in Pine River.

The lock was old and recalcitrant, but it turned, and Elisabeth opened the door and walked into the familiar entryway, lugging her suitcase with her.

There were those who believed this house was haunted—it had been the stuff of legend in and around Pine River for a hundred years—but for Elisabeth, it was a friendly place. It had been her haven since the summer she was fifteen, when her mother had died suddenly and her grieving, overwhelmed father had sent her here to stay with his somewhat eccentric widowed sister-in-law, Verity.

Inside, she leaned back against the sturdy door, remembering. Rue's wealthy parents had been divorced that same year, and Elisabeth's cousin had joined the fold. Verity Claridge, who told fabulous stories of ghosts and magic and people traveling back and forth between one century and another, had taken both girls in and simply loved them.

Elisabeth bit her lower lip and hoisted her slender frame away from the door. It was too much to hope, she thought with a beleaguered smile, that Aunt Verity might still be wandering these spacious rooms.

With a sigh, she hung her shoulder bag over the newel post at the base of the stairway and hoisted the suitcase. At the top of the stairs were three bedrooms, all on the right-hand side of the hallway. Elisabeth paused, looking curiously at the single door on the left-hand side and touched the doorknob.

Beyond that panel of wood was a ten-foot drop to the sun-porch roof. The sealed door had always fascinated both her and Rue, perhaps because Verity had told them such convincing stories about the world that lay on the other side of it.

Elisabeth smiled and shook her head, making her chin-length blond curls bounce around her face. "You may be gone, Auntie," she said softly, "but your fanciful influence lives on."

With that, Elisabeth opened the door on the opposite

side of the hallway and stepped into the master suite that had always been Verity's. Although the rest of the house was badly in need of cleaning, the real-estate agent had sent a cleaning crew over in anticipation of Elisabeth's arrival to prepare the kitchen and one bedroom.

The big four-poster had been uncovered and polished, made up with the familiar crocheted ecru spread and pillow shams, and the scent of lemon furniture polish filled the air. Elisabeth laid the suitcase on the blue-velvet upholstered bench at the foot of the bed and tucked her hands into the back pockets of her jeans as she looked around the room.

The giant mahogany armoire stood between two floor-to-ceiling windows covered by billowing curtains of Nottingham lace, waiting to receive the few clothes Elisabeth had brought with her. A pair of Queen Anne chairs, upholstered in rich blue velvet, sat facing the little brick fireplace, and a chaise lounge covered in cream-colored brocade graced the opposite wall. There was also a desk—Verity had called it a secretary— and a vanity table with a seat needle-pointed with pale roses.

Pushing her tousled tresses back from her face with both hands, Elisabeth went to the vanity and perched on the bench. A lump filled her throat as she recalled sitting here while Verity styled her hair for a summer dance.

With a hand that trembled slightly, Elisabeth opened

the ivory-inlaid jewel box. Verity's favorite antique necklace, given to her by a friend, lay within.

Elisabeth frowned. *Odd,* she reflected. She'd thought Rue had taken the delicate filigree necklace, since she was the one who loved jewelry. Verity's modest estate—the house, furnishings, a few bangles and a small trust fund—had been left to Elisabeth and Rue in equal shares, and then the cousins had made divisions of their own.

Carefully, Elisabeth opened the catch and draped the necklace around her neck. She smiled sadly, recalling Verity's assertions that the pendant possessed some magical power.

Just then, the telephone rang, startling her even though the agent at the real-estate office had told her service had been connected and had given her the new number.

"Hello?" she said into the receiver of the French phone sitting on the vanity table.

"So you made it in one piece." The voice belonged to Janet Finch, one of Elisabeth's closest friends. She and Janet had taught together at Hillsdale Elementary School in nearby Seattle.

Elisabeth sagged a little as she gazed into the mirror. The necklace looked incongruous with her Seahawks sweatshirt. "You make it sound like I crawled here through a barrage of bullets," she replied. "I'm all right, Janet. Really."

Janet sighed. "Divorce is painful, even if it was your own idea," she insisted quietly. "I just think it would have been better if you'd stayed in Seattle, where your friends are. I mean, who do you know in that town now that your aunt is gone and Rue is off in South Africa or Eastern Europe or wherever she is?"

Through the windows, Elisabeth could see the neighbor's orchard. It was only too true that most of her friends had long since moved away from Pine River and her life had been in Seattle from the moment she'd married Ian. "I know myself," she answered. "And the Buzbee sisters."

Despite her obvious concerns, Janet laughed. Like Elisabeth, she was barely thirty, but she could be a real curmudgeon at times. "The Buzbee sisters? I don't think you've told me about them."

Elisabeth smiled. "Of course, I have. They live across the road. They're spinsters, but they're also card-carrying adventurers. According to Aunt Verity, they've been all over the world."

"Fascinating," Janet said, but Elisabeth couldn't tell whether she meant it or not.

"When you come down to visit, I'll introduce you," Elisabeth promised, barely stifling a yawn. Lately, she'd tired easily; the emotional stresses and strains of the past year were catching up with her.

"If that's an invitation, I'm grabbing it," Janet said quickly. "I'll be down on Friday night to spend the weekend helping you settle in."

Elisabeth smiled, looking around the perfectly furnished room. There wasn't going to be a tremendous amount of "settling in" to do. And although she wanted to see Janet, she would have preferred to spend that first weekend alone, sorting through her thoughts and absorbing the special ambiance of Aunt Verity's house. "I'll make spaghetti and meatballs," she said, resigned. "Call me when you get to Pine River and I'll give you directions."

"I don't need directions," Janet pointed out reasonably. "You were married in that house, in case you've forgotten, and I was there." Her voice took on a teasing note. "You remember. Rue and I and two of your friends from college were all dressed alike, in floaty pink dresses and your cousin said it was a shame we couldn't sing harmony."

Elisabeth chuckled and closed her eyes. How she missed Rue, with her quick, lethal wit. She drew a deep breath, let it out, and made an effort to sound cheerful so Janet wouldn't worry about her any more than she already did. "I'll be looking for you on Friday, in time for dinner," Elisabeth said. And then, after quick good-byes, she hung up.

With a sigh of relief, Elisabeth crossed the room to the enormous bed, kicked off her sneakers and stretched out, her hands cupped behind her head. Looking up at the intricately crocheted canopy, she felt a sense of warm well-being wash over her.

She would make a list and shop for groceries later, she promised herself. Right now she needed to rest her eyes for a few moments.

She must have drifted off, because when the music awakened her, the spill of sunlight across the hooked rug beside the bed had receded and there was a slight chill in the air.

Music.

Elisabeth's heart surged into her throat as she sat up and looked around. There was no radio or TV in the room, and yet the distant, fairylike notes of a piano still teased her ears, accompanied by a child's voice.

"Twinkle, twinkle, little star
how I wonder what you are...."

Awkwardly, Elisabeth scrambled off the bed to pursue the sound, but it ceased when she reached the hallway.

All the same, she hurried downstairs.

The small parlor, where Aunt Verity's spinet was kept, was empty, and the piano itself was hidden beneath a large canvas dust cover. Feeling a headache begin to pulse beneath her right temple, Elisabeth checked the big, old-fashioned radio in the large parlor and the portable TV set on the kitchen counter.

Neither was on.

She shoved her hands through her already-mussed hair. Maybe her friends were right to be concerned. Maybe the divorce was affecting her more deeply than she'd ever guessed.

The thing to do, she decided after a five-minute struggle to regain her composure, was to get her purse and drive into Pine River for groceries. Since she'd left her shoes behind, she started up the rear stairway.

An instant after Elisabeth reached the second floor,

the piano music sounded clearly again, thunderous and discordant. She froze, her fingers closed around Aunt Verity's pendant.

"I don't want to practice anymore," a child's voice said petulantly. "It's sunny out, and Vera and I are having a picnic by the creek."

Elisabeth closed her eyes, battling to retain her equilibrium. The voice, like the music, was coming from the other side of the door Aunt Verity had told so many stories about.

As jarring as the experience was, Elisabeth had no sense of evil. It was her own mental state she feared, not the ghosts that supposedly populated this old house. Perhaps in her case, the result of a broken dream had been a broken mind.

She walked slowly along the hallway, gripped the doorknob and rattled it fiercely. The effort to open the door was hopeless, since the passage had been sealed long ago, but Elisabeth didn't let up. "Who's there?" she cried.

She wasn't crazy. Someone, somewhere, was playing a cruel joke on her.

Finally exhausted, she released her desperate hold on the knob, and asked again plaintively, "Please. Who's there?"

"Just us, dear," said a sweet feminine voice from the top of the main stairway. The music had died away to an echo that Elisabeth thought probably existed only in her mind.

She turned, a wan smile on her face, to see the Buzbee sisters, Cecily and Roberta, standing nearby.

Roberta, the taller and more outgoing of the two, was holding a covered baking dish and frowning. "Are you quite all right, Elisabeth?" she asked.

Cecily was watching Elisabeth with enormous blue eyes. "That door led to the old part of the house," she said. "The section that was burned away in 1892."

Elisabeth felt foolish, having been caught trying to open a door to nowhere. She managed another smile and said, "Miss Cecily, Miss Roberta—it's so good to see you."

"We've brought Cecily's beef casserole," Roberta said, practical as ever. "Sister and I thought you wouldn't want to cook, this being your first night in the house."

"Thank you," Elisabeth said shakily. "Would you like some coffee? I think there might be a jar of instant in one of the cupboards...."

"We wouldn't *think* of intruding," said Miss Cecily.

Elisabeth led the way toward the rear stairway, hoping her gait seemed steady to the elderly women behind her. "You wouldn't be intruding," she insisted. "It's a delight to see you, and it was so thoughtful of you to bring the casserole."

From the size of the dish, Elisabeth figured she'd be able to live on the offering for a week. The prospective monotony of eating the same thing over and over didn't trouble her; her appetite was small these days, and what she ate didn't matter.

In the kitchen, Elisabeth found a jar of coffee, probably left behind by Rue, who liked to hole up in the house every once in a while when she was working on a big story. While water was heating in a copper kettle on the stove, Elisabeth sat at the old oak table in the breakfast nook, talking with the Buzbee sisters.

She neatly skirted the subject of her divorce, and the sisters were too well-mannered to pursue it. The conversation centered on the sisters' delight at seeing the old house occupied again. Through all of it, the child's voice and the music drifted in Elisabeth's mind, like wisps of a half-forgotten dream. *Twinkle, twinkle...*

Trista Fortner's small, slender fingers paused on the piano keys. Somewhere upstairs, a door rattled hard on its hinges. "Who's there?" a feminine voice called over the tremendous racket.

Trista got up from the piano bench, smoothed her freshly ironed poplin pinafore and scrambled up the front stairs and along the hallway.

The door of her bedroom was literally clattering in its frame, the knob twisting wildly, and Trista's brown eyes went wide. She was too scared to scream and too curious to run away, so she just stood there, staring.

The doorknob ceased its frantic gyrations, and the woman spoke again, "Please. Who's there?"

"Trista," the child said softly. She found the courage to touch the knob, to twist her wrist. Soon, she was peering around the edge.

There was nothing at all to see, except for her bed,

her dollhouse, the doorway that led to her own private staircase leading into the kitchen and the big, wooden wardrobe that held her clothes.

At once disappointed and relieved, the eight-year-old closed the door again and trooped staunchly back downstairs to the piano.

She sighed as she settled down at the keyboard again. If she mentioned what she'd heard and seen to Papa, would he believe her? The answer was definitely no, since he was a man of science. He would set her down in his study and say, "Now, Trista, we've discussed this before. I know you'd like to convince yourself that your mother could come back to us, but there are no such things as ghosts. I don't want to hear any more of this foolishness from you. Is that clear?"

She began to play again, dutifully. Forlornly.

A few minutes later, Trista glanced at the clock on the parlor mantel. Still half an hour left to practice, then she could go outside and play with Vera. She'd tell her best friend there was a ghost in her house, she supposed, but only after making her swear to keep quiet about it.

On the other hand, maybe it would be better if she didn't say anything at all to anybody. Even Vera would think Trista was hearing things just because she wanted her mama to come back.

"Twinkle, twinkle," she muttered, as her fingers moved awkwardly over the keys.

"My, yes," Roberta Buzbee went on, dusting nonexistent crumbs from the bosom of her colorful jersey print dress. "Grandma was just a little girl when this house burned."

"She was nine," Miss Cecily put in solemnly. She shuddered. "It was a dreadful blaze. The doctor and his poor daughter perished in it, you know. And, of course, that part of the house was never rebuilt."

Elisabeth swallowed painfully, thinking of the perfectly ordinary music she'd heard—and the voice. "So there was a child," she mused.

"Certainly," Roberta volunteered. "Her name was Trista Anne Fortner, and she was Grandma's very best friend. They were close in age, you know, Grandma being a few months older." She paused to make a tsk-tsk sound. "It was positively tragic—Dr. Fortner expired trying to save his little girl. It was said the companion set the fire—she was tried for murder and hanged, wasn't she, Sister?"

Cecily nodded solemnly.

A chill moved through Elisabeth, despite the sunny warmth of that April afternoon, and she took a steadying sip from her coffee cup. *Get a grip, Elisabeth,* she thought, giving herself an inward shake. *Whatever you heard, it wasn't a dead child singing and playing the piano. Aunt Verity's stories about this house were exactly that—stories.*

"You look pale, my dear," Cecily piped up.

The last thing Elisabeth needed was another person to worry about her. Her friends in Seattle were doing enough of that. "I'll be teaching at the Pine River school this fall," she announced, mainly to change the subject.

"Roberta taught at the Cold Creek school," Cecily said proudly, pleased to find some common ground, "and I was the librarian in town. That was before we went traveling, of course."

Before Elisabeth could make a response, someone slammed a pair of fists down hard on the keys of a piano.

This time, there was no possibility that the sound was imaginary. It reverberated through the house, and both the Buzbee sisters flinched.

Very slowly, Elisabeth set her coffee cup on the counter. "Excuse me," she said when she was able to break the spell. The spinet in the parlor was still draped, and there was no sign of anyone.

"It's the ghost," said Cecily, who had followed Elisabeth from the kitchen, along with her sister. "After all this time, she's still here. Well, I shouldn't wonder."

Elisabeth thought again of the stories Aunt Verity had told her and Rue, beside the fire on rainy nights. They'd been strange tales of appearances and disappearances and odd sounds, and Rue and Elisabeth had never passed them on because they were afraid their various parents would refuse to let them go on spending their summers with Verity. The thought of staying in their boarding schools year round had been unbearable.

"Ghost?" Elisabeth croaked.

Cecily was nodding. "Trista has never rested properly, poor child. And they say the doctor looks for her still. Folks have seen his buggy along the road, too."

Elisabeth suppressed a shudder.

"Sister," Roberta interceded somewhat sharply. "You're upsetting Elisabeth."

"I'm fine," Elisabeth lied. "Just fine."

"Maybe we'd better be going," said Cecily, patting Elisabeth's arm. "And don't worry about poor little Trista. She's quite harmless, you know."

The moment the two women were gone, Elisabeth hurried to the old-fashioned black telephone on the entryway table and dialed Rue's number in Chicago.

An answering machine picked up on the third ring. "Hi, there, whoever you are," Rue's voice said energetically. "I'm away on a special project, and I'm not sure how long I'll be gone this time. If you're planning to rob my condo, please be sure to take the couch. If not, leave your name and number and I'll get in touch with you as soon as I can. Ciao, and don't forget to wait for the beep."

Elisabeth's throat was tight; even though she'd known Rue was probably away, she'd hoped, by some miraculous accident, to catch her cousin between assignments. "Hi, Rue," she said. "It's Beth. I've moved into the house and—well—I'd just like to talk, that's all. Could you call as soon as you get in?" Elisabeth recited the number and hung up. She thought about calling Rue's cell phone, but didn't want to bother her when she was working.

She pushed up the sleeves of her shirt and started for the kitchen. Earlier, she'd seen cleaning supplies in the broom closet, and heaven knew, the place needed some attention.

* * *

Jonathan Fortner rubbed the aching muscles at his nape with one hand as he walked wearily through the darkness toward the lighted house. His medical bag seemed heavier than usual as he mounted the back steps and opened the door.

The spacious kitchen was empty, though a lantern glowed in the center of the red-and-white-checked tablecloth.

Jonathan set his bag on a shelf beside the door, hung up his hat, shrugged out of his suitcoat and loosened his string tie. Sheer loneliness ached in his middle as he crossed the room to the stove with its highly polished chrome.

His dinner was congealing in the warming oven, as usual. Jonathan unfastened his cuff links, dropped them into the pocket of his trousers and rolled up his sleeves. Then, taking a kettle from the stove, he poured hot water into a basin, added two dippers of cold from the bucket beside the sink and began scrubbing his hands with strong yellow soap.

"Papa?"

He turned with a weary smile to see Trista standing at the bottom of the rear stairway, wearing her nightgown. "Hello, Punkin," he said. A frown furrowed his brow. "Ellen's here, isn't she? You haven't been home alone all this time?"

Trista resembled him instead of Barbara, with her dark hair and gray eyes, and it was a mercy not to be reminded of his wife every time he looked at his daughter.

"Ellen had to go home after supper," Trista said, drawing back a chair and joining Jonathan at the table as he sat down to eat. "Her brother Billy came to get her. Said the cows got out."

Jonathan's jawline tightened momentarily. "I don't know how many times I've told that girl…"

Trista laughed and reached out to cover his hand with her own. "I'm big enough to be alone for a few hours, Papa," she said.

Jonathan dragged his fork through the lumpy mashed potatoes on his plate and sighed. "You're eight years old," he reminded her.

"Maggie Simpkins is eight, too, and she cooks for her father and all her brothers."

"And she's more like an old woman than a child," Jonathan said quietly. It seemed he saw elderly children every day, though God knew things were better here in Pine River than in the cities. "You just leave the house-keeping to Ellen and concentrate on being a little girl. You'll be a woman soon enough."

Trista looked pointedly at the scorched, shriveled food on her father's plate. "If you want to go on eating that awful stuff, it's your choice." She sighed, set her elbows on the table's edge and cupped her chin in her palms. "Maybe you should get married again, Papa."

Jonathan gave up on his dinner and pushed the plate away. Just the suggestion filled him with loneliness— and fear. "And maybe you should get back to bed," he said brusquely, avoiding Trista's eyes while he took his watch from his vest pocket and frowned at the time. "It's late."

His daughter sighed again, collected his plate and scraped the contents into the scrap pan for the neighbor's pigs. "Is it because you still love Mama that you don't want to get another wife?" Trista inquired.

Jonathan went to the stove for a mug of Ellen's coffee, which had all the pungency of paint solvent. There were a lot of things he hadn't told Trista about her mother, and one of them was that there had never really been any love between the two of them. Another was that Barbara hadn't died in a distant accident, she'd deliberately abandoned her husband and child. Jonathan had gone quietly to Olympia and petitioned the state legislature for a divorce. "Wives aren't like wheelbarrows and soap flakes, Trista," he said hoarsely. "You can't just go to the mercantile and buy one."

"There are plenty of ladies in Pine River who are sweet on you," Trista insisted. Maybe she was only eight, but at times she had the forceful nature of a dowager duchess. "Miss Jinnie Potts, for one."

Jonathan turned to face his daughter, his cup halfway to his lips, his gaze stern. "To bed, Trista," he said firmly.

She scampered across the kitchen in a flurry of dark hair and flannel and threw her arms around his middle. "Good night, Papa," she said, squeezing him, totally disarming him in that way that no other female could. "I love you."

He bent to kiss the top of her head. "I love you, too," he said, his voice gruff.

Trista gave him one last hug, then turned and hurried up the stairs. Without her, the kitchen was cold and empty again.

Jonathan poured his coffee into the iron sink and reached out to turn down the wick on the kerosene lantern standing in the center of the table. Instantly, the kitchen was black with gloom, but Jonathan's steps didn't falter as he crossed the room and started up the stairs.

He'd been finding his way in the dark for a long time.

Chapter 2

Apple-blossom petals blew against the dark sky like snow as Elisabeth pulled into her driveway early that evening, after making a brief trip to Pine River. Her khaki skirt clung to her legs as she hurried to carry in four paper bags full of groceries.

She had just completed the second trip when a crash of thunder shook the windows in their sturdy sills and lightning lit the kitchen.

Methodically, Elisabeth put her food away in the cupboards and the refrigerator, trying to ignore the sounds of the storm. Although she wasn't exactly afraid of noisy weather, it always left her feeling unnerved.

She had just put a portion of the Buzbee sisters' casserole in the oven and was preparing to make a green salad when the telephone rang. "Hello," she said, balancing the receiver between her ear and shoulder so that she could go on with her work.

"Hello, darling," her father said in his deep and always slightly distracted voice. "How's my baby?"

Elisabeth smiled and scooped chopped tomatoes into the salad bowl. "I'm fine, Daddy. Where are you?"

He chuckled ruefully. "You know what they say—if it's Wednesday, this must be Cleveland. I'm on another business trip."

That was certainly nothing new. Marcus Claridge had been on the road ever since he had started his consulting business when Elisabeth was little. "How are Traci and the baby?" she asked. Just eighteen months before, Marcus had married a woman three years younger than Elisabeth, and the couple had an infant son.

"They're terrific," Marcus answered awkwardly, then cleared his throat. "Listen, I know you're having a rough time right now, sweetheart, and Traci and I were thinking that… well…maybe you'd like to come to Lake Tahoe and spend the summer with us. I don't like to think of you burrowed down in that spooky old house…."

Elisabeth laughed, and the sound was tinged with hysteria. She didn't dislike Traci, who invariably dotted the *i* at the end of her name with a little heart, but she didn't want to spend so much as an hour trying to make small talk with the woman, either. "Daddy, this house isn't spooky. I love the place, you know that. Who told you I was here, anyway?"

Her father sighed. "Ian. He's very worried about you, darling. We all are. You don't have a job. You don't know a soul in that backwoods town. What do you intend to do with yourself?"

She smiled. Trust Ian to make it sound as if she were hiding out in a cave and licking her wounds. "I've been substitute teaching for the past year, Daddy, and I *do* have a job. I'll be in charge of the third grade at Pine River Elementary starting in early September. In the meantime, I plan to put in a garden, do some reading and sewing—"

"What you need is another man."

Elisabeth rolled her eyes. "Even better, I could just step in front of a speeding truck and break every bone in my body," she replied. "That would be quicker and not as messy."

"Very funny," Marcus said, but there was a grudging note of amused respect in his tone. "All right, baby, I'll leave you alone. Just promise me that you'll take care of yourself and that you'll call and leave word with Traci if you need anything."

"I promise," Elisabeth said.

"Good."

"I love you, Daddy—"

The line went dead before Elisabeth had completed the sentence. "Say hello to Traci and the baby for me," she finished aloud as she replaced the receiver.

After supper, Elisabeth washed her dishes. By then, the power was flickering on and off, and the wind was howling around the corners of the house. She decided to go to bed early so she could get a good start on the cleaning come morning.

Since she'd showered before going to town, Elisabeth simply exchanged her skirt and blouse for an oversize red football jersey, washed her face, scrubbed her teeth and went to bed. Her hand curved around the delicate pendant on Aunt Verity's necklace as she settled back against her pillows.

Lightning filled the room with an eerie light, but Elisabeth felt safe in the big four-poster. How many nights had she and Rue come squealing and giggling to this bed, squeezing in on either side of Aunt Verity to beg her for a story that would distract them from the thunder?

She snuggled down between crisp, clean sheets, closed her eyes and sighed. She'd been right to come back here; this was home, the place where she belonged.

The scream brought her eyes flying open again.

"Papa!"

Elisabeth bolted out of bed and ran into the hallway. Another shriek sounded, followed by choked sobs.

It wasn't the noise that paralyzed Elisabeth, however; it was the thin line of golden light glowing underneath the door across the hall. That door that opened onto empty space.

She leaned against the jamb, one trembling hand resting on the necklace, as though to conjure Aunt Verity for a rescuer. "Papa, Papa, where are you?" the child cried desperately from the other side.

Elisabeth pried herself away from the woodwork

and took one step across the hallway, then another. She found the knob, and the sound of her own heartbeat thrumming in her ears all but drowned out the screams of the little girl as she turned it.

Even when the door actually opened, Elisabeth expected to be hit with a rush of rainy April wind. The soft warmth that greeted her instead came as a much keener shock.

"My God," she whispered as her eyes adjusted to a candle-lit room where there should have been nothing but open air.

She saw the child, curled up at the very top of a narrow bed. Then she saw what must be a dollhouse, another door and a big, old-fashioned wardrobe. As she stood there on the threshold of a world that couldn't possibly exist, the little girl moved, her form illuminated by the light that glowed from an elaborate china lamp on the bedside table.

"You're not Papa," the child said with a cautious sniffle, edging farther back against the intricately carved headboard.

Elisabeth swallowed. "N-no," she allowed, extending one toe to test the floor. Even now, with this image in front of her, complete in every detail, her five senses were telling her that if she stepped into the room, she would plummet onto the sun-porch roof and break numerous bones.

The little girl dragged the flannel sleeve of her nightgown across her face and sniffled again. "Papa's probably in the barn. The animals get scared when there's a storm."

Elisabeth hugged herself, squeezed her eyes tightly shut and stepped over the threshold, fully prepared for a plunge. Instead, she felt a smooth wooden floor beneath her feet. It seemed to her that "Papa" might have been more concerned about a frightened daughter than frightened animals, but then, since she had to be dreaming the entire episode, that point was purely academic.

"You're the lady, aren't you?" the child asked, drawing her knees up under the covers and wrapping small arms around them. "The one who rattled the doorknob and called out."

This isn't happening, Elisabeth thought, running damp palms down her thighs. *I'm having an out-of-body experience or something.* "Y-yes," she stammered after a long pause. "I guess that was me."

"I'm Trista," the girl announced. Her hair was a dark, rich color, her eyes a stormy gray. She settled comfortably against her pillows, folding her arms.

Trista. The doctor's daughter, the child who died horribly in a raging house fire so many years before Elisabeth was even born. "Oh, my God," she whispered again.

"You keep saying that," Trista remarked, sounding a little critical. "It's not truly proper to take the Lord's name in vain, you know."

Elisabeth swallowed hard. "I k-know. I'm sorry."

"It would be perfectly all right to give me yours, however."

"What?"

"Your name, goose," Trista said good-naturedly.

"Elisabeth. Elisabeth McCartney—no relation to the Beatle." As she spoke, Elisabeth was taking in the frilly chintz curtains at the window, the tiny shingles on the roof of the dollhouse.

Trista wrinkled her nose. "Why would you be related to a bug?"

Elisabeth would have laughed if she hadn't been so busy questioning her sanity. *I refuse to have a breakdown over you, Ian McCartney,* she vowed silently. *I didn't love you that much.* "Never mind. It's just that there's somebody famous who has the same last name as I do."

Trista smoothed the colorful patchwork quilt that covered her. "Which are you?" she demanded bluntly. "My guardian angel, or just a regular ghost?"

Now Elisabeth did laugh. "Is there such a thing as a 'regular ghost'?" she asked, venturing farther into the room and sitting down on the end of Trista's bed. At the moment, she didn't trust her knees to hold her up. "I'm neither one of those things, Trista. You're looking at an ordinary, flesh-and-blood woman."

Trista assessed Elisabeth's football jersey with a puzzled expression. "Is that your nightdress? I've never seen one quite like it."

"Yes, this is my—nightdress." Elisabeth felt lightheaded and wondered if she would wake up with her face in the rain gutter that lined the sun-porch roof. She ran one hand over the high-quality workmanship of the quilt. If this was an hallucination, she reflected, it was a remarkably vivid one. "Go to sleep now, Trista. I'm sure it's very late."

Thunder shook the room and Trista shivered visibly. "I won't be able to sleep unless I get some hot milk," she said, watching Elisabeth with wide, hopeful eyes.

Elisabeth fought an urge to enfold the child in her arms, to beg her to run away from this strange house and never, ever return. She stood, the fingers of her right hand fidgeting with the necklace. "I'll go and make some for you." She started back toward the door, but Trista stopped her.

"It's that way, Elisabeth," she said, pointing toward the inner door. "I have my own special stairway."

"This is getting weirder and weirder," Elisabeth muttered, careful not to stub her toe on the massive dollhouse as she crossed to the other door and opened it. "Let's see just how far this delusion goes," she added, finding herself at the top of a rear stairway. Her heart pounded so hard, she thought she'd faint as she made her way carefully down to the lower floor.

She wouldn't have recognized the kitchen, it was so much bigger than the one she knew. A single kerosene lantern burned in the center of the oak table, sending up a quivering trail of sooty smoke. There were built-in cabinets and bins along one wall, and the refrigerator and the stove were gone. In their places were an old-fashioned wooden icebox and an enormous iron-and-chrome monster designed to burn wood. The only thing that looked familiar was the back stairway leading into the main hallway upstairs.

Elisabeth stood in the middle of the floor, holding herself together by sheer force of will. "This is a dream, Beth," she told herself aloud, grasping the brass latch on the door of the icebox and giving it a cautious wrench. "Relax. This is *only a dream*."

The door opened and she bent, squinting, to peer inside. Fortunately, the milk was at the front, in a heavy crockery pitcher.

Elisabeth took the pitcher out of the icebox, closed the door with a distracted motion of one heel and scanned the dimly lit room again. "Wait till you tell Rue about this," she chattered on, mostly in an effort to comfort herself. "She'll want to do a documentary about you. You'll make the cover of the tabloids and TV will have a heyday—"

"Who the hell are you?"

The question came from behind her, blown in on a wet-and-frigid wind. Elisabeth whirled, still clutching the pitcher of cream-streaked milk to her bosom, and stared into the furious gray eyes of a man she had never seen before.

A strange sensation of being wrenched toward him spiritually compounded Elisabeth's shock.

He was tall, close to six feet, with rain-dampened dark hair and shoulders that strained the fabric of his suitcoat. He wore a vest with a gold watch chain dangling from one pocket, and his odd, stiff collar was open.

For some confounding reason, Elisabeth found herself wanting to touch him—tenderly at first, and then with the sweet, dizzying fury of passion.

She gave herself an inward shake. "This is really authentic," Elisabeth said. "I hope I'll be able to remember it all."

The stranger approached and took the endangered pitcher from Elisabeth's hands, setting it aside on the table. His eyes raked her figure, taking in every fiber of the long football jersey that served as her favorite nightgown, leaving gentle fire in their wake.

"I asked you a question," he snapped. "Who the devil are you?"

Elisabeth gave an hysterical little burst of laughter. The guy was a spirit—or more likely a delusion—and she felt a staggering attraction to him. She *must* be 'round the bend. "Who I am isn't the question at all," she answered intractably. "The question is, are you a ghost or am *I* a ghost?" She paused and spread her hands, reasoning that there was no sense in fighting the dream. "I mean, who ya gonna call?"

The man standing before her—Elisabeth could only assume he was the "Papa" Trista had been screaming for—puckered his brow in consternation. Then he felt her forehead with the backs of four cool fingers.

His touch heated Elisabeth's skin and sent a new shock splintering through her, and Elisabeth fairly leapt backward. Hoping it would carry her home to the waking world, like some talisman, she brought the pendant from beneath her shirt and traced its outline with her fingers.

"What is your name?" the man repeated patiently, as though speaking to an imbecile.

Elisabeth resisted an impulse to make a suitable noise with a finger and her lower lip and smiled instead. She had a drunken feeling, but she assured herself that she was bound to wake up any minute now. "Elisabeth McCartney. What's yours?"

"Dr. Jonathan Fortner," was the pensive answer. His steely eyes dropped to the pendant she was fiddling with and went wide. In the next instant, before Elisabeth had had a chance even to brace herself, he'd gripped the necklace and ripped it from her throat. "Where did you get this?" he demanded, his voice a terrifying rasp.

Elisabeth stepped back again. Dream or no dream, she'd felt the pull of the chain against her nape, and she was afraid of the suppressed violence she sensed in this man. "It—it belonged to my aunt—and now it belongs to my cousin and me." She gathered every shred of courage she possessed just to keep from cowering before this man. "If you'll just give it back, please...."

"You're a liar," Dr. Fortner spat out, dropping the necklace into the pocket of his coat. "This pendant was my wife's—it's been in her family for generations."

Elisabeth wet her lips with the tip of her tongue. This whole experience, whatever it was, was getting totally out of hand. "Perhaps it belonged to your—your wife at one time," she managed nervously, "but it's mine now. Mine and my cousin's." She held out one palm. "I want it back."

He looked at her hand as though he might spit in it, then pressed her into a chair. Her knees were like jelly, and she couldn't be sure whether this was caused by her situation or the primitive, elemental tug she felt toward this man.

"Papa?" Trista called from upstairs.

Dr. Fortner's lethal glance followed the sound. He stood stock still for a long moment, then shrugged out of his coat and hung it from a peg beside the door. "Everything is all right," he called back. "Go to sleep."

Elisabeth swallowed the growing lump in her throat and started to rise from the chair. At one quelling glance from Dr. Fortner, however, she thought better of it and sank back to her seat. She watched with rounded eyes as her reluctant host sat down across from her.

"Who are you?" he asked sternly.

He was a remarkable man, ruggedly handsome and yet polished, in a Victorian sort of way. The sort Elisabeth had fantasized about since puberty.

She tried to keep her voice even and her manner calm. "I told you. I'm Elisabeth McCartney."

"All right, Elisabeth McCartney—what are you doing here, dressed in that crazy getup, and why were you wearing my wife's necklace?"

"I was—well, I don't know what I'm doing here, actually. Maybe I'm dreaming, maybe I'm a hologram or an astral projection…."

His dark eyebrows drew together for a moment. "A what?"

She sighed. "Either I'm dreaming or you are. Or

maybe both of us. In any case, I think I need Aunt Verity's necklace to get back where I belong."

"Then it looks like you won't be going anywhere for a while. And I, for one, am not dreaming."

Elisabeth gazed into his hard, autocratic face. Doubtless, the pop-psychology gurus would have something disturbing to say about the irrefutable appeal this man held for her. "You're probably right. I don't see how you could possibly have the sensitivity to dream. It must be me."

"Papa, is Elisabeth still here?"

The doctor's eyes scoured Elisabeth, then softened slightly. "Yes, Punkin, she's still here."

"She was going to bring me some warm milk," Trista persisted.

Jonathan glowered at Elisabeth for a moment, then gestured toward the pitcher. She stumbled out of her chair and proceeded to the wall of cupboards where, with some effort, she located a store of mugs and a small pan.

She poured milk into the kettle, shaking so hard, it was a wonder she didn't spill the stuff all over the floor, and set it on the stove to heat. She glanced toward the doctor's coat, hanging nearby on a peg, and gauged her chances of getting the necklace without his noticing.

They didn't seem good.

"If you want that milk to heat, you'll have to stoke up the fire," he said.

Elisabeth stiffened. The stove had all kinds of lids and doors, but she had no idea how to reach in and "stoke" the flames to life. And she really didn't want to bend over in her nightshirt. "Maybe you could do that," she said.

He took a chunk of wood from a crude box beside the stove, opened a little door in the front and shoved it inside. Then he reached for a poker that rested against the wall and jabbed at the embers and the wood until a snapping blaze flared up.

Elisabeth, feeling as stirred and warm as the coals at the base of the rejuvenated fire, lifted her chin to let him know she wasn't impressed and waited for the milk to heat.

Dr. Fortner regarded Elisabeth steadily. "I'm sure you're some kind of lunatic," he said reasonably, "though I'll be damned if I can figure out how you ended up in Pine River. In any case, you'll have to spend the night. I'll turn you over to the marshal in the morning."

Elisabeth was past wondering when this nightmare was going to end. "You'd actually keep me here all night? I'm a lunatic, remember? I could take an ax and chop you to bits while you sleep. Or put lye down your well."

By way of an answer, he strode across the room, snatched the pan from the stove and poured the milk into a mug. Then, after setting the kettle in the sink, he grasped Elisabeth's elbow in one hand and the cup in the other and started toward the stairs, stopping only to blow out the lamp.

The suitcoat, Elisabeth noticed, was left behind, on its peg next to the door.

He hustled Elisabeth through the darkness and up the steep, narrow, enclosed staircase ahead of him. Her knees trembled with a weird sort of excitement as she hustled along. "I'm not crazy, you know," she insisted, sounding a little breathless.

He opened the door to Trista's room and carried the milk inside, only to find his daughter sleeping soundly, a big, yellow-haired rag doll clutched in her arms.

A fond smile touched Jonathan Fortner's sensual mouth, and he bent to kiss the child lightly on the forehead. Then, after setting the unneeded milk on the bedstand, he motioned for Elisabeth to precede him into the hallway.

The fact that she'd originally entered the Twilight Zone from that door was not lost on Elisabeth. She rushed eagerly through it, certain she'd awaken on the other side in her own bed.

Instead, she found herself in a hallway that was familiar and yet startlingly different from the one she knew. There was a painted china lamp burning on a table, and grim photographs stuck out from the walls, their wire hangers visible. The patterned runner on the floor was one Elisabeth had never seen before.

"It must have been the beef casserole," she said.

Dr. Fortner gave her a look and propelled her down the hall to the room next to the one she was supposed to be sleeping in. "Get some rest, Miss McCartney. And remember—if you get up and start wandering around, I'll hear you."

"And do what?" Elisabeth said as she pushed open the door and stepped into a shadowy room. In the real world, it would be the one she and Rue had always shared during their visits.

"And lock you in the pantry for the rest of the night," he replied flatly.

Even though the room was almost totally dark, Elisabeth knew the doctor wasn't kidding. He *would* lock her in the pantry, like a prisoner. But then, all of this was only happening in her imagination anyway.

He pulled back some covers on a bed and guided her into it, and Elisabeth went without a struggle, pursued by odd and erotic thoughts of him joining her. None of this was like her at all; Ian had always complained that she wasn't passionate enough. She decided to simply close her eyes and put the whole crazy episode out of her mind. In the morning, she would wake up in her own bed.

"Good night," Dr. Fortner said. The timbre of his voice was rich and deep, and he smelled of rain and horses.

Elisabeth felt a deep physical stirring, but she knew nothing was going to come of it because, unfortunately, this wasn't that kind of dream. "Good night," she responded in a dutiful tone.

She lay wide awake for a long time, listening. Somewhere in the room, a clock was ticking, and rain pattered against the window. She heard a door open and close, and she imagined Dr. Fortner taking off his clothes. He'd do it methodically, with a certain rough, masculine grace.

Elisabeth closed her eyes firmly, but the intriguing images remained and her body began to throb. "Good grief, woman," she muttered, "this is a *dream*. Do you realize what Rue will say when she hears about this— and I know you'll be fool enough to tell her, too—she'll say, 'Get a life Bethie. Better yet, get a shrink.'"

She waited for a long time, then crept out of bed, grimacing as she opened the door. Fortunately, it didn't squeak on its hinges nor did the floorboards creak. Holding her breath, Elisabeth groped her way down the hall in the direction of the main staircase.

So much for your threats, Dr. Fortner, she thought smugly as she hurried through the large parlor and the dining room.

In the kitchen, she stubbed her toe trying to find the matches on the table and cried out in pain before she could stop herself. The fire was out in the stove and the room was cold.

Elisabeth snatched the coat from the peg and pulled it on, cowering in the shadows by the cabinets as she waited for Jonathan Fortner to storm in and follow up on his threat to lock her in the pantry.

When an estimated ten minutes had ticked past and he still hadn't shown up, Elisabeth came out of hiding, her fingers curved around the broken necklace in the coat's pocket. Slowly, carefully, she crept up the smaller of the two stairways and into Trista's room.

There she stood beside the bed for a moment, seeing quite clearly now that her eyes had adjusted again, looking down at the sleeping child. Trista was beautiful and so very much alive. Tears lined Elisabeth's lashes as she thought of all this little girl would miss by dying young.

She bent and kissed Trista's pale forehead, then crossed the room to the other door, the one she'd unwittingly stumbled through hours before. Eyes closed tightly, fingers clutching the necklace, she turned the knob and stepped over the threshold.

For almost a full minute she just stood there in the hallway, trembling, afraid to open her eyes. It was the feel of plush carpeting under her bare feet that finally alerted her to the fact that the dream was over and she was back in the real world.

Elisabeth began to sob softly for joy and relief. And maybe because she missed a man who didn't exist. When she'd regained some of her composure, she opened the door of her own room, stepped inside and flipped the switch. Light flooded the chamber, revealing the four-poster, the fireplace, the vanity, the Queen Anne chairs.

Suddenly, Elisabeth was desperately tired. She switched off the lights, stumbled to the bed and fell onto it face-first.

When she awakened, the room was flooded with sunlight and her nose itched. Elisabeth sat up, pushing back her hair with one hand and trying to focus her eyes.

The storm was over, and she smiled. Maybe she'd

take a long walk after breakfast and clear her head. That crazy dream she'd had the night before had left her with a sort of emotional hangover, and she needed fresh air.

She was passing the vanity table on her way to the bathroom when her image in the mirror stopped her where she stood. Shock washed over her as she stared, her eyes enormous, her mouth wide open.

She was wearing a man's suitcoat.

Her knees began to quiver and for a moment, she thought she'd be sick right where she stood. She collapsed onto the vanity bench and covered her face with both hands, peeking through her fingers at her reflection.

"It wasn't a dream," she whispered, hardly able to believe the words. She ran one hand down the rough woolen sleeve of the old-fashioned coat. "I was really there."

For a moment, the room dipped and swayed, and Elisabeth was sure she was going to faint. She pushed the bench back from the table and bent to put her head between her knees. "Don't swoon, Beth," she lectured herself. "There's a perfectly logical explanation for this. Okay, it beats the hell out of me what it could be, but there *is* an answer!"

Once she was sure she wasn't going to pass out, Elisabeth sat up again and drew measured breaths until she had achieved a reasonable sense of calm. She stared at her pale face in the mirror and at her startled blue eyes. But mostly she stared at Dr. Jonathan Fortner's coat.

She put her hand into the right pocket and found the necklace. Slowly lifting it out, she spread it gently on the vanity table. The necklace was broken near the catch, but the pendant was unharmed.

Elisabeth pulled in a deep breath, let it out slowly. Then, calmly, she stood up, removed Dr. Fortner's coat and proceeded into the bathroom.

During her shower and shampoo, she almost succeeded in convincing herself that she'd imagined the suitcoat as well as the broken necklace. But when she came out, wrapped in a towel, they were where she'd left them, silent proof that something very strange had happened to her.

With a lift of her chin, Elisabeth dressed in gray pants and a raspberry sweater, then carefully blew her hair dry and styled it. She took the necklace with her when she went out of the room, but left the suitcoat behind.

In the hallway, her eyes locked on the door across the hall. She tried the knob, but it was rusted in place, and the plastic seal that surrounded the passage was unbroken.

"Trista?" she whispered.

There was no answer.

Elisabeth went slowly down the back staircase, recalling that there had been two of them in her "dream." She ate cereal, coffee and fruit while staring at the kitchen table, fetched her purse, got into her car and drove slowly along the puddled driveway toward the main road.

The house still needed cleaning, but Elisabeth's priorities had been altered slightly. Before she did anything else, she meant to have the necklace repaired.

Chapter 3

"It should be ready by Friday morning," said the clerk in Pine River's one and only jewelry store, dropping Aunt Verity's necklace into a small brown envelope.

Elisabeth felt oddly deflated. She didn't know what was happening to her, but she suspected that the antique pendant was at the core of things, given Aunt Verity's stories, and she didn't want to let it out of her sight. "Thank you," she said with a sigh, and left the shop.

After doing a little more shopping at the supermarket, she drove staunchly back to the house, changed into old clothes, covered her hair with a bandanna and set to work dusting and sweeping and scrubbing.

She'd finished the large parlor and was starting on the dining room when the doorbell sounded. Elisabeth straightened her bandanna and smoothed her palms down the front of her frayed flannel shirt, then answered the rather peremptory summons.

Ian was standing on the porch, looking dapper in his crisp cotton pants and dress shirt. His eyes assessed Elisabeth's work clothes with a patronizing expression that made her want to slap him.

Ironic as it was, he seemed to have no texture, no reality. It was as though *he* were the other-worldly being, not Jonathan.

"Hello, Bethie," he said.

She made no move to invite him in. "What do you want?" she asked bluntly. Her ex-husband was handsome, with his glossy chestnut hair and dark blue eyes, but Elisabeth had no illusions where he was concerned. To think she'd once believed he was an idealist!

He patted the expensive briefcase he carried under one arm. "Papers to sign," he said with a guileless lift of his eyebrows. "No big deal."

Reluctantly, Elisabeth stepped back out of the doorway. Since she didn't feel up to a sparring match with Ian, she didn't state the obvious: if Ian had left his very profitable seminars and taping sessions to deliver these papers personally, they were, indeed, a "big deal."

She saw his gaze sweep over the valuable antique furnishings as he stepped into the main parlor. Had his brain been an adding machine, it would have been spitting out paper tape.

"Your father called," he said, perching in a leather wing chair near the fireplace. "He's been worried about you."

Elisabeth kept her distance, standing with her arms folded. "I know. I talked to him."

Ian sighed and opened the briefcase on his lap, taking out a sheaf of papers. "I'm concerned about your inheritance, Bethie,—"

"I'll just bet you are," she interjected, holding her shoulders a little straighter.

He gave her a look of indulgent reprimand. "I have no intention of trying to take anything from you," he told her, shaking a verbal finger in her face. "It's just that I have questions about your ability to manage your share of the estate." He looked around again at the paintings, the substantial furniture and the costly knickknacks. "I don't think you realize what a bonanza you have here. You could easily be taken in."

"And your suggestion is…?" Elisabeth prompted dryly.

"That you allow my accountant to run an audit and give you some advice on how to manage—"

"Put the papers back in your briefcase, Ian. Neither Rue nor I want to sell this place or anything that's in it. Besides that, Rue's father had everything appraised soon after the will was read."

Ian's chiseled face was flushed. Clearly he was annoyed that he'd taken time away from his motivational company to visit his hopelessly old-fashioned ex-wife. "Elisabeth, you can't be serious about keeping this cavernous, drafty old house. Why, you could live anywhere in the world on your share of the take…."

Elisabeth walked to the front door and opened it,

and Ian followed, somewhat unwillingly. Not for one moment did she believe the man had ever had her best interests at heart—he'd been planning to file for changes in the divorce agreement and get a piece of what he called "the take."

"Goodbye," she said.

"I'm getting married next Saturday," he replied, almost smugly, as he swept through the doorway.

"Congratulations," Elisabeth answered. "You'll understand if I don't send a sterling-silver pickle dish?" With that, she shut the door firmly and leaned against it, her arms folded.

Her throat thickened as she remembered her own wedding, right here in this marvelous old house, nearly a decade before. There had been flowers, old-fashioned dresses and organ music. Somehow, she'd missed the glaring fact that Ian didn't fit into the picture, with his supersophistication and jet-set values.

In retrospect, she saw that Ian had always been emotionally unavailable, just like her father, and she'd seen his cool distance as a challenge, something to surmount with her love.

After a few years, she'd realized her mistake—Ian didn't want children or a real home the way she did, and he cared far more about money than the ideals he touted in his lectures and books. Furthermore, there would be no breaching the emotional wall he'd built around his soul.

Elisabeth had quietly returned to teaching school, biding her time and saving her money until she'd built up the courage to file for a divorce and move out of Ian's luxury condo in Seattle.

With a sigh, she thrust herself away from the door and went back to her cleaning. The road to emotional maturity had been a painful, rocky one for her, but she'd learned who she was and what she wanted. To her way of thinking, that put her way out in front of the crowd.

Carefully, she removed Dresden figurines and Haviland plates from the big china closet in the dining room. As she worked, Elisabeth cataloged the qualities she would look for in a second husband. She wanted a gentle man, but he had to be strong, too. Tall, maybe, with dark hair and broad shoulders—

Elisabeth realized she was describing Jonathan Fortner and put down the stack of dessert plates she'd been about to carry to the kitchen for washing. Her hands were trembling.

He's not real, she reminded herself firmly. But another part of her mind argued that he was. She had his suitcoat to prove it.

Didn't she?

What with all the things that had been happening to her since her return to Pine River, Elisabeth was beginning to wonder if she really knew what was real and what wasn't. She hurried up the back stairs and along the hallway to her bedroom, ignoring the sealed doorway in the outside wall, and marched straight to the armoire.

After opening one heavy door, she reached inside

and pulled out the coat, pressing it to her face with both hands. It still smelled of Jonathan, and the mingled scents filled Elisabeth with a bittersweet yearning to be near him.

Which was downright silly, she decided, since the man obviously lived in some other time—or some other universe. She would probably never see him again.

Sadly, she put the jacket back on its hanger and returned it to the wardrobe.

By Friday morning, Elisabeth had almost convinced herself that she *had* dreamed up Dr. Fortner and his daughter. Probably, she reasoned, she'd felt some deep, subconscious sympathy for them, learning that they'd both died right there in Aunt Verity's house. Her ideal man had no doubt been woven from the dreams, hopes and desperate needs secreted deep inside her, where a man as shallow as Ian could never venture.

As for the suitcoat, well, that had probably belonged to Verity's long-dead husband. No doubt, she had walked in her sleep that night and found the jacket in one of the trunks in the attic. But if that was true, why was the garment clean and unfrayed? Why didn't it smell of mothballs or mildew?

Elisabeth shook off the disturbing questions as she parked her car in front of Carlton Jewelry, but another quandary immediately took its place. Why was she almost desperately anxious to have Aunt Verity's necklace back in her possession again? Granted, it was very old and probably valuable, but she had never been much for bangles and beads, and money hardly mattered to her at all.

She was inordinately relieved when the pendant was poured from its brown envelope into the palm of her hand, fully restored to its former glory. She closed her fingers around it and shut her eyes for a second, and immediately, Jonathan's face filled her mind.

"Ms. McCartney?" the clerk asked, sounding concerned.

Elisabeth remembered herself, opened her eyes and got out her wallet to pay the bill.

When she arrived home an hour later with the makings for spaghetti, garlic bread and green salad, the moving company was there with her belongings. The two men carried in her books, CD collection, stereo, microwave oven, TV sets and boxes of seasonal clothes and shoes.

Elisabeth paid the movers extra to connect her DVD player and set up the stereo, and made them tuna sandwiches and vegetable soup for lunch. When they were gone, she put on Mozart and let the music swirl around her while she did up the lunch dishes and put away some of her things.

Knowing it would probably take hours or even days to find places for everything, Elisabeth stored her seasonal clothes in the small parlor and set about making her special spaghetti sauce.

Seeing her practical friend Janet again would surely put to rest these crazy fancies she was having, once and for all.

As promised, Janet arrived just when the sauce was ready to be poured over the pasta and served. She had straight reddish-brown hair that just brushed her shoulders and large hazel eyes.

Elisabeth met her friend on the porch with a hug. "It's so good to see you."

Janet's expression was troubled as she studied Elisabeth. "You're pale, and I swear you've lost weight," she fretted.

Elisabeth grinned. "I'm *fine,*" she said pointedly, bending to grasp the handle of the small suitcase Janet had set down moments before. "I hope you're hungry, because the sauce is at its peak."

After putting Janet's things in an upstairs bedroom, the two women returned to the kitchen. There they consumed spaghetti and salad at the small table in the breakfast nook, while an April sunset settled over the landscape.

From the first, Elisabeth wanted to confide in her friend, to show her the suitcoat and tell her all about her strange experience a few nights before, but somehow, she couldn't find the courage. They talked about Janet's new boyfriend and Rue's possible whereabouts instead.

After the dishes were done, Janet brought a DVD from her room and popped it into the player, while Elisabeth built a fire on the parlor hearth, using seasoned apple wood she'd found in the shed out back. An avid collector of black-and-white classics, Janet didn't rent movies, she bought them.

"What's tonight's feature?" Elisabeth asked, curling up at one end of the settee, while Janet sat opposite her, a bowl of the salty chips they both loved between them.

Janet gave a little shudder and smiled. *"The Ghost and Mrs. Muir,"* she replied. "Fitting, huh? I mean, since this house is probably haunted."

Elisabeth practically choked on the chip she'd just swallowed. "Haunted? Janet, that is really silly." The FBI warning was flickering on the television screen, silently ominous.

Her friend shrugged. "Maybe so, but a funny feeling came over me when I walked in here. It happened before, too, when I came to your wedding."

"That was a sense of impending doom, not anything supernatural," Elisabeth said.

Janet laughed. "You're probably right."

As they watched the absorbing movie, Elisabeth fiddled with the necklace and wondered if she wouldn't just turn around one day, like Mrs. Muir with her ghostly captain, and see Jonathan Fortner standing behind her.

The idea gave her a delicious, shivery sensation, totally unrelated to fear.

After the show was over and the chips were gone, Elisabeth and Janet had herbal tea in the kitchen and gossiped. When Elisabeth mentioned Ian's visit and his plans to remarry, Janet's happy grin faded.

"The sleazeball. How do you feel about this, Beth? Are you sad?"

Elisabeth reached across the table to touch her

friend's hand. "If I am, it's only because the marriage I thought I was going to have never materialized. Like so many women, I created a fantasy world out of my own needs and desires, and when it collapsed, I was hurt. But I'm okay now, Janet, and I want you to stop worrying about me."

Janet looked at Elisabeth for a long moment and then nodded. "All right, I'll try. But I'd feel better if you'd come back to Seattle."

Elisabeth pushed back her chair and carried her empty cup and Janet's to the sink. "I played a part for so many years," she said with a sigh. "Now I need solitude to sort things out." She turned to face her friend. "Do you understand?"

"Yes," Janet answered, albeit reluctantly, getting out of her chair.

Elisabeth turned off the downstairs lights and started up the rear stairway, which was illuminated by the glow of the moon flooding in from a fanlight on the second floor. The urge to tell Janet about Jonathan was nearly overwhelming, but she kept the story to herself. There was no way practical, ducks-in-a-row Janet was going to understand.

Reaching her room, Elisabeth called out a good-night to her friend and closed the door. Everything looked so normal and ordinary and *real*—the four-poster, the vanity, the Queen Anne chairs, the fireplace.

She went to the armoire, opened it and ferreted out the suitcoat that was at once her comfort and her torment. She held the garment tightly, her face pressed to the fabric. The scent of Jonathan filled her spirit as well as her nostrils.

If she told Janet the incredible story and then showed her the coat—

Elisabeth stopped in midthought and shook her head. Janet would never believe she'd brought the jacket back from another era. Most of the time, Elisabeth didn't believe that herself. And yet the coat was real and her memories were so vivid, so piquant.

After a long time, Elisabeth put the suitcoat back in its place and exchanged her T-shirt and jeans for another football jersey. Her fingers strayed to the pendant she took off only to shower.

"Jonathan," she said softly, and just saying his name was a sweet relief, like taking a breath of fresh air after being closed up in a stuffy house.

Elisabeth performed the usual ablutions, then switched off her lamp and crawled into bed. Ever since that morning when she'd recovered the necklace, a current of excitement had coursed just beneath the surface of her thoughts and feelings. She ached for the magic to take her back to that dream place, even though she was afraid to go there.

It didn't happen.

Elisabeth awakened the next morning to the sound of her clock radio. She put the pendant on the dresser, stripped off her jersey and took a long, hot shower. When she'd dressed in pink capris and a rose-colored sweater, she hurried downstairs to find Janet in the kitchen, sipping coffee.

Janet was wearing shorts, sneakers and a hooded sweatshirt, and it was clear that she'd already been out for her customary run. She smiled. "Good morning."

"Don't speak to me until I've had a jolt of caffeine," Elisabeth replied with pretended indignation.

Her friend laughed. "I saw a notice for a craft show at the fairgrounds," she said as Elisabeth poured coffee. "Sounds like fun."

Elisabeth only shrugged. She was busy sipping.

"We could have lunch afterward."

"Fine," Elisabeth said. "Fine." She was almost her normal self by the time they'd had breakfast and set out for the fairgrounds in Elisabeth's car.

Blossom petals littered the road like pinkish-white snow, and Janet sighed. "I can see why you like the country," she said. "It has a certain serenity."

Elisabeth smiled, waving at Miss Cecily, who was standing at her mailbox. Miss Cecily waved back. "You wouldn't last a week," Elisabeth said with friendly contempt. "Not enough action."

Janet leaned her head back and closed her eyes. "I suppose you're right," she conceded dreamily. "But that doesn't mean I can't enjoy the moment."

They spent happy hours at the craft show, then dined on Vietnamese food from one of the many concession booths. It was when they paused in front of a quilting display that Elisabeth was forcibly reminded of the Jonathan episode.

The slender, dark-haired woman behind the plank-board counter stared at her necklace with rounded eyes and actually retreated a step, as though she thought it would zap her with an invisible ray. "Where did you get that?" she breathed.

Janet's brow crinkled as she frowned in bewilderment, but she just looked on in silence.

Elisabeth's heart was beating unaccountably fast, and she felt defensive, like a child caught stealing. "The necklace?" At the woman's nervous nod, she went on. "I inherited it from my aunt. Why?"

The woman was beginning to regain her composure. She smiled anxiously, but came no closer to the front of the booth. "Your aunt wouldn't be Verity Claridge?"

A finger of ice traced the length of Elisabeth's backbone. "Yes."

Expressive brown eyes linked with Elisabeth's blue-green ones. "Be careful," the dark-haired woman said.

Elisabeth had dozens of questions, but she sensed Janet's discomfort and didn't want to make the situation worse.

"What was that all about?" Janet asked when she and Elisabeth were in the car again, their various purchases loaded into the back. "I thought that woman was going to faint."

Chastity Pringle. Elisabeth hadn't made an effort to remember the name she'd read on the woman's laminated badge; she'd known it would still burn bright in her mind after nine minutes or nine decades. Whoever Ms. Pringle was, she knew Aunt Verity's necklace was no ordinary piece of jewelry, and Elisabeth meant to find out the whole truth about it.

"Elisabeth?"

She jumped slightly. "Hmm?"

"Didn't you think it was weird the way that woman acted?"

Elisabeth was navigating the early-afternoon traffic, which was never all that heavy in Pine River. "The world is full of weird people," she answered.

Having gotten the concession she wanted, Janet turned her mind to the afternoon's entertainment. She and Elisabeth rented a stack of movies at the convenience store, put in an order for a pizza to be delivered later and returned to the house.

By the time breakfast was over on Sunday morning, Janet was getting restless. When noon came, she loaded up her things, said goodbye and hastened back to the city, where her boyfriend and her job awaited.

The moment Janet's car turned onto the highway, Elisabeth dashed to the kitchen and began digging through drawers. Finding a battered phone book, she flipped to the *P*'s. There was a Paul Pringle listed, but no Chastity.

After taking a deep breath, Elisabeth called the man and asked if he had a relative by the name of Chastity. He barked that nobody in his family would be fool enough to give an innocent little girl a name like that and hung up.

Elisabeth got her purse and drove back to the fairgrounds. The quilting booth was manned by a chunky, gray-haired grandmother this time, and sunlight was reflected in the rhinestone-trimmed frames of her glasses as she smiled at Elisabeth.

"Chastity Pringle? Seems like a body couldn't forget a name like that one, but it appears as if I have, because it sure doesn't ring a bell with me. If you'll give me your phone number, I'll have Wynne Singleton call you. She coordinated all of us, and she'd know where to find this woman you're looking for."

"Thank you," Elisabeth said, scrawling the name and phone number on the back of a receipt from the cash machine at her Seattle bank.

Back at home, Elisabeth changed into old clothes again, but this time she tackled the yard, since the house was in good shape. She found an old lawn mower in the shed and fired it up, after making a run to the service station for gas, and spent a productive afternoon mowing the huge yard.

When that was done, she weeded the flower beds. At sunset, weariness and hunger overcame her and she went inside.

The little red light on the answering machine she'd hooked up to Aunt Verity's old phone in the hallway was blinking. She pushed the button and held her breath when she heard Rue's voice.

"Hi, Cousin, sorry I missed you. Unless you get back to me within the next ten minutes, I'll be gone again and I won't have internet, so no emails. No cell service either. Wish I could be there with you, but I've got another assignment. Talk to you soon. Bye."

Hastily, Elisabeth dialed Rue's home number, but the

prescribed ten minutes had apparently passed. Rue's machine picked up, and Elisabeth didn't bother to leave a message. She felt like crying as she went wearily up the stairs to strip off her dirty jeans and T-shirt and take a bath.

When she came downstairs again, she heated a piece of leftover pizza in the microwave and sat down for a solitary supper. Beyond the breakfast nook windows, the sky had a sullen, heavy look to it. Elisabeth hoped there wouldn't be another storm.

She ate, rinsed her dishes and went upstairs to bed, bringing along a candle and matches in case the power were to go out. Stretched out in bed, her body aching with exhaustion from the afternoon's work, Elisabeth thoroughly expected to fall into a fathomless sleep.

Instead, she was wide awake. She tossed from her left side to her right, from her stomach to her back. Finally, she got up, shoved her feet into her slippers and reached for her bathrobe.

She made herself a cup her herbal tea downstairs, then settled at the desk in her room. Going the old-fashioned route, she reached for a few sheets of Aunt Verity's vellum writing paper and a pen.

"Dear Rue," she wrote. And then she poured out the whole experience of meeting Jonathan and Trista, starting with the first time she'd heard Trista's piano. She put in every detail of the story, including the strange attraction she'd felt for Jonathan, ending with the fact that she'd awakened the next morning to find herself wearing his coat.

She spent several hours going over the letter, re-writing parts of it, making it as accurate an account of her experience as she possibly could. Then she folded the missive, tucked it into an envelope, scrawled Rue's name and address and applied a stamp.

In the morning, she would put it in the mailbox down by the road, pull up the little metal flag and let the chips fall where they may. Rue was the best friend Elisabeth had, but she was also a pragmatic newswoman. She was just as likely to suggest professional help as Elisabeth's father would be. Still, Elisabeth felt she had to tell somebody what was going on or she was going to burst.

She was just coming upstairs, having carried the letter down and set it in the middle of the kitchen table so she wouldn't forget to mail it the next morning, when she heard the giggles and saw the glow of light on the hallway floor.

Elisabeth stopped, her hand on the necklace, her heart racing with scary exhilaration. They were back, Jonathan and Trista—she had only to open that door and step over the threshold.

She went to the portal and put her ear against the wood, smiling as Trista's voice chimed, "And then I said to him, Zeek Filbin, if you pull my hair again, I'll send my papa over to take your tonsils out!"

Elisabeth's hand froze on the doorknob when another little girl responded with a burst of laughter and, "Zeek Filbin needed his wagon fixed, and you did it right and proper." Vera, she thought. Trista's best friend. How would the child explain it if Elisabeth simply walked into the room, appearing from out of nowhere?

She knew she couldn't do that, and yet she felt a longing for that world and for the presence of those people that went beyond curiosity or even nostalgia.

The low, rich sound of Jonathan's voice brought her eyes flying open. "Trista, you and Vera should have been asleep hours ago. Now settle down."

There was more giggling, but then the sound faded and the light gleaming beneath the door dimmed until the darkness had swallowed it completely. Elisabeth had missed her chance to step over the threshold into Jonathan's world, and the knowledge left her feeling oddly bereft. She went to bed and slept soundly, awakening to the jangle of the telephone early the next morning.

Since the device was sitting on the vanity table on the other side of the room, Elisabeth was forced to get out of bed and stumble across the rug to snatch up the receiver.

"Yes?" she managed sleepily.

"Is this Elisabeth McCartney?"

Something about the female voice brought her fully awake. "Yes."

"My name is Wynne Singleton, and I'm president of the Pine River County Quilting Society. One of our members told me you were anxious to get in touch with Ms. Pringle."

Elisabeth sat up very straight and waited silently.

"I can give you her address and telephone number, dear," Mrs. Singleton said pleasantly, "but I'm afraid it won't do you much good. She and her husband left just this morning on an extended business trip."

Disappointed, Elisabeth nonetheless wrote down the number and street address—Chastity Pringle apparently lived in the neighboring town of Cotton Creek— and thanked the caller for her help.

After she hung up, Elisabeth dressed in a cotton skirt and matching top, even though the sky was still threatening rain, and made herself a poached egg and a piece of wheat toast for breakfast.

When she'd eaten, she got into her car and drove to town. If Rue were here, she thought, she'd go to the newspaper office and to the library to see what facts she could gather pertaining to Aunt Verity's house in general and Jonathan and Trista Fortner in particular.

Only it was early and neither establishment was open yet. Undaunted, Elisabeth bought a bouquet of simple flowers at the supermarket and went on to the well-kept, fenced graveyard at the edge of town.

She left the flowers on Aunt Verity's grave and then began reading the names carved into the tilting, discolored stones in the oldest part of the cemetery. Jonathan and Trista were buried side by side, their graves surrounded by a low iron fence.

Carefully, Elisabeth opened the gate and stepped through it, kneeling to push away the spring grass that nearly covered the aging stones. "Jonathan Stevens Fortner," read the chiseled words. "Born August 5, 1856. Perished June 1892."

"What day?" Elisabeth whispered, turning to Trista's grave. Like her father's, the little girl's headstone bore only her name, the date of her birth and the sad inscription, "Perished June 1892."

There were tears in Elisabeth's eyes as she got to her feet again and left the cemetery.

Chapter 4

After leaving the Pine River graveyard, Elisabeth stopped by the post office to mail the letter she'd written to Rue the night before. Even though she loved and trusted her cousin, it was hard to drop the envelope through the scrolled brass slot, and the instant she had, she wanted to retrieve it.

All she'd need to do was ask the sullen-looking man behind the grilled window to fetch the letter for her, and no one would ever know she was having delusions.

Squaring her shoulders, Elisabeth made herself walk out of the post office with nothing more than a polite, "Good morning," to the clerk.

The library was open, but Elisabeth soon learned that there were virtually no records of the town's history. There was, however, a thin, self-published autobiography called, *My Life in Old Pine River,* written by a Mrs. Carolina Meavers.

While the librarian, a disinterested young lady with spiky blond hair and a mouthful of gum, issued a borrower's card and entered Elisabeth's name in the computer system, Elisabeth skimmed the book. Mrs. Meavers herself was surely dead, but it was possible she had family in the area.

"Do you know anyone named Meavers?" she asked, holding up the book.

The child librarian popped her gum and shrugged. "I don't pay a lot of attention to old people."

Elisabeth suppressed a sigh of exasperation, took the book and her plastic library card and left the small, musty building. She and Rue had visited the place often during their summer visits to Pine River, devouring books they secretly thought they should have been too sophisticated to like.

Feeling lonely again, Elisabeth crossed the wide street to the newspaper office, where the weekly *Pine River Bugle* was published.

This time she was greeted by a competent-looking middle-aged man with a bald spot, wire-rimmed glasses and a friendly smile. "How can I help you?" he asked.

Elisabeth returned his smile. "I'm doing research," she said, having rehearsed her story as she crossed the street. "How long has the *Bugle* been in publication?"

"One of the oldest newspapers in the state," the man replied proudly. "Goes back to 1876."

Elisabeth's eyes widened. "Do you have the old issues on microfilm?"

"Most of them. If you'll just step this way, Ms....?"

"McCartney," she answered. "Elisabeth McCartney."

"I'm Ben Robbins. Are you writing a book, Ms. McCartney?"

Elisabeth smiled, shook her head and followed him through a small but very noisy press room and down a steep set of stairs into a dimly lit cellar.

"They don't call these places morgues for nothing," Mr. Robbins said with a sigh. Then he gestured toward rows of file cases. "Help yourself," he said. "The microfilm machine is over there, behind those cabinets. The last fifty years are on the computer, but anything older than that is still on microfilm."

Elisabeth nodded, feeling a little overwhelmed, and found the long table where the machine waited. After putting down her purse and the library book, she went to work.

The four issues of the *Bugle* published in June of 1892 were on one spool of film, and once Elisabeth found that and figured out how to work the elaborate projection apparatus, the job didn't seem so difficult.

During the first week of that long-ago year, Elisabeth read, Anna Jean Maples, daughter of Albert and Hester Eustice Maples, had been married to Frank Peterson on the lawn of the First Presbyterian church. Kelsey's Grocery had offered specials on canned salmon and "baseball goods."

The *Bugle* was not void of national news. It was rumored that Grover Cleveland would wrest the presidency back from Benjamin Harrison come November, and the people of Chicago were busy preparing for the World Columbian Exposition, to open in October.

Elisabeth skimmed the second week, then the third. A painful sense of expectation was building in the pit of her stomach when she finally came upon the headline she'd been searching for.

DR. FORTNER AND DAUGHTER PERISH IN HOUSE FIRE

She closed her eyes for a moment, feeling sick. Then she anxiously read the brief account of the incident.

No exact date was given—the article merely said, "This week, the people of Pine River suffered a tragic double loss." The reporter went on to state that no bodies or remains of any kind had been found, "so hot did the hellish blazes burn."

Practically holding her breath, Elisabeth read on, feeling just a flicker of hope. She'd watched enough reruns of *CSI* to know just how stubbornly indestructible human bones could be. If Jonathan's and Trista's remains had not been found, they probably hadn't died in the fire.

She paused to sigh and rub her eyes. If that was true, where had they gone? And why were there two graves with headstones that bore their names?

Elisabeth went back to the article, hoping to find a specific date. Near the end she read, "Surviving the inferno is a young and apparently indigent relative of the Fortners, known only as Lizzie. Marshal Farley Haynes has detained her for questioning."

After scanning the rest of that issue and finding nothing but quilting-bee notices and offers to sell bulls, buggies and nursery furniture, Elisabeth went on to late July of that fateful year.

MYSTERIOUS LIZZIE TO BE TRIED FOR MURDER OF PINE RIVER FAMILY

Pity twisted Elisabeth's insides. Her head was pounding, and she was badly in need of some fresh air. After finding several coins in the bottom of her purse, she made copies of the last newspaper of June 1892, to read later. Then she carefully put the microfilm reel back in its cabinet and turned off the machine.

Upstairs, she found Ben Robbins in a cubicle of an office, going over a stack of computer printouts.

"I want to thank you for being so helpful," Elisabeth said. Her mind was filled with dizzying thoughts. Had Trista and Jonathan died in that blasted fire or hadn't they? And who the heck was this Lizzie person?

Ben smiled and took off his glasses. "Find what you were looking for?"

"Yes and no," Elisabeth answered distractedly, frowning as she shuffled the stack of microfilm copies and the library book resting in the curve of her arm. "Did you know this woman—Carolina Meavers?"

"Died when I was a boy," Ben said with a shake of

his head. "But she was good friends with the Buzbee sisters. If you have any questions about Carolina, they'd be the ones to ask."

The Buzbee sisters. Of course. She guessed this was a case of overlooking the obvious. Elisabeth thanked him again and went out.

Belying the glowering sky of the night before, the weather was sunny and scented with spring. Elisabeth got into her car and drove home.

By the time she arrived, it was well past noon and she was hungry. She made a chicken-salad sandwich, took a diet cola from the refrigerator, found an old blanket and set out through the orchard behind the house in search of a picnic spot.

She chose the grassy banks of Birch Creek, within sight of the old covered bridge that was now strictly off limits to any traffic. Elisabeth and Rue had come to this place often with Aunt Verity to wade in the sparkling, icy stream and listen to those endless and singularly remarkable stories.

Elisabeth spread the blanket out on the ground and sat down to eat her sandwich and drink her soda. When she'd finished her lunch, she stretched out on her stomach to read about Lizzie's arrest. Unfortunately, the piece had been written by the same verbose and flowery reporter who had covered the fire, and beyond the obvious facts, there was no real information.

Glumly, Elisabeth set aside the photocopies and flipped through the library book. There were pictures in the center, and she stopped to look at them. The author, with her family, posing on the porch—if those few rough planks of pine could be described as a porch—of a ramshackle shanty with a tarpaper roof. The author, standing on the steps of a country schoolhouse that had been gone long before Elisabeth's birth, clutching her slate and spelling primer to her flat little chest.

Elisabeth turned another page and her heart leapt up into her sinus passages to pound behind her cheeks. Practically the entire town must have been in that picture, and Elisabeth could see one side of the covered bridge. But it wasn't that structure that caught her eye and caused her insides to go crazy with a strange, sweet anxiety.

It was Jonathan's image, smiling back at her from the photograph. He was wearing trousers and a vest, and his dark hair was attractively rumpled. Trista stood beside him, a basket brimming with wildflowers in one hand, regarding the camera solemnly.

Elisabeth closed her eyes. She had to get a hold on her emotions. These people had been dead for over a century. And whatever fantasies she might have woven around them, they could not be a part of her life.

She gathered the book and the photocopies and the debris of her lunch, then folded the blanket. Despite the self-lecture, Elisabeth knew she would cross that threshold into the past again if she could. She wanted to see Jonathan and warn him about the third week in June.

In fact, she just plain wanted to see Jonathan.

Back at the house, Elisabeth found she couldn't settle

down to the needlework or reading she usually found so therapeutic. There were no messages on the answering machine.

Restless, she took the Buzbees' covered casserole dish, now empty and scrubbed clean, and set out for the house across the road.

An orchard blocked the graceful old brick place from plain view, and the driveway was strewed with fragrant velvety petals. Elisabeth smiled to herself, holding the casserole dish firmly, and wondered how she had ever been able to leave Pine River for the noise and concrete of Seattle.

Miss Cecily came out onto the porch and waved, looking pleased to have a visitor. "I *told* Sister you'd be dropping in by and by, but she said you'd rather spend your time with young folks."

Elisabeth chuckled. "I hope I'm not interrupting anything," she said. "I really should have called first."

"Nonsense." Cecily came down the walk to link Elisabeth's arm with hers. "Nobody calls in the country. They just stop by. Did you enjoy the casserole, dear?"

Elisabeth didn't have the heart to say she'd put most of it down the disposal because there had been so much more than she could eat. "Yes," she said. "Every bite was delicious."

They proceeded up fieldstone steps to the porch, where an old-fashioned swing swayed in the mid-afternoon breeze. The ponderous grandfather clock in the entryway sounded the Westminster chimes, three o'clock, and Elisabeth was surprised that it was so late.

"Sister!" Cecily called, leading Elisabeth past the staircase and down a hallway. There was a note of triumph in her voice, an unspoken "I told you she would come to visit!"

"Oh, Sister! We have company!"

Roberta appeared, looking just a little put out. Obviously, she preferred being right to being visited. "Well," she huffed, in the tone of one conceding grudging defeat, "I'll get the lemonade and the molasses cookies."

Soon the three women were settled at the white iron ice-cream table on the stone-floored sun porch, glasses of the Buzbee sisters' incomparable fresh-squeezed lemonade brimming before them.

"Elisabeth thought the casserole was delicious," Cecily announced with a touch of smugness, and Elisabeth resisted a smile, wondering what rivalries existed between these aging sisters.

"Wait until she tastes my vegetable lasagne," said Roberta, pursing her lips slightly as she reached for the sampler she was embroidering.

"I'd like to," Elisabeth said, to be polite. She took a molasses cookie, hoping that would balance things out somehow. "Mr. Robbins at the newspaper told me you probably knew Mrs. Carolina Meavers."

"My, yes," said Roberta. "She was our Sunday-school teacher."

"The old crow," muttered Cecily.

Elisabeth nibbled at her cookie. "She wrote a book

about Pine River, you know. I checked it out of the library this morning."

Roberta narrowed her eyes at Elisabeth. "It's that crazy house. That's what's got you so interested in Pine River history, isn't it?"

"Yes," Elisabeth answered, feeling as though she'd been accused of something.

"There are some things in this world, young woman, that are better left alone. And the mysteries of that old house are among them."

"Don't be so fractious, Sister," Cecily scolded. "It's natural to be curious."

"It's also dangerous," replied Roberta.

Elisabeth could see that this visit was going to get her nowhere in unraveling a century of knotted truths, so she finished her cookie and her lemonade and made chitchat until she could politely leave. As Cecily was escorting her through the parlor, Elisabeth was jolted out of her reveries by a brown and hairy shrunken head proudly displayed on the back of the upright piano.

"Chief Zwilu of the Ubangis," Cecily confided, having followed Elisabeth's horrified gaze. "Since the dastardly deed had already been done, Sister and I could see no reason not to bring the poor fellow home as a souvenir."

Elisabeth shivered. "The customs people must have been thrilled."

Cecily shook her head and answered in a serious tone, "Oh, no, dear. They were quite upset. But Sister was uncommonly persuasive and they allowed us to bring the chief into the country."

Just before the two women parted at the Buzbee gate, Cecily patted Elisabeth's arm and muttered, "Don't mind Sister, now. She was just put out because she's always considered my beef casserole inferior to her vegetable lasagna."

"I won't give it another thought," Elisabeth promised. She didn't smile until she was facing away from Cecily, walking down the long driveway.

Reaching the downstairs hallway of her own house, Elisabeth found the light blinking on the answering machine and eagerly pushed the play button.

"Hello, Elisabeth." The voice belonged to Traci, her father's wife. "Marcus asked me to call and find out if you need any money and if there's anything we can do to convince you to come and spend the summer in Tahoe with us. If I don't hear from you, I'll assume you're all right. Bye-ee."

"Bye-ee," Elisabeth chimed sweetly, just as another message began to play.

"Elisabeth? It's Janet. Just wanted to say I had a great time visiting. How about coming to Seattle next weekend? Give me a call."

Elisabeth turned off the machine and went slowly up the stairs. On a whim, she continued up a second flight to the attic.

There was one way to find out if she'd walked in her sleep that night and found a man's coat to use as proof of the unprovable.

The attic door squeaked loudly on its hinges, and Elisabeth thought to herself that the shrill sound should have awakened the dead, let alone a sleepwalker. A flip of the switch located just inside the door illuminated the dust-covered trunks, bureaus, boxes and chairs.

Even from where she stood, Elisabeth could see that neither she nor anyone else had visited this chamber in a very long time. There were no tracks in the thick dust on the floor.

Taking the necklace out from under her sweater, Elisabeth returned to the second floor and stood opposite the sealed door. Her heart was beating painfully fast, and the pit of her stomach was jittery. "Be there," she whispered. "Please, Jonathan. Be there."

Elisabeth tried the knob, but even before she touched it, she knew it wasn't going to turn. Obviously, she could not enter the world on the other side of that door at will, even wearing the necklace. Other forces, all well beyond Elisabeth's comprehension, had to be present.

"I have to tell you about the fire," she said sadly, sliding down the wooden framework to sit on the hallway floor, her knees drawn up, her forehead resting on her folded arms. "Please, Jonathan. Let me in."

She must have dozed off right there on the floor. She came to herself with a start when she heard her name being whispered.

"Elisabeth! Elisabeth, come back! I *need* to talk to you!"

Elisabeth glanced wildly toward the fanlight at the end of the hall and saw that it was still light outside. Then she scrambled to her feet.

"Trista?" She reached for the doorknob, and it turned easily in her hand. On the other side of the door, she found the child who was a lifetime her senior.

Trista was sitting on the floor of her room, next to the big dollhouse, and her lower lip protruded. "I'm being punished," she said.

Elisabeth knelt beside the little girl and gave her a heartfelt hug, hoping she wouldn't feel the trembling. "What did you do?"

"Nothing." Jonathan's daughter handed Elisabeth a tiny china doll as she sat beside her on the rag rug, and Elisabeth smiled at its little taffeta dress and painted hair.

"Come on, Trista," she said. "Your father wouldn't restrict you to your room for no reason."

"Well, it wasn't a very *good* reason."

Elisabeth raised her eyebrows, waiting, and Trista's little shoulders rose and fell in a heavy sigh.

"I couldn't help it," she said. "I told my friend Vera about you, and she told everybody in the county that Papa had a naked woman here. Now I have to come straight to my room after school every day for a solid month!"

Elisabeth touched the child's glossy dark pigtail. "I'm sorry, sweetheart. I didn't mean to get you in trouble. I do, however, feel duty bound to point out that I wasn't naked—I was wearing a football jersey."

"You didn't get me into trouble," Trista said. "Vera did. And what's a football jersey?"

"A very fancy undershirt. Is your papa at home, Trista?" Elisabeth couldn't help the little shiver of excitement that passed through her at the prospect of encountering Jonathan again, though God knew he probably wouldn't be thrilled to see *her*.

Glumly, Trista nodded. "He's out in the barn, I think. Maybe you could tell him that a month is too long to restrict a girl to her bedroom."

Elisabeth chuckled and kissed the child's forehead. "Sorry, short person. It isn't my place to tell your father how to raise his daughter."

With care, Elisabeth unclasped the necklace and put it in a little glass bowl on Trista's bureau. "You'll keep this safe for me, won't you?"

Trista nodded, watching Elisabeth with curious eyes. "I've never seen a lady wear pants before," she said. "And I'll bet you haven't got a corset on, neither."

Elisabeth grinned over one shoulder as she opened the door. "That's one bet you're bound to win," she said. And then she was moving down the hallway.

The pictures of glowering men in beards and steely eyed, calico-clad women were back, and so was the ghastly rose-patterned runner on the floor. Elisabeth felt exhilarated as she hurried toward the back stairway, also different from the one she knew, and walked through the kitchen.

There was a washtub hanging on the wall outside the back door, and chickens clucked and scratched in the yard. A woman was standing nearby, hanging little calico pinafores and collarless white shirts on a clothesline. She didn't seem to notice Elisabeth.

Wife? Housekeeper? Elisabeth decided on the latter. When Jonathan had snatched the necklace from Elisabeth's neck during her first visit, he'd spoken of his spouse in the past tense.

When she stepped through the wide doorway of the sturdy, unpainted barn—which was a teetering ruin in her time—she saw golden hay wafting down from a loft. A masculine voice was singing a bawdy song that made Elisabeth smile.

"Jonathan?" she called, waiting for her eyes to adjust to the dimmer light. The singing instantly stopped.

Jonathan looked down at her from the hayloft, his chest shirtless and glistening with sweat, a pitchfork in one hand. His dark hair was filled with bits of straw. Something tightened inside Elisabeth at the sight of him.

"You." His tone was so ominous, Elisabeth took a step backward, ready to flee if she had to. "Stay right there!" he barked the moment she moved, shaking an index finger at her.

He tossed the pitchfork expertly into the hay and climbed down rough-hewn rungs affixed to the wall beside the loft. Standing within six feet of Elisabeth, he dragged his stormy-sky eyes over her in angry wonderment, then dragged a handkerchief from his hip pocket and dried his brow.

Elisabeth found the sight and scent of him inexplicably erotic, even though if she could have described her primary emotion, she would have said it was pure terror.

"Trousers?" he marveled, stuffing the handkerchief back into his pocket. "Who are you, and where the devil did you disappear to the other night?"

Elisabeth entwined her fingers behind her back, hiding the crazy, nonsensical joy she felt at seeing him again. "Where I come from, lots of women wear—trousers," she said, stalling.

He went to a bucket on a bench beside the wall and raised a dipperful of water to his mouth. Elisabeth watched the muscles of his back work, sweaty and hard, as he swallowed and returned the dipper to its place.

"You don't look Chinese," he finally said, dryly and at length.

"Listen, if I tried to tell you where I really came from, you'd never believe me. But I—I know the future."

He chuckled and shook his head, and Elisabeth was reminded of his medical degree. The typical man of science. Jonathan probably believed only in things he could reduce to logical components. "No one knows the future," he replied.

"I do," Elisabeth insisted, "because I've been there. And I'm here to warn you." She swallowed hard as he regarded her with those lethally intelligent eyes. Somehow she couldn't get the words out; they'd sound too insane.

"About what?"

Elisabeth closed her eyes and forced herself to answer. "A fire. There's going to be a terrible fire, the third week of June. Part of the house will be destroyed, and you and Trista will—will disappear."

Jonathan's hand shot out and closed around her elbow, tight as a steel manacle. "Who are you, and what asylum did you escape from?" he snapped.

"I told you before—my name is Elisabeth McCartney. And I'm *not* insane!" She paused, biting her lip and futilely trying to pull out of his grasp. "At least, I don't think I am."

He dragged her into the dusty, fading sunlight that filled the barn's doorway and examined her as though she were a creature from another planet. "Your hair," he muttered. "No woman I've ever seen wears her hair sheared off at the chin like that. And your clothes."

Elisabeth sighed. "Jonathan, I'm from the future," she said bluntly. "Women dress like this in my time."

He touched her forehead, just as he had once before. "No fever," he murmured, as though she hadn't spoken at all. "This is the damnedest thing I've ever seen."

"I guess they didn't cover this in medical school, huh?" Elisabeth said, getting testy because he seemed to see her as more of a white mouse in a laboratory than a flesh-and-blood woman. "Well, here's another flash for you, Doc—they're not bleeding people with leeches anymore, but there's still no cure for psoriasis."

Jonathan's grip on her arm didn't slacken. "Who are you?" he repeated, and it was clear to Elisabeth that her host was running out of patience. If he'd ever possessed any in the first place.

"Julia Roberts," she snapped. "Damn it, Fortner, will you let go of my arm! You're about to squeeze it off at the elbow!"

He released her. "You said your name was Elisabeth," he said in all seriousness.

"Then why did you have to ask who I am? It isn't as though I haven't told you more than once!"

He crossed the barn, snatched a shirt from a peg on the wall and slipped his arms into it. "How did you manage to vanish from my house last week, Miss McCartney?"

Elisabeth waited for him in the doorway, knowing she'd never be able to outrun him. "I told you. There's a passageway between your time and mine. You and I are roommates, in a manner of speaking."

Jonathan placed a hand on the small of Elisabeth's back and propelled her toward the house. There was no sign of the woman who had been hanging clothes on the line. The set of his jaw told Elisabeth he was annoyed with her answers to his questions.

Which wasn't surprising, considering.

He steered her up the back steps and through the door into the kitchen. "They must have cut your hair off while you were in the asylum," he said.

"I've never been in an asylum," Elisabeth informed him. "Except in college, once. We visited a mental hospital as part of a psychology program."

Jonathan's teeth were startlingly white against his dirty face. "Sit down," he said.

Elisabeth obeyed, watching as he took a kettle from the stove and poured hot water into a basin. He added cold from the pump over the sink and then began to wash himself with pungent yellow soap. She found she couldn't look away, even though there was something painfully intimate in the watching.

By the time he turned to her, drying himself with a damask towel, Elisabeth's entire body felt warm and achy, and she didn't trust herself to speak. The man was so uncompromisingly masculine, and his very presence made closed places open up inside her.

Jonathan took his medical bag from a shelf beside the door, set it on the table with a decisive thump and opened the catch. "The first order of business, Miss McCartney," he said, taking out a stethoscope and a tongue depressor, "is to examine you. Open your mouth and say awww."

"Oh, brother," Elisabeth said, but she opened her mouth.

Chapter 5

"Are you satisfied?" Elisabeth demanded when Dr. Jonathan Fortner had finished the impromptu examination. "I'm perfectly healthy—physically *and* mentally."

There were freshly ironed shirts hanging from a hook on the wall behind a wooden ironing board, and Jonathan took one down and shrugged into it. Elisabeth tried to ignore the innately male grace in the movements of his muscles.

He didn't look convinced of her good health. "I suppose it's possible you really believe that," he speculated, frowning.

Elisabeth sighed. "If all doctors are as narrow-minded as you are, it's a real wonder they ever managed to wipe out diphtheria and polio."

She had Jonathan's undivided attention. "What did you say?"

"Diphtheria and polio," Elisabeth said seriously. But inside, she was enjoying having the upper hand for once. "They're gone. No one gets them anymore."

The desire to believe such a miracle could be accomplished was plain in Jonathan's face, but so was his skepticism and puzzlement. He dragged back a chair at the table and sat in it, staring at Elisabeth.

She was encouraged. "You were born in the wrong century, Doc," she said pleasantly. "They say more medical advances were made in the twentieth century than in all the rest of time put together."

He was watching her as if he expected her head to spin around on her shoulders.

Elisabeth was enjoying the rare sense of being privy to startling information. "Not only that, but people actually walked on the moon in 1969, and—"

"Walked on the moon?" He shoved back his chair, strode across the room and brought back a dipperful of cold well water. "Drink this very slowly."

Disappointment swept over Elisabeth when she realized she wasn't convincing him after all. It was followed by a sense of hopelessness so profound, it threatened to crush her. If she didn't find some way to influence Jonathan, he and Trista might not survive the fire. And she would never be able to bear knowing they'd died so horribly, because they were real people to her and not just figures in an old lady's autobiography.

She tasted the water, mostly because she knew he

wouldn't leave her alone until she had, and then turned her head away. "Jonathan, you must listen to me," she whispered, forgetting the formalities. "Your life depends on it, and so does Trista's."

He returned the dipper to the bucket, paying no attention to her words. "You need to lie down."

"I don't...."

"If you refuse, I can always give you a dose of laudanum," Jonathan interrupted.

Elisabeth's temper flared. "Now just a minute. *Nobody* is giving me laudanum. The stuff was—is—made from opium, and that's addictive!"

Jonathan sighed. "I know full well what it's made of, Miss McCartney. And I wasn't proposing to make you dependent and sell you into white slavery. It's just that you're obviously agitated—"

"I am *not* agitated!"

His slow, leisurely smile made something shift painfully inside her. "Of course, you're not," he said in a patronizing tone.

Now it was Elisabeth who sighed. She'd known Jonathan Fortner, M.D., for a very short time, but one thing she had learned right off was that he could be mule stubborn when he'd set his mind on a certain course of action. Arguing with him was useless. "All right," she said sweetly, even managing a little yawn. "I guess I would like to rest for a while. But you've got to promise not to send for the marshal and have me arrested."

She saw a flicker of amusement in his charcoal eyes. "You have my word, Elisabeth," he told her, and she loved the way he said her name. He took her arm and led her toward the back stairs, and she allowed that, thinking how different Dr. Fortner was from Ian, from *any* man she knew in her own time. There was a courtly strength about him that had evidently been lost to the male population as the decades progressed.

He deposited her in the same room she'd had during her last visit, settling her expertly on the narrow iron bed, slipping off her shoes, covering her with a color-ful quilt. His gentle, callused hand smoothed her hair back from her forehead.

"Rest," he said hoarsely, and then he was gone, clos-ing the door quietly behind him.

Elisabeth tensed, listening for the click of a key in the lock, but it never came. She relaxed, soaking up the atmosphere of this world that apparently ran parallel to her own. Everything was more substantial, somehow, more vivid and richly textured. The ordinary sound of an errant bee buzzing and bumping against the window, the support of the feather-filled mattress beneath her, the poignant blue of the patch of sky visible through the lace curtains at the window—all of it blended together to create an undeniable reality.

She was definitely not dreaming and, strangely, she was in no particular hurry to get back to her own cen-tury. There was no one there waiting for her, while here, she had Trista and Jonathan. She would stay a few days, if Jonathan would let her, and perhaps find some way to avert the disaster that lay ahead.

When the door of her room opened, she was only

a little startled. Trista peered around the edge, her Jonathan-gray eyes wide with concerned curiosity. "Are you sick?" she asked.

Elisabeth sat up and patted the mattress. "No, but your father thinks I am. Come and sit here."

Shyly, Trista approached the bed and sat on the edge of the mattress, her small, plump hands folded in her lap.

"I've heard you practicing your piano lessons," Elisabeth said, settling back against her pillows and folding her arms.

Trista's eyes reflected wonder rather than the disbelief Elisabeth had seen in Jonathan's gaze. "You have?"

"I don't think you like it much," Elisabeth observed.

The child made a comical face. "I'd rather be outside. But Papa wants me to grow up to be a lady, and a lady plays piano."

"I see."

Trista smiled tentatively. "Do you like music?"

"Very much," Elisabeth answered. "I studied piano when I was about your age, and I can still play a little."

The eight-year-old's gapped smile faded to a look of somber resignation. "Miss Calderberry will be here soon to give me my lesson. I'm allowed to leave my room for that, of course."

"Of course," Elisabeth agreed seriously.

"Would you care to come down and listen?"

"I'd better not. Something tells me your father wouldn't want me to be quite so—visible. I'm something of a secret, I think."

Trista sighed, then nodded and rose to go down-stairs and face her music teacher. She had the air of Anne Boleyn proceeding to the Tower. "Your neck-lace is in the dish on my bureau, just where you left it," she whispered confidentially, from the doorway. "You won't leave without saying goodbye, will you?"

Elisabeth felt her throat tighten slightly. "No, sweet-heart. I promise I won't go without seeing you first."

"Good," Trista answered. And then she left the room.

After a few minutes, Elisabeth got out of bed and wandered into the hallway. At the front of the house was a large, arched window looking down on the yard, and she couldn't resist peering around the curtains to watch a slender woman dressed in brown sateen climb delicately down from the seat of a buggy.

Miss Calderberry wore a feathered hat that hid her face from Elisabeth, but when Jonathan approached from the direction of the barn, smiling slightly, delight seemed to radiate from the piano teacher's countenance. Her trilling voice reached Elisabeth's ears through the thick, bubbled glass.

"Dr. Fortner! What a pleasure to see you."

In the next instant, Jonathan's gaze rose and seemed to lock with Elisabeth's, and she remembered that she was supposed to be lying down, recovering from her odious malady.

She stepped back from the window, but only because she didn't want Miss Calderberry to see her and carry a lot of gossip back to the fine folks of Pine River. It wouldn't do to ruin whatever might be left of the good doctor's reputation following Vera's accounts of a naked lady in residence.

When Trista's discordant efforts at piano playing started to rise through the floorboards, Elisabeth grew restless and began to wander the upstairs, though she carefully avoided Jonathan's room.

She made sure the necklace was still in Trista's crystal dish, then peeked into each of the other bedrooms, where she saw brass beds, chamberpots, pitchers and basins resting on lovely hardwood washstands. From there, she proceeded to the attic.

The place gave her a quivery feeling in the pit of her stomach, being a mirror image of its counterpart in her own time. Of course, the contents were different.

She opened a trunk and immediately met with the scent of lavender. Setting aside layers of tissue paper, she found a delicate ivory dress, carefully folded, with ecru-lace trim on the cuffs and the high, round collar.

Normally, Elisabeth would not have done what she did next, but this was, in a way, her house. And besides, all her actions had a dreamlike quality to them, as though they would be only half-remembered in the morning.

She took the dress out of the trunk, held it against her and saw that it would probably fit, then she stripped off her slacks and sweater. Tiny buttons covered in watered silk graced the front of the gown, fastening through little loops of cloth.

When she had finished hooking each one, Elisabeth looked around for a mirror, but there was none in sight.

She dipped into the trunk again and found a large, elegantly shaped box, which contained a confection of a hat bursting with silk flowers—all the color of rich cream—and tied beneath the chin with a wide, ivory ribbon.

Elisabeth couldn't resist adding the hat to her costume.

Holding up her rustling skirts with one hand, she made her way cautiously down the attic steps and along the hallway to her room. She was inside, beaming with pleasure and turning this way and that in front of the standing mirror, when she sensed an ominous presence and turned to see Jonathan in the doorway.

He leaned against the jamb, the sleeves of his white shirt rolled up to reveal muscle-corded forearms folded across his chest.

"Make yourself right at home, Miss McCartney," he urged in an ill-tempered tone. An entirely different emotion was smoldering in his eyes, however.

Elisabeth had been like a child, playing dressup. Now her pleasure faded and her hands trembled as she reached up to untie the ribbon that held the hat in place. "I'm so sorry," she whispered, mortified, realizing that the clothes had surely belonged to his wife and that seeing someone else wearing them must be painful for him. "I don't know what came over me...."

Jonathan stepped into the room and closed the door against the distant tinkle of piano keys, probably not wanting their voices to carry to Trista and Miss Calderberry. His eyes were narrowed. "When I first met you, you were wearing my wife's necklace, and when it disappeared, so did you. Tell me, Elisabeth...do you know Barbara?"

Elisabeth shook her head. "H-how could I, Jonathan? She—I live in another century, remember?"

He arched one dark eyebrow and hooked his thumbs in the pockets of his black woolen vest. "Yet, somehow, my wife's necklace came to be here. Without Barbara. She never let it out of her sight, you know. She claimed it had powers."

A hard lump formed in Elisabeth's throat, and she swallowed. If Barbara Fortner had known about the necklace's special energy and had used it, she could have crossed the threshold into the modern world....

"This is all getting pretty far-fetched," Elisabeth said, squaring her shoulders. "I didn't know your wife, Jonathan." She looked down at the lovely dress. "I truly am sorry for presuming on your hospitality this way, though."

"Keep the dress," he told her with a dismissive gesture of one hand. "It will raise a lot fewer questions than those trousers of yours."

Elisabeth felt as though she'd just been given a wonderful gift. "Thank you," she breathed softly, running her hands down the satiny skirt.

"You'd better hunt up some calico and sateen for everyday," he finished, moving toward the door. "Naturally, women don't cook and clean in such fancy getup."

"Jonathan?" Elisabeth approached him as he waited, his hand on the doorknob. She stood on tiptoe to kiss his now-stubbly cheek, and again she felt a powerful charge of some mystical electricity. "Thank you. But I won't need special clothes if I go back to my own time."

He rolled his eyes, but there was a look of tenderness in their depths. "Something tells me you're going to be here for a while," he said, and then his gaze moved slowly over Elisabeth, from her face to the incongruous toes of her sneakers and back again. His hands rested lightly on the sides of her waist, and she felt a spiritual jolt as he looked deeply into her eyes, as though to find her soul behind them.

It seemed natural when his lips descended toward hers and brushed lightly against them, soft and warm and moist. A moment later, however, he was kissing her in earnest.

With a whimper, Elisabeth put her arms around his neck and held on, afraid she would sink to the floor. The gentle assault on her senses continued; her mouth was open to his, and even through the dress and the bra beneath, her nipples hardened against the wall of his chest. A sweet, grinding ache twisted in the depths of her femininity, a wild need she had never felt with Ian, and if Jonathan had asked her, she would have surrendered then and there.

Instead, he set her roughly away from him and avoided her eyes. Trista's labored piano playing filled their ears.

"There's obviously no point in keeping you locked up in your room," he said hoarsely. "If you encounter Miss Calderberry, kindly introduce yourself as my wife's sister."

With that, he was gone. Elisabeth stood there in the center of her room, her cheeks flaring with color because he'd kissed her as no other man ever had—and because he was ashamed to have her under his roof. She wanted to laugh and cry, both at the same time, but in the end she did neither.

She crept down the back stairway and out the kitchen door and headed in the direction of the stream where she had picnicked by herself over a hundred years in the future. The scent of apple blossoms filled her spirit as she walked through the recently planted orchard. Birds sang in the treetops, and in the near distance, she could hear the rustling song of the creek.

It occurred to her then that she could be blissfully happy in this era, for all its shortcomings. On some level, she had always yearned for a simpler, though certainly not easier, life and a man like Jonathan.

Elisabeth hurried along, the soft petals billowing around her like fog in a dream, and finally reached the grassy bank.

The place was different and yet the same, and she stood in exactly the spot where she'd spread her blanket to eat lunch and read. The covered bridge towered nearby, but its plank walls were new, and the smell of freshly sawed wood mingled with the aromas of spring grass and the fertile earth.

In order to protect her dress from green smudges, Elisabeth sat on a boulder overlooking the stream instead of on the ground. She removed the hat and set it beside her, then lifted her arms to her hair, winding it into a French knot at the back of her head even though she had no pins to hold it. Her reflection smiled back at her from the crystal-bright waters of the creek, looking delightfully Victorian.

A clatter on the road made her lift her head, her hands still cupped at her nape, and she watched wide-eyed as a large stagecoach, drawn by eight mismatched horses, rattled onto the bridge. The driver touched his hat brim in a friendly way when the coach reappeared, and Elisabeth waved, laughing. It was like playing a part in a movie.

And then the wind picked up suddenly, making the leaves of the birch and willow trees whisper and lifting Elisabeth's borrowed hat right off the rock. She made a lunge, and both she and the bonnet went straight into the creek.

With a howl of dismay, Elisabeth felt the slippery pebbles on the bottom of the icy stream give way beneath the soles of her sneakers. As the luscious hat floated merrily away, she tumbled forward and landed in the water with a splash.

Jonathan was standing on the bank when she floundered her way back to shore, her lovely dress clinging revealingly to her form, and though he offered his hand, Elisabeth ignored it.

"What are you doing?" she sputtered furiously, her teeth already chattering, her hair hanging in dripping tendrils around her face. "Following me?"

He grinned and shrugged. "I saw you walking this way, and I thought you might be planning to hitch a ride on the afternoon stage. It seems you've been swimming instead."

Elisabeth glared at him and crossed her arms over her breasts. Because of the unexpected dip in the creek, her nipples were plainly visible beneath the fabric. "It isn't funny," she retorted, near tears. "This is the prettiest dress I've ever had, and now it's ruined!"

He removed his suitcoat and laid it over her shoulders. "I suppose it is," he allowed. "But there are other dresses in the world."

"Not like this one," Elisabeth said despairingly.

Jonathan's arm tightened briefly around her before falling to his side. "That's what you think," he countered. "Go through the trunks again. If you don't find anything you like, I'll *buy* you another dress."

Elisabeth gave him a sidelong look, shivering inside his coat as they walked toward the orchard and the house beyond. No one needed to tell her that nineteenth-century country doctors didn't make a lot of money; many of Jonathan's patients probably paid him in chickens and squash from the garden. "Did this dress belong to your wife?" she ventured to ask, already knowing the answer, never guessing how much she would regret the question until it was too late to call it back.

Jonathan's jawline tightened, then relaxed again. He did not look at her, but at the orchard burgeoning with flowers. "Yes," he finally replied.

"Doesn't it bother you to see another woman wearing her things?"

He rubbed his chin, then thrust both hands into the pockets of his plain, practical black trousers. "No," he answered flatly.

Elisabeth thought of the two graves inside the little fence, back in modern-day Pine River, and her heart ached with genuine grief to think of Jonathan and Trista lying there. At the same time, she wondered why Jonathan's mate wasn't buried in the family plot. "Did she die, Jonathan? Your wife?"

They had reached the grove of apple trees, and petals clung to the hem of Elisabeth's spoiled dress. Jonathan's hands knotted into fists in his trouser pockets. "As far as Trista and I are concerned," he replied some moments later, "yes."

Pressing him took all Elisabeth's courage, for she could sense the controlled rage inside him. And yet she had to know if she was feeling all these crazy emotions for another woman's husband. "She left you?"

"Yes."

"Then, technically, you're a married man."

Jonathan's eyes sliced to Elisabeth's face and the expression she saw in them brought color pulsing to her cheeks. "Technically?" He chuckled, but there wasn't a trace of humor in the sound. "An odd word. No, Elisabeth, I'm not the rogue you think I am. When it became clear that Barbara didn't plan to return, I went to Olympia and petitioned the legislature for a divorce. It was granted."

"All of this must have been very difficult for Trista," Elisabeth observed, wondering why Barbara Fortner hadn't taken her daughter along when she left. Perhaps Jonathan had prevented that by some legal means, or maybe the woman had doubted her own ability to support a child in such a predominantly male world.

The house was within sight now, and twilight was beginning to fall over the fragrant orchard. Elisabeth felt a tug in her heart as they walked toward the glow of lantern light in the kitchen windows. She knew she'd been homesick for this time, this place, this man at her side, all of her life.

He shocked her with his reply to her remark about the effect the divorce had had on Trista. "My daughter believes her mother died in an accident in Boston, while visiting her family, and I don't want anyone telling her differently. Since the Everses have disinherited their daughter, I don't think there's any danger that they'll betray the secret."

Elisabeth stopped to stare at him, even though it was chilly and her wet dress was clinging to her skin. "But it's a lie."

"Sometimes a lie is kinder than the truth." Having spoken these words, Jonathan picked up his stride and Elisabeth was forced to follow him into the kitchen or stand in the yard until she caught her death.

Inside, Jonathan turned the wicks up in the lamps so that the flames burned brightly, then he opened a door in the stove and began shoving in wood from the box beside it. Elisabeth huddled nearby, gratefully soaking up the warmth.

"A lie is never better than the truth," she said, having finally worked up the courage to contradict him so bluntly. He was bull stubborn in his opinions; Rue would have said he was surely a Republican.

He wrenched a blue enamel pot from the back of the stove, carried it to the sink and used the hand pump to fill it with water. Then he set the pot on to heat. "You'll be wanting tea," he remarked, completely ignoring her statement. "I'll go and find you a dressing gown."

Elisabeth drew closer to the stove, wanting the heat to reach the marrow of her bones. She had stopped shivering, at least, when Jonathan returned with a long flannel nightgown and a heavy blue corduroy robe to go over it.

"You can change in the pantry," he said, shoving the garments at Elisabeth without meeting her eyes.

She took them and went into the little room—where the washer and drier were kept in her time—and stripped in the darkness. The virginal nightgown felt blissfully warm against her clammy, goose-pimpled skin.

She was tying the belt on the robe when she came out of the pantry to find Jonathan pouring hot water into a squat, practical-looking brown teapot. "I'd be happy to cook supper," she said, wanting to be useful and, more than that, to belong in this kitchen, if only for an hour.

"Good," he said with a sigh, going to the wall of

cupboards for mugs, which he carried back to the table. "Trista doesn't cook, and Ellen—that's our house-keeper—tends to be undependable on occasion. She was here earlier, but she wandered off and probably won't be back until tomorrow."

Elisabeth opened the icebox she'd discovered the first night and squatted to look inside it. Two large brook trout stared at her from a platter, and she carried them to the counter nearest the stove. "Did you catch these fish?" she asked, mostly because it gave her a soft, bittersweet sensation to be cooking and chatting idly with Jonathan.

He poured tea into the cups and went to the base of the back stairs to call Trista down. Evidently, she'd dutifully returned to her room after Miss Calderberry left.

"They were given to me," he answered presently, "in payment for a nerve tonic."

Elisabeth found a skillet in the pantry, along with jars of preserved vegetables and fruit. She selected a pint of sliced carrots and one of stewed pears, and carried them into the kitchen. By this time, Trista was setting the table with Blue Willow dishes, and Jonathan was nowhere in sight.

"He went out to the barn to feed the animals," Trista offered without being asked.

Elisabeth smiled. "Did you enjoy your piano lesson?"

"No," Trista answered. "How come your hair is all wet and straggly like that?"

Elisabeth put the trout into the skillet, minus their

heads. "I fell into the creek," she replied. "Is there any bread?"

Trista went to a maple box on the far counter and removed a loaf wrapped in a checkered dish towel. She set it on a plate, then brought a bowl of butter from the icebox. "I fell in the creek once," she confided. "I was only two, and I think maybe I would have drowned if my mama hadn't pulled me right out."

Elisabeth felt a small pull in the tenderest part of her soul. "It's a good thing she was around," she said gently, remembering a small tombstone with Trista's name carved into it. She had to look away to hide sudden tears that burned hot along her lashes.

"Maybe you could play the piano for us, after supper," Trista said.

Subtly, Elisabeth dried her eyes with the soft sleeve of the wrapper Jonathan had brought to her. Like the spoiled dress, it smelled faintly of lavender. "I haven't touched a keyboard in weeks, so I'm probably out of practice," she said with a cheerful sniffle. She took her first sip of the tea Jonathan had made for her and found it strong and sweet.

Trista laughed. "You couldn't sound worse than I do, no matter how long it's been since you've practiced."

Elisabeth laughed, too, and hugged the little girl. Through the window, she saw Jonathan moving toward the house in the last dim light of day. In that moment, she was as warm as if the noontime sun had been shining unrestrained on her bare skin.

She dished up the fish and the preserved carrots

while Jonathan washed at the sink, then they all sat down at the table.

Elisabeth was touched when Trista offered a short grace, asking God to take special care that her mama was happy in heaven. At this, Elisabeth opened her eyes for an accusing peek at Jonathan and found him staring defiantly back at her, his jawline set.

When the prayer was over, Jonathan immediately cut three perfect slices from the loaf of bread and moved one to his plate.

"Don't you have any cows?" Elisabeth asked. She'd noticed that Jonathan hadn't carried in a bucket of fresh milk, the way farmers did in books and movies.

He shook his head. "Don't need one," he replied. "I get all the butter and cream we can use from my patients."

"Do any of them give you money?" Elisabeth inquired, careful not to let so much as a trace of irony slip into her tone.

Still, Jonathan's look was quick and sharp. "We manage," he replied crisply.

After that, Trista carried the conversation, chattering cheerfully about the upcoming spelling bee at school and how she'd be sure to win it because she had so much time to practice her words. When supper was over, she and Elisabeth washed the dishes while Jonathan put on his suitcoat—it had been drying on the back of a chair near the stove—and reached for his medical bag.

"I won't be long," he said, addressing his words to

Trista. "I want to check and see if Mrs. Taber is any closer to delivering that baby."

Trista nodded and hung up the dish towel neatly over the handle on the oven door, but Elisabeth followed Jonathan outside.

"You mean you're leaving your daughter all alone here, with a total stranger?" she demanded, her hands on her hips.

Jonathan took a lantern from the wall of the back porch and lit it after striking a wooden match. "You're not a stranger," he said. "You and I are old friends, though I admit I don't remember exactly where we met." He bent to kiss her lightly on the cheek. "In case I don't see you before morning, good night, Lizzie."

Chapter 6

Lizzie.

Being called by that name made Elisabeth sway on her feet. She grasped at the railing beside the porch steps to steady herself.

Jonathan didn't notice her reaction, which was probably just as well because Elisabeth was in no condition to offer more explanations. She watched, stricken, as he strode toward the barn, the lantern in one hand, his medical bag in the other.

The moment he disappeared from sight, Elisabeth sank to the steps and just sat there, trembling, her hands over her face. Dear God in heaven, why hadn't she guessed? Why hadn't she known that *she* was the woman accused of setting the fire that probably killed Jonathan and Trista?

"Elisabeth?" Trista's voice was small and full of concern. "Is something the matter?"

Elisabeth drew in a deep breath and made herself speak in a normal tone of voice. "No, sweetheart," she lied, "everything is just fine."

The child hovered in the doorway behind her. "Are you going to play for me?" she asked hopefully. "I'm still in trouble, but I know Papa wouldn't mind my staying downstairs for just one song."

Elisabeth rose from the step, feeling chilly even in the warm robe and nightgown Jonathan had brought her. What a scandal her state of dress would cause in Victorian Pine River, she thought in a wild effort to distract herself. But there was no forgetting—if she didn't do something to change history, two people she already cherished would die tragically and she would be blamed for their deaths.

"One song," she answered sadly, taking Trista's hand and holding it tightly in her own.

"Elisabeth played a boogie," Trista told her father the next morning as she ate the oatmeal Ellen had made for her. Jonathan frowned, and the housekeeper stiffened slightly in disapproval, her shoulders going rigid under her cambric dress.

"A what?" His head ached; deception did not come naturally to him. And he knew Ellen hadn't believed his story about his late wife's sister arriving suddenly for a visit.

"Land sakes," muttered Ellen, slamming the fire door after shoving another stick of wood into the stove.

"A boogie-woogie," Trista clarified, and it was clear from her shining face that she enjoyed just saying the word.

Just then, Elisabeth came somewhat shyly down the back stairs and Jonathan's sensible heart skittered over two full beats when he saw her. She'd pinned her hair up in back, but it still made soft, taffy-colored curls around her face, and she was wearing a blue-and-white-flowered dress he didn't remember seeing on Barbara.

She smiled as she advanced toward the kitchen table, where Trista had set a place for her. "Good morning."

Remembering his manners, Jonathan rose and stood until Elisabeth was seated. "Ellen," he said, "This is my—sister-in-law, Miss Elisabeth McCartney. Elisabeth, our housekeeper, Ellen Harwood."

Ellen, a plain girl with a freckled face and frizzy red-brown hair, nodded grudgingly but didn't return Elisabeth's soft hello.

Jonathan waited until Ellen had gone upstairs to clean to ask, "What in the devil is a boogie-woogie?"

Elisabeth and Trista looked at each other and laughed. "Just a lively song," Elisabeth answered.

"A *very* lively song," Trista confirmed.

Jonathan sighed, pushed back his plate and pulled his watch from his vest pocket to flip open the case. He should have been gone an hour already, but he'd waited for a glimpse of Elisabeth, needing the swelling warmth that filled his bruised, stubborn heart when he looked at her. He could admit that to himself, if not out loud to her. "If you're ready, Trista, I'll drop you off at the schoolhouse on my way into town."

His daughter cast a sidelong glance at their strange but undeniably lovely guest. "I thought I'd walk this morning, Papa," Trista answered. "Elisabeth wants to see where I go to school."

Jonathan narrowed his eyes as he regarded Elisabeth, silently issuing warnings he could not say in front of Trista. "I'm sure she wouldn't be foolish enough to wander too far afield and get herself lost."

"I'm sure she wouldn't," Elisabeth said wryly, watching him with those blue-green eyes of hers. Their beauty always startled him, caught him off guard.

Jonathan left the table, then, and took his suitcoat from the peg beside the back door. Trista was ready with his medical bag, looking up at him earnestly. "Don't worry, Papa," she confided in a stage whisper. "I'll take very good care of Elisabeth."

He bent to kiss the top of her head, then tugged lightly at one of her dark pigtails. "I'm sure you will," he replied. After one more lingering look at Elisabeth, he left the house to begin his rounds.

Elisabeth marveled as she walked along, Trista's hand in hers. In the future, this road was a paved highway, following a slightly different course and lined with telephone poles. It was so quiet that she could hear the whisper of the creek on the other side of the birch, cedar and Douglas fir trees that crowded its edges.

A wagon loaded with hay clattered by, drawn by two weary-looking horses, and Elisabeth stared after it. By then, she'd given up the idea that this experience was any kind of hallucination, but she still hadn't gotten used to the sights and sounds of a century she'd thought was gone forever.

Trista gazed up at her speculatively. "Where did you go when you went away before?"

"Back to my own house," Elisabeth replied after careful thought.

"Are you going to stay with Papa and me from now on?"

Elisabeth had to avert her eyes, thinking of the fire. She'd spent most of the night tossing and turning, trying to come up with some way to evade fate. For all she knew, it could not be changed.

Again, she took her time answering. "Not forever," she said softly.

Trista's strong little fingers tightened around Elisabeth's. "I don't want you to go."

In that moment, Elisabeth realized that she didn't want to leave...ever. For all its hard realities, she felt that she belonged in this time, with these people. Indeed, it was her other life, back in twentieth-century Washington state, that seemed like a dream now. "Let's just take things one day at a time, Trista," she told the child.

They rounded a wide bend in the road and there was the brick schoolhouse—nothing but a ruin in Elisabeth's day—with glistening windows and a sturdy shake roof. The bell rang in the tower while a slender woman with dark hair and bright blue eyes pulled exuberantly on the rope.

Elisabeth stood stock-still. "It's wonderful," she whispered.

Trista laughed. "It's only a schoolhouse," she said indulgently. "Do you want to meet my teacher, Miss Bishop?" The child gazed up at Elisabeth, gray eyes dancing, and dropped her voice to a confidential whisper. "She's sweet on the blacksmith, and Ellen says she probably won't last out the term!"

Elisabeth smiled and shook her head. "It's time for class to start, so I'll meet Miss Bishop later."

Trista nodded and hurried off to join the other children surging up the steps and through the open doorway of the schoolhouse. A few of them looked back over their shoulders at Elisabeth, freckled faces puzzled.

She stood outside, listening, until the laughter and noise faded away. Being a teacher herself, she relished the familiar sounds.

The weather was bright and sunny, and Elisabeth had no particular desire to go back to Jonathan's house and face that sullen housekeeper, so she continued on toward town. As she neared the outskirts, the metallic squeal of a steam-powered saw met her ears and her step quickened. Even though she was scared—her situation gave new meaning to the hackneyed term "a fish out of water"—she was driven by a crazy kind of curiosity that wouldn't allow her to turn back.

Her first glimpse of the town stunned her, even though she'd thought she was prepared. The main street seemed to be composed of equal measures of mud and manure, and the weathered buildings clustered alongside were like something out of a *Bonanza* rerun. Any minute now, Hoss and Little Joe were sure to come ambling out through the swinging doors of the Silver Lady Saloon....

There were horses and wagons everywhere, and the noisy machinery in the sawmill screeched as logs from the timber-choked countryside were fed through its blades. Elisabeth wandered past a forge worked by a man wearing a heavy black apron. and she sidestepped two lumberjacks who came out of the general store to stand in the middle of the sidewalk, leering.

When she saw Jonathan's shingle up ahead, jutting out from the wall of a small, unpainted building, she hurried toward it. There was a blackboard on the wall beside the door, with the word *In* scrawled on it in white chalk. Elisabeth smiled as she opened the door.

A giant man in oiled trousers and a bloody flannel shirt sat on the end of an old-fashioned examining table. Jonathan was winding a clean bandage around the patient's arm, but he paused, seeing Elisabeth, took off his gold-rimmed spectacles and tucked them into his shirt pocket.

A tender whirlwind spun in her heart and then her stomach.

"Is there a problem?" he asked.

Elisabeth was feeling a little queasy, due to the sight

and smell of blood. She groped for a chair and sank into the only seat available—the hard wooden one behind Jonathan's cluttered desk. "No," she answered. "I was just exploring Pine River."

The lumberjack smiled at her, revealing gaps between his crooked, tobacco-stained teeth. "This must be the lady you've been hidin' away out at your place, Doc," he said.

Jonathan gave his patient an annoyed glance and finished tying off the bandage. "I haven't been hiding anything," he replied. "And don't go telling the whole damn town I have, Ivan, or I'll sew your mouth shut, just like I did your arm."

Ivan stood and produced a coin from the pocket of his filthy trousers, but even as he paid Jonathan, he kept his eyes on Elisabeth. "Good day to you, ma'am," he said, and then he reluctantly left the office.

Jonathan began cleaning up the mess Ivan and his blood had made. "Coming here was probably not the most intelligent thing you ever did," he observed presently.

Elisabeth's attention had strayed to the calendar page on the wall. April 17, 1892. It was incredible. "I was curious," she said distractedly, thinking of a documentary she'd watched on public television recently. "In a few more months—August, if I remember correctly— a woman in Fall River, Massachusetts, will be accused of murdering her father and stepmother with an ax. Her name is Lizzie Borden. She'll be acquitted of the crime because of a lack of evidence."

His gaze held both pity and irritation. "Is that supposed to have some kind of significance—the fact that
she has the same first name as you do?"

A chill went through Elisabeth; she hadn't thought
of that. "No. Besides, nobody ever calls me Lizzie."

"I do," Jonathan answered flatly, pouring water into
a clean basin and beginning to wash his hands.

"I'm glad to see that you're taking antisepsis seriously," Elisabeth said, as much to change the subject
as anything. She still had that jittery feeling that being
around Jonathan invariably gave her. "Most disease is
caused by germs, you know."

Jonathan leaned forward slightly and rounded his
eyes. "No," he said, pretending to be surprised.

"I guess maybe you've figured that out already,"
Elisabeth conceded, folding her hands in her lap.

"Thank you for that," he answered, drying his hands
on a thin, white towel and laying it aside.

Just then, the door opened and a tall man wearing
a cowboy hat and a battered, lightweight woolen coat
strode in. He needed a shave, and carried a rifle in his
right hand, holding it with such ease that it seemed a
part of him. When he glanced curiously at Elisabeth,
she saw that his eyes were a piercing turquoise blue.
Pinned to his coat was a shiny nickel-plated badge in
the shape of a star.

Wow, Elisabeth thought. *A real, live lawman.*

"'Morning, Farley," Jonathan said. "That boil still
bothering you?"

Farley actually flushed underneath that macho five-o'clock shadow of his. "Now, Jon," he complained in his low drawl, "there was no need to mention that in front of the lady. It's personal-like."

Elisabeth averted her face for a moment so the marshal wouldn't see that she was smiling.

"Sorry," Jonathan said, but Elisabeth heard the amusement in his voice even if Farley didn't. He gave her a pointed look. "The lady is just leaving. Let's get on with it."

Elisabeth nodded and bolted out of her chair. They wouldn't have to tell her twice—the last thing she wanted to do was watch Jonathan lance a boil on some private part of the marshal's body. "Goodbye," she said from the doorway. "And it was very nice to meet you, Mr. Farley."

"Just Farley," rumbled the marshal.

"Whatever," Elisabeth answered, ducking out and closing the door. There was something summarial in the way Jonathan pulled the shades on both windows.

Since her senses were strained from all the new things she was trying to take in, Elisabeth was getting tired. She walked back through town, nodding politely to the women who stared at her from the wooden sidewalks and pointed, and she hoped she hadn't ruined Jonathan's practice by marching so boldly into town and walking right into his office.

Reaching Jonathan's house, she found Ellen in the backyard. She'd hung a rug over the clothesline and was beating it with a broom.

Elisabeth smiled in a friendly way. "Hello," she called.

"If you want anything to eat," the housekeeper retorted, "you'll just have to fix it yourself!"

With a shrug, Elisabeth went inside and helped herself to a piece of bread, spreading it liberally with butter and strawberry jam. Then she found a blanket, helped herself to a book from Jonathan's collection in the parlor and set out for her favorite spot beside the creek.

She supposed Janet was probably getting worried, if she'd tried to call, and the Buzbee sisters would be concerned, too, if they went more than a few days without seeing her. She spread the blanket on the ground and sat down, tucking her skirts carefully around her.

A sigh escaped Elisabeth as she watched the sunlight making moving patterns on the waters of the creek. She was going to have to go back soon, back where she belonged. Her throat went tight. Before she could do that, she had to find some way to convince Jonathan that he and Trista were in very real danger.

The book forgotten at her side, Elisabeth curled up on the blanket and watched the water flow by, shimmering like a million liquid diamonds in the bright sunshine. And her sleepless night caught up with her.

When she awakened, it was to the sound of children's laughter echoing through the trees. Elisabeth rose, automatically smoothing her hair and skirts, and left the blanket and book behind to follow the path of the stream, walking beneath the covered bridge.

Presently, she could see the schoolhouse across the narrow ribbon of water. The children were all outside at recess. While the boys had divided up into teams for baseball, the girls pushed each other in the rustic swings and played hopscotch. She spotted Trista and wondered if the plain little girl at her side was Vera, who would eventually give birth to Cecily and Roberta Buzbee's mother.

Deciding that her presence would just raise a lot of awkward questions for Trista, Elisabeth slipped away and, after fetching the blanket and Jonathan's book, went back to the house.

By this time, there was a nice stew simmering on the stove and fresh bread cooling on the counter under a spotless dishtowel. Ellen had apparently left for the day.

Relieved, Elisabeth opened the icebox and peered inside. There was a bowl of canned pears left over from breakfast, so she dished up a serving and went out onto the back step to eat them. She was enjoying the glorious spring afternoon when Jonathan pulled up alongside the barn, driving his horse and buggy. He sprang nimbly down from the seat and walked toward her, his medical bag in one hand.

Elisabeth felt a sweet tightening in the most feminine part of her as he approached. "Must have been an easy day," she said when he sat down beside her.

He chuckled ruefully. "'Easy' isn't the word I would use to describe it," he said. "I couldn't stop thinking about you, Elisabeth."

Elisabeth drew a deep breath, and suddenly her heart and her spirit and all of her body were full of springtime. She lifted one eyebrow and forced herself to speak in a normal tone. "I suppose you were wondering if I was chasing poor Ellen all over the farm with an ax."

Jonathan laughed and shook his head. "No, I've considered doing that myself." His expression turned solemn in the next moment, however, and his sure, callused hand closed over one of Elisabeth's. "Who are you?" he rasped out. "And what spell have you cast over me?"

Never before had Elisabeth guessed that tenderness toward another person could run so deep as to be painful. "I'm just a woman," she said softly. "And I wouldn't have the first idea how to cast a spell."

He stood slowly, drawing Elisabeth with him, discounting her words with a shake of his head. She knew where he meant to take her, but she couldn't protest because it seemed to her that she'd been moving toward this moment all of her life. Maybe even for all of eternity.

She closed her eyes as he held her hand to his mouth and placed featherlight kisses on her knuckles.

Once they were inside the house, he lifted her easily into his arms and started up the back stairs. Elisabeth buried her face in his muscular neck, loving the smell and the strength and the substance of him. She looked up when she heard the creak of a door and found herself in a version of her room back in the world she knew.

The bed, made of aged, intricately carved oak, stood between the windows facing the fireplace. The walls were unpapered, painted a plain white, and Elisabeth didn't recognize any of the furniture.

Jonathan set her on her feet and just as she would have found the wit to argue that what they were about to do was wrong, he kissed her. So great was his skill and his innate magnetism that Elisabeth forgot her objections and lost herself in his mastery.

He unpinned her hair, combing it through with his fingers, and then very slowly began unbuttoning the front of her dress. Uncovering the lacy bra beneath, he frowned, and Elisabeth reached up to unfasten the front catch, revealing her full breasts to him.

Jonathan drew in his breath, then lifted one hand to caress her lightly. The pad of his thumb moved over her nipple, turning it button hard and wrenching a little cry of pleasure and surrender from Elisabeth.

She tilted her head back in glorious submission as he bent his head to her breast, pushing the dress down over her hips as he suckled. Elisabeth entwined her fingers in his thick, dark hair, her breathing shallow and quick.

When both her nipples were wet from his tongue, Jonathan laid her gently on the bed, taking no notice of her sneakers as he pulled them off and tossed them away. She crooned and arched her back as he slipped her panties down over her legs and threw them aside, too. He caressed her until she was damp, her body twisting with readiness.

His clothes seemed to disappear as easily as hers had, and soon he was stretched out on the mattress beside her. The April breeze ruffled the curtains at the windows and passed over their nakedness, stirring their passion to even greater heights rather than cooling it.

Elisabeth moaned as Jonathan claimed her mouth in another consuming kiss, his tongue sparring with hers. Her fingers dug into the moist flesh on his back as he moved his lips down over her breasts and her belly. Then he gripped her ankles and pressed her heels to the firm flesh of her bottom. Boldly, he burrowed through the silken barrier and tasted her.

Elisabeth's head moved from side to side on the pillow. "Oh, Jonathan—please—it's too much—"

"I want you to be ready for me," he told her gruffly, and then he enjoyed her in earnest, as greedy as if she were covered in honey.

The exercise moistened Elisabeth's skin, making small tendrils of hair cling to her face, and her breath came hard as she rose and fell in time with the rhythm Jonathan set for her. A low, guttural cry escaped her when he set her legs over his shoulders and teased her into the last stages of response.

She called his name when a sweet volcano erupted within her, her body arched like a bow drawn tight to launch an arrow. He spoke gently as he laid her, quivering, upon the bed and poised himself over her. She was still floating when he began kissing her collarbone.

"Shall I make love to you, Elisabeth?" he asked quietly, and a new tenderness swept over her in that moment because she knew he would respect her decision, whatever it might be.

"Yes," she whispered, twisting one finger in a lock of his hair. "Oh, yes."

He touched her with his manhood, and Elisabeth trembled with anticipation and a touch of fear. After all, there had only been one other man in her life and her experience was limited.

"I promise I won't hurt you," Jonathan said, and she was diffused with heat when he teased her by giving her just the tip of his shaft.

She clutched at his back. "Jonathan!"

He gave her a little more, and she marveled that he filled her so tightly. "What?"

"I want you—I need you—"

In a long, smooth glide, he gave her his length, and Elisabeth uttered a muffled shout of triumph. An instant later, she was in the throes of release, buckling helplessly beneath Jonathan, sobbing as her body worked out its sweet salvation.

She was embarrassed when she could finally lie still, and she would have turned her head away if Jonathan hadn't caught her chin in his hand and made her look at him.

"You were beautiful," he said. "So—beautiful."

Elisabeth's eyes brimmed with tears. Jonathan had given her a kind of pleasure she'd never dreamed existed, and she wanted to do the same for him. She cupped his face in her hands, moving her thumbs slowly over his jawbones, and she began to move beneath him.

He uttered a strangled moan and his powerful frame tensed, then he began to meet her thrusts with more and more force, until he finally exploded within her, filling her with his warmth. When it was over, he collapsed beside her, his head on her chest, one leg sprawled across her thighs, and Elisabeth held him.

After a long time, he asked quietly, "Who was he?"

Elisabeth braced herself, knowing men of Jonathan's generation expected women to come to their beds as virgins. "My husband," she said.

Instantly, Jonathan raised his head to stare into her eyes. "Your what?"

Her face felt hot. "Your honor is safe, Doctor," she assured him. "Ian and I were divorced a year ago."

He cleared his throat and sat up, reaching for his clothes. The distance in his manner wounded Elisabeth; she felt defensive. "Now I suppose I'm some kind of social pariah, just because my marriage didn't last," she said. "Well, things are different where I come from, Jonathan. Divorced women aren't branded as sinners for the rest of their lives."

Jonathan didn't answer, he just kept dressing.

There was a black-and-blue-plaid lap robe folded across the foot of the bed. Elisabeth snatched it up to cover herself. "Jonathan Fortner, if you walk out of here without speaking to me, I swear I'll never forgive you!"

He watched as she tried to dress without letting the lap robe slip. "Why did he divorce you?"

Elisabeth was furious; her cheeks ached with color. "He *didn't*—the choice was mine!"

Jonathan's shoulders slackened slightly, as though pressed under some great weight, and he sat down on the edge of the bed with a sigh. When he extended a hand to Elisabeth, she took it without thinking, and he settled her gently beside him, buttoning the front of her dress as he spoke.

"I'm sorry. I was judging what you did in terms of my own experience, and that's unreasonable."

Elisabeth couldn't resist touching the dark, rumpled hair at his nape. "Did she hurt you so badly, Jonathan?" she whispered.

"Yes," he answered simply. And then he stood and started toward the door. "Trista will be home soon," he said, without looking back. And he was gone.

Barely fifteen minutes later, when Elisabeth was in the kitchen brewing tea, Trista came in, carrying her slate and a spelling primer. The child set her school things down and went to the icebox for the crockery pitcher.

"How was school?" Elisabeth asked.

Trista's gray eyes sparkled as she poured milk into a glass and then helped herself to cookies from a squat china jar. "When Miss Bishop opened her lunch pail, there was a love letter inside—from Harvey Kates."

"The blacksmith?" Elisabeth took a cookie and joined Trista at the table.

The little girl nodded importantly, and there was now a milk mustache on her upper lip. "His sister Phyllis is in the seventh grade, and he gave her a penny to put the note where Miss Bishop would be sure to find it."

"And, of course, Phyllis told all of you exactly what her brother had written," Elisabeth guessed.

Trista nodded. "He said he was crazy for her."

Before Elisabeth could respond to that, Jonathan came into the kitchen. He gave Trista a distracted kiss on the top of her head, without so much as glancing at the houseguest he'd taken to bed only a short time before. "You've paid your debt to society," he said to the child. "You don't have to spend any more afternoons in your room."

Trista's face glowed with delight and gratitude. "Thank you, Papa."

Elisabeth might have been invisible for all the attention Jonathan was paying her.

"I'll be on rounds. Would you like to go along?"

The child shook her head. "I want to practice my piano lessons," she said virtuously.

Jonathan looked amused, but he made no comment. His gray eyes touched Elisabeth briefly, questioningly, and then he was gone. Sadness gripped her as she realized he now regretted what had happened between them.

While Trista trudged bravely through her music, Elisabeth made her way slowly up the back stairs and into the little girl's room. She was becoming too enmeshed in a way of life that could never be hers, and she had to put some space between herself and Jonathan before she fell hopelessly in love with him.

The decision was made. She would say goodbye to Trista, go back to her own time and try to make herself believe that all of this had been a dream.

Chapter 7

The necklace was gone.

Elisabeth dried her eyes with the back of one hand as relief and panic battled within her. After drawing a very deep breath and letting it out slowly, she made her way downstairs to the parlor, where Trista was struggling through *Ode to Joy* at the piano.

Elisabeth paused in the doorway, watching the little girl practice and marveling that she'd come to love this child so deeply in such a short time. "Trista?"

Innocent gray eyes linked with Elisabeth's and the notes reverberated into silence. "Yes?"

"I can't find my necklace. Have you seen it?"

Trista's gaze didn't waver, though her lower lip trembled slightly. "Papa has it. He said the pendant was valuable and might get lost if we left it lying around."

"I see," Elisabeth replied as righteous indignation welled up inside her. The fact that they'd been so gloriously intimate made Jonathan's action an even worse betrayal than it would ordinarily have been. "Do you know where he put it?"

Moisture brimmed along Trista's lower lashes; somehow, Trista had guessed that Elisabeth meant to leave and that the necklace had to go with her. She shook her head. "I don't," she sniffled. "Honest."

Elisabeth's heart ached, and she went to sit beside Trista on the piano bench, draping one arm around the little girl's shoulders. "There are people in another place who will be worrying about me," Elisabeth said gently. "I have to go and let them know I'm all right."

A tear trickled down Trista's plump cheek. "Will you be back?"

Elisabeth leaned over and lightly kissed the child's temple. "I don't know, sweetheart. Something very strange is happening to me, and I don't dare make a lot of promises, because I'm not sure I can keep them." She thought about the impending fire and a sense of hopelessness swept over her. "I'll tell you this, though—if I have any choice in the matter, I *will* see you again."

Trista nodded and rested her head against Elisabeth's shoulder. "Most times, when grown-up people go away, they don't come back."

Knowing the child was referring to her lost mother, Elisabeth hugged her again. "If I don't return, Trista, I want you to remember that it was only because I couldn't, and not because I didn't want to." She stood.

"Now, you go and finish your practicing while I look for the necklace."

Elisabeth searched Jonathan's study, which was the small parlor in modern times, and found nothing except a lot of cryptic notes, medical books jammed with bits of paper and a cabinet full of vials and bottles and bandage gauze. From there, she progressed to the bedroom where he had made such thorough love to her only that afternoon.

She was still angry, but just being in that room again brought all the delicious, achy sensations rushing back, and she was almost overwhelmed with the need of him. She began with the top drawer of his bureau, finding nothing but starched handkerchiefs and stiff celluloid collars.

"Did you lose something?"

Jonathan's voice startled Elisabeth; like a hard fall, it left her breathless. She turned, her cheeks flaming, to face him.

"My necklace," she said, keeping her shoulders squared. "Where is it, Jonathan?"

He went to the night table beside his bed, opened the drawer and took out a small leather box. Lifting the lid, he looped the pendant over his fingers and extended it to Elisabeth.

"I'm going back," she said, unable to meet his eyes. For the moment, it was all she could do to cope with the wild emotions this man had brought to life inside her. He had taught her one thing for certain: she had never truly loved Ian or any other man. Jonathan Fortner had first claim on both her body and her soul.

He kept his distance, perhaps sensing that she would fall apart if he touched her. "Why?"

"We made love, Jonathan," she whispered brokenly, her hands trembling as she opened the catch on the pendant and draped the chain around her neck. "That changed things between us. And I can't afford to care for you."

Jonathan sighed. "Elisabeth—"

"No," she said, interrupting, holding up one hand to silence him. "I know you think I'm eccentric or deluded or something, and maybe you're right. Maybe this is all some kind of elaborate fantasy and I'm wandering farther and farther from reality."

He came to her then and took her into his arms. She felt the hard strength of his thighs and midsection. "I'm real, Elisabeth," he told her with gentle wryness. "You're not imagining me, I promise you."

She pushed herself back from the warm solace of him. "Jonathan, I came here to warn you," she said urgently. "There was—will be—a fire. You've got to do something, if not for your own sake, then for Trista's."

He kissed her forehead. "I know you believe what you're saying," he replied, his tone gentle and a little hoarse. "But it's simply not possible for a human being to predict the future. Surely you understand that I cannot throw my daughter's life into an uproar on the basis of your...premonitions."

Elisabeth stiffened as a desperate idea struck her.

"Suppose I could prove that I'm from the future, Jonathan—suppose I could show you the article that will be printed in the *Pine River Bugle?*"

Jonathan was frowning at her, as though he feared she'd gone mad. "That would be impossible."

She gave a brief, strangled laugh. "Impossible. You know, Jonathan, until just a short while ago, I would have said it was *impossible* to travel from my century to yours. I thought time was an orderly thing, rolling endlessly onward, like a river. Instead, it seems that the past, present and future are all of a piece, like some giant celestial tapestry."

All the while she was talking, Jonathan was maneuvering her toward the bed, though this time it was for a very different reason. "Just lie down for a little while," he said reasonably. His bag was close at hand, like always, and he snapped it open.

"Jonathan, I'm quite all right...."

He took out a syringe and began filling it from a vial.

Elisabeth's eyes went wide and she tried to bolt off the bed. "Don't you dare give me a shot!" she cried, but Jonathan put his free hand on her shoulder and pressed her easily back to the mattress. "Ouch!" she yelled when the needle punctured her upper arm. "Damn you, Jonathan, I'm not sick!"

He withdrew the needle and reached for the plaid lab robe Elisabeth had tried to hide behind after their lovemaking that afternoon. "Just rest. You'll feel better in a few hours," he urged, laying the blanket over her.

Elisabeth sat up again, only to find that all her muscles had turned to water. She sagged back against the pillows. "Jonathan Fortner, what did you give me? Do you realize that there are laws against injecting things into people's veins?"

"Be quiet," he ordered sternly.

The door creaked open and Trista peered around the edge. "What's wrong with Elisabeth?" she asked in a thin, worried voice.

Jonathan sighed and closed his medical bag with a snap. "She's overwrought, that's all," he answered. "Run along and do your spelling lesson."

"Pusher!" Elisabeth spat out once the door had closed behind the little girl. The room was starting to undulate, and she felt incredibly weak. "I should get that Farley person out here and have you arrested."

"Don't you think you're being a little childish?" Jonathan asked, bending over the bed. "I admit I shouldn't have shoved you down that way, but you didn't give me much choice, did you?"

Elisabeth rolled her eyes. "A pusher is... Oh, never mind! But you mark my words, *Doctor*—I'm filing a complaint against you!"

"And I'm sure Marshal Haynes will track me down and throw me in the hoosegow the minute his boil is healed and he can sit a horse again." In the next moment, Jonathan was gone.

Struggling to stay awake, Elisabeth wondered how she could ever expect to get through to this man if he was going to hold her down and drug her every time she talked about her experience. She drifted off into a restless sleep, waking once to find Trista standing beside the bed, gently bathing her forehead with a cool cloth.

Elisabeth felt a surge of tenderness and, catching hold of Trista's hand, she gave it a little squeeze. Then she was floating again.

The house was dark when the medication finally wore off, and the realization that this was Jonathan's bed came to her instantly. She lay very still until she was sure he wasn't beside her.

Her hand rose to her throat, and she was relieved to find the necklace was still there. Another ten minutes passed before she had the wit to get out of bed and grope her way through the blackness to the door.

In the hallway, she carefully took the pendant off and tossed it over Trista's threshold. Only when she was on the other side did she put it on again.

There was pale moonlight shining in through the little girl's window, and Elisabeth went to her bedside and gently awakened her.

"You're leaving," Trista whispered, holding very tightly to her rag doll.

Elisabeth bent to kiss her forehead. "Yes, darling, I'm going to try. Remember my promise—if I can come back to you, I will."

Trista sighed. "All right," she said forlornly. "Goodbye, Elisabeth."

"Goodbye, sweetheart." Elisabeth put her arms around Trista and gave her a final hug. "No matter what happens, don't forget that I love you."

Trista's eyes were bright with tears as she sank her teeth into her lower lip and nodded.

Elisabeth drew a deep breath and went back to the door, closing her eyes as she reached for the knob, turned it and stepped through.

She was back in her own time. Elisabeth opened her eyes to find herself in a carpeted hallway, then reached out for a switch and found one. Suddenly the electric wall sconces glared.

She opened the door to her room and peeked in. A poignant, bitter loneliness possessed her because there was no trace, no hint of Jonathan's presence. After lingering for a moment, she turned and went downstairs to the telephone table in the hallway.

Not surprisingly, the little red light on her answering machine was blinking.

There were three messages from Janet, each more anxious than the last, and several other friends had called from Seattle. Elisabeth shoved her fingers through her hair, sighed and padded into the kitchen, barefoot. She was still wearing the cambric dress Jonathan had given her, and she smiled, thinking what a sensation it would cause if she wore it to the supermarket.

Since she hadn't had dinner, Elisabeth heated a can of soup before finding the microfilm copies she'd made in the *Bugle* offices. It gave her a chill to think of showing Jonathan a newspaper account of his own death and that of his daughter.

While she huddled at the kitchen table, eating, Elisabeth read over the articles. It still troubled her that no bodies had been found, but then, such investigations hadn't been very thorough or scientific in the nineteenth century. Maybe the discovery had even been hushed up, out of some misguided Victorian sense of delicacy.

Flipping ahead in the sheaf of copies, Elisabeth came to her own trial for the murder of Jonathan and Trista Fortner. With a growing sense of unreality, she read that Lizzie McCartney, who "claimed to be" the sister of the late Barbara McCartney Fortner, had been found guilty of the crime of arson, and thus murder, and sentenced to hang.

Elisabeth pushed away the last of her soup, feeling nauseous. Destiny had apparently decreed her death, as well as Jonathan's and Trista's, and she had no way of knowing whether or not their singular fates could be circumvented.

She took her bowl to the sink and rinsed it, then went upstairs to take a long, hot shower. When that was finished Elisabeth brushed her teeth, put on a lightweight cotton nightgown and crawled into bed.

Unable to sleep, she lay staring up at the ceiling. It would be easy to avoid being tried and hanged—all she would have to do was drop the necklace down a well somewhere and never go back to Jonathan's time. But even as she considered this idea, Elisabeth knew she would discard it. She loved Trista and, God help her,

Jonathan, too. And she could not let two human beings die without trying to save them.

Throughout the rest of the night, Elisabeth slept only in fits and starts. The telephone brought her summarily into a morning she wasn't prepared to face.

"Hello?" she grumbled into the ornate receiver of the French telephone on the vanity table. Having stubbed her toe on a chest while crossing the room, Elisabeth made the decision to move the instrument closer to the bed.

"There you are!" Janet cried, sounding both annoyed and relieved. "Good heavens, Elisabeth—*where have you been?*"

Elisabeth sighed and sank down onto the vanity bench. "Relax," she said. "I was only gone for a couple of days."

"A couple of days? Give me a break, Elisabeth, I've been trying to reach you for *two weeks!* You were supposed to come to Seattle and spend a weekend with me, remember?"

Two weeks? Elisabeth gripped the edge of the vanity table. The question was out of her mouth before she could properly weigh the effect it would have. "Janet, what day is it?"

Her friend's response was a short, stunned silence, followed by, "It's the first of May. I'm on my way. Don't you set foot out of that house, Elisabeth McCartney, until I get there."

Elisabeth's mind was still reeling. If there was no logical correlation between her time and Jonathan's, she might return to find that the fire had already happened. The idea set her trembling, but she knew she had to keep Janet from coming to visit and get back to 1892.

She ran the tip of her tongue quickly over her dry lips. "Listen, Janet, I'm all right, really. It's just that I met this fascinating man." That much, at least, was true. Bullheaded though he might be, Jonathan *was* fascinating. "I guess I just got so caught up in the relationship that I wasn't paying attention to the calendar."

Janet sounded both intrigued and suspicious. "Who is this guy? You haven't mentioned any man to me."

"That's because I just met him." She thought quickly, desperately. "We were away for a while."

"Something about this doesn't ring true," Janet said, but she was weakening. Elisabeth could hear it in her voice.

"I—I really fell hard for him," she said.

"Who is he? What does he do?"

Elisabeth took a deep breath. "His name is Jonathan Fortner, and he's a doctor."

"I'd like to meet him."

Elisabeth stifled an hysterical giggle. "Yes—well, he and I are taking off for a vacation. But maybe I can arrange something after I—we get back."

"Where are you going?" Janet asked quickly, sounding worried again.

"San Francisco." It was the first place that came to mind.

"Oh. Well, I'll just come to the airport and see you off. That way, you could introduce Jonathan and me."

"Umm," Elisabeth stalled, biting her lower lip. "We're going by car," she finally answered. "I promise faithfully that I'll call you the instant I step through the doorway."

Janet sighed. "All right but, well, there isn't anything wrong with this guy, is there? I mean, it's almost like you're hiding something."

"You've pried it out of me," Elisabeth teased. "He's a vampire. Even as we speak, he's lying in a coffin in the basement, sleeping away the daylight hours."

The joke must have reassured Janet, because she laughed. A moment later, though, her tone was serious again. "You'd tell me if you weren't all right, wouldn't you?"

Elisabeth hesitated. As much as she loved Janet, Rue was the only person in the world she could have talked to about what was happening to her. "If I thought there was anything you could do to help, yes," she answered softly. "Please don't worry about me, Janet. I'll call you when I get back." *If I get back.* "And we'll make plans for my visit to Seattle."

Mollified at least for the moment, Janet accepted Elisabeth's promise, warned her to be careful and said goodbye.

She showered and put on white pants and a sea green tank top, along with a pair of plastic thongs. Then after a hasty trip to the mailbox—there were two postcards from Rue, one mailed from Istanbul, the other from

Cairo, along with a forwarded bank statement and a sales flier addressed to "occupant"—Elisabeth made preparations to return to Jonathan and Trista.

As she looked at the copies of the June 1892 issue of the *Bugle,* however, she began to doubt that Jonathan would see them as proof of anything. He was bound to say that, while the printing admittedly looked strange, she could have had the articles made up.

Elisabeth laid the papers down on the kitchen table and went up the back stairs and along the hallway to her room. In the bathroom medicine cabinet, she found the half-filled bottle of penicillin tablets she'd taken for a throat infection a few months before.

The label bore a typewritten date, along with Elisabeth's name, but it was the medicine itself that would convince Jonathan. After all, he was a doctor. She dropped the bottle into the pocket of her pants and went back out to the vanity.

Aunt Verity's necklace was lying there, where she'd left it before taking her shower that morning. Her fingers trembled with mingled resolution and fear as she put the chain around her neck and fastened the clasp.

Reaching the hallway, Elisabeth went directly to the sealed door and clasped the knob in her hand.

Nothing happened.

"Please," Elisabeth whispered, shutting her eyes. "Please."

Still, that other world was closed to her. Fighting down panic, she told herself she had only to wait for the "window" to open again. In the meantime, there was something else she wanted to do.

After riffling through a variety of scribbled notes beside the hallway phone, she found the name and number she wanted. She dialed immediately, to keep herself from having time to back out.

"Hello?" a woman's voice answered.

Elisabeth had a clear picture of Chastity Pringle in her mind, standing in that quilting booth at the craft show, looking at the necklace as though it was something that had slithered out of hell. "Ms. Pringle? This is Elisabeth McCartney. You probably don't remember me, but we met briefly at the craft fair, when you were showing your quilts—"

"You were wearing Verity's necklace," Chastity interrupted in a wooden tone.

"Yes," Elisabeth answered. "Ms. Pringle, I wonder if I could see you sometime today—it's important."

"I won't set foot in that house" was the instant response.

"All right," Elisabeth agreed quietly, "I'll be happy to come to you. If that's convenient, of course."

"I'll meet you at the Riverview Café," Chastity offered, though not eagerly.

"Twelve-thirty?"

"Twelve-thirty," the woman promised.

The Riverview Café was about halfway between Pine River and Cotton Creek, the even smaller town where Chastity lived. Elisabeth couldn't help wondering, as she stared blankly at a morning talk show to pass the time, why Ms. Pringle was being so cloak-and-dagger about the whole thing.

At twelve-fifteen, Elisabeth pulled into the restaurant parking lot, got out of her car and went inside. Chastity hadn't arrived yet, but Elisabeth allowed a waitress to escort her to a table with a magnificent view of the river and ordered herbal tea to sip while she waited.

Chastity appeared, looking anxious and rushed, at exactly twelve-thirty. She was trim and very tanned, and her long, dark hair was wound into a single, heavy braid that rested over one shoulder. She focused her gaze on Elisabeth's necklace and shuddered visibly.

Elisabeth waited until the waitress had taken their orders before bracing her forearms against the table edge and leaning forward to ask bluntly, "What was your connection with my aunt Verity, and why are you afraid of this necklace?"

"Verity was my friend," Chastity answered, "at a time when I needed one very badly." The waitress brought their spinach and smoked salmon salads, then went away again. "As for the pendant..."

"It was yours once," Elisabeth ventured, operating purely on instinct. "Wasn't it...Barbara?"

The woman's dark eyes were suddenly enormous, and the color drained from her face. "You know? About the doorway, I mean?"

Elisabeth nodded.

Barbara Fortner reached for her water glass with an unsteady hand. "You've met Jonathan, then, I suppose, and Trista." She paused to search Elisabeth's face anxiously. "How is my little girl?"

"She believes you're dead," Elisabeth answered, not unkindly.

Barbara flinched. Misery was visible in every line of her body. "Jonathan would have told her something like that. He'd be too proud to admit to the truth, that he drove me away."

Elisabeth's hands tightened on the arms of her chair. Her entire universe had been upended, but here was a woman who understood. Whatever Elisabeth's personal feelings about Barbara might be, she was relieved to find a person who knew about the world beyond that threshold.

"Did he divorce me?" Barbara asked quietly, after a long moment.

Elisabeth hesitated. "Yes."

Jonathan's ex-wife took several sips of water and then shrugged, although Elisabeth could see that she was shaken. "How is Trista?"

Elisabeth opened her purse and took out the folded copies of the newspaper articles. "She's in a lot of danger, Barbara, and so is Jonathan. They need your help."

Barbara's face blanched as she scanned the newspaper accounts. "Oh, my God, my baby...I knew I should have found a way to bring her with me."

A quivering sensation in the pit of her stomach kept Elisabeth constantly on edge. She was aware of every tick of the clock, and the idea that it might already be too late to help Jonathan and Trista tormented her.

"Sometimes I can make the trip back and sometimes I can't," she said in a low voice. "Do you know if there's some way to be sure of connecting?"

Tears glimmered in Barbara's eyes as she met Elisabeth's gaze. "I—I don't know—I only did it a couple of times—but I think there has to be some sort of strong emotion. Are you going back?"

Elisabeth nodded. "As soon as I can manage it, yes."

Barbara sat up very straight in her chair, her salad forgotten. "You're in love with Jonathan, aren't you?"

The answer came immediately; Elisabeth didn't even need to think about it. "Yes."

"Fine. Then the two of you will have each other." She leaned forward, her eyes pleading. "Elisabeth, I want you to send Trista over the threshold to me. It might be the only way to save her."

Barbara's statement was undeniable, but it caused Elisabeth tremendous pain. If she put the necklace on Trista and sent her through the doorway, she would disappear forever. Jonathan would be heartbroken, and he'd never believe the truth. No, he'd think Elisabeth had harmed the child, and he'd hate her for it.

And that wasn't all. Without the necklace, Elisabeth would be trapped in the nineteenth century, friendless and despised. Why, she might even be blamed for Trista's disappearance and hanged or sent to prison.

She swallowed hard. "Jonathan loves Trista, and he's a good father. Besides, your daughter believes you died in Boston, while visiting your family."

Barbara's perfectly manicured index finger stabbed

at the stack of photocopies lying on the tabletop. "If you don't send her to me, she'll burn to death!"

Elisabeth looked away, toward the river flowing past. "I'll do what I can," she said. Presently, she met Barbara's eyes again, and she was calmer. "How could you have left her in the first place?" she asked, no longer able to hold the question back.

The other woman lowered her eyes for a moment. "I was desperately unhappy, and I'd had a glimpse of this world. I couldn't stop thinking about it. It was like a magnet." She sighed. "I wasn't cut out to live there, to be the wife of a country doctor. I had a lover, and Jonathan found out. He was furious, even though Matthew and I had broken off. I was afraid he was going to kill me, so I came here to stay. Verity took me in and helped me establish an identity, and I left the necklace with her because I knew I'd never want to go back."

"Not even to help your daughter?"

Color glowed in Barbara's cheeks. "I don't dare step over that threshold," she said, almost in a whisper. "I'm too afraid of Jonathan."

Although Elisabeth would never have denied that Jonathan was imposing, even arrogant and opinionated, she didn't believe for a moment that he would ever deliberately hurt another person. He was a doctor, after all, and an honorable man. She changed the subject.

"How long have you been here?"

Barbara dried her eyes carefully with a cloth napkin. "Fifteen years," she answered. "And I've been happy."

Elisabeth felt another chill. Fifteen years. And yet

Trista was only eight—or she had been, when Elisabeth had seen her last. She gave up trying to figure out these strange wrinkles in time and concentrated on what was important: saving Trista and Jonathan.

"If I can find a way to protect Trista while still keeping her there, that's what I'm going to do," she warned, rising and reaching for her purse and the check. "Jonathan adores his daughter, and it would crush him to lose her."

Barbara lifted one eyebrow, but made no move to stand. "Are you really thinking of Jonathan, Elisabeth? Or is it yourself you're worried about?"

It was a question Elisabeth couldn't bear to answer. She paid for the lunches neither she nor Barbara had eaten and hurried out of the restaurant.

Chapter 8

By the time Elisabeth arrived at home, she was in a state of rising panic. She had to reach Jonathan and Trista, had to know that they were all right. She glanced fitfully at the telephone and answering machine on the hallway table, not pausing even though the message light was blinking.

Could you please connect me with someone in 1892? she imagined herself asking a bewildered operator.

Shaking her head, Elisabeth went on into the kitchen and tossed her purse onto the table. Then she crossed the room to switch the calendar page from April to May. She was still standing there staring, her teeth sunk into her lower lip, when a loud pounding at the back door startled her out of her wonderment.

Miss Cecily Buzbee peered at her through the frosted

oval glass, and Elisabeth smiled as she went to admit her neighbor, who had apparently come calling alone.

"I don't mind telling you," the sweet-natured spinster commented after Elisabeth had let her in and offered a glass of ice tea, "that Sister and I have been concerned about you, since we don't see hide nor hair of you for days at a time."

Elisabeth busied herself with the tasks of running cold water into a pitcher and adding ice and powdery tea. "I'm sorry you were worried," she said quietly. She carried the pitcher to the table, along with two glasses. "I don't mean to be a recluse—I just need a lot of solitude right now."

Cecily smiled forgivingly. "I don't suppose there's any lemon, is there, dear?"

Elisabeth shook her head regretfully. Even if she'd remembered to buy lemons the last time she'd shopped, which she hadn't, that had been two weeks before and they would probably have spoiled by now. "Miss Cecily," she began, clasping her hands together on her lap so her visitor wouldn't see that they were trembling, "how well did you know my aunt Verity?"

"Oh, very well," Cecily trilled. "Very well, indeed."

"Did she tell you stories about this house?"

Cecily averted her cornflower blue eyes for a moment, then forced herself to look at Elisabeth again. "You know how Verity liked to talk. And she *was* a rather fanciful sort."

Elisabeth smiled, remembering. "Yes, she was. She told Rue and me lots of things about this house, about people simply appearing, seemingly out of nowhere, and other things like that."

The neighbor nodded solemnly. "Sister and I believe that young Trista Fortner haunts this house, poor soul. Her spirit never rested because she died so horribly."

Unable to help herself, Elisabeth shuddered. If she did nothing else, she had to see that Trista wasn't trapped in that fire. "I can't buy the ghost theory," she said, sipping the tea and barely noticing that it tasted awful. "I mean, here are these souls, supposedly lost in the scheme of things, wandering about, unable to find their way into whatever comes after this life. Why would God permit that, when there is so much order in everything else, like the seasons and the courses of the planets?"

"My dear," Cecily debated politely, "reputable people have seen apparitions. They cannot all be dismissed as crackpots."

Elisabeth sighed, wondering which category she would fall into: crackpot or reputable person. "Isn't it just possible that the images were every bit as real as the people seeing them? Perhaps there are places where time wears thin and a person can see through it, into the past or the future, if only for a moment."

Miss Buzbee gave the idea due consideration. "Well, Elisabeth, as the bard said, there are more things in heaven and earth…"

Anxiety filled Elisabeth as her mind turned back to Jonathan and Trista. Would she return to 1892 only to find them gone—if she was able to reach them at all?

"More tea?" she asked, even though she was desperate to be alone again so that she could make another attempt at crossing the threshold.

Trista's friend, Vera, had apparently trained her granddaughters not to overstay their welcome. "I really must be running along," Cecily said. "It's almost time for Sister and I to take our walk. Two miles, rain or shine," she said with resignation, frowning grimly as she looked out through the windows. Storm clouds were gathering on the horizon.

"I've enjoyed our visit," Elisabeth replied honestly, following Miss Cecily to the door. She wondered what Cecily would say if told Elisabeth had had a glimpse of Vera, the Buzbee sisters' grandmother, as a little girl playing on the school grounds.

A light rain started to fall after Cecily had gone, and Elisabeth stood at the back door for a long moment, her heart hammering as she gazed at the orchard. The beautiful petals of spring were all gone now, replaced by healthy green leaves—another reminder that two weeks of her life had passed without her knowing.

When thunder rolled down from the mountains and lightning splintered the sky, Elisabeth shuddered and closed the door. Then she hurried up the back stairs and along the hallway.

"Trista!" she shouted, pounding with both fists at the panel of wood that separated her from that other world. "Trista, can you hear me?"

There was no sound from the other side, except for the whistle of the wind, and Elisabeth sagged against the wood in frustrated despair. "Oh, God," she whispered, "don't let them be dead. *Please* don't let them be dead."

After a long time, she turned away and went back down the stairs to the kitchen. She put on a rain coat and dashed out to the shed for an armload of kindling and aged apple wood, which she carried to the hearth in the main parlor.

There, she built a fire to bring some warmth and cheer to that large, empty room. When the wood was crackling and popping in the grate, she put the screen in place and went to the piano, lifting the keyboard cover and idly striking middle C with her index finger.

"Hear me, Trista," she pleaded softly, flexing her fingers. "Hear and wish just as hard as you can for me to come back."

She began to play the energetic tune she'd described to Trista as a boogie-woogie, putting all her passion, all her hopes and fears into the crazy, racing, tinkling notes of the song. When she finally stopped, her fingers exhausted, the sound of another pianist attempting to play the song met her ears.

Elisabeth nearly overturned the piano bench in her eagerness to run upstairs to the door that barred her from the place where she truly belonged. She wrenched hard on the knob, and breathtaking exultation rushed into her when it turned.

Trista's awkward efforts at the piano tune grew louder and louder as Elisabeth raced through the little girl's bedroom and down the steps. When she burst into the parlor, Trista's face lit up.

She ran to Elisabeth and threw her arms around her.

Elisabeth embraced her, silently thanking God that she wasn't too late, that the fire hadn't already happened, then knelt to look into Trista's eyes. "Sweetheart, this is important. How long have I been gone?"

Trista bit her lip, seeming puzzled by the question. "Since last night, when you came in and kissed me goodbye. It's afternoon now—school let out about an hour ago."

"Good," Elisabeth whispered, relieved to learn that days or weeks hadn't raced by in her absence. "Was your father upset to find that I wasn't here?"

"He cussed," Trista replied with a solemn nod. "It reminded me of the day Mama went away to Boston. Papa got angry then, too, because she didn't say goodbye to us."

Elisabeth sat down on the piano bench and took Trista onto her lap, recalling her talk with Barbara Fortner in the Riverview Café. Sending Trista over the threshold to her mother might be the only way to save her, but Jonathan would never understand that. "Where is he now?"

Trista sighed. "In town. There was a fight at one of the saloons, and some people needed to be stitched up."

Elisabeth winced and said, "Ouch!" and Trista laughed.

"Papa's going to be happy when he sees you're

back," the child said after an interval. "But he probably won't admit he's pleased."

"Probably not," Elisabeth agreed, giving Trista's pigtail a playful tug. She looked down at her slacks and tank top. "I guess I'd better change into something more fitting," she confided.

Trista nodded and took Elisabeth's hand. They went upstairs together, and the little girl's expression was thoughtful. "I wish Papa would let *me* wear trousers," she said. "It would be so much better for riding a horse. I hate sitting sideways in the saddle, like a priss."

"Do you have a horse?" Elisabeth asked as they reached the second floor, but continued on to the attic, where Barbara's clothes were stored.

"Yes," Trista answered, somewhat forlornly. "Her name is Estella, she's about a thousand years old, and she's a ninny."

Elisabeth laughed. "What a way to talk about the poor thing!" The attic door creaked a little as they went in, and the bright afternoon sunlight was flecked with a galaxy of tiny dust particles. "Most little girls love their horses, if they're lucky enough to have one."

Trista dusted off a short stool and sat down, smoothing the skirts of her flowered poplin pinafore as she did so. "Estella just wants to wander around the pasture and chew grass, and she won't come when I call because she doesn't like to be ridden. Do you have your own horse, Elisabeth?"

Opening the heavy doors of the cedar-lined armoire, Elisabeth ran her hand over colorful, still-crisp skirts of lawn and cambric and poplin and satin and even velvet. "I don't," she said distractedly, "but my cousin Rue does. When her grandfather died, she inherited a ranch in Montana, and I understand there are lots of horses there." She took a frothy pink lawn gown from the wardrobe and held it against her, waltzing a little because it was so shamelessly frilly.

"Wasn't he your grandfather, too, if you and Rue are cousins?"

Elisabeth bent to kiss the child's forehead, while still enjoying the feel of the lovely dress under her hands. "Our fathers were brothers," she explained. "The ranch belonged to Rue's mother's family."

"Could we visit there sometime?" The hopeful note in Trista's voice tugged at Elisabeth's heart, and unexpected tears burned in her eyes.

She shook her head, turning her back so Trista wouldn't see that she was crying. "It's very far away," she said after a long time had passed.

"Montana isn't so far," Jonathan's daughter argued politely. "We could be there in three days if we took the train."

But we wouldn't see Rue, Elisabeth thought sadly. *She hasn't even been born yet.* She stepped behind a dusty folding screen and slipped off her tank top and slacks, then pulled the pink dress on over her head. "I don't think your papa would want you to go traveling without him," she said, having finally found words, however inadequate, to answer Trista.

When Elisabeth came out from behind the screen,

Trista drew in her breath. "Thunderation, Elisabeth—you look beautiful!"

Elisabeth laughed, put her hands on her hips and narrowed her eyes. "Thanks a heap, kid, but did you just swear?"

Trista giggled and scurried around behind Elisabeth to begin fastening the buttons and hooks that would hold the dress closed in back. "*Thunderation* isn't a swear word," she said indulgently. "But I don't suppose it's very ladylike, either."

The light was fading, receding across the dirty floor toward the windows like an ebbing tide, so the two went down the attic steps together, Elisabeth carrying her slacks and tank top over one arm. She felt a sense of excitement and anticipation, knowing she would see Jonathan again soon.

In her room, Elisabeth brushed her hair and pinned it up, while Trista sat on the edge of the bed, watching with her head tilted to one side and her small feet swinging back and forth.

Downstairs, Elisabeth checked the pot roast Ellen had left to cook in the oven. She found an apron to protect her gown, then set to work washing china from the cabinet in the dining room. In a drawer of the highboy, she found white tapers and silver candle sticks, and she set these on the formal table.

"We never eat in here," Trista said.

Outside, twilight was falling, and with it came a light spring rain. "We're going to tonight," Elisabeth replied.

"Why? It isn't Christmas or Easter, and it's not any-body's birthday."

Elisabeth smiled. "I want to celebrate being home," she said, and only when the words were out of her mouth did she realize how presumptuous they sounded. Jonathan had made love to her, but it wasn't as though he'd expressed a desire for a lifelong commitment or anything like that. This wasn't her home, it was Barbara's, as was the china she was setting out and the dress she was wearing.

As were the child and the man she loved so fiercely.

"Don't be sad," Trista said, coming to stand close to Elisabeth in a show of support.

Elisabeth gave her a distracted squeeze, and said brightly, "I think we'd better get some fires going, since it's so dreary out."

"I'll do it," Trista announced. "So you don't ruin your pretty dress." With that, she fetched wood from the shed out back and laid fires in the grates in the parlor and the dining room. Rain was pattering at the windows and blazes were burning cheerily on the hearths when Elisabeth saw Jonathan drive his buggy through the wide doorway of the barn.

It was all she could do not to run outside, ignoring the weather entirely, and fling herself into his arms. But she forced herself to remain in the kitchen, where she and Trista had been sipping tea and playing Go Fish while they waited for Jonathan.

When he came in, some twenty minutes later, he was

wet to the skin. The look in his gray eyes was grim, and Elisabeth felt a wrench deep inside when she saw him.

"You," he said, tossing his medical bag onto the shelf beside the door and peeling off his coat. He wasn't wearing a hat, and his dark hair streamed with rain water. His shirt was so wet, it had turned transparent.

Elisabeth refused to be intimidated by his callous welcome. "Yes, Dr. Fortner," she said, "I'm back."

He glared at her once, then stormed up the stairs. When he came down again, he was wearing plain black trousers and an off-white shirt, open at the throat to reveal a wealth of dark chest hair. But then, Elisabeth knew all about that wonderful chest...

"Go stand by the fire," she told him as she lifted the roasting pan from the oven. Inside was a succulent blend of choice beef, a thin but aromatic gravy and perfectly cooked potatoes and carrots. "You'll catch your death."

Trista was in the dining room, lighting the candles.

"Where were you?" Jonathan demanded in a furious undertone. "I searched every inch of this house and the barn and the woodshed...."

Elisabeth shrugged. "I've explained it all before, Jonathan, and you never seem to believe me. And, frankly, I'd rather not risk having you throw me down on a bed and inject some primitive sedative into my veins because you think I'm hysterical."

He rolled his wonderful gray eyes in exasperation. *"Where did you go?"*

"Believe it or not, most of the time I was right here

in this house." She wanted to tell him about seeing Barbara, but the moment wasn't right, and she couldn't risk having Trista overhear what she said. "For now, Jonathan, I'm afraid you're going to have to be satisfied with that answer."

He glared at her, but there was a softening in his manner, and Elisabeth knew he was glad she'd come back—a fact that made her exultant.

The three of them ate dinner in the dining room, then Trista volunteered to clear the table and wash the dishes. While she was doing that, Elisabeth sat at the piano, playing a medley of the Beatles ballads.

Jonathan stood beside the fireplace, one arm braced against the mantelpiece, listening with a frown. "I've never heard that before," he said.

Elisabeth smiled but made no comment.

He came to stand behind her, lightly resting his hands on her shoulders, which the dress left partially bare. "Lizzie," he said gruffly, "please tell me who you are. Tell me how you managed to vanish that way."

She stopped playing and turned slightly to look up at him. Her eyes were bright with tears because the name Lizzie had brought the full gravity of the situation down on her again, though she'd managed to put it out of her mind for a little while.

"There's something I want to show you," she said. "Something I brought back from—from where I live. We'll talk about it after Trista goes to bed."

He bent reluctantly and gave her a brief, soft kiss.

He'd barely straightened up again when his daughter appeared, her round little cheeks flushed with pride.

"I did the dishes," she announced.

Jonathan smiled and patted her small shoulder. "You're a marvel," he said.

"Can we go to the Founder's Day picnic tomorrow, Papa?" she asked hopefully. "Since Elisabeth would be there to take me home, it wouldn't matter if you had to leave early to set a broken bone or deliver a baby."

Jonathan's gaze shifted uncertainly to Elisabeth, and she felt a pang, knowing he was probably concerned about the questions her presence would raise. "Would you like to go?" he asked.

Elisabeth thrived on this man's company, and his daughter's. She wanted to be wherever they were, be it heaven or hell. "Yes," she said in an oddly choked voice.

Pleasure lighted Jonathan's weary eyes for just a moment, but then the spell was broken. He announced that he had things to do in the barn and went out.

Elisabeth exchanged the pink gown for her slacks and tank top and began heating water on the stove for Trista's bath. Once the little girl had scrubbed from head to foot, dried herself and put on a warm flannel nightgown, she and Elisabeth sat near the stove, and Elisabeth gently combed the tangles from Trista's hair.

"I wish you were my mama," Trista confessed later, when Elisabeth was tucking her into bed, after reading her a chapter of *Huckleberry Finn*.

Touched, Elisabeth kissed the little girl's cheek. "I

wish that, too," she admitted. "But I'm not, and it's no good pretending. However, we can be the very best of friends."

Trista beamed. "I'd like that," she said.

Elisabeth blew out Trista's lamp, then sat on the edge of the bed until the child's breathing was even with sleep. Her eyes adjusted now to the darkness, Elisabeth made her way to the inner door that led down to the kitchen.

Jonathan was seated at the table, drinking coffee. His expression and his bearing conveyed a weariness that made Elisabeth want to put her arms around him.

"What were you going to show me?"

Elisabeth put one hand into the pocket of her slacks and brought out the prescription bottle. "Nothing much," she said, setting it on the table in front of him. "Just your ordinary, everyday, garden-variety wonder drug."

He picked up the little vial and squinted at the print on the label. "Penicillin." His eyes widened, and Elisabeth thought he was probably reading the date. As she sat down next to him, he looked at her in skeptical curiosity.

"In proper doses," she said, "this stuff can cure some heavy hitters, like pneumonia. They call it an antibiotic."

Jonathan tried to remove the child-proof cap and failed, until Elisabeth showed him the trick. He poured the white tablets into his palm and sniffed them, then picked one up and touched it to his tongue.

Elisabeth watched with delight as he made a face and dropped all the pills back into the bottle. "Well? Are you convinced?"

Still scowling, the country doctor tapped the side of the bottle with his finger nail. "What is this made of?"

"Plastic," Elisabeth answered. "Another miracle of the twentieth century. Take it from me, Jonathan, the twentieth century was full of them. I just wish I could show you everything."

He studied her for a moment, then shoved the bottle toward her. It was obvious that, while he didn't know what to think, he'd chosen not to believe Elisabeth. "The twentieth century," he scoffed.

"Actually, now it's the early twenty-first," Elisabeth insisted implacably. No matter what this guy said or did, she wasn't going to let him rile her again. There was simply too much at stake. She let her eyes rest on the penicillin. "When you use that, do it judiciously. The drug causes violent reactions, even death, in some people."

Jonathan shook his head scornfully, but Elisabeth noticed that his gaze kept straying back to the little vial. It was obvious that he was itching to pick it up and examine it again.

She sighed, allowing herself a touch of exasperation. "All right, so you can dismiss the pills as some kind of trick. But what about the bottle? You admitted it yourself—you've never seen anything like it. And do you know why, Jonathan? Because it doesn't exist in your world. It hasn't been invented yet."

Clearly, he could resist no longer. He reached out and snatched up the penicillin as if he thought Elisabeth would try to beat him to it, dropping the bottle into the pocket of his shirt.

"Where did you go?" he demanded in an impatient whisper.

Elisabeth smiled. "Why on earth would I want to tell you that?" she asked. "You'll just think I'm having a fit and pump my veins full of dope."

"Full of what?"

"Never mind." She reached across the table and patted his hand in a deliberately patronizing fashion. "From here on out, just think of me as a…guardian angel. Actually, that should be no more difficult to absorb than the truth. I have the power to help you and Trista, even save your lives, if you'll only let me."

Jonathan surprised her with a slow smile. "A guardian angel? More likely, you're a witch. And I've got to admit, I'm under your spell."

Elisabeth glanced nervously toward the rear stairway, half expecting to find Trista there, listening. "Jonathan, while I was—er—where I was, I talked with Barbara."

The smile faded, as Elisabeth had known it would. "Where? Damn it, if that woman has come back here, meaning to upset my daughter—"

"She's over a century away," Elisabeth said. "And Trista is her daughter, too."

"Are you telling me that Barbara…"

"Went to the future?" Elisabeth finished for him.

"Yes. She was wearing my necklace at the time, though, of course, it was *her* necklace then."

Jonathan erupted from his chair with such force that it clattered to the floor. Elisabeth watched as he went to the stove to refill his coffee mug, and even through the fabric of his shirt, she could see that the muscles in his shoulders were rigid. "You're insane," he accused without facing Elisabeth.

"I saw her. She said she had a lover, and you'd found out about him. She was afraid of what you might do to her."

Jonathan went to the stairway and looked up to make sure his daughter wasn't listening. "Is that why you're here?" he snapped cruelly when he was certain they were alone. "Did Barbara send you to spy on me?"

It was getting harder and harder to keep her temper. Elisabeth managed, although her hands trembled slightly as she lifted her cup to her mouth and took a sip. "No. I stumbled onto this place quite by accident, I assure you—rather like Alice tumbling into the rabbit hole. That story has been written, I presume?"

He gave her a look of scalding sarcasm. "Every schoolchild knows it," he said. "Where are those newspaper accounts you mentioned? The ones that cover my death?"

Elisabeth ran the tip of her tongue over dry lips. "Well, I had them, but in the end I decided you would only say I'd had them printed up somewhere myself. What I can't understand is why you think I would want to pull such an elaborate hoax in the first place. Tell me exactly what you think I would have to gain by making up such a story."

He took her cup, rather summarily, and refilled it. "You probably believe what you're saying."

She threw her hands out from her sides in a burst of annoyance. "If you think I'm a raving lunatic, why do you allow me to stay here? Why do you trust me with your daughter?"

Jonathan smiled and sat down again. "Because I think you're a *harmless* lunatic."

Elisabeth shoved her fingers through her hair, completely ruining the modified Gibson Girl style. "Thank you, Sigmund Freud."

"Sigmund Who?"

"Forget it. It's too hard to explain."

Her host rolled his eyes and then leaned forward ominously, in effect ordering her to try.

"Listen, you're bound to read about Dr. Freud soon, and all your questions will be answered. Though you shouldn't take his theories concerning mothers and sons too seriously."

Jonathan rubbed his temples with a thumb and forefinger and sighed in a long-suffering way.

"How are you going to explain me to the good citizens of Pine River at that picnic tomorrow?" Elisabeth asked, not only because she wanted to change the dead-end subject, but because she was curious. "By telling them I'm your wife's sister?"

"I'm not about to change my story now," he said. "Of

course, Ellen's told half the county you're a witch, popping in and out whenever it strikes your fancy."

Close, Elisabeth thought with grim humor, *but no cigar.* "Maybe it would be simpler if I just stayed here."

"We can't hide you away forever, especially after that visit you paid to my office."

Elisabeth fluttered her eyelashes. "I think I have an admirer in the big fella," she teased. "What was his name again? Moose? Svend?"

Jonathan laughed. "Ivan." He pushed back his chair and carried his cup and Elisabeth's to the sink, leaving them for Ellen to wash in the morning. Then he waited, in that courtly way of his, while Elisabeth stood. "Will you disappear again tonight?" he asked.

"You wouldn't tease if you knew how uncertain it is," she answered. "I could get stuck on the other side and never find my way back."

He escorted her to the door of the spare room and gave her a light, teasing kiss that left her wanting more. Much more. "Good night, Lizzie," he said. "I'll see you in the morning—I hope."

Chapter 9

Elisabeth was pleasantly surprised to learn that the Founder's Day picnic was to be held in one of her favorite places—the grassy area beside the creek, next to the covered bridge. All that sunny Saturday morning, while she and Trista were frying chicken and making a version of potato salad, wagons and buggies rattled past on the road.

When Jonathan returned from his morning rounds, the three of them walked through the orchard to the creek, Jonathan carrying the food in a big wicker basket. Elisabeth, wearing a demure blue-and-white checked gingham she'd found in one of the attic trunks, was at his side. Though her chin was at a slightly obstinate angle, there was no hiding her nervousness.

There were rigs lining the road on both sides of the

bridge, and dozens of blankets had been spread out on the ground alongside the creek. Boys in caps and short pants chased each other, pursued in turn by little girls with huge bows in their hair. The ladies sat gracefully on their spreads, their skirts arranged in modest fashion. Some used ruffle-trimmed parasols to shelter their complexions from the sun, while others, clad in calico, seemed to relish the light as much as the children did.

Most of the men wore plain trousers and either flannel or cotton shirts, and Jonathan was the only one without a hat. They stood in clusters, talking among themselves, but when the Fortner household arrived, it seemed they all turned to look, as did the women.

Elisabeth was profoundly aware of the differences between herself and these people and, for one terrible moment, she had to struggle to keep from turning and running back to the shelter of the house.

Vera came over, a tiny emissary with flowing brown hair and freckles, and looked solemnly up into Elisabeth's face. "You don't look like a witch to me," she remarked forthrightly.

"Does this mean they won't burn me at the stake?" Elisabeth whispered to Jonathan, who chuckled.

"She's not a witch," Trista said, arms akimbo, her gray gaze sweeping the crowd and daring any detractor to step forward. Her youthful voice rang with conviction. "Elisabeth is my friend."

Jonathan set the picnic basket down and began unfolding the blanket he'd been carrying under one arm, while Elisabeth waited, staring tensely at the population of Pine River, her smile wobbling on her mouth.

Finally, one of the women in calico came forward, returning Elisabeth's smile and offering her hand. "I'm Clara Piedmont," she said. "Vera's mother."

"Lizzie McCartney," Jonathan said, making the false introduction smoothly, just a moment after Trista and Vera had run off to join the other kids, "my wife's sister."

"How do you do?" Clara asked as a shiver went down Elisabeth's back. As long as she lived, which might not be very long at all, she would never get used to being called Lizzie.

This show of acceptance reassured her, though, and her smile was firm on her lips, no longer threatening to come unpinned and fall off. She murmured a polite response.

"Will you be staying in Pine River?" Clara inquired.

Elisabeth glanced in Jonathan's direction, not certain how to respond. "I—haven't decided," she said lamely.

Although Clara was not a pretty woman, her smile was warm and open. She patted Elisabeth's upper arm in a friendly way. "Well, you come over for tea one day this week. Trista will show you where we live." She turned to Jonathan. "Would it be all right if Trista stayed at our house tonight? Vera's been plaguing me about it all day."

Jonathan didn't look at Elisabeth, which was a good thing, because even a glance from him would have brought the color rushing to her cheeks. With Trista away, the two of them would be alone in the house.

"That would be fine," he said.

Elisabeth felt a rush of anticipation so intense that it threatened to lift her off the ground and spin her around a few times, and she was mortified at herself. She didn't even want to think what modern self-help books had to say about women who wanted a particular man's love-making that much.

Over the course of the afternoon, she managed to blend in with the other women, and after eating, everyone posed for the town photographer, the wooden bridge looming in the background. Later, while the boys fished in the creek, girls waded in, deliberately scaring away the trout. The men puffed on their cigars and played horseshoes, and the ladies gossiped.

Toward sunset, when people were packing up their children, blankets and picnic baskets, the hooves of a single horse hammered over the plank floor of the bridge. The rider paused on the road above the creek bank and called, "Is Doc Fortner here? There's been a man cut up pretty bad, over at the mill."

Jonathan waved to the rider. "I'll get my bag and meet you there in ten minutes," he said. Then, after giving Elisabeth one unreadable look, he disappeared into the orchard, headed toward the house.

Elisabeth finished gathering the picnic things, feeling much less a part of the community now that Jonathan was gone. She was touched when Trista came to say goodbye before leaving with Vera's family. "I'll see you tomorrow, in church," she promised. "Could I have a kiss, please?"

With a smile, Elisabeth bent to kiss the child's smudged, sun-warmed cheek. "You certainly may." She was painfully conscious of how short her time with this child might be and of how precious it was. "I love you, Trista," she added.

Trista gave her a quicksilver, spontaneous hug, then raced off to scramble into the Piedmonts' wagon with Vera. Carrying the picnic basket, now considerably lighter, and the blanket, Elisabeth turned and started for home.

Although Jonathan had left a lamp burning in the kitchen, its glow pushing back the twilight, he had, of course, already left for the sawmill. Elisabeth shivered to think what horrors might be awaiting him in that noisy, filthy place.

Taking pitchy chunks of pine from the woodbox beside the stove, Elisabeth built up the fire and put a kettle on for tea. Then, because she knew Jonathan would be tired and shaken when he returned, she filled the hot-water reservoir on the stove and put more wood in to make the flames burn hotter.

His clothes were covered with blood when he came in, nearly two hours later, and his gray eyes were haunted. "I couldn't save him," Jonathan muttered as Elisabeth took his bag and set it aside, then began helping him out of his coat. "He had a wife and four children."

Elisabeth stood on tiptoe to kiss Jonathan's cheek,

which was rough with a new beard. "I'm so sorry," she said gently. She'd set the oblong tin bathtub in the center of the kitchen floor earlier, and scouted out soap and a couple of thin, coarse towels. While Jonathan watched her bleakly, she began filling the tub with water from the reservoir and from various kettles on the stove. "Take off your clothes, Jon," she urged quietly when he didn't seem to make the connection. "I'll get you a drink while you're settling in."

He was unbuttoning his shirt with the slow, distracted motions of a sleepwalker when Elisabeth went into the dining room. Earlier, she'd found virtually untouched bottles of whiskey and brandy behind one of the doors in the china cabinet, and she took her time deciding which would be most soothing.

When she returned to the kitchen with the brandy, Jonathan was in the bathtub, his head back, his eyes closed. His bloody shirt and trousers were draped neatly over the back of a chair.

"You were telling the truth," he said when she knelt beside the tub and handed him a glass, "when you claimed to be a guardian angel."

Elisabeth wasn't feeling or thinking much like an angel. She was painfully, poignantly conscious of Jonathan's powerful body, naked beneath the clear surface of the water. "We all need someone to take care of us once in a while—no matter how strong we are."

"I half expected you to be gone when I got back," Jonathan confessed, lifting the glass to his lips. He took a healthy swallow and then set the liquor aside on the floor. "I figured you might not want to be here, without Trista to act as an unofficial chaperone."

Elisabeth couldn't quite meet his eyes. "I don't think I want to be chaperoned," she said.

Jonathan's chuckle was a raw sound, conveying despair and weariness, as well as amusement. "Ladies must be very forward where you come from," he teased. Elisabeth could feel him watching her, caressing her with his gaze.

She made herself look at him. "I guess compared to Victorian women, they are." She reached for soap and a wash cloth and made a lather. Jonathan looked pleasantly bewildered when she began washing his back. "The term 'Victorian,'" she offered, before he could ask, "refers to the time of Queen Victoria's reign."

"I deduced that," Jonathan said with a sigh, relaxing slightly under Elisabeth's hand.

Bathing him was so sensual an experience that Elisabeth's head was spinning, and the warm ache between her legs had already reached such a pitch that it was nearly painful.

"You know, of course," Jonathan told her, leaning back as she began to wash his chest, "that I mean to take you directly from here to my bed and make love to you until you've given me everything?"

Elisabeth swallowed. Her heart was beating so hard, she could hear it. "Yes, Jon," she replied. "I know."

He took the soap and cloth from her hand and, after watching her face for a long moment, set about finishing his bath. Elisabeth left the kitchen, climbing the stairs to his bedroom.

As soon as the door closed behind her, she began undressing. She had barely managed to wash and put on a thin white eyelet chemise she'd found when Jonathan entered the room.

His dark hair was rumpled, and he was naked except for the inadequate towel wrapped around his waist. Thunder rattled the windows suddenly, like some kind of celestial warning, and Jonathan went to the fireplace and struck a match to the shavings that waited in the grate. On top of them, he laid several sticks of dry wood.

Elisabeth trembled, shy as a virgin, when he turned down the kerosene lamps on the mantelpiece, leaving the room dark except for the primitive crimson glow of the fire. He came to her, resting his strong, skilled hands on the sides of her waist.

"Thank you," he said.

Heat was surging through Elisabeth's system, and she could barely keep from swaying on her feet. "For what?" she managed to choke out as Jonathan began to caress her breasts through the fabric of the chemise.

He bent, nibbling at her neck even as his thumbs chafed her covered nipples into hard readiness for his mouth. "For being here, now, tonight, when I need you so much."

Elisabeth gave a little moan and ran her hands up and down his muscled, still-damp back. He smelled of soap and brandy and manhood. "I need you, too, Jonathan," she admitted in a whisper.

Jonathan drew back far enough to raise the chemise over her head and toss it aside. His charcoal eyes seemed to smolder as he took in the curves and valleys of her body, bare except for the rhythmic flicker of the firelight. He let the towel fall away.

She hadn't meant to be bold, but he was so magnificent that she couldn't resist touching him. When her fingers closed around his heated shaft, he tilted his head back and gave a low growl of fierce surrender. With one hand, she pressed him gently backward into a chair, while still caressing him with the other.

"Dear God, *Elisabeth*..." he moaned as she knelt between his knees and began kissing the bare skin of his upper thighs. "Stop..."

"I'm not going to stop," she told him stubbornly between flicks of her tongue that made his flesh quiver. "I haven't even begun to pleasure you."

He uttered a raspy shout of shock and delight when she took him, his fingers entangling themselves in her hair. "Lizzie," he gasped. "Oh...Lizzie...my God..."

Elisabeth lightly stroked the insides of his thighs as she enjoyed him.

Finally, with a ragged cry, he clasped her head in his hands and forced her to release him. In a matter of seconds, he'd lifted her from the floor so that she was standing in the chair itself, her feet on either side of his hips. He parted her with the fingers of one hand and then brought her down onto his mouth.

There was no need to be quiet, since they were alone in the house, and that was a good thing, because such pleasure knifed through Elisabeth that she burst out with a throaty yell. Her hands gripped the back of the chair in a desperate bid for balance as Jonathan continued to have her.

She began to pant as her hips moved back and forth of their own accord, and a thin film of perspiration broke out over every inch of her. She could feel tendrils of her hair clinging to her cheeks as she blindly moved against Jonathan's mouth.

When she felt release approaching, she tried to pull away, wanting her full surrender to happen when Jonathan was inside her, but he wouldn't let her go. Gripping her hips in his work-roughened hands, he held her to him even as the violent shudders began, making her fling her head back and moan without restraint.

He was greedy, granting her absolutely no quarter, and Elisabeth's captured body began to convulse with pleasure. The firelight and the darkness blurred as she gave up her essence and then collapsed against the back of the chair, exhausted.

But Jonathan wasn't about to let her rest. Within five minutes her cries of delighted fury again rang through the empty house.

"Now you're ready for me," he informed her in a husky voice as he lowered her to his lap and then stood, carrying her to the bed.

Elisabeth's two releases had been so violent, so all-consuming, that she was left with no breath in her lungs. She lay gasping, gazing up at Jonathan as he arranged her in the center of the bed and put two fluffy pillows under her bottom.

He lay down beside her on the mattress, slightly lower so that he could take her nipple into his mouth while his hand stroked her tender mound.

"Jonathan," she managed to whisper. "Please—*oh*—please…"

Jonathan spread her legs and knelt between them, parting her to give her one more teasing stroke. Then he poised himself over her. He had played her body so skillfully that in the instant his shaft glided inside her, she came apart.

While she buckled under the slow, deliberate strokes of his manhood, her head tossed back and forth on the mattress and she sobbed his name over and over again.

Her vindication came when the last little whimper of satisfied surrender had been wrung from her, because that was when Jonathan's release began. She toyed with his nipples and talked breathlessly of all the ways she meant to pleasure him in the future. With a fevered groan and a curse, he quickened his pace.

"I'll put you back in that chair again," she told him as he moved more and more rapidly upon her, his head thrust back. "Only next time, I won't let you stop me…."

Jonathan gave a strangled shout and stiffened, his eyes glazed, his teeth bared as he filled Elisabeth with his warmth. She stroked his back and buttocks until he'd given up everything. He sank to the bed beside her, resting his head on her breasts.

A blissful hour passed and the fire was burning low before Jonathan rose on one elbow to look into her face. "Stay with me, Elisabeth," he whispered. "Be my wife, so that I can bring you to this room, this bed, in good conscience."

She plunged her fingers into his dark, freshly washed hair. "Jon," she sighed, "I'm a stranger. You have no idea what marrying me would mean."

He parted her thighs and touched her brazenly in that moist, silken place where small tremors of passion were already starting to stir again. "It would mean," he drawled, his eyes twinkling, "that I would either have to put a gag over your mouth or move Trista to a room downstairs."

Elisabeth blushed hotly, glad of the darkness. It wasn't like her to carry on the way she had; with Ian, she'd hardly made a sound. But then, there had been no reason to cry out. "You're a very vain man, Jon Fortner."

He laughed and kissed her. "Maybe so," he answered, "but you make me feel like something more than a man."

She blinked and tried to turn her head, but Jonathan clasped her chin in his hand and prevented that.

"Don't you think I'm—I'm cheap?" she whispered, only too aware of Victorian attitudes toward sex.

Jonathan got up and fed the fire, and then Elisabeth heard the chink of china. Only when he brought a basin of tepid water back to the bed and began gently washing her did he reply. "Because you enjoy having a man make love to you?" He continued to cleanse her, using a soft cloth. "Lizzie, it was refreshing to see you respond like that." He set the cloth and basin aside on the floor, but would not let her close her legs. "Did you mean what you said about the next time I sit in that chair?"

Elisabeth's face pulsed with heat, but she nodded, unable to break the link between his eyes and hers. "I meant it," she said hoarsely.

At that, he kissed her, his tongue teasing her lips until they parted to take him in. "I meant what I said, too," he told her presently, moving his lips downward, toward her waiting breasts. "I want you to be my wife. And I won't let you put me off forever."

God help us, Elisabeth thought, just before she succumbed to the sweet demands of her body, *we don't have forever.*

Elisabeth felt like a fraud, sitting there in church beside Jonathan the next morning, pretending to be his sister-in-law. Maybe these good people didn't know she'd spent most of the night tossing in his bed, but God did, and He was bound to demand an accounting.

All she could do was hope it made a difference, her loving Jonathan the way she did.

After the service, she and Jonathan and Trista went home, the three of them crowded into Jonathan's buggy. He saw to the horses while Elisabeth and Trista went inside to put a fresh ham in the oven.

When Jonathan appeared, just as they finished peeling potatoes to go with the pork, he was carrying two simple bamboo fishing poles. Trista's eyes lit up at the prospect of a Sunday afternoon beside the creek, and Elisabeth's heart was touched. Jonathan led a busy, demanding life, and he and Trista probably didn't have a lot of time together.

"You'll come with us, won't you?" the little girl cried, whirling to look up into Elisabeth's face with an imploring expression.

Elisabeth glanced at Jonathan, who winked almost imperceptibly, then nodded. "If you don't think I'll be interrupting," she agreed.

The creek bank was theirs again, now that yesterday's picnickers had all gone home, taking their blankets and scraps with them. Elisabeth sat contentedly on her favorite rock while Jonathan and Trista dug worms from the loamy ground and then threw their lines into the water.

Trista's laughter was liquid crystal, like the creek sparkling in the sunshine, and Elisabeth's heart climbed into her throat. It wasn't fair that this beautiful child was destined to die in just a few short weeks—she'd never had a chance to live!

Neither Jon nor Trista noticed when Elisabeth got down from the boulder and walked away, trying to distract herself by gathering the wild daisies and tiger lilies that hadn't been crushed by the picnickers the day before. She was under the bridge, watching the water flow by, when Jonathan suddenly materialized at her side.

"Where's Trista?" she asked, looking away quickly in hopes that he wouldn't read too much from her eyes.

"She went back to the house to make a pitcher of lemonade," Jonathan answered sleepily, taking one of the tiger lilies from Elisabeth's bouquet and brushing its fragrant orange petals against the underside of her chin. When she turned her head, he kissed her and the tangle of flowers tumbled to the smooth pebbles at her feet. "I want to bring you here," he told her when he'd finally released her mouth, "and make love to you in the moonlight."

Elisabeth trembled as his fingers found the pins in her hair and removed them, letting the soft blond tresses fall around her face. His name was all the protest she managed before he kissed her again.

By the time Trista returned with the lemonade, Elisabeth was badly in need of something that would cool her off. She sat in the grass with the man and the child, sipping the tart drink and hoping she wasn't flushed. Trista chattered the whole time about how they'd have the trout they'd caught for breakfast, firmly maintaining that Vera and *her* father had certainly never caught so many fine fish in one single day.

They returned to the house in midafternoon to eat the lovely ham dinner, and Jonathan was called away before he could have dessert. He seemed to be contemplating whether to leave or stay with them as he kissed

Trista on top of the head and gave Elisabeth's shoulder a subtle squeeze.

Just that innocent contact sent heated shards through her, and she couldn't help recalling what Jonathan had said about making love to her in the moonlight under the covered bridge.

She and Trista cleared the table when they were finished eating, then they went out to the orchard and sat on the same thick, low branch of a gnarled old tree. Elisabeth listened and occasionally prompted while Trista practiced her spelling.

They were back in the house, seated together on the piano bench and playing a duet that wouldn't be composed for another several decades or so, when Jonathan returned. He was in much better spirits than he had been the night before.

"Susan Crenshaw had a baby girl," he said, his eyes clear.

Elisabeth wanted to kiss him for the happiness she saw in his face, but she didn't dare because Trista was there and because she wasn't entirely sure the air wouldn't crackle. "I guess delivering a healthy baby makes up for a lot of bad things, doesn't it?"

"That it does," he agreed, and his fingers touched her shoulder again, making her breasts ache. Elisabeth watched Jonathan as he walked away, disappearing into his study, and she dared to consider what it would be like to be his wife and share his bed every night.

"Your face is red," Trista commented, jolting her back to matters at hand. "Are you getting a fever?"

Elisabeth smiled. "Maybe," she replied, "but it isn't the kind you have to worry about. Now, let's trade places, and you can play harmony while I do the melody."

Trista nodded eagerly and moved to the spot Elisabeth had occupied.

Because Trista had had an exciting weekend—the picnic, spending the night with Vera and going fishing with her father and Elisabeth—she went to bed early. Jonathan read to his daughter, then came downstairs to join Elisabeth in the parlor.

Standing behind her chair in front of the fireplace, he bent and kissed the crown of her head. "Play something for me," he urged, and Elisabeth went immediately to the piano. Strange as it seemed, making music for his ears was a part of their lovemaking; it warmed Elisabeth's blood and made her heart beat faster and her breathing quicken.

She played soft, soothing Mozart, and she was almost able to believe that she belonged there in that untamed century, where life was so much more difficult and intense. When she'd finished, she turned on the piano bench to gaze at Jonathan, who was standing at the window.

"Have you decided?" he asked after a long interval of comfortable silence had passed.

Elisabeth didn't need to ask what he meant; she knew. Although Jonathan had never once said he loved her, he wanted her to marry him. She smoothed her skirts. "I've decided," she said.

He arched one eyebrow, waiting.

"I'll marry you," Elisabeth said, meeting his eyes. "But only on one condition—you have to promise that we'll go away on a wedding trip. We'll be gone a full month, and Trista will be with us."

Jonathan's expression was grim. "Elisabeth, I'm the only doctor between here and Seattle—I can't leave these people without medical care for a month."

"Then I have to refuse," Elisabeth said, although it nearly killed her.

Dr. Fortner held out a hand to her. "It seems you need a little convincing," he told her in a low voice that set her senses to jumping.

Elisabeth couldn't help herself; she went to him, let him enfold her fingers in his. "May I remind you," she said in a last-ditch effort at behaving herself, "that there's a child only a few rooms away?"

"That's why I'm taking you to the bridge." Jonathan led her through the dining room and the kitchen and out into the cool spring night. There was a bright silver wash of moonlight glimmering in the grass.

She had to hurry to keep up with his long, determined strides. She thought fast. "Jonathan, what if someone needs you...?"

"You need me," he answered without missing a beat, pulling her through the orchard, where leaves rustled overhead and crushed petals made a soft carpet under her feet. "I'm about to remind you how much."

In the shadow of the covered bridge, Jonathan dragged Elisabeth against his chest and kissed her soundly, and the mastery of his lips and tongue made her knees go weak beneath her. He pressed her gently into the fragrant grass, his fingers opening the tiny buttons of her high-collared blouse. He groaned when he found her breasts bare underneath, waiting for him, their sweet tips reaching.

Elisabeth surrendered as he closed his mouth around one nipple, sucking eagerly, and she flung her arms back over her head to make herself even more vulnerable. While he made free with her breasts, Jonathan raised Elisabeth's skirts and, once again, found no barrier between him and what he wanted so much to touch.

"Little witch," he moaned, clasping her in his hand so that the heel of his palm ground against her. "Show me your magic."

He'd long since aroused Elisabeth with words and looks and touches, and she tugged feverishly at his clothes until he helped her and she could feel bare flesh under her palms. Finally, he lay between her legs, and she guided him into her, soothing Jonathan even as she became his conqueror.

Chapter 10

"Prove it," Jonathan challenged in a whisper when he and Elisabeth had finally returned to the house. They were standing in the upstairs hallway, their clothes rumpled from making love on the ground beside the creek. Jonathan had lit the lamp on the narrow table against the wall. A light spring rain was just beginning to fall. "If you can leave this century at will, then show me."

Elisabeth paused, her hand resting on the knob of the door to the spare bedroom. "It's not a parlor trick, Jon," she told him with sad annoyance. "I don't have the first idea how or why it works, and there's always the chance that I won't be able to get back."

His eyes seemed to darken, just for a moment, but his gaze was level and steady. "If you want me to believe what you've been saying, Lizzie, then you'll have to give me some evidence."

"All right," she agreed with a forlorn shrug. She didn't like the idea of leaving Jonathan, even if it was only a matter of stepping over a threshold and back. "But first I want a promise from you. If I don't return, you have to take Trista away from this house and not set foot in it again until after the first of July."

Jonathan watched her for a moment, his arms folded, and then nodded. "You have my word," he said with wry skepticism in his eyes.

Elisabeth went silently into her room to collect the necklace from its hiding place. Then she went into Trista's room. After casting one anxious look at the sleeping, unsuspecting child, Elisabeth put the chain around her neck. She could see Jonathan clearly, standing in the hallway.

She took a deep breath, closed her eyes, and stepped over the threshold.

In one instant, Elisabeth had been there, closing her eyes and wishing on that damned necklace as though it were some sort of talisman. In the next, she was gone.

Shock consumed Jonathan like a brushfire, and he sank against the wall, squinting at the darkened doorway, hardly daring to trust his own vision.

"Lizzie," he whispered, running one hand down his face. Then reason overcame him. It had to be a trick.

He thrust himself away from the wall and plunged through Trista's quiet room. The inner door was fastened tightly. Jonathan wrenched it open and bounded down the steep steps to the kitchen.

"Elisabeth!" he rasped, his patience wearing thin, his heart thrumming a kind of crazy dread.

Jonathan searched every inch of the downstairs, then carrying a lantern, he went out into the drizzling rain to look in all the sheds and check the barn. Finding nothing, he strode through the orchard and even went as far as the bank of the creek.

There was no sign of her, and fear pressed down on him as he made his way slowly back to the house, his hair dripping, his shirt clinging wetly to his skin. "Elisabeth," he said. Despair echoed in the sound.

Elisabeth stood smugly on the back porch of Jonathan's house, watching him cross the rainy yard with the lantern and waiting for him to look up and see her standing there on the step.

When he raised his eyes, he stopped and stared at her through the downpour.

"Get in here," she said, scurrying out to take Jonathan's free hand and drag him toward the door. "You'll catch something!"

"How did you do that?" he demanded, setting the lantern on the kitchen table and gaping at Elisabeth while she fed wood into the stove and urged him closer to the heat.

She tapped the side of the blue enamel coffeepot with her fingertips to see if it was still hot and gave an exasperated sigh. "Your guess is as good as mine," she said, fetching a mug from the cabinets and filling it with the stout coffee. "You must have seen *something,* Jonathan. Did I fade out, or was I gone in a blink?"

Jonathan sank into a chair at the table and she set the mug before him. He didn't even seem to be aware of his sodden shirt and hair. "You simply—disappeared."

This was no time for triumph; Jonathan's teeth were already chattering. Elisabeth got a dry shirt from his room and a towel from the linen chest upstairs and returned to the kitchen.

He was standing close to the stove, bare chested, sipping his coffee. "I've had enough nonsense from you, Lizzie," he said, shaking a finger at her. "You fooled me, and I want to know how."

Elisabeth laughed and shook her head. "I always thought my father was stubborn," she replied, "but when it comes to bullheaded, you beat him all to hell." Her eyes danced as she approached Jonathan, laying her hands on his shoulders. "Face it, Jon. I vanished into thin air, and you saw it happen with your own eyes."

His color drained away and he rubbed his temples with a thumb and forefinger. "Yes. Good God, Lizzie, am I losing my mind?"

She slipped her arms around his waist. "No. It's just that there's a lot more going on in this universe than we poor mortals know."

Jonathan pressed her head against his bare shoulders, and she felt a shudder go through him. "I want to try it," he said. "I want to see the other side."

It was as though Elisabeth had stepped under a

pounding, icy waterfall. "No," she whispered, stepping away from him.

He allowed her to go no farther than arm's length. "Yes," he replied, his gaze locked with hers. "If this world you've been telling me about is really there, I want a glimpse of it."

Elisabeth began to shake her head slowly from side to side. "Jonathan, no—you'd be taking a terrible chance...."

His deft, doctor's fingers reached beneath her tousled hair to unclasp the necklace. Then, holding it in one hand, he rounded Elisabeth and started up the short stairway that led to Trista's room.

"Jonathan!" Elisabeth cried, scrambling after him. "Jonathan, *wait,* there are things I need to tell you...."

She reached the first door just as he got to the one leading out into the main hallway. Her eyes widened when he stepped across the threshold. Like a rippling reflection on the surface of a pond, he diffused into nothingness. Elisabeth clasped one hand over her mouth and went to stand in the empty doorway.

She sagged against the jamb, half-sick with the fear that she might never see him again. Heaven knew how she would explain his absence to Trista or to Marshal Haynes and the rest of the townspeople. And then there was the prospect of living without him.

It was the damnedest thing Jonathan had ever seen. A second ago, he'd been standing in Trista's bedroom, on a rainy night. Now, a fierce spring sun was shining and the familiar hallway had changed drastically.

There were light fixtures on the walls, and beneath his feet was a thick rug the color of ripe wheat. For a few moments, he just stood there, gripping the necklace, trying to understand what was happening to him. He was scared, but not badly enough to turn around and go back without seeing what kind of world Elisabeth lived in.

Once he'd regained his equilibrium, he crossed the hall and opened the door to the master bedroom.

Like the hallway, it was structurally the same, but there the similarities ended. Jonathan's scientific heart began to beat faster with excitement.

When the shrill sound of a bell filled the air, he jumped and almost bolted. Then he realized the jangle was coming from a telephone.

He looked around, but there was no instrument affixed to the wall. Finally, he tracked the noise to a fussy-looking gadget resting on the vanity table and he lifted the earpiece.

"Hello!" he snapped, frowning. There were telephones in Seattle, of course, but the lines hadn't reached Pine River yet, and Jonathan hadn't had much practice talking into a wire.

"Who is this?" a woman's voice demanded.

"This is Jonathan Fortner," he answered, fascinated. "Who are you, and why are you telephoning?"

There was a pause. "I'm Janet Finch, Elisabeth's friend. Is she there?"

A slow grin spread across Jonathan's mouth. "I'm afraid not," he replied. And then he laid the receiver in its cradle and walked away.

Almost immediately, the jarring noise began again, but Jonathan ignored it. There were things he wanted to investigate.

Just as he was descending the front stairway, an old woman with fussy white hair and enormous blue eyes peered through one of the long windows that stood on either side of the door. At the sight of Jonathan, she gave a little shriek, dropped something to the porch floor with a clatter and turned to run away.

Jonathan went to the window, grinning, and watched her trot across the road, her legs showing beneath her short dress. If this was truly the future, the elderly lady probably thought he was a ghost.

He just hoped he hadn't scared her too badly.

With a sigh of resignation, Jonathan proceeded to the kitchen, where he made an amazed inspection. He figured out the icebox right away, and he identified the thing with metal coils on top as a stove by process of elimination. He turned one of the knobs and then moved on to the sink, frowning at the gleaming spigots. When he gave one a twist, water shot out of a small pipe, startling him.

One of the spirals on the stove was red hot when he looked back, and Jonathan held his palm over it, feeling the heat and marveling.

By far the most interesting thing in the room, however, was the box that sat on the counter. It had little buttons and a window made out of the same stuff as Elisabeth's medicine bottle, only clear.

Jonathan tampered with the buttons and suddenly the window flashed with light and the face of an attractive African woman with stiff hair loomed before him.

"Are you tired of catering to your boss's every whim?" she demanded, and Jonathan took a step backward, speechless. The woman was staring at him, as if waiting for an answer, and he wondered if he should speak to her. "Today's guests will tell you how to stand up for yourself and still keep your job!" she finished.

"What guests?" Jonathan asked, looking around the kitchen. Music poured out of the box, and then a woman with hair the same color as Elisabeth's appeared, holding up a glass of orange juice.

"No, thank you," Jonathan said, touching the button again. The window went dark.

He ambled outside to look at the barn—it had fallen into a shameful state of disrepair—and stood by the fence watching automobiles speed by. They were all colors now, instead of just the plain black he'd seen on the streets of Boston and New York.

When half an hour passed and he still hadn't seen a single horse, Jonathan shook his head and turned toward the house. He walked around it, noting the changes.

The section that contained Trista's room and the second rear stairway was gone, leaving no trace except for a door in the second-story wall. Remembering what

Elisabeth had said about a fire, he shoved splayed fingers through his hair and strode inside.

He could hear her calling to him the moment he entered, and he smiled as he started up the rear stairs.

"Damn you, Jonathan Fortner, you get back here! Now!"

Jonathan took the necklace from his pocket and held it in one hand. Then he opened the door and stepped over the threshold.

Elisabeth was wearing different clothes—a black sateen skirt and a blue shirtwaist—and there were shadows under her eyes. "Oh, Jonathan," she cried, thrusting herself, shuddering, into his arms.

He kissed her temple, feeling pretty shaken himself. "It's all right, Lizzie," he said. "I'm here." He held her tightly.

She raised her eyes to his face. "People were starting to ask questions," she fretted. "And I had to lie to Trista and tell her you'd gone to Seattle on business."

Jonathan was stunned. "But I was only gone for an hour or so...."

Elisabeth shook her head. "Eight days, Jonathan," she said somberly. She pressed her cheek to his chest. "I was sure I'd never see you again."

He was distracted by the way she felt in his arms, all soft and warm. With a fingertip, he traced the outline of her trembling lips. "Eight days?" he echoed.

She nodded.

The mystery was more than he could assimilate all at once, so he put it to the back of his mind. "You must have missed me something fierce in that case," he teased.

A spark of the old fire flickered in her eyes, and a corner of her mouth quivered, as though she might forgive him for frightening her and favor him with a smile. "I didn't miss you at all," she said, raising her chin.

He spread his hands over her rib cage, letting the thumbs caress her full breasts, feeling the nipples jut against the fabric in response. "You're lying, Lizzie," he scolded. His arousal struck like a physical blow; suddenly he was hard and heavy with the need of her. He bent and kissed the pulse point he saw throbbing under her right ear. "Are we alone?"

Her breath caught, and her satiny flesh seemed to tremble under his lips. "For the moment," she said, her voice breathless and muffled. "Trista isn't home from school yet, and Ellen is out in the vegetable garden, weeding."

"Good," Jonathan said, thinking what an extraordinarily long time an hour could be. And then he lost himself in Elisabeth's kiss.

Elisabeth knew her cheeks were glowing and, despite her best efforts, her hair didn't look quite the same as it had before Jonathan had taken it down from its pins.

"Imagine that," Ellen said, breaking open a pod and expertly scraping out the peas with her thumbnail. "The doctor came back from wherever he's been, but I didn't hear no wagon nor see a sign of a horse. Come to that, he never took his rig with him in the first place." She paused to cluck and shake her head. "Strange doin's."

Elisabeth was sitting on the front step, while Ellen occupied the rocking chair. Watching the road for Trista, Elisabeth brushed a tendril of pale hair back from her cheek. "There are some things in this life that just can't be explained," she informed the housekeeper in a moderate tone. She was tired of the woman's suspicious glances and obvious disapproval.

Ellen sniffed. "If you ask me—"

"I *didn't* ask you," Elisabeth interrupted, turning on the step to fix the housekeeper with a look.

Color seeped into Ellen's sallow cheeks, but she didn't say anything more. She just went on shelling peas.

When Elisabeth saw Trista coming slowly down the road from the schoolhouse, her head lowered, she smoothed her sateen skirts and stood. She met the child at the gate with a smile.

"Your papa is back from his travels," she said.

The transformation in Trista stirred Elisabeth's heart. The little girl fairly glowed, and a renewed energy seemed to make her taller and stronger in an instant. With a little cry of joy, Trista flung herself into Elisabeth's arms.

Elisabeth held the child, near tears. Over the past eight trying days, she'd seen the depths of the bond this child had with her father. To separate them permanently by sending Trista to Barbara, so far in the future, was no longer an option.

"I thought maybe he'd stay away forever, like Mama," Trista confided as the two of them went through the gate together.

Elisabeth had known what Trista was thinking, of course, but there hadn't been much she could do to reassure the uneasy child. She squeezed Trista's shoulders. "He'll be home for supper—if there isn't a baby ready to be born somewhere."

Ellen, in the meantime, had finished shelling the peas and returned to the kitchen, where she was just putting a chicken into the oven to roast. She sniffed again when she saw Elisabeth.

"I don't imagine I'll be needed around here much longer," she said to no one in particular.

So that was it, Elisabeth reflected. Ellen's tendency to be unkind probably stemmed from her fear of losing her job, now that the doctor's sister-in-law seemed to be a permanent fixture in the house. The problem was really so obvious, but Elisabeth had been too worried about Jonathan's disappearance into the future to notice.

Even now, Elisabeth couldn't reassure the woman because she didn't know what Jonathan thought about the whole matter. He had talked about marriage, and he could well expect Elisabeth to take on all the duties Ellen was handling then. He might have been more progressive than most men of his era, but he wouldn't be taking up the suffrage cause anytime soon.

"I'll let Jon—the doctor know you're concerned," Elisabeth finally said, and Ellen paused and looked back at her in mild surprise. "And for what it's worth, I think you do a very good job."

Ellen blinked at that. Clearly, she'd had Elisabeth tagged as an enemy and didn't know how to relate to her as a friend. "I'd be obliged," Ellen allowed at last. "The family depends on me, and if there ain't going to be a place for me here, I need to be finding another position."

Elisabeth nodded and went back into the house to look about. Lord knew, there weren't any labor-saving devices, and she'd never been all that crazy about housework, but the idea of being a wife to Jonathan filled her with a strange, sweet vigor. Maybe she *was* crazy, she thought with a crooked little smile, because she really wanted to live out this life fate had handed to her.

Twilight had already fallen when Jonathan returned, and the kitchen was filled with the succulent aroma of roasting chicken and the cheery glow of lantern light. Trista was working out her fractions while Elisabeth mashed the potatoes.

The moment she heard her father's buggy in the yard, Trista tossed down her schoolwork and bolted for the back door, her face flushed and wreathed in smiles.

Elisabeth watched with her heart in her throat as the child launched herself from the back step into Jonathan's arms, shrieking, "Papa!"

He laughed and caught her easily, planting a noisy kiss on her forehead. "Hello, sweetheart," he said.

There was a suspicious glimmer in his eyes, and his voice was a little hoarse.

Trista's small arms tightened around his neck. "I missed you so much!" she cried, hugging him tightly.

Jonathan returned the child's embrace, told her he loved her and set her back on the steps. Only then did Elisabeth notice how tired he looked.

"I imagine your patients missed you, too," she said as he followed Trista into the house and set his bag in the customary place. One of the greatest sources of Elisabeth's anxiety, during Jonathan's absence, was the fact that people had constantly come by looking for him. It hadn't been easy, knowing patients who needed his professional attention were being left to their own devices.

He sighed, and Elisabeth could see the strain in his face and in the set of his shoulders. "There are times," he said, "when I think being a coal miner would be easier."

Although she wanted to touch him, to take him into her arms and offer comfort, Elisabeth was painfully aware that she didn't have that option—not with Trista in the room.

It was bad enough that they'd lied to the child, telling her Elisabeth was Barbara's sister. For the past week, Trista had been begging for stories of the childhood Elisabeth had supposedly shared with her mother.

"Sit down, Jon," Elisabeth said quietly, letting her hands rest on his tense shoulders for a moment after he sank into a chair at the kitchen table.

Trista, delighted that her father was home, rushed to get his coffee mug, but it was Elisabeth who filled it from the heavy enamel pot on the stove.

The evening passed pleasantly—by some miracle, no one came to call Jonathan away—and after Trista had been settled in bed, he came into the kitchen and began drying dishes as Elisabeth washed them.

That reminded her of Ellen's concerns. "You need to have a talk with your housekeeper," she said. "She wants to look for another job if you're planning to let her go."

Jonathan frowned. "Isn't her work satisfactory?"

Elisabeth couldn't help smiling, seeing this rugged doctor standing there with an embroidered dishtowel in his hands. "Her work is fine. But you have given the community—and me, I might add—the impression that I might be staying around here permanently." She paused, blushing because the topic was a sensitive one. "I mean, if I'm to be your wife...."

He put down the towel and the cup he'd been drying and turned Elisabeth to face him. Her hands were dripping suds and water, and she dried them absently on her apron.

His expression was wry. "I'm not as destitute as you seem to think," he said. "I had an inheritance from my father and I invested it wisely, so I can afford to keep a housekeeper *and* a wife."

Elisabeth flushed anew; she hadn't meant to imply that he was a pauper.

Her reaction made Jonathan laugh, but she saw love

in his eyes. "My sweet Lizzie—first and foremost, I want you to be a wife and partner to me. And I hope you'll be a mother to Trista. But running a house is a lot of work, and you're going to need Ellen to help you." He tilted his head to one side, studying her more soberly now. "Does this mean you're going to agree to marry me?"

Elisabeth sighed. The motion left her partially deflated, like a balloon the day after a party. There was still the specter of the fire looming over them, and the question had to be resolved. "That depends, Jonathan," she said, grieving when he took his hands away from her shoulders. "You've been over the threshold now, you've experienced what I have. I guess it all distills down to one question—do you believe me now?"

She saw his guard go up, and her disappointment was so keen and so sudden that it made her knees go weak.

Jonathan shoved one hand through his dark, rumpled hair. "Lizzie…"

"You *saw* it, Jonathan!" she cried in a ragged whisper as panic pooled around her like tidewater, threatening to suck her under. "Damn it, *you were there!*"

"I imagined it," he said, and his face was suddenly hard, his eyes cold and distant.

Elisabeth strode over to the sidetable where his medical bag awaited and snapped it open, taking out the prescription bottle and holding it up. "What about this, Jonathan? Did you imagine this?"

He approached her, took the vial from her hands

and dropped it back into the bag. "I experienced *something*," he said, "but that's all I'm prepared to admit. The human mind is capable of incredible things—it could all have been some sort of elaborate illusion."

Elisabeth was shaking. Jonathan was the most important person in her topsy-turvy universe, and he didn't believe her. She felt she would go mad if she couldn't make him understand. "Are you saying we both had the same hallucination, Jon? Isn't that a little far-fetched?"

Again, Jonathan raked the fingers of one hand through his hair. "No more than believing that people can actually travel back and forth between centuries," he argued, making an effort to keep his voice down for Trista's sake. "Lizzie, the past is gone, and the future doesn't exist yet. All we have is *this moment*."

Elisabeth was in no mood for an esoteric discussion. For eight days she'd been mourning Jonathan, worrying about him, trying to reassure his daughter and his patients. She was emotionally exhausted and she wanted a hot bath and some sleep.

"I'd like the kitchen to myself now, if you don't mind," she said wearily, lifting the lid on the hot-water reservoir to check the supply inside. "I need a bath."

Jonathan's eyes lighted with humor and love. "I'd be happy to help you."

Elisabeth glared at him. "Yes, I imagine you would," she said, "but I don't happen to want your company just now, Dr. Fortner. As far as I'm concerned, you're an imbecile and I'd just as soon you kept your distance."

He smiled and lingered even after Elisabeth had dragged the big tin bathtub in from the combination pantry and storage room. His arms were folded across his chest. It was obvious that he was stifling a laugh.

Elisabeth brought out the biggest kettle in the kitchen, slammed it down in the sink and began pumping icy well water into it. It was amazing, she thought furiously, that she wanted to stay in this backward time with this backward man, when she could have hot and cold running water and probably a Democrat with an M.B.A. if she just returned to the future. She lugged the heavy kettle to the stove and set it on the surface with a ringing thump.

When she turned to face Jonathan, her hands were on her hips and her jaw was jutting out obstinately. "I wouldn't give a flying *damn* whether you believed me or not," she breathed, "if it weren't for the fact that your life is hanging in the balance—and so is Trista's! Half of this house is going to burn in the third week in June, and they're not going to find a trace of you or your daughter. What they are going to do is try *me* for your murders!"

It hurt that the concern she saw in his face was so obviously for her sanity and not for his safety and Trista's. "Lizzie, there are doctors back in Boston and New York—men who know more than I do. They might be able to—"

"Just get out of here," Elisabeth spat out, tensing up like a cat doused in ice water, "and let me take my bath in peace."

Instead, Jonathan brought out more kettles and filled them at the pump, then set them on the stove. "You took care of me when I needed you," he said finally, his voice low, his expression brooking no opposition, "and I'm going to do what I have to do to take care of you, Lizzie. I love you."

Elisabeth had never been so confused. He'd said the words she most wanted to hear, but it also sounded as though he was planning to pack her off to the nearest loony bin the first chance he got. "If you love me," she said evenly, "then trust me, Jon. You didn't believe your own eyes and ears and... well...I'm all out of ways to convince you."

He sat her down in a chair, then fed more wood to the fire so her bathwater would heat faster. He didn't look at her when he spoke. "There isn't going to be a fire, Lizzie—you'll see. The third week of June will come and go, just like it always does."

She stared at his back. "You're going to pretend it didn't happen, aren't you?" she said in a thick whisper. "Jonathan, you were gone for *eight days*. How do you explain that—as a memory lapse?"

Heat began to surge audibly through the pots of water simmering on the stove. "Frankly," he answered, "I'm beginning to question *my* sanity."

Chapter 11

Frantic pounding at the front door roused Elisabeth from a sound, dreamless sleep. She reached for the robe she'd left lying across the foot of the bed and hurried into the hallway, where she saw Jonathan leaving his room. He was buttoning his shirt as he descended the stairs.

She remembered the proprieties of the century and held back, sitting on one of the high steps and gripping a banister post with one hand.

"It's my little Alice," a man's voice burst out after Jonathan opened the door. "She can't breathe right, Doc!"

"Just let me get my bag," Jonathan answered with grim resignation. A few moments later, he was gone, rattling away into the night in the visitor's wagon.

Elisabeth remained on the stairway, even though it was chilly and her exhausted body yearned for sleep. She was still sitting there, huddled in her nightgown and robe when Jonathan returned several hours later.

He lit a lamp in the entryway and started upstairs, halting when he saw Elisabeth.

"What happened?" she asked, wondering if she was going to be in this kind of suspense every time Jonathan was summoned out on a night call. "Is the little girl…"

Jonathan sighed raggedly and shook his head. "Diphtheria," he said.

Elisabeth's knowledge of old-fashioned diseases was limited, but she'd heard and read enough about this one to know it was deadly. And very contagious. "Is there anything I can do to help?" she asked lamely, knowing there wasn't.

He advanced toward her, and his smile was rueful and sad. "Just be Lizzie," he said hoarsely.

They went back to their separate beds then, but it wasn't long before someone else came to fetch the doctor for *their* sick child. When Elisabeth finally gave up on sleeping somewhere around dawn and got up, Jonathan had still not returned.

She built up the kitchen fire and put coffee on to brew. And then she waited. This, she supposed, would be an integral part of being the wife of a nineteenth-century country doctor—if, indeed, destiny allowed her to marry Jonathan at all.

Sipping coffee, her feet resting on the warm, chrome

footrail on the front of the stove, Elisabeth thought of her old life with Ian. It was like a half-remembered dream now, but once, that relationship had been the focal point of her existence.

Tilting her head back and closing her eyes, Elisabeth sighed and contemplated the hole her leaving would rend in that other world. Her disappearence would make one or two local newscasts, but after a while, she'd just be another nameless statistic, a person the police couldn't find.

Ian would cock an eyebrow, say it was all a pity and call his lawyer to see if he and the new wife had any claim on Elisabeth's belongings.

Her father would suffer, but he had his career and Traci and the new baby. In the long run, he'd be fine.

Janet and Elisabeth's other friends in Seattle would probably be up in arms for a time, bugging the police and speculating among themselves, but they all had their own lives. Eventually, they'd go back to living them, and it would be as though Elisabeth had died.

Rue, of course, was an entirely different matter. She would come home from her travels, read the letter Elisabeth had written about her first experience with the threshold and be on the next plane for Seattle. Within an hour of landing, she'd be right here in this house, looking for any trace of her cousin, following up every lead, making the police wish they'd never heard of Elisabeth McCartney.

So close, Elisabeth thought, imagining Rue in these

very rooms, her throat thickening with emotion, *and yet so far*.

The sound of Trista coming down the steps roused Elisabeth from her thoughts.

"What are you doing up so early?" Elisabeth asked, taking the child onto her lap.

Trista snuggled close. Although she was wearing a pinafore, black ribbed stockings and plain shoes with pointy toes, her dark hair hadn't been brushed or braided, and she was still warm and flushed from sleep. She yawned. "I kept hearing people knock on the door. Is Papa out?"

Elisabeth nodded, noting with a start that Trista's forehead felt hot against her cheek. *God, no,* she thought, pressing her palms to either side of the child's face. *No!* She made herself speak in an even tone of voice. "He's been gone for several hours," she said. "Trista—do you feel well?"

"My throat's sore," she said, "and my chest hurts."

Tears of alarm sprang to Elisabeth's eyes, but she forced them back. This was no time to lose her head. "Were you sick during the night?" She tightened her arms around the child, as if preparing to resist some giant, unseen hand that might wrench her away.

Trista looked up at Elisabeth. "I wanted to get into bed with you," she said shyly.

Elisabeth bit her lip and made herself speak calmly. "Well, I think we'd better forget about school and make you a nice, comfortable bed right here by the stove.

We'll read stories and I'll play the piano for you. How would that be?"

A tremor ran through the small body in Elisabeth's arms. "I have to go to school," Trista protested. "There's a spelling bee today, and you know how hard I've been practicing."

There was an element of the frantic in the quick kiss Elisabeth planted on Trista's temple. "It would be my guess that there won't be any school today, sweetheart. And it's possible, you know, to practice too hard. Sometimes, you have to just do your best and then stand back and let things happen."

Trista sighed. "I *would* like to have a bed in the kitchen and hear stories," she confessed.

"Then let's get started," Elisabeth said with false cheer as she set Trista in a chair and automatically felt the child's face for fever again. "You stay right there," she ordered, waggling a finger. "And don't you dare think of even *one* spelling word!"

Trista laughed, but the sound was dispirited.

Elisabeth dragged a leather-upholstered Roman couch from Jonathan's study to the kitchen and set it as close to the stove as she dared. Then she hurried upstairs and collected Trista's nightgown and the linens from her bed.

By the time Jonathan came through the back door, looking hollow eyed and weary to the very center of his soul, his daughter was reclining on the couch, listening to Elisabeth read from *Gulliver's Travels*. The expression on his face as he made the obvious deduction was terrible to see.

Immediately, he came to his daughter's bedside, touched her warm face, examined her ears and throat. Then his eyes linked with Elisabeth's, over Trista's head, and she knew it might not matter that there was going to be a fire the third week in June. Not to this little girl, anyway.

They went into Jonathan's study to talk.

"Diphtheria?" Elisabeth whispered, praying he'd say Trista just had the flu or common cold. But then, those maladies weren't so harmless in the nineteenth century, either. There were so many medical perils at this time that a child would never encounter in Elisabeth's.

Jonathan was standing at one of the windows, gazing past the lace curtain at the new, bright, blue-and-gold day. He shook his head. "It's a virus I've never seen before—and there seems to be an epidemic."

Elisabeth's fingers were entwined in the fabric of her skirts. "Isn't there anything we can do?"

He shrugged miserably. "Give them quinine, force liquids...."

She went and stood behind him, drawn by his pain and the need to ease it. She rested her hands on his tense shoulders. "And then?"

"And then they'll probably die," he said, walking away from her so swiftly that her hands fell to her sides.

"Jon, the penicillin—there wouldn't be enough for all the children, but Trista..." Her sentence fell away, unfinished, when Jonathan walked out of the study and let the door close crisply behind him. Without uttering a word, he'd told Elisabeth he had neither the time nor the patience for what he considered delusions.

He'd left his bag on his cluttered desk in the corner. Elisabeth opened it and rummaged through until she'd found the bottle of penicillin tablets. Removing the lid, she carefully tipped the pills into her palm and counted them.

Ten.

She scooped the medicine back into its bottle and dropped it into her pocket.

Jonathan was stoking the fire in the kitchen stove when Elisabeth joined him, while Trista watched listlessly from the improvised bed. Elisabeth could see the child's chest rise and fall unevenly as breathing became more difficult for her.

Elisabeth began pumping water into pots and kettles and carrying them to the stove, and soon the windows were frosted with steam and the air was dense and hot.

"Let me take her over the threshold, Jon," Elisabeth pleaded in a whisper when Trista had slipped into a fitful sleep an hour later. "There are hospitals and modern drugs…"

He glowered at her. "For God's sake, don't start that nonsense now!"

"You must have seen the cars going by on the road. It's a much more advanced society! Jonathan, I can help Trista—I know I can!"

"Not another word," he warned, and his gray eyes looked as cold as the creek in January.

"The medicine, then—"

The back door opened and Ellen came in, looking flushed and worried. When her gaze fell on Trista, however, the high color seeped from her face. "I'm sorry I couldn't come sooner, but it's the grippe—we've got it at our place, and Seenie's so hot, you can hardly stand to touch her!"

Jonathan's eyes strayed to Trista for a moment, but skirted Elisabeth completely. "I'll be there in a few minutes," he said.

Ellen hovered near the door, looking as though she might faint with relief, but Elisabeth felt nothing but frustration and despair.

"I'll get your bag," she said to Jonathan, and disappeared into the study.

When she returned, the doctor had already gone outside to hitch up his horse and buggy. Elisabeth gave the bag to Ellen, but there seemed to be no reassuring words to offer. A look passed between the two women, and then Ellen hurried outside to ride back to her family's farm with Jonathan.

Throughout the afternoon, Elisabeth kept the stove going at full tilt, refilling the kettles and pots as their contents evaporated. The curtains, the tablecloth, Trista's bedclothes—everything in the room was moist.

Elisabeth found fresh sheets and blankets and a clean nightgown for Trista. The child hardly stirred as the changes were made. Her breathing was a labored rattle, and her flesh was hot as a stove lid.

Elisabeth knelt beside the couch, her head resting

lightly on Trista's little chest, her eyes squeezed shut against tears of grief and helplessness. This, too, was part of being a Victorian woman—watching a beloved child slip toward death because there were no medicines, no real hospitals. Now, she realized that she'd taken the vaccinations and medical advances of her own time for granted, never guessing how deadly a simple virus could be.

Presently, Elisabeth felt the pharmacy bottle pressing against her hip and reached into her pocket for it, turning it in her fingers. She was no doctor—in fact, she had virtually no medical knowledge at all, except for the sketchy first-aid training she'd been required to take to get her teaching certificate. But she knew that penicillin was a two-edged sword.

For most people, it was perfectly safe and downright magical in its curative powers. For others, however, it was a deadly poison, and if Trista had an adverse reaction, there would be nothing Elisabeth could do to help. On the other hand, an infection was raging inside the child's body. She probably wouldn't live another forty-eight hours if someone didn't intercede.

Resolutely, Elisabeth got to her feet and went to the sink. A bucket of cold water sat beside it, pumped earlier, and Elisabeth filled a glass and carried it back to Trista's bedside.

"Trista," she said firmly.

The child's eyes rolled open, but Trista didn't seem to recognize Elisabeth. She made a strangled, moaning sound.

The prescription bottle recommended two tablets every four hours, but that was an adult dose. Frowning, Elisabeth took one pill and set it on Trista's tongue. Then, holding her own breath, she gave the little girl water.

For a few moments, while Trista sputtered and coughed, it seemed she wouldn't be able to hold the pill down, but finally she settled back against the curved end of the couch and closed her eyes. Elisabeth sensed that the child's sleep was deeper and more comfortable this time, but she was so frightened and tense, she didn't dare leave the kitchen.

She was sitting beside Trista's bed, holding the little girl's hand, when the back door opened and Jonathan dragged in. "Light cases," he said, referring, Elisabeth hoped, to the children in Ellen's sizable family. "They'll probably be all right." He was at his daughter's side by then, setting his bag on the table, taking out his stethoscope and putting the earpiece in place. He frowned as he listened to Trista's lungs and heart.

Elisabeth wanted to tell him about the penicillin, but she was afraid. Jonathan was not exactly in a philosophical state of mind, and he wouldn't be receptive to updates on modern medicine. "You need some rest and something to eat," she said.

He smiled grimly as he straightened, pulling off the stethoscope and tossing it back into his bag. "This is a novelty, having somebody worry about me," he said. "I think I like it."

"Sit," Elisabeth ordered wearily, rising and pressing

him into the chair where she'd been keeping her vigil over Trista. She poured stout coffee for him, adding sugar and cream because he liked it that way, and then went to the icebox for eggs she'd gathered herself the day before and the leftovers from a baked ham.

Jonathan's gaze rested on his daughter's flushed face. "She hasn't been out of my thoughts for five minutes all day," he said with a sigh. "I didn't want to leave her, but you were here, and the others—"

Elisabeth stopped to lay a hand on his shoulder. "I know, Jon," she said softly. She found an onion and spices in the pantry and, minutes later, an omelette was bubbling in a pan on the stove.

"Her breathing seems a little easier," Jonathan commented when Elisabeth dished up the egg concoction and brought it to the table for him.

She didn't say anything, but her fingers closed around the little bottle of penicillin in the pocket of her skirt. Soon, when Jonathan wasn't looking, she would give Trista another pill.

He seemed almost too tired to lift his fork, and Elisabeth's heart ached as she watched him eat. When he finished his meal, she knew he wouldn't collapse into bed and sleep, as he needed to do. No, Jonathan would head for the barn, where he would feed and water animals for an hour. Then, provided another frantic father didn't come to fetch him, he'd sit up the rest of the night, watching over Trista.

Elisabeth woke the child while he was in the barn and made her swallow another penicillin tablet. By that time, her own body was aching with fatigue and she wanted to sink into a chair and sob.

She didn't have time for such luxuries, though, for the fire was waning and the water in the kettles was boiling away. Elisabeth found the wood box empty and, after checking Trista, she wrapped herself in a woolen shawl and went outside to the shed. There, she picked up the ax and awkwardly began splitting chunks of dry apple wood.

Jonathan was crossing the yard when she came out, her arms loaded, and he took the wood from her without a word.

Inside, he fed the fire while she pumped more water to make more steam. Suddenly, she ran out of fortitude and sank against Jonathan, weeping for all the children who could not be saved, both in this century and in her own.

Jonathan embraced her tightly for a moment, kissed her forehead and then lifted her into his arms and started toward the stairs. "You're going to lie down," he announced in a stern undertone. "I'll bring you something to eat."

"I want to stay with Trista."

"You're no good to her in this condition," Jonathan reasoned, opening the door to her room and carrying her inside. He laid her gently on the bed and pulled off her sneakers, so incongruous with her long skirt and big-sleeved blouse. "I'll bring you a tray."

Elisabeth opened her mouth to protest, but it was

too late. Jonathan had already closed the door, and she could hear his footsteps in the hallway.

She had to admit it felt gloriously, decadently good to lie down. She would rest for a few minutes, to shut Jonathan up, and then go back to Trista.

The doctor returned, as promised, bringing a ham sandwich and a glass of milk. Elisabeth ate, even though she had virtually no appetite, knowing she needed the food for strength.

Filling her stomach had a peculiar tranquilizing effect, and she sagged against her pillows and yawned even as she battled her weariness. She would just close her eyes long enough to make them stop burning, Elisabeth decided, then go back downstairs to sit with Trista.

There were shadows in the room and the bedside lamp was burning low when Elisabeth awakened with a start. Her throat was sore when she swallowed, but she didn't take time to think about that because she was too anxious to see Trista.

She was holding her breath as she made her way down the back stairway.

The kitchen lamps were lit, and Jonathan sat at the table, his head resting on his folded arms, sound asleep. Trista was awake, though, and she smiled shakily as Elisabeth approached the bed and bent to kiss her forehead.

"Feeling better?"

Trista nodded, though she was still too weak to talk.

"I'll bet you'd like some nice broth, wouldn't you?" Elisabeth asked, remembering the chicken Ellen had killed and plucked yesterday. And even though Trista shook her head and wrinkled her nose, Elisabeth took the poultry from the icebox and put it on the stove to boil.

Although she tried to be quiet, the inevitable clatter awakened Jonathan and he lifted his head to stare at Elisabeth for a few seconds, seeming not to recognize her. Then his gaze darted to his daughter.

Trista smiled wanly at the startled expression on his face.

A study in disbelief, Jonathan grabbed his bag and hastily donned his stethoscope. His eyes were wide with surprise when he looked at Elisabeth, who was grinning at him and holding up the little medicine bottle.

Jonathan snatched it out of her hands. "You gave her this?"

Elisabeth's delight faded. "Yes," she answered with quiet defiance. "And it saved her life."

He looked from the pills to his daughter's placid, if pale, face. "My God."

"It's safe to say He's involved here somewhere," Elisabeth ventured a little smugly. "You should give her one every four hours, though, until she's out of danger."

Jonathan groped for a chair and sank into it. He opened the bottle, this time with no assistance from Elisabeth, and dumped the remaining tablets out onto the table to stare at them as though he expected a magic beanstalk to sprout before his eyes. "Peni— What did you call them?"

"Penicillin," Elisabeth said gently.

"I didn't dream it," he whispered.

She shook her head and spread her hands over his shoulders. A glance at Trista showed her that the child was sleeping again, this time peacefully. "No, Jon—you were really there." She began to work the rigid muscles with her fingers. "You never told me what you saw, you know."

A tremor went through him. "There was a box with women inside," he said woodenly. "They spoke to me."

At the same time she was stifling a laugh, tears of affection burned in Elisabeth's eyes. "The television set," she said. "They weren't talking to you Jon—they were only pictures, being transmitted through the air."

"What else do they have in your world," Jonathan inquired wearily, "besides automobiles that travel too fast?"

Elisabeth smiled. So he *had* seen something of the real modern world. "We're exploring outer space," she said, continuing with the massage and knowing an ancient kind of pleasure as Jonathan's muscles began to relax. "And there have been so many inventions that I couldn't list them all—the most significant being a machine called a computer."

Jonathan listened, rapt, while Elisabeth told him what she knew about computers. She went on to explain modern society as best she could. "There are still social problems, I'm afraid," she told him. "For instance, we have a serious shortage of housing for the poor, and there's a lot of drug and alcohol abuse."

He arched an eyebrow. "Which must be why you were so angry when I sedated you," he ventured.

Elisabeth's achy throat was tight as she nodded. He finally believed her, and if she'd had the energy, she would have jumped up and clicked her heels together to celebrate.

Jonathan sighed. "There are people now who use opium, but thank heaven it's not prevalent."

Elisabeth sat down beside him and cupped her chin in her hands. "Don't be too cocky, Dr. Fortner. You've got a lot of laudanum addicts out there, taking a tipple when nobody's looking. And the saloons are brimming with alcoholics. In approximately 1935, two men will start an organization to help drunks get and stay sober."

He rubbed his beard-stubbled chin, studying Elisabeth as though she were of some unfamiliar species. "Let's talk about that fire you've been harping on ever since you first showed up," he said. Then, remembering Trista, he caught Elisabeth's elbow in one hand and ushered her out of the kitchen and into the parlor, where he proceeded to build a fire against the evening chill. "You said Trista and I died in it."

"I said the authorities—Marshal Farley Haynes, to be specific—believed I killed you by setting the blaze. If—" she swallowed as bile rushed into her throat "—if bodies were found, the fact was hushed up. And the newspaper didn't give a specific date."

Jonathan rubbed the back of his neck and shook his head, watching as the fire caught on the hearth, sending orange and yellow flames licking around the applewood logs. "You'll understand," he said, still crouching before the grate, "if I find this whole thing a little hard to accept."

"I think I would in your place," Elisabeth conceded, taking a seat in a leather wing chair and folding her hands in her lap. "Jonathan, we can leave now, can't we? We can move to the hotel in town, at least during that week?"

To her surprise, he shook his head again as he rose to stand facing her, one shoulder braced against the mantelpiece. "We'll be especially careful," he said. "Surely being warned ahead of time will make a difference."

Elisabeth wasn't convinced; she had a sick feeling in the pit of her stomach, a sense of dire urgency. "Jonathan, please—you must have seen that the house was different in my time. If that isn't evidence that there really was a fire..."

Jonathan came to stand before her chair, bending to rest one hand on each of its arms and effectively trapping her. "There won't be a fire," he said, "because you and I are going to prevent it."

She closed her eyes tightly, defeated for the moment.

Jonathan's breath was warm on her face as he changed the subject. "I'm tired of lying in my bed at night, Elisabeth, aching for you. I want to get married."

She felt her cheeks heat as she glared up at him. "Now, that's *romantic!*" she murmured, moving to push him away and rise, but he stood fast, grinning at her. Raw pain burned her throat as she spoke, and the amusement faded from Jonathan's eyes.

He touched her forehead with his hand. "If you come from a time where some of our diseases no longer exist," he breathed, "you haven't built up any kind of immunity." Jonathan stepped back and drew Elisabeth to her feet, and she was instantly dizzy, collapsing against him. Her first thought was that the rigors of the past twenty-four hours had finally caught up with her.

As easily as before, Jonathan lifted her into his arms. The next thing she knew, she was upstairs and he was stripping her, tucking her into bed. He brought water and two of the precious pills, which Elisabeth wanted to save for Trista.

She shook her head.

But Jonathan forced her to swallow the medicine. She watched, her awareness already wavering, as he constructed a sort of tent around the bed, out of blankets. Presently, the air grew close and moist, and Elisabeth dreamed she was lost in a jungle full of exotic birds and flowers.

In the dream, she knew Jonathan was looking for her—she could hear him calling—but he was always just out of sight, just out of reach.

Chapter 12

Jonathan's fear grew moment by moment as he watched Elisabeth lapse further and further into the depths of the illness. As strong and healthy as she was, her body had no apparent defenses against the virus, and within a matter of hours, she was near death. Even the wonder pills she'd brought with her from the future didn't seem to be helping.

He was searching her dresser before he consciously acknowledged the desperate decision he'd made. Finding the necklace in a top drawer, under a stack of carefully laundered and folded pantaloons, he went back to Elisabeth's bedside and fastened the tarnished chain around her neck.

For a long time, he just stood there, staring down at her, marveling at how deeply he'd come to cherish her in the short time they'd had together. Even when he'd thought she was demented, he'd loved her.

The daylight was fading at the windows when he finally looked up. He turned and went rapidly down the rear stairway to check on Trista.

Earlier, he'd given her a bowl of Elisabeth's chicken broth. He found her sleeping now, and her fever had finally broken.

Jonathan bent and, smoothing back his daughter's dark hair with a gentle hand, kissed her forehead. "I'll be back as soon as I can," he promised in a husky whisper.

Upstairs again, he lifted Elisabeth from the bed and carried her down the back stairs into the kitchen and then up the other set of steps leading to Trista's room. Within moments, they were standing at the threshold.

Although he'd never been a religious man, Jonathan prayed devoutly in those moments. Then he closed his eyes and stepped across.

The immediate lightness in his arms swung a hoarse cry of despair from his throat. He was still in his time—the same pictures hung from the walls and the familiar runner was under his feet.

But Elisabeth was gone.

Miss Cecily Buzbee hovered and fretted while the young men from the county hospital lifted Elisabeth's inert form onto a gurney and started an IV flowing into a vein in her left hand.

"It's a lucky thing I came by to check on her, that's

all I can say," Miss Cecily said, following as Elisabeth was carried down the stairs and out through the front door. "There's something strange going on in this house, you mark my words, and Sister and I have a good mind to telephone the sheriff...."

The paramedics lifted the stretcher into the back of the ambulance, and one of them climbed in with it.

"Heaven only knows how long she's been lying there in that hallway," Cecily babbled on, trailing after the second man as he walked around to get behind the wheel.

"Does Ms. McCartney have any allergies that you know about?" he asked, speaking to her through the open window on the driver's side of the ominous-looking vehicle.

Cecily had no idea and it was agony that she couldn't help.

The young man shifted the ambulance into gear. "Well, if she's got any family, you'd better get in touch with them right away."

The words struck Cecily like a blow. She didn't know Elisabeth well, but she cared what happened to her. Merciful heavens, the poor thing was too young and beautiful to die—she hadn't had a proper chance to live.

Cecily watched until the ambulance had turned onto the main road, lights slicing the twilight, siren blaring. Then she hurried back into the house and began searching for Elisabeth's address book.

* * *

"Jonathan?" The name hurt Elisabeth's throat as she said it, and she wasn't sure whether she was whispering or shouting. She tried to sit up, but she was too weak. And she was immediately pressed back to her pillows by a nurse anyway.

A nurse.

Every muscle in Elisabeth's limp and aching body tensed as a rush of alarm swept through her. Her eyes darted about the room wildly, looking for the one face that would make everything all right.

But there was no sign of Jonathan, and the reason was painfully obvious. Somehow, she'd found her way back into the future, though she had no conscious memory of making the transition. And that meant she was separated from the man she loved.

The nurse was a young woman, tall, with short, curly, brown hair and friendly eyes. "Just relax," she said. "You're safe and sound in the county hospital."

Elisabeth could barely control the panic that seized her. "How long have I been here?" she rasped, as the nurse—the tag on her uniform said her name was Vicki Webster—held a glass of cool water up so that Elisabeth could drink through a straw.

"Just a couple of days," Vicki replied. "One of your friends has been here practically the whole time. Would you like to see her?"

For a moment, Elisabeth soared with the hope that Rue had come back from her assignment, but in the next instant, she knew better. Rue was family and she would never have introduced herself to the staff as a friend.

Minutes later, Janet appeared, looking haggard. Her hair was a mess, her raincoat was crumpled and there were dark smudges under her eyes. "Do you know how worried I've been?" she demanded, coming to stand beside the bed. "First I talked to that strange man on the telephone, and then I couldn't get anyone to answer at all...."

Elisabeth gripped Janet's hand. "Janet, what day is this?"

Janet's brow furrowed with concern and she bit her lips. "It's the tenth of June," she said.

"The tenth..." Elisabeth closed her eyes, too drained to go on. Time was racing by, not only here, but in the nineteenth century, as well. Perhaps Jonathan and Trista were trapped in a burning house at that very moment— perhaps they were already dead!

Janet snatched a tissue from the box on the bedside stand and gently wiped away tears Elisabeth hadn't even realized she was shedding. "Beth, I know you're sick, and it's obvious you're depressed, but you can't give up. You've got to keep putting one foot in front of the other until you get past whatever it is that's troubling you so much."

Elisabeth was too tired to say any more, and Janet stayed a while longer, then left again. The next morning, a big bouquet of flowers arrived from Elisabeth's father, along with a note saying that he and Traci hoped she was feeling better.

As it happened, Elisabeth was feeling stronger, if not better, and she was growing more and more desperate to return to Jonathan and Trista. But here she was, too frail even to walk to the bathroom by herself. She fought off rising panic only because she knew it would drain her and delay the time when she'd be able to leave the hospital.

"I'm taking you home with me," Janet announced three evenings later. A true friend, she'd been making the drive to Pine River every day after she finished teaching her classes. "The term is almost over, so I'll have lots of time to play nurse."

Elisabeth smiled wanly and shook her head. "I want to go home," she said in a quiet voice. *To Jonathan, and Trista—please, God.*

Janet cleared her throat and averted her eyes for just a moment. When she looked back at Elisabeth, her gaze was steady. "Who was that man, Bethie—the one who answered the telephone when I called that day?"

Elisabeth imagined Jonathan glaring at the instrument as it rang, and she smiled again. "That was Jonathan," she said. "The man I love."

"So where is he?" Janet demanded, somewhat impatiently. "If you two are so wild about each other, why haven't I had so much as a glimpse of the guy?" She waved one hand to take in the flowers that banked the room—even Ian and his new bride had sent carnations. "Where's the bouquet with his name on the card?"

Elisabeth sighed. She was too tired to explain about Jonathan, and even if she attempted it, Janet would never believe her. In fact, she would probably go straight to the nearest doctor and the next thing Elisabeth knew, she'd be in the psychiatric ward, weaving potholders. "He's out of the...country," she lied, staring up at the ceiling so she wouldn't have to meet Janet's eyes. "And he's called every day."

When Elisabeth dared look at Janet again, she saw patent disbelief in her friend's face. "There's something very weird here," Janet said.

You don't know the half of it, Elisabeth thought. She was relieved when Janet left a few minutes later.

Almost immediately, however, the Buzbee sisters appeared with colorful zinnias from their garden and a stack of books that probably came from their personal library.

"I saw the ghost through the front window one day," Cecily confided to Elisabeth in a whisper, when her sister had gone down the hall to say hello to a friend who was recovering from gall-bladder surgery.

Elisabeth felt herself go pale. "The ghost?"

Cecily nodded. "Dr. Fortner it was—I'd know him anywhere." She took one of the books from the pile she'd brought, thumbed through it and held it out to Elisabeth. "See? He's standing second from the left, beside the little girl."

Elisabeth's throat tightened as she stared at the old picture, taken by the Pine River Bridge on Founder's Day 1892. Jonathan gazed back at her, and so did Trista, but that wasn't really what shook her, since this was a copy of the same book she'd checked out from the library and she'd seen the picture before. No, it was the fact that her own image had been added, standing just to Jonathan's right. Cecily probably hadn't noticed because Elisabeth looked very different in period clothes and an old-fashioned hairstyle, and because she'd been looking at the picture with the careless eyes of familiarity.

"You've seen this man, haven't you?" Cecily challenged, though not unkindly. She poured water for Elisabeth and held the straw to her lips, as though alarmed by Elisabeth's sudden pallor.

Tears squeezed past Elisabeth's closed eyelids and tickled in her lashes. "Yes," she said. "I've seen him."

Cecily patted Elisabeth's forehead. "There, there, dear. I'm sorry if I upset you. You've probably been frightened half out of your mind these past few weeks, and then you let yourself get run-down and you caught—what is it you caught?"

Elisabeth's disease had been diagnosed simply as a "virus," and she knew the medical community was puzzled by it. "I—I guess it's pneumonia," she said. She put her hand to her throat and turned pleading eyes on Cecily. "They took my necklace."

"I'll just get it right back for you," Cecily replied briskly. And she went out into the hallway, calling for a nurse.

Half an hour later, Elisabeth had her necklace back. Just wearing it made her feel closer to Jonathan and Trista.

That evening when the doctor came by on his evening rounds, he took the IV needle from Elisabeth's hand and pronounced her on the mend. His kindly eyes were full of questions as to where she could have contracted a virus modern medicine couldn't identify, but he didn't press her for answers.

"I want to go home," she announced when he'd finished a fairly routine examination. Weak as she was, she was conscious of every tick of the celestial clock, and it was hell not knowing what was happening to Jonathan and Trista.

The physician smiled and shook his head. "Not for a few more days, I'm afraid. You're in a very weakened state, Ms. McCartney."

"But I can recover just as well there as here...."

"Let's see how you feel on Friday," he said, overruling her. And then he moved on to the next room.

Elisabeth waited until it was dark before getting out of bed, staggering over to the door and peering down the lighted hallway to the nurses' station. One woman was there, her head bent over some notes she was making, but other than that, the coast was clear.

With enormous effort, Elisabeth put on the jeans and sweatshirt Janet had brought her from the house, brushed her tangled hair and crept out into the hallway. A city hospital would have been more difficult to escape, but this one was small and understaffed, and Elisabeth made it into the elevator without being challenged.

She leaned back, clutching the metal railing in both hands and summoning up all her strength. She still had to get to her house, which was several miles away. And Pine River wasn't exactly bustling with available taxi cabs.

Elisabeth didn't have her purse—that was locked away for safekeeping in the hospital and, of course, she didn't dare ask for it—but there was a spare house key hidden in the woodshed.

She started walking, and it soon became apparent that she was simply too weak to walk all the way home. Praying she wouldn't find herself hooked up with a serial killer, like women she'd read about, she stuck out her thumb.

Presently a rattly old pickup truck with one missing fender came to a stop beside her and a young man leaned across the seat to push open the door. His smile was downright ingenuous.

"Your car break down?" he asked.

Elisabeth eyed him wearily, waiting for negative vibes to strike her, but there weren't any. The kid kind of reminded her of Wally Cleaver. She nodded, not wanting to explain that she'd just sprung herself from the hospital, and climbed into the truck.

Just that effort exhausted her and she collapsed against the back of the lumpy old seat, terrified that she would pass out.

"Hey," the teenage boy began, shifting the vehicle into gear and stepping on the gas with enthusiasm. "You sick or something? There's a hospital right back there...." He cocked his thumb over one shoulder.

Elisabeth shook her head. "I'm fine," she managed,

rallying enough to smile. "I live out on Schoolhouse Road."

The young man looked at her with amused interest. "You don't mean that haunted place across from the Buzbees, do you?"

Elisabeth debated between laughing and crying, and settled on the former, mostly to keep from alarming her rescuer. "Sure do," she said.

He uttered an exclamation, and Elisabeth could see that he was truly impressed. "Ever see any spooks or anything like that?"

They were passing through the main part of town, and Elisabeth felt a bittersweet pang as she looked at the lighted windows and signs. She hoped to be back with Jonathan soon, and when that happened, the modern world would be a memory. If something that didn't exist yet could be called a memory.

"No," she said, pushing back her hair with one hand. "To tell you the truth, I don't believe in ghosts. I think there's a scientific explanation for everything—it's just that there are so many natural laws we don't understand."

"So you've never seen nothing suspicious, huh?"

As a teacher, Elisabeth winced at his grammar. "I've seen things I can't explain," she admitted. She figured she owed him that much, since he was giving her a ride home.

"Like what?"

Elisabeth sighed, unsure how much to say. After all, if he went home and told his parents she'd talked about traveling between one century and the next, the authorities would probably come and cart her off to a padded room. "Just—things. Shadows. The kind of stuff you catch a glimpse of out of the corner of an eye and wonder what you really saw."

Her companion shuddered as he turned into Elisabeth's driveway. She could tell the sight of the dark house looming in the night didn't thrill him.

"Thanks," she said, opening the door and getting out of the truck. Her knees seemed to have all the substance of whipped egg whites, and she clung to the door for a moment to steady herself.

The boy swallowed. "No problem," he answered. He gunned the engine, though it was probably an unconscious motion. "Want me to stick around until you're inside?"

Elisabeth looked back over her shoulder at the beloved house that had always been her refuge. "I'll be perfectly all right," she said. And then she turned and walked away.

Her young knight in shining armor wasted no time in backing out of the driveway and speeding away down the highway. Elisabeth smiled as she made her way around the house to the woodshed to extract the back door key from its hiding place.

The lights in the kitchen glowed brightly when she flipped the switch, and Elisabeth felt the need of a cup of tea to brace herself, but she didn't want to take the time. Her strength was about to give out, and she yearned to be with Jonathan.

Upstairs, however, she found the door to the past sealed against her, even though she was wearing the necklace. After a half hour of trying, she went into the master bedroom and collapsed on the bed, too weary even to cry out her desolate frustration.

In the morning, she tried once again to cross the threshold, and once again, the effort was fruitless. She didn't let herself consider the possibility that the window in time had closed forever, because the prospect was beyond bearing.

She listened listlessly to the messages on her answering machine—the last one was from her doctor, urging her to return to the hospital—then shut off the machine without returning any of the calls. She thumbed through her mail and, finding nothing from Rue, tossed the lot of it into the trash, unopened. Quickly checking her email again, she found nothing from Rue.

In the kitchen, she brewed hot tea and made toast with a couple slices of bread from a bag in the freezer. She was feeling a little better this morning, but she knew she hadn't recovered a tenth of her normal strength.

After finishing her toast, she wrote another long letter to Rue, stamped it and carried it out to the mailbox. By the time she returned, carrying a batch of fourth-class mail with her, she was on the verge of collapse.

Numbly, Elisabeth climbed the stairs again, found herself a fresh set of clothes and ran a deep, hot bath. After shampooing her hair, she settled in to soak. The heat revived her, and she had some of her zip back when she got out and dressed in black jeans and a T-shirt with a picture of planet Earth on the front.

Pausing in the hallway, she leaned against the door, both palms resting against the wood, and called, "Jonathan?"

There was no answer, and Elisabeth couldn't help wondering if that was because there was no longer a Jonathan. There were tears brimming in her eyes when she went back downstairs and stretched out on the sofa.

The jangle of the hallway telephone awakened her and, for a moment, Elisabeth considered not answering. Then she decided she'd caused people enough worry as it was, without ignoring their attempts to reach her.

She was shaky and breathless when she picked up the receiver in the hallway and blurted, "Hello?"

"What are you doing home?" Janet demanded. "Your doctor expressly told me you were supposed to stay until Friday, at least."

Elisabeth wound her finger in the cord, smiling sadly. She was going to miss Janet, and she hoped her friend wouldn't suffer too much over her disappearance. "I was resting until you called," she said, making an effort to sound like her old self.

"I'm wasting my time trying to get you to come to Seattle, aren't I?"

"Yes," Elisabeth answered gently. "But don't think your kindness doesn't mean a lot to me, Janet, because it does. It's just that, well, I'm up against something I have to work out for myself."

"I understand," Janet said uncertainly. "You'll call if you change your mind?"

Elisabeth promised she would, hung up and immediately dialed her father's number at Lake Tahoe. These conversations would be remembered as goodbyes, she supposed, if she managed to make it back to 1892.

The call was picked up by an answering machine, though, and Elisabeth was almost relieved. She identified herself, said she was out of the hospital and feeling fine, and hung up.

Early that afternoon, while Elisabeth was heating a can of soup at the stove, a light rain began to fall and the electricity flickered. She glanced uneasily at the darkening sky and wondered if it was about to storm where Jonathan and Trista were.

Just the thought of them brought a tightness to her throat and the sting of tears to her eyes. She was eating her soup and watching a soap opera on TV when a courier brought her purse from the hospital. Later, if she felt better and she still couldn't get across the threshold, she would get into her car and drive to town for groceries. Because she'd been away so much, she had practically nothing in the cupboards except for canned goods.

Thunder shook the walls, lightning flashed and the TV went dead. Not caring, Elisabeth went upstairs. Once again, longingly, she paused in front of the door.

There was nothing beyond it, she told herself sternly, besides a long fall to the roof of the sun porch. She was having a nervous breakdown or something, that was all, and Jonathan and Trista were mere figments of her imagination. They were the family she'd longed for but never really had.

She leaned against the door, her shoulders shaking with silent sobs. The hope of returning was all she had to cling to, and even that was fading fast.

Presently, Elisabeth grew weary of crying and straightened. She knotted one fist and pounded. "Jonathan!" she yelled.

Nothing.

She splashed her face with cold water at the bathroom sink, then went resolutely downstairs. Amazed at how simple exertions could exhaust her, she got her purse and forced herself out to her car.

Shopping was an ordeal, and Elisabeth felt so shaky, she feared she'd fall over in a dead faint right there in the supermarket. Hastily, she bought fruit and a stack of frozen entrées and left the store.

At home, she found the electricity had been restored, and she put one of the packaged dinners into the microwave. She hardly tasted the food.

Following her solitary meal, Elisabeth spent a few disconsolate minutes at the piano, running her fingers over the keys. The songs she played reminded her too much of Trista, though, and of Jonathan, and she finally had to stop. And she had to admit she'd been hoping to hear the sound of Trista's piano echoing back across the century that separated them.

Figuring she might as well give up on getting back to 1892—for that day at least—Elisabeth gathered an armload of Aunt Verity's journals from one of the book-shelves in the parlor and took herself upstairs. After building a fire with the last of the wood, she curled up in the middle of the bed and began to read.

At first, the entries were ordinary enough. Verity talked about her marriage, how much she loved her husband, how she longed for children. After her mate's untimely death in a hunting accident, she wrote about sadness and grief. And then came the account of Barbara Fortner's appearance in the upstairs hallway.

Elisabeth sat bolt upright as she read about the woman's baffled disbelief and Verity's efforts to make her feel at home. The words Elisabeth's aunt had written shed new light on the stories Verity had told her teenage nieces during their summer visits, and Elisabeth felt the pang of grief.

By midnight, Elisabeth's eyes were drooping. She closed the journals and stacked them neatly on the bed-side table, then changed into a nightshirt, brushed her teeth and crawled into bed. "Jonathan," she whispered. His name reverberated through her heart.

She was never sure whether minutes had passed or hours when the sound of a child's sobs prodded her awake. *Trista.*

Elisabeth sat up and flung the covers back, her fingers gripping the necklace as she hurried into the hall-way. Her hand trembled violently as she reached for the knob on the sealed door, praying with all her heart that it would open.

The child's name left her throat in a rush, like a sigh

of relief, when the knob turned under her hand and the hinges creaked.

There was a lamp burning on Trista's bedside table, and she stared at Elisabeth as though she couldn't believe she was really seeing her. Then her small face contorted with childish fury. "Where were you? Why did you leave me like that?"

Elisabeth sat down on the edge of the bed and gathered the little girl into her arms, holding her very close. "I was sick, sweetheart," she said as joyous tears pooled in her eyes. "Believe me, the last thing I wanted to do was leave you."

"You'll stay here now?" Trista sniffled, pulling back in Elisabeth's embrace to look up into her face. "You won't leave us again?"

Elisabeth thought of Rue, her father, Janet. She would miss them all, but she knew she belonged here in this time, with these people. She kissed Trista's forehead. "I won't leave you again," she promised. "Were you all alone? Is that why you were crying?"

Trista nodded. "I was scared."

"Where's your papa?"

Jonathan's daughter allowed herself to be settled back on the pillows and tucked in. "He's just out in the barn, but I heard noises and I imagined Mr. Marley was coming down the hall, rattling his chains and moaning."

Elisabeth smiled at the reference to the Dickens ghost. "I'm the only apparition in this house tonight," she said. Then she kissed Trista again, turned down the wick in the lamp and went downstairs.

Before she went to Jonathan and told him she'd marry him if he still wanted her, before she threw herself into his arms, there was something she had to find out.

Chapter 13

Elizabeth stood in the kitchen, staring helplessly at Jonathan's calendar. Never before had it been so crucial to know the exact date, but the small numbered squares told her nothing except that it was still June.

The sudden opening of the back door and a rush of cool, night air made her turn. Pure joy caused her spirit to pirouette within her. Jonathan was standing there, looking at her as though he didn't quite dare to trust his eyes.

With a strangled cry, she launched herself across the room and into his embrace, her arms tight around his neck.

"Lizzie," he rasped, holding her. "Thank God you're all right."

She tilted her head back and kissed him soundly

before replying, "It was hell not knowing what was happening here. I was terrified I wouldn't be able to get back, and I was even more frightened by what I might find if I did."

Jonathan laughed and gave her a squeeze before setting her on her feet. His hand smoothed her hair with infinite gentleness, and his gaze seemed to caress her. "Are you well again?"

She shrugged, then slipped her arms around his lean waist. "I'm a little shaky, but I'm going to make it."

A haunted expression crossed his face. "I wanted to go with you, to make sure you got help, but when I stepped over the threshold, you vanished from my arms."

Elisabeth glanced back at the calendar. "Jonathan…"

He smiled and crooked a finger under her chin. "That's one thing you were wrong about," he said. "It's the twenty-third of June—Thursday, to be exact—and there's been no fire."

His words lessened Elisabeth's dread a little. After all, she knew next to nothing about this phenomenon, and it was possible that she or Jonathan had inadvertently changed fate somehow.

In the next instant, however, another matter involving dates and cycles leapt into her mind, and the shock made her sway in Jonathan's arms.

He eased her into a chair. "Elisabeth, what is it?"

"I…" Her throat felt dry and she had to stop and swallow. "My…Jonathan, I haven't had my…I could be pregnant."

His eyes glowed bright as the kerosene lantern in the middle of the table. "You not only came back to me," he smiled. "You brought someone with you."

Tears of happiness gathered on Elisabeth's lashes. Once, during her marriage, she'd gotten pregnant and then miscarried, and Ian had been pleased. He'd said it was for the best and that he hoped Elisabeth wouldn't take too long getting her figure back.

"Y-you're glad?"

Jonathan crouched in front of her chair and took her hands in his. A sheen of moisture glimmered in his eyes. "What do you think? I love you, Lizzie. And a child is the best gift you could give me." He frowned. "You won't leave again, will you?"

Elisabeth reached back to unclasp the necklace and place it in his palm. "For all I care, you can drop this down the well. I'm here to stay."

He put the pendant into his shirt pocket and stood, drawing Elisabeth with him. "I'd like to take you straight to bed," he said, "but you're still looking a little peaky, and we have to think about Trista." Jonathan paused and kissed her. "Will you marry me in the morning, Lizzie?"

She nodded. "I know it wouldn't be right for us to make love," she said shyly, "but I need for you to hold me. Being apart from you was awful."

He put an arm around her waist and ushered her toward the rear stairs. "I'm not going to let you out of my sight," he answered gruffly.

In the spare room, he settled Elisabeth under the

covers and then began stripping off his own clothes. She was grateful it was dark so she couldn't see what she was missing and *he* couldn't see her blushing like a virgin bride.

A few moments later, Jonathan climbed into the bed and enfolded Elisabeth in his arms, fitting her close against the hard warmth of his body. Despite the lingering effects of her illness and their decision not to make love again until they were man and wife, desire stirred deep within Elisabeth.

When his hand curved lightly over her breast, she gave an involuntary moan and arched her back. She felt Jon come to a promising hardness against her thigh and heard the quickening of his breath.

"I suppose we could be quiet," she whispered as he lifted her nightshirt and spread one hand over her quivering belly as though to claim and shelter the child within.

Jonathan chuckled, his mouth warm and moist against the pulsepoint at the base of Elisabeth's throat. "You?" he teased. "The last time I had you, Lizzie, you carried on something scandalous."

She reached back over her head to grasp the rails in the headboard as he began kissing her breasts. "I g-guess I'll just have to trust you to be a...to be a gentleman."

"You're a damn fool if you do," he said, just before he took a nipple into his mouth and scraped it lightly with his teeth.

Elisabeth flung her head from one side to the other,

struggling with all her might to keep back the cries of surrender that were already crowding her throat. Rain pelted the window, and a flash of lightning lit the room with an eerie explosion of white. "Jonathan..." she cried.

He brought his mouth down onto hers at the same moment that he parted her legs and entered her. While their tongues sparred, her moans of impending release filled his throat.

Their bodies arched high off the mattress in violent fusion, twisting together like ribbons in the wind. Then, after long, exquisite moments of fiery union, they sank as one to the bed, both gasping for breath.

"We agreed not to do that," Elisabeth said an eternity later, when she was able to speak again.

Jonathan smoothed damp tendrils of hair back from her forehead, sighed and kissed her lightly. "It's a little late for recriminations, Lizzie. And if you're looking for an apology, you're wasting your time."

She blushed and settled close against his chest, which was still heaving slightly from earlier exertions. Thunder rattled the roof above their heads, immediately followed by pounding and shouting at the front door and a shriek from Trista's room.

"I'll see to her," Elisabeth said, reaching for her nightshirt while Jon scrambled into his clothes. "You get the door."

Trista was sobbing when Elisabeth stumbled into her room, lit the lamp on her bedside stand and drew the child into her arms. "It's all right, baby," she whispered. "You were just having a bad dream, that's all."

"I saw Marley's ghost," Trista wailed, shuddering against Elisabeth as she scrambled toward reality. "He was standing at the foot of my bed, calling me!"

Elisabeth kissed the little girl's forehead. "Darling, you're awake now and I'm here. And Marley's ghost isn't real—he's only a story character. You don't need to be afraid."

Trista clung to Elisabeth's shoulders, but she wasn't trembling so hard now, and her sobs had slowed to irregular hiccups. "I don't want to leave you and Papa," she said. "I don't want to die."

The words were like the stab of a knife, reminding Elisabeth of the fire. "You aren't going to die, sweetheart," she vowed fiercely, stretching out on top of Trista's covers, still holding the child. "Not for many, many years. Someday, you'll marry and have children of your own." Tears of determination scalded Elisabeth's eyes, and she reached to turn down the wick in the lamp, letting the safe darkness enfold them.

Trista sniffled, clutching Elisabeth as though she feared she would float unanchored through the universe if she let go. "Will you promise to stay here with us?" she asked in a small voice. "Are you going to marry Papa?"

Elisabeth kissed her cheek. "Yes and yes. Nothing could make me leave you again, and your father and I are getting married tomorrow."

"Then you'll be my mother."

"I'll be your stepmother," Elisabeth clarified gently. "But I swear I love you as much as I would if you'd been born to me."

Trista yawned. It was a reassuring, ordinary sound that relieved a lot of Elisabeth's anxieties. "Will there be babies? I'm very good with them, you know."

Elisabeth chuckled and smoothed the child's hair. "Yes, Trista, I think you'll have a little brother or sister before you know it. And I'll be depending on your help."

She yawned again. "Did Papa go out?"

Elisabeth nodded. "I think so. We'll just go to sleep, you and I, and when we wake up, he'll be home again."

"All right," Trista sighed. And then she slipped easily into a quiet, natural sleep.

Jonathan had still not returned when Elisabeth and Trista rose the next morning, but Elisabeth didn't allow the fact to trouble her. He was a doctor, and he would inevitably be away from home a great deal.

While Ellen prepared oatmeal downstairs in the kitchen, Elisabeth brushed and braided Trista's thick, dark hair. After eating breakfast, the two of them went up to the attic to go through the trunks again. The school term was over, and Trista, who was still a little wan and thin from her illness, had a wealth of time on her hands.

Elisabeth found a beautiful midnight blue gown in the depths of one of the trunks and decided that would be her wedding dress.

Trista's brow crumpled. "Don't brides usually wear white?"

Draping the delicate garment carefully over her arm, Elisabeth went to sit beside Trista on the arched lid of one of the trunks. "Yes, sweetheart," she replied after taking a breath and searching her mind for the best words. "But I was married once before, and even though I wasn't very happy then, I don't want to deny that part of my life by pretending it didn't happen. Do you understand?"

"No," Trista said with a blunt honesty that reminded Elisabeth of Jonathan. The child's smile was sudden and blindingly bright. "But I guess I don't need to. You're going to stay and we'll be a family. That's what matters to me."

Elisabeth smiled and kissed Trista's forehead. It was odd to think that this child was her elder in the truest sense of the word. The dress in her arms and the dusty attic and the little girl had become her reality, however, and it was that other world that seemed like an illusion. "We are definitely going to be a family," she agreed. "Now, let's take my wedding gown outside and let it air on the clothesline, so I won't smell like mothballs during the ceremony."

Trista wrinkled her nose and giggled, but when her gaze traveled to the grimy window, she frowned. "It looks like it's about to rain."

There had been so much sunshine in Elisabeth's heart since she'd awakened to the realization that this was her wedding day, she hadn't noticed the weather at all. Now, with a little catch in her throat, she went over and peered out through the dirty panes of glass.

Sure enough, the sky was dark with churning clouds, and now that she thought of it, there was a hot, heavy, brooding feeling to the air. From where she stood, Elisabeth could see the weathered, unevenly shaped shingles on the roof of the front porch. They looked dry as tinder.

She tried to shake off a feeling of foreboding. Jonathan was right, she insisted to herself—if there was truly going to be a fire, it would have happened before this. Still, she was troubled, and she wished she and Jonathan and Trista were far away from that place.

They took the dress down to Elisabeth's room and hung it near a window she'd opened slightly, then descended to the kitchen. Since Ellen was busy with the ironing, Elisabeth and Trista decided to gather the eggs.

Fetching a basket, she hurried off toward the hen house, expecting to be drenched by rain at any moment. But the sullen sky retained its burden, and the air fairly crackled with the promise of violence. *Jonathan,* Elisabeth thought nervously, *come home. Now.*

But she laughed with Trista as they filled the basket with brown eggs. Surprisingly, considering the threat of a storm, Vera appeared, riding her pony and carrying a virtually hairless doll. After settling the horse in the barn, the two children retreated to Trista's room to play.

Elisabeth joined Ellen in the kitchen and volunteered to take a turn at pressing Jonathan's shirts. The cumber-

some flatirons were heated on the stove, and it looked
like an exhausting task.

"You just sit down and have a nice cup of tea," Ellen
ordered with a shake of her head. "It wasn't that long
ago that you were sick and dying, you know."

There was a kind of grudging affection in Ellen's
words, and Elisabeth was pleased. She was also en-
lightened; obviously, her disappearance had been easily
explained. Jonathan had probably said she was lying in
bed and mustn't be disturbed for any reason. "I'm better
now," she allowed.

Ellen stopped ironing the crisp white shirts long
enough to get the china teapot down from a shelf and
spoon loose tea leaves into it. She added hot water from
the kettle and brought the teapot and a cup and saucer
to the table. "I guess you and the doctor will be getting
married straight away."

Elisabeth nodded. "Yes."

The housekeeper frowned, but her expression showed
curiosity rather than antagonism. "I can't quite work out
what it is, but there's something different about you,"
she mused, touching the tip of her index finger to her
tongue and then to the iron.

The resultant sizzle made Elisabeth wince. "I'm—
from another place," she said, making an effort at cor-
diality.

Ellen ironed with a vehemence. "I know. Boston. But
you don't talk much like she did."

By "she," Elisabeth knew Ellen meant Barbara Fortner, who was supposed to be Elisabeth's sister. Unfor-

tunately, the situation left Elisabeth with no real choice but to lie. Sort of. "Well, I've lived in Seattle most of my adult life."

The housekeeper rearranged a shirt on the wooden ironing board and began pressing the yoke, and a pleasant, mingled scent of steam and starch rose in the air. "She never talked about you," the woman reflected. "Didn't keep your photograph around, neither."

Elisabeth swallowed, contemplating the tangled web that stretched before her. "We weren't close," she answered, and that was true, though not for the reasons Ellen would probably invent on her own. Elisabeth took a sip of tea and then boldly inquired, "Did you like her?"

"No," Ellen answered with a surprising lack of hesitation. "The first Mrs. Fortner was always full of herself. What kind of a woman would go away for months and leave her own child behind?"

Elisabeth wasn't about to touch that one. After all, she'd made a few unscheduled departures herself, and it hadn't been because she didn't care about Trista. "Maybe she was homesick, being so far from her family."

The housekeeper didn't look up from her work, but her reply was vibrant, like a dart quivering in a bull's eye. "She had you, right close in Seattle. Seems like that should have helped."

There was nothing Elisabeth could say to that. She carried her cup and saucer to the sink and set them carefully inside. Beyond the window, with its pristine,

white lace curtains, the gloomy sky waited to remind
her that there were forces in the universe that operated
by laws she didn't begin to understand. Far off on the
horizon, she saw lightning plunge from the clouds in
jagged spikes.

If only the rain would start, she fretted silently. Perhaps that would alleviate the dreadful tension that per-
vaded her every thought and move.

"I'd like to leave early today, if it's all the same to
you," Ellen said, startling Elisabeth a little. "Don't want
to get caught in the rain."

Elisabeth caught herself before she would have offered to drive Ellen home in her car. If she hadn't felt
so anxious, she would have smiled at the near lapse.
"Maybe you'd better leave now," she said, hoping Ellen
didn't have far to go.

Agreeing quickly, the housekeeper put away the
ironing board and the flatirons and took Jonathan's
clean shirts upstairs. Soon she was gone, but there was
still no rain and no sign of Jonathan.

Elisabeth was more uneasy than ever.

She climbed the small stairway that led up to Trista's
room and knocked lightly.

"Come in," a youthful voice chimed.

Smiling, Elisabeth opened the door and stepped
inside. Her expression was instantly serious, however,
when her gaze went straight to the pendant Vera was
wearing around her neck. It took all her personal control not to lunge at the child in horror and snatch away
the necklace before it could work its treacherous magic.

Vera preened and smiled broadly, showing a giant vacant space where her front teeth should have been. "Don't you think I look pretty?" she asked, obviously expecting an affirmative answer. It was certainly no mystery that her grandchildren had grown up to be adventurous; they would inherit Vera's innate self-confidence.

"I think you look very pretty," Elisabeth said shakily, easing toward the middle of the room, where the two little girls sat playing dolls on the hooked rug. She sank to her knees beside them, her movements awkward because of her long skirts.

Vera beamed into Elisabeth's stricken face. "I guess I shouldn't have tried it on without asking you," she said, reaching back to work the clasp. Clearly, she was giving no real weight to the idea that Elisabeth might have objections to sharing personal belongings. "Here."

Elisabeth's hand trembled slightly as she reached out to let Vera drop the chain and pendant into her palm. Rather than make a major case out of the incident, she decided she would simply put the necklace away somewhere, out of harm's way. "Where did you find this?" she asked moderately, her attention on Trista.

Her future stepdaughter looked distinctly uncomfortable. "It was on top of Papa's dresser," she said.

Elisabeth simply arched an eyebrow, as if inviting Trista to explain what she'd been doing going through someone else's things, and the child averted her eyes.

Dropping the necklace into the pocket of her skirt,

Elisabeth announced, "It's about to rain. Vera, I think you'd better hurry on home."

Trista looked disappointed, but she didn't offer a protest. She simply put away her doll and followed Vera out of the room and down the stairs.

Afraid to cross the threshold leading into the main hallway with the necklace anywhere on her person, Elisabeth tossed it over. Only as she was bending to pick the piece of jewelry up off the floor did it occur to her that she might have consigned it to a permanent limbo, never to be seen again.

She carried the necklace back to the spare room and dropped it onto her bureau, then went downstairs and out onto the porch to scan the road for Jonathan's horse and buggy. Instead, she saw the intrepid Vera galloping off toward home, while Trista swung forlornly on the gate.

"There was *supposed* to be a wedding today," she said, her lower lip jutting out just slightly.

Elisabeth smiled and laid a hand on a small seersucker-clad shoulder. "I'm sorry you're disappointed, honey. If it helps any, so am I."

"I wish Papa would come home," Trista said. She was gazing toward town, and the warm wind made tendrils of dark hair float around her face. "I think there's going to be a hurricane or something."

Despite her own uneasiness and her yearning to see Jonathan, Elisabeth laughed. "There won't be a hurricane, Trista. The mountains make a natural barrier."

As if to mock her statement, lightning struck behind

the house in that instant, and both Trista and Elisabeth cried out in shock and dashed around to make sure the chicken house or the woodshed hadn't been struck.

Elisabeth's heart hammered painfully against her breastbone when she saw the wounded tree at the edge of the orchard. Its trunk had been split from top to bottom, and its naked core was blackened and still smoldering. In the barn, Jonathan's horses neighed, sensing something, perhaps smelling the damaged wood.

And for all of it, the air was still bone-dry and charged with some invisible force that seemed to buzz ominously beneath the other sounds.

"We'd better get inside," Elisabeth said.

Trista turned worried eyes to her face. "What about Vera? What if she doesn't get home safely?"

It was on the tip of Elisabeth's tongue to say they'd phone to make sure, but she averted the slip in time. She wished she knew how to hitch up a wagon and drive a team, but she didn't, and she doubted that Trista did, either.

She could ride, though not well. "Let's get out the tamest horse you own," she said. "I'll ride over to Vera's place and make sure she got home okay."

"Okay?" Trista echoed, crinkling her nose at the unfamiliar word.

"It means 'all right,'" Elisabeth told her, picking up her skirts and heading toward the barn. Between the two of them, she and Trista managed to put a bridle on the recalcitrant Estella, Trista's aging, swaybacked mare. Elisabeth asked for brief directions and set off down the road, toward the schoolhouse.

Overhead, black clouds roiled and rolled in on each other, and thunder reverberated off the sides of distant hills. Elisabeth thought of the splintered apple tree and shivered.

As she reached the road, she waved at the man who lived in an earlier incarnation of the house the Buzbee sisters shared. Heedless of the threatened storm, he was busy hammering a new rail onto his fence.

Just around the bend from the schoolhouse, Elisabeth found Vera sitting beside the road, her face streaked with dust, sobbing. The pony was galloping off toward a barn on a grassy knoll nearby.

"Are you hurt?" Elisabeth asked. She didn't want to get down from the horse if she could help it, because getting back on would be almost impossible, dressed as she was. It was bad enough riding with her skirts hiked up to show her bare legs.

Vera gulped and got to her feet, dragging one sun-tanned arm across her dirty face. Evidently, the sight of Elisabeth riding astride in a dress had been enough of a shock to distract her a little from the pain and indignity of being thrown. "I scraped my elbow," she said with a voluble sniffle.

Elisabeth rode closer and squinted at the wound. "That looks pretty sore, all right. Would you like a ride home?"

Vera gestured toward the sturdy-looking, weathered farmhouse five hundred yards from the barn. "I live close," she said. It appeared she'd had enough of horses for one day, and Elisabeth didn't blame her.

"I'll just ride alongside you then," she said gently as lightning ripped the fabric of the sky again and made her skittish mount toss its head and whinny.

Vera nodded and dried her face again, this time with the skirt of her calico pinafore. "I don't usually cry like this," she said as she walked along the grassy roadside, Elisabeth and the horse keeping pace with her. "I'm as tough as my brother."

"I'm sure you are," Elisabeth agreed, hiding a smile.

Vera's mother came out of the house and waved, smiling, apparently unruffled to see her daughter approaching on foot instead of on the back of her fat little pony. "It's good to see you're feeling better, Elisabeth," she called over the roar of distant thunder. "You're welcome to come in for pie and coffee if you have the time."

"I'd better get back to Trista," Elisabeth answered, truly sorry that she couldn't stay and get to know this woman better. "And I suppose the storm is going to break any minute now."

The neighbor nodded her head pleasantly, shepherding Vera into the house, and Elisabeth reined the mare toward home and rode at the fastest pace she dared, given her inexperience. As it was, she needn't have hurried, for even after she'd put Trista's horse back in the barn and inspected the unfortunate tree that had been struck by lightning earlier, there was no rain.

She muttered as she climbed the back steps and

opened the kitchen door. The forlorn notes of Trista's piano plunked and plodded through the heavy air.

The rest of the afternoon passed, and then the evening, and there was still no word from Jonathan. The sky remained as black and irritable as ever, but not so much as a drop of rain touched the thirsty ground.

After a light supper of leftover chicken, Elisabeth and Trista took turns reading aloud from *Gulliver's Travels,* the book they'd begun when Trista had fallen ill. When they tired of that, they played four games of checkers, all of which Trista won with smug ease.

And Jonathan did not come through the door, tired and hungry, longing for the love and light of his home.

Elisabeth was beginning to fear that something had happened to him. Perhaps there had been an accident, or he'd had a heart attack from overwork, or some drunken cowboy had shot him....

Trista, who had already put on her nightgown, scrubbed her face and washed her teeth, was surprisingly philosophical—and perceptive—for an eight-year-old. "You keep going to the window and looking for Papa," she said. "Sometimes he's gone a long time when there's a baby on its way or somebody's real sick."

Self-consciously, Elisabeth let the curtain above the sink fall back into place. "What if you'd been here alone?" she asked, frowning.

Trista shrugged. "Ellen would probably have taken me home with her." She beamed. "I like going to her house because there's so much noise."

The old clock on the shelf ticked ponderously, emphasizing the quiet. And it occurred to Elisabeth that Trista had been very lonely, with no brothers and sisters and no mother. "You like noise, do you?" Elisabeth teased. And then she bolted toward Trista, her hands raised, fingers curled, like a bear's claws.

Trista squealed with delight and ran through the dining room to the parlor and up the front stairway, probably because that was the long way and the pursuit could be drawn out until the last possible moment.

In her room, Trista collapsed giggling on the bed, and Elisabeth tickled her for a few moments, then kissed her soundly on the cheek, listened to her prayers and tucked her into bed.

Later, in the parlor, she sat down at the piano and began to play soft and soothing songs, tunes Rue would have described as cocktail-party music. All the while, Elisabeth listened with one ear for the sound of Jonathan's footsteps.

Chapter 14

The touch of Jonathan's lips on her forehead brought Elisabeth flailing up from the depths of an uneasy sleep. The muscles in her arms and legs ached from her attempt to curl around Trista in a protective crescent.

For a moment, wild fear seized her, closing off her throat, stealing her breath. Then she realized that except for the rumble of distant thunder, the world was quiet. She and Trista were safe, and Jonathan was back from his wanderings.

She started to rise, but he pressed her gently back to the mattress and, in the thin light of the hallway lamp, she saw him touch his lips with an index finger.

"We'll talk in the morning," he promised, his low voice hoarse with weariness. "I trust you're still inclined to become my wife?"

Elisabeth stretched, smiled and nodded.

"Good." He bent and kissed her forehead again. "Tomorrow night you'll sleep where you belong—in my bed."

A pleasant shiver went through Elisabeth at the thought of the pleasures Jonathan had taught her to enjoy. She nodded again and then snuggled in and went contentedly back to sleep, this time without tension, without fear.

Jonathan couldn't remember being more tired than he was at that moment—not even in medical school, when he'd worked and studied until he was almost blind with fatigue. He'd spent most of the past twenty-four hours struggling to save the lives of a mother and her twins, losing the woman and one of the infants. The remaining child was hanging on to life by the thinnest of threads, and there was simply nothing more Jonathan could do at this point.

In his room, he poured tepid water from the pitcher into the basin, removed his shirt and washed, trying to scrub away the smell of sickness and despair. When he could at least stand the scent of himself, he turned toward the bed.

God knew, he was so exhausted, he couldn't have made love to Elisabeth even if the act somehow averted war or plague, but just having her lie beside him would have been the sweetest imaginable comfort. He ached to extend a hand and touch her, to breathe deeply and fill his lungs with her fragrance.

Wearily, Jonathan made his way toward his bed and then stopped, knowing he would lapse into virtual unconsciousness once he stretched out. Before he did that, he had to know Elisabeth wouldn't get it into her head to vanish again.

Picking up a small kerosene lamp, he forced himself out into the hallway and along the runner to the door of the spare room, where she normally slept. The necklace, left carelessly on top of the bureau, seemed to sparkle in the night, drawing Jonathan to it by some inexplicable magic.

Although he knew he would be ashamed of the action in the morning, he scooped the pendant into his hand and went back to his own room, where he blew out the lamp and sank into bed.

Even in sleep, his fingers were locked around the necklace, and the hot, thunderous hours laid upon him like a weight.

Somewhere in the blackest folds of that starless night, Elisabeth awakened with a wrench. She had to go to the bathroom, and that meant a trip to the outhouse if she didn't want to use a chamber pot—which she most assuredly didn't.

Yawning, she rose and pulled on a robe—Ellen and Trista always spoke of the garment as a wrapper—and, after her eyes had adjusted, made her way toward the inner door and down the back steps to the kitchen.

There was no wind, she noticed when she stepped out onto the back step, and certainly no rain. The air was ominously heavy, and it seemed to reverberate with unspoken threats. With a little shiver, Elisabeth forced herself down the darkened path and around behind the woodshed to the privy.

She was returning when the unthinkable happened, paralyzing her in the middle of the path. As she watched, her eyes wide with amazement and horror, a bolt of lightning zigzagged out of the dark sky, like a laser beam from an unseen spacecraft, and literally splintered the roof of the house. For one terrible moment, the entire landscape was aglow, the trees and mountains like dazed sleepers under the glare of a flashlight.

Immediately, flames shot up from the roof, and Elisabeth screamed. The animals in the barn had heard the crash and had probably caught the scent of fire. They were going wild with fear. Elisabeth dared not take the time to calm them. She had to reach Jonathan and Trista.

She hurled herself through the barrier of terrified inertia that had blocked her way and ran into the house, coughing and shrieking Jonathan's and Trista's names.

The short stairway leading to Trista's room was filled with black, roiling smoke. The stuff was so noxious that it felt greasy against Elisabeth's skin. Breathing was impossible.

Beyond the wall of smoke, she could hear Trista screaming, "Papa! Papa!"

Elisabeth dragged herself a few more steps upward, but then she couldn't go farther. Her lungs were empty, and she was becoming disoriented, unsure of which way was up and which was down. She began to sob, and felt herself slipping, the stairs bruising her as she lost her grip.

The next thing she knew, someone was grasping her by her flannel nightgown. Strong hands hoisted her into steely arms, and for a moment she thought Jonathan had found her and Trista, and that the three of them were safe.

But then Elisabeth heard a voice. She didn't recognize it. She felt a huge drop of rain strike her face, warm as bathwater, and opened her eyes to look into the haunted features of Farley Haynes.

Looking around her, she saw the man from across the road, along with his five sons. The shapes of other men moved through the hellish, flickering light of the flames, and Elisabeth saw that they'd formed a bucket brigade between the well and the house. Frantic horses had been released from the endangered barn into the pasture.

The barn won't burn, Elisabeth thought with despondent certainty, remembering the newspaper accounts she'd read in that other world, so far away. *Only the house.*

Marshal Haynes set her down, and she stood trembling in the silky grass, her nightgown streaked with soot.

"Jonathan—Trista—" she gasped hoarsely, starting back toward the house.

But the marshal encircled her waist with one arm

and hauled her back. "It's too late," he said, his voice a miserable rasp. "All three stairways are blocked."

At that moment, part of the roof fell in with a fierce crash, and Elisabeth screamed, struggled wildly in the marshal's grasp and then lost consciousness.

When she awakened, gasping, sobbing before she even became fully aware of her surroundings, Elisabeth found herself in a wagon, bumping and jostling along the dark road that led to town. She sat up, twisting to look at the man who sat in the box, driving the team.

She raised herself to her knees, hair flying wildly around her face, filthy nightgown covered with bit of hay and straw, and clasped the low back of the wagon seat. "Jonathan and Trista," she managed to choke out. "Did you get them out? Did anyone get them out?"

Marshal Haynes turned slightly to look back at her, but the night was moonless and she could see only the outline of his tall, brawny figure and Western hat. The rain that had begun to fall after she'd been pulled from the house started to come down in earnest in that moment, so that he had to raise his voice to be heard.

"That's somethin' you and I are going to have to talk about, little lady," he said.

Elisabeth remembered the sight of the roof of Jonathan's house caving in, and she closed her eyes tightly, heedless of the drops that were wetting her hair and her dirty nightgown. Nothing mattered, nothing in the universe, except Jonathan and Trista's safety. She knelt there, unable to speak, holding tightly to the back of the wagon seat, letting the temperate summer rain drench her.

Only when Farley brought the wagon to a stop in front of the jailhouse did Elisabeth's state of shock begin to abate. Bile rushed into her throat as she recalled the events she'd read about—the fire, no bodies found in the ruins, her own arrest and trial for murder.

And despite the horror of what she faced, Elisabeth felt the first stirring of hope. *No bodies.* Perhaps, just perhaps, Jonathan had found the necklace and he and Trista had managed to get over the threshold into the safety of the future.

The marshal hoisted her down from the wagon and hustled her into his office. While Elisabeth stood shivering and looking around—the place was like something out of a museum—Marshal Haynes hung his sodden hat on a peg beside the door and crouched in front of the wood stove to get a fire going.

"Now, I suppose you're going to arrest me for murder," Elisabeth said, her teeth chattering.

Farley looked back at her over one shoulder, his expression sober. "Actually, ma'am, I just brought you here to wait for the church ladies. They'll be along to collect you any minute now, I reckon."

The guy was like something out of the late show. "You'll try me for murder," Elisabeth said with dismal conviction, stepping a little closer to the stove as the blaze caught and Farley closed the metal door with a clank. "I read it in the newspaper."

"I heard you were a little crazy," the marshal said

thoughtfully. His eyes slid over Elisabeth's nightgown, which was probably transparent, and he brought her a long canvas coat that had been draped over his desk chair. "Here, put this on and go sit there next to the fire. All I need is for the Presbyterians to decide I've been mistreating you."

Elisabeth's knees were weak, and she couldn't keep her thoughts straight. She sank into the rocking chair he indicated, closing the coat demurely around her legs. "I didn't kill anybody," she said.

"Nobody is claiming you did," Farley answered, pouring syrupy black coffee into a metal mug and handing it to her. But he was staring at Elisabeth as though she were a puzzle he couldn't quite solve, and she wondered hysterically if she'd already said too much.

The chair creaked as Elisabeth rocked, and the heat from the stove and the terrible coffee began to thaw out her frozen senses. "Jonathan and Trista are not dead," she insisted, speaking over the rim of the cup. She had to cling to that, to believe it, or she would go mad, right then and there.

Farley looked pained as he finally shrugged out of his own coat and came to stand near the stove, giving Elisabeth a sidelong glance and pouring himself a cup of coffee. His beard-stubbled face was gray with grief, and his brown hair was rumpled from repeated rakings of his fingers and wet with the rain. His green-blue eyes reflected weariness and misery. "There's no way anybody could have survived a blaze like that, Miss

Lizzie," he said with gruff gentleness. "They're dead, all right." He paused and sighed sadly. "We'll get their bodies out tomorrow and bury them proper."

Elisabeth felt the coffee back up into her throat in an acid rush, and it was only by monumental effort that she kept herself from throwing up on the marshal's dirty, plankboard floor. "No, you won't," she said when she could manage it. "You won't find their bodies because they're not there."

Farley sidled over and touched Elisabeth's forehead with the back of one big hand, frowning. Then he went back to his place by the stove. "What do you mean they're not there? Me and four other men tried to get in, and all the staircases were blocked. We couldn't get to Jonathan and the little girl, and we damn near didn't get to you."

A headache throbbed under Elisabeth's temples, and she could feel her sinus passages closing up. "Don't think I'm not grateful, Marshal," she said. "As for what I meant—well, I—" What could she say? That Jonathan and Trista might have disappeared into another time, another dimension? "I believe they got out and that they're wandering somewhere, perhaps not recalling who they are."

"I've known Jonathan Fortner for ten years," Farley answered, staring off at some vision Elisabeth couldn't see. "He wouldn't have left that house unless he was taking everybody inside with him. He wasn't that kind of man."

Elisabeth felt tears burn her eyes. No one was ever

going to believe her theory that Jonathan and Trista had taken the only escape open to them, and she would have to accept the fact. Furthermore, even though the man she loved, the father of the baby growing inside her at that very moment, had not died, he might well be permanently lost to her. Perhaps he wouldn't be able to find his way back, or perhaps the mysterious passageway, whatever it was, had been sealed forever....

Farley fetched a bottle from his desk drawer and poured a dollop of potent-smelling whiskey into Elisabeth's coffee. "You mentioned murder a few minutes ago," he said, "and you talked of reading about what happened in the papers. What did you mean by that?"

Elisabeth normally didn't drink anything stronger than white wine, but she lifted the whiskey-laced coffee gratefully to her mouth, her hands shaking. "There hasn't been a murder. It's just that you're going to *think*..." Her voice failed as she realized how crazy any explanation she could make would sound. She squirmed in the chair. "You won't find any bodies in that house, Marshal, because no one is dead."

A metallic ring echoed through the small, cluttered office when Farley set his cup on the stove top and disappeared into the single cell to drag a blanket off the cot. "Put this around you," he ordered, returning to shove the cover at Elisabeth. "You're out of your head with the shock of what you've been through."

Elisabeth wrapped herself in the blanket. By that time, her mixed-up emotions had undergone another radical shift and she was convinced that Jonathan would come walking through the door at any moment, his clothes blackened and torn, to collect her and prove to the marshal that he was alive. Trista, she decided, was safe at Vera's house.

Farley stooped to peer into her face. "You didn't set that fire, did you?"

She jerked her head back, as though the words had been a physical blow. "Set it? Marshal, the roof was struck by lightning—I saw it happen!"

"Seems to me something like that would be pretty unlikely," he mused, rubbing his chin with a thumb and two fingers as he considered the possibilities.

"Oh, really?" Elisabeth demanded, frightened now because the scenario was beginning to go the way she'd feared it would. "Well, it split one of the apple trees in the orchard right down the middle. Maybe you'd like to go and see for yourself."

"Who are you?" Farley inquired, and Elisabeth was sure he hadn't heard a word she said. "Where did you come from?"

She swallowed. Jonathan had told various people in the community that she was his late wife's sister, and now Elisabeth had no choice but to maintain the lie. If—*when*—she saw him again, she was going to give him hell for getting her into this mess. "My name is Lizzie McCartney, and I was born in Boston," she said, her chin quivering.

"Yes, I remember that Barbara's family lived in Boston," the marshal answered calmly. "If you'll just give me your father's name and street address, I'll get in touch with your family and tell them you're going to need some help."

Elisabeth felt the color drain from her face. She couldn't relay the information the marshal wanted because she didn't know the answers to his questions. "I'd rather handle this on my own," she said after a hesitation that was a fraction too long.

The marshal took a watch from the pocket of his trousers, flipped the case open with his thumb and frowned at the time. "Now where do you suppose those Presbyterians are?" he muttered.

"I don't imagine they'll be coming by for me at all," Elisabeth ventured to say, and her throat felt thick because Jonathan and Trista were gone and she might have to live out what was left of her life alone in a strange place. "My guess would be the ladies of Pine River don't entirely approve of the fact that I've been staying in Jonathan's house."

"Well, you'd better get some sleep. You can bunk in there, on the cot." He pointed toward the cell and Elisabeth shuddered to think of some of the types who might have used it before her. "In the morning, we'll contact your people."

Elisabeth was shaking, and not in her wildest imaginings would she have expected to sleep, but she went obediently into the cell all the same. When the marshal had blown out all the lamps and disappeared into his own undoubtedly humble quarters out back, she stripped off the wet nightgown, wrapped herself tightly in the blanket and lay down on the rickety bed.

* * *

Two sleepless hours passed, during which Elisabeth alternately listened for Jonathan to storm the citadel and cried because she knew the modern world would never surrender him. She was tortured by worries about how he was faring and whether he and Trista had been hurt or not. Jonathan was a doctor and an extremely intelligent man, but Elisabeth wasn't sure he'd know how to get help in her world.

What if Jonathan and Trista were in pain? What if they weren't in her time at all, but some weird place in between? Worst of all, what if they *had* died in the fire and their remains simply hadn't been found yet?

The cell was brimming with sunshine when the marshal appeared, bearing an ugly brown calico dress in one hand. "You can put this on," he said, shoving it through the bars. Actually, he looked rather handsome in an Old West sort of way, with his brown hair brushed shiny, his jaw shaved and his substantial mustache trimmed.

"At least have the courtesy to turn your back," Elisabeth said, rising awkwardly in her scratchy blanket to reach for the garment.

Farley obliged, folding his beefy arms in front of his chest. "Looks like you'll be staying with us for a while," he said with a sort of grim heartiness. "I had a talk with Jon's housekeeper, and she managed to find some family papers in the part of the house that didn't burn. Then I sent a telegram to Barbara's family, back there in Massachusetts. They wired me that they never had a daughter named Lizzie."

Elisabeth felt panic sweeping her toward the edge like a giant broom, but somehow she contrived to keep her voice even. "I guess I'm just lucky I didn't end up in the 1600s," she said, pulling on the charity dress and fastening the buttons. The thing was a good three sizes too big. "They probably would have burned me at the stake as a witch."

"I'd be careful about how I talked," Farley advised, turning around to face her. "The people around here don't hold much with witches and the like."

"I don't imagine they do," Elisabeth remarked sweetly, wondering how the heck she was going to get out of this one. "Tell me, whose dress is this?"

"Belongs to Big Lil over at the Phifer Hotel. She's the cook."

"And she's in the habit of lending her clothes to prisoners?"

Farley's powerful shoulders moved in an offhanded shrug. "Not really. I believe she left that here the last time I had to run her in for disturbing the peace."

Elisabeth gripped the bars in both hands and peered through with guileless eyes. "I hardly dare ask what Big Lil was wearing when she left."

To her satisfaction, the marshal's neck went a dull red, and he averted his eyes for a moment. "She had her daughter bring her some things," he mumbled.

If it hadn't been for the gravity of her situation and all the dreadful possibilities she was holding at bay,

Elisabeth might have smiled. As it was, her sense of humor was strained to the breaking point.

"Exactly what am I charged with?" she asked as Farley went to the stove and touched the big enamel coffeepot with an inquiring finger. "You can't pin a murder on somebody if there aren't any bodies."

Farley stared at her, looking bewildered and just a touch sick. "What makes you so sure we didn't find... remains?"

He'd never buy the truth, of course. "I just know," Elisabeth said with a little shrug. She wriggled her eyebrows. "Maybe I am a witch."

The marshal hooked his thumbs under his suspenders and regarded Elisabeth somberly. "What did you do with them? Drop 'em down the well? Dump 'em into the river?"

Elisabeth spread her hands wide of her body and the horrendous brown dress that was practically swallowing her. "Do I look big enough to overcome a man Jonathan's size?"

Farley arched an eyebrow. "You could have poisoned him or hit him over the head. As for disposing of the bodies, you might even have had an accomplice."

Knowing the townspeople were going to believe some version of that story, Elisabeth cringed inwardly. Still, she had to at least try to save her skin. "What motive would I have for doing that?"

"What motive did you have for lying about who you are?" Farley countered, rapid-fire. "I'll bet you lied to

Jonathan, too—told him you were family, so to speak. He took you in, and you repaid him by—"

"Before you whip out a violin," Elisabeth interrupted, "let me say that Jonathan *does* know who I am. And telling people I was Barbara's sister was his idea, not mine."

"Unfortunately, we don't have anybody's word for that but yours. And it wouldn't make a damn bit of difference if we did." He came to the cell door and glared at her through the bars, his hands gripping the black iron so hard that his knuckles went white. "What did you do to Dr. Fortner and his little girl?"

Elisabeth backed away from the bars because, suddenly, Farley looked fierce. "Damn it, I didn't do *anything* to them," she whispered. "To me, Jonathan and Trista are the most important people in the world!"

Glowering, Farley turned away. "Big Lil will be by with your breakfast pretty soon," he said, taking a gun belt down from a hook on the wall and strapping it on with disturbing deftness. "See you don't try to escape or anything. Lil is mean as a wet badger and tall enough to waltz with a bear."

Again, Elisabeth had the feeling that she would have been amused, if her circumstances hadn't been so dire. "I'll be sure I don't try to dance with her," she replied, slumping forlornly on the edge of the cot.

Farley gave her a look over one broad shoulder and walked out, calmly closing the door behind him.

Elisabeth cupped her chin in her hands and tried to remember if the *Pine River Bugle* had said anything about a lynch mob. "Jonathan," she whispered, "where are you?"

When the door slammed open a few minutes later, however, it wasn't Jonathan filling the chasm. In fact, it could only have been Big Lil, so tall and broadly built was this woman who strode in, carrying a basket covered with a checked table napkin. She wore trousers, boots, suspenders and a rough-spun shirt. Her gray hair was tied back into a severe knot at the nape of her neck.

It occurred to Elisabeth that Big Lil might begrudge her the calico dress, and she reached back to pull the garment tight with one hand, hoping that effort would disguise it.

Big Lil fetched a ring of keys from the desk, unlocked the door and brought the basket into the cell. Her regard was neither friendly nor condemning, but merely steady. "So, you're the little lady what roasted the doctor like a trussed turkey," she said.

Elisabeth's appetite fled, and she swallowed vile-tasting liquid as she stared at the covered food. She jutted out her chin and glared defiantly at Big Lil, refusing to dignify the remark with an answer.

Big Lil gave a raucous, crowing laugh, then went out of the cell and locked the door again. "Folks around here liked the doc," she said. "I don't reckon they'll take kindly to what you did."

Still, Elisabeth was silent, keeping her eyes fixed on the wall opposite her cot until she heard the door close behind the obnoxious woman.

Elisabeth was in the worst fix of her life, but in the

next few moments, her appetite returned, wooed back by the luscious smells coming from inside the basket. She pushed aside the napkin to find hot buttered biscuits inside, along with two pieces of fried chicken and a wedge of goopy cherry pie.

She consumed the biscuits, then the chicken and half the piece of pie before Farley returned, followed by a hard-looking woman with dark hair, small, mean eyes and a pockmarked complexion.

"This is Mrs. Bernard," Farley said, cocking his thumb toward the lady. "She's a Presbyterian."

At last, Elisabeth thought, *the lynch mob.*

Mrs. Bernard stood at a judicious distance from the bars and told Elisabeth in on uncertain terms how God dealt harshly with harlots and liars and had no mercy at all for murderers.

Elisabeth's rage drew her up off the cot and made her stand tall, like a puppet with its strings pulled too tight. "There will certainly be no need to bring in a judge and try me fairly," she said. "This good woman apparently feels competent to pronounce sentence herself."

Mrs. Bernard's face turned an ugly, mottled red. "Jonathan Fortner was a fine man," she said after a long, bitter silence. She pulled a handkerchief from under her sleeve and dabbed at her beady eyes with it.

"I know that, Mrs. Bernard," Elisabeth replied evenly. The marshal made something of a clatter as he went about his business at the desk, opening drawers and shuffling papers and books.

"Which is not to say he didn't make his share of

errors in judgment," the woman went on, as if Elisabeth hadn't spoken. She snuffled loudly. "In any case, the Ladies' Aid Society wishes to extend Christian benevolence. For that reason, I'll be bringing by some decent clothes for you to wear, and some of my companions will drop in to explain the wages of sin."

Elisabeth let her forehead rest against the cold bars. "And I thought I didn't have anything but a hanging to look forward to," she sighed.

If Mrs. Bernard heard, she gave no response. She merely said a stiff goodbye to the marshal and went out.

"If you'll just bring a doctor in from Seattle," Elisabeth said, "he'll testify that human bones can't be destroyed in an ordinary house fire and you'll have to let me go."

"I'm not letting you go until you tell me what you did with the doc and that poor little girl of his," Farley replied, and although he didn't look up from his paperwork, Elisabeth saw his fist tighten around his nibbed pen.

"Well, at least send someone out to look for my necklace," Elisabeth persisted, but the situation was hopeless and she knew it. Farley simply wasn't listening.

Chapter 15

It was the second week in July before the circuit judge showed up to conduct Elisabeth's trial, and by that time, she'd lost all hope that Jonathan and Trista would ever return. The townspeople were spoiling for a hanging, and even Elisabeth's defense attorney, a smarmy little man in an ill-fitting suit, made it clear that he would have preferred working for the prosecution.

If it hadn't been for the child nature was knitting together beneath her heart, Elisabeth wouldn't have minded dying so much. After all, she was in a harsh and unfamiliar century, separated from practically everyone who mattered to her, and even if she managed to be acquitted of killing Jonathan and Trista, she would always be an outcast.

And she would probably be convicted.

The thought of the innocent baby dying with her tightened her throat and made her stomach twist as she sat beside her lawyer in the stuffy courtroom—which was really the schoolhouse with the desks all pushed against the walls.

The judge occupied the teacher's place, and there was nothing about his appearance or manner to reassure Elisabeth. In fact, his eyes were red rimmed, and the skin of his face settled awkwardly over his bones, like a garment that was too large. The thousands of tiny purple-and-red veins in his nose said even more about the state of his character.

"This court will now come to order," he said in a booming voice, after clearing his throat.

Elisabeth shifted uncomfortably in her chair beside Mr. Rodcliff, her attorney, recalling her reflection in the jailhouse mirror that morning. Her blond hair had fallen loose around her shoulders, her face looked pallid and gaunt, and there were purple smudges under her eyes.

She was the very picture of guilt.

Farley stood over by the wainscoted wall, slicked up for the big day, his hat in his hands. He caught Elisabeth's eye and gave a slight nod, as if to offer encouragement.

She looked away, knowing Farley's real feelings. He wanted to see her dangle, because he believed she'd willfully murdered his friend.

The first witness called to the stand was Ellen, Jonathan's erstwhile housekeeper. Tearfully, the plain woman told how Elisabeth had just appeared one day, seemingly out of nowhere, and somehow managed to bewitch the poor doctor.

Mr. Rodcliff asked a few cursory questions when his turn came, then sat down again.

Elisabeth folded her arms and sat back in her chair, biting down hard on her lower lip. Vera was the next to testify, saying Trista had told her some very strange things about Elisabeth—that she was really an angel come from heaven, and that she had a magic necklace and played queer music on the piano and claimed to know exactly what the world would be like in a hundred years.

Mr. Rodcliff gave Elisabeth an accusing sidelong glance, as if to ask how she expected him to defend her against such charges. When the prosecuting attorney sat down behind his table, Elisabeth's lawyer rose with a defeated sigh and told the judge he had nothing to say.

Elisabeth watched a fly buzzing doggedly against one of the heavy windows and empathized. She felt hot and ugly in her brown dress, and even though she'd borrowed a needle and thread from Farley and taken tucks in it, it still fit badly.

Hearing Farley's name called, Elisabeth jerked her attention back to the front of the room. He wouldn't meet her eyes, though his gaze swept over the jury of six men lined up under the world map. He cleared his throat before repeating the oath, then testified that he'd been summoned to the Fortner farm, along with the volunteer fire department, by one of Efriam Lute's sons, who'd awakened because the livestock was fretful and seen the flames.

When he'd arrived, Farley said, he immediately tried to get up the main staircase, knowing the members of the household would be sleeping, it being the middle of the night and all. He allowed as how his way had been blocked by flames and smoke, so he'd tried both the other sets of stairs and met with the same frustration. He had, however, found Miss Lizzie half-conscious in the kitchen and had carried her out.

It was only later, he related, when she began saying odd things, that he started to suspect that something was wrong. When he'd learned she was lying about her identity, he'd filed charges.

While Farley talked, Elisabeth stared at him, and he began to squirm in his chair.

Mr. Rodcliff didn't even bother to offer a question when he was given the opportunity and, at last, Elisabeth was called to the stand. She was terrified, but she stood and walked with regal grace to the front of the crowded schoolroom and laid her left hand on the offered Bible, raising her right.

Benches had been brought in for the spectators, and the place was packed with them. The smell of sweat made Elisabeth want to gag.

"Do you solemnly swear to tell the truth, the whole truth and nothing but the truth?" asked the bailiff, who was really Marvin Hites, the man who ran the general store.

"I do," Elisabeth said clearly, even though she knew she couldn't tell the "whole truth" because these relatively primitive minds would never be able to absorb it. She would be committed, and Elisabeth's limited knowledge of nineteenth-century mental hospitals told her it would be better to hang.

There followed a long inquisition, during which Elisabeth was asked who she was. "Lizzie" was the only answer she would give to that. She was asked where she came from, and she said Seattle, which caused murmurs of skepticism among the lookers-on.

Finally, the prosecutor inquired as to whether Elisabeth had in fact "ignited the blazes that consumed one Dr. Jonathan Fortner and his small daughter, Trista."

The question, even though Elisabeth had expected it, outraged her. "No," she said reasonably, but inside she was screaming her anger and her innocence. "I loved Dr. Fortner. He and I were planning to be married."

The townswomen buzzed behind their fans at this statement, and it occurred to Elisabeth that many of them had probably either hoped to marry Jonathan themselves or had wanted to land him for a son-in-law or a nephew by marriage.

"You *loved* him," the prosecutor said in a voice that made Elisabeth want to slap his smug face. "And yet you did murder, Miss—Lizzie. You killed the man and his child *as they slept,* unwitting, in their beds!"

A shape moved in the open doorway, then a familiar voice rolled over the murmurs of the crowd like a low roll of thunder. "If I'm dead, Walter," Jonathan said, "I think it's going to come as a big shock to both of us."

He stood in the center aisle, his clothes ripped and covered in soot, one arm in a makeshift sling made from one of the silk scarves Elisabeth had collected in her other incarnation. His gray eyes linking with hers, he continued, "I'm alive, obviously, and so is Trista."

Women were fainting all over the room, and some of the men didn't look too chipper, either. But Elisabeth's shock was pure, undiluted joy. She flung herself at Jonathan and embraced him, being careful not to press against his injured arm.

He kissed her, holding her unashamedly close, his good hand pressed to the small of her back. And even after he lifted his mouth from hers, he seemed impervious to the crowd stuffing the schoolhouse.

It was Farley who shouldered his way to Jonathan and demanded, "Damn it, Jon, *where the hell have you been?*"

Jonathan's teeth were startlingly white against his soot-smudged face. He slapped the marshal's shoulder affectionately. "Someday, Farley, when we're both so old it can't make a difference, I may just tell you."

"Order, order!" the judge was yelling, hammering at the desk with his trusty gavel.

The mob paid no attention. They were shouting questions at Jonathan, but he ignored them, ushering a stunned Elisabeth down the aisle and out into the bright July sunshine.

"It seems time has played another of its nasty tricks

on us," he said when he and Elisabeth stood beneath the sheltering leaves of a maple tree. He traced her jawline with the tip of one index finger. "Let's make a vow, Lizzie, never to be apart again."

Tears were trickling down Elisabeth's cheeks, tears of joy and relief. "Jonathan, what happened?"

He held her close, and she rested her head against his shoulder, not minding the acrid, smoky smell of him in the least. "I'm not really sure," he replied, his breath moving in her hair. "I woke up, Trista was screaming and there was no sign of you. I had the necklace in my hand. All three stairways were closed off, and the roof was burning, too. I grabbed up my daughter, offered a prayer and went over the threshold."

Elisabeth clung to him, hardly able even then to believe that he'd really come back to her. "How long were you there?" she asked.

He propped his chin on top of her head, and the townspeople kept their distance, though they were streaming out of the schoolhouse, chattering and speculating. "That's the crazy part, Elisabeth," he said. "A few hours passed at the most—I waited until I could be fairly sure the fire would be out, then I came over again, this time carrying Trista on my back. Climbing down through the charred ruins took some time."

"How did you know where to look for me?"

His powerful shoulders moved in a shrug. "There were a lot of horses and wagons going past. I stopped old Cully Reed, and he about spit out his teeth when he saw me. Then he told me what was going on and brought me here in his hay wagon."

Elisabeth stiffened, looking up into Jonathan's face, searching for any sign of a secret. "And Trista wasn't hurt?"

He shook his head. "She's already convinced the whole thing was a nightmare, brought on by swallowing so much smoke. Maybe when she's older, we can tell her what really happened, but I think it would only confuse her now. God knows, it confuses me."

The judge, who had been ready to send Elisabeth to the gallows only minutes before, dared to impinge upon the invisible circle that had kept the townspeople back. He laid a hand to Jonathan's shoulder and smiled. "Looks like you need some medical attention for that arm, son."

"The first thing I need," Jonathan answered quietly, his eyes never leaving Elisabeth's face, "is a wife. Think you could perform the ceremony, Judge? Say in an hour, out by the covered bridge?"

The judge agreed with a nod, and Elisabeth thought how full of small ironies life is, not to mention mysteries.

"Will you marry me, Lizzie?" Jonathan asked, a little belatedly. "Will you throw away the necklace and live with me forever?"

Elisabeth thought only briefly of that other life, in that other, faraway place. She might have dreamed it, for all the reality it had, though she knew she would miss Rue and her friends. "Yes, Jon."

He kissed her again, lifting her onto her toes to do it, and the spectators cheered. Elisabeth forgave them for their fickleness because a lifetime of love and happiness lay before her, because Jonathan was back and she was carrying his baby, and because Trista would grow up to raise a family of her own.

As Elisabeth caught a glimpse of the half-burned house, what in her mind had been the very symbol of shattered hopes now, miraculously, became a place where children would laugh and run and work, a place where music would play.

"Oh, Jonathan, I love you," Elisabeth said, her arm linked with his as Cully Reed's hay wagon came to a stop in the side yard. They'd been sitting in the back, their feet dangling.

Jonathan kissed her smartly, jumped to the ground and lifted her after him with one arm. "I love you, too," he answered huskily, and his eyes brushed over her, making her flesh tingle with the anticipation of his lovemaking. He waved at the driver. "Thanks, Cully. See you at the wedding."

Practical concerns closed around Elisabeth like barking dogs as she and Jonathan went up the front steps and into the house. "What am I going to wear?" she fretted, holding wide the skirts of Big Lil's brown calico dress. "I can't be married in this!"

Jonathan assessed the outfit and laughed. "Why not, Lizzie? This certainly isn't going to be a conventional wedding day anyhow."

Elisabeth sighed. There was no denying that. Nonetheless, she diligently searched the upstairs and was heartbroken to find nothing that wasn't in even worse condition than what she was wearing.

In his bedroom, Jonathan sank into a chair and unwrapped his wounded arm. Elisabeth winced when she saw the angry burn.

"Oh, Jon," she whispered, chagrined. She fell to her knees beside his chair. "Here I am, worrying about a stupid dress, when you're hurt...."

He bent to kiss her forehead. "I'll be all right," he assured her gruffly. "But after the wedding, I'd like to go first to Seattle and then San Francisco. There's a doctor in Seattle who might be able to help me keep full use of the muscles in my hand and wrist."

Elisabeth's eyes filled with tears. "I'll go anywhere, as long as I can be with you. You know that. But who will look after your patients here?" Even as she voiced the question, she thought of the young, red-haired physician who had been summoned from Seattle after Jonathan's disappearance.

"Whoever's been doing it in my absence," Jonathan replied, and there was pain in his eyes, and distance. "I won't be of use to anybody if I can't use my right hand, Lizzie."

Elisabeth watched unflinchingly as he began treating the burns with a smelly ointment. "That's not true. You're so important to me that I can't even imagine what I'd have done without you."

Before Jonathan could respond to that, Trista bolted

into the room and hurled herself into Elisabeth's waiting arms.

"Vera said there was a trial and that she testified," the child chattered. Her brow was crimped into a frown when she drew back to search Elisabeth's face. "How could so much have happened while I was sleeping?"

Elisabeth kissed her cheek. "I don't think I can explain, sweetheart," she said truthfully enough, "because I don't understand, either. I'm just glad we're all together again."

"Vera's mother says there's going to be a wedding, and she's bringing over her own dress for you to wear. She says the least Pine River can do for you is see that things are done properly."

Soon Vera's mother did, indeed, arrive with a dress, and Elisabeth was so grateful that she forgot how the woman's child had practically called her a witch that very morning. She bathed in the privacy of the spare room, and brushed her hair until it shone, pinned it into a modified Gibson-girl and put on the lace-trimmed ivory silk dress her neighbor had so generously offered. The fabric made a rustling sound as Elisabeth moved, and smelled pleasantly of lavender. Trista gathered wildflowers and made a garland for Elisabeth's hair, and when the two of them reached the site Jonathan had chosen, next to the covered bridge, the doctor was waiting there with a handful of daisies and tiger lilies.

The townsfolk crowded the hillside and creek bank, and several schoolboys even sat on the roof of the bridge. Elisabeth marveled that she'd come so close to losing her life and then had gained everything she'd ever wanted, all in the space of a single day.

To be married by the very judge who would probably have handed down her death sentence was a supreme irony.

The ceremony passed in a sort of sparkling daze for Elisabeth; it seemed as though she and Jonathan were surrounded by an impenetrable white light, and the ordinary sounds of a summer afternoon blended into a low-key whir.

Only when Jonathan kissed her did Elisabeth realize she was married. When the kiss ended, she was flushed with the poignant richness of life. Instead of tossing her bouquet, she handed it to Trista and hugged the child.

"Now we're a family," Trista said, her gray eyes glowing as she looked up at her stepmother.

"We are, indeed," Elisabeth agreed, her throat choked with happy tears.

After the ceremony, there was corn bread and coffee at the hotel. There hadn't been enough advance warning for a cake, but Elisabeth didn't care. What stories she'd be able to tell her and Jonathan's grandchildren!

Trista would spend the night with Vera, it was agreed, and the Fortner family would leave on their trip the following morning. Once all the corn bread had been consumed and Jonathan and Elisabeth had been wished the best by everyone, from the judge who had married them to the man who swept out the saloon, the newlyweds retired to the room Jonathan had rented.

Beyond the window and the door, ordinary life went

on. Buggies and wagons rattled by, and the piano player hammered out bawdy tunes in the saloon across the road. But Jonathan and Elisabeth were alone in a world no one else could enter.

She trembled with love and wanting as he slowly, gently undressed her, and it was an awkward process, since his right arm was still in a sling. "I'm going to have your baby, Jon," she said in a breathless whisper as he unbuttoned her muslin camisole and pushed it back off her shoulders, baring her breasts. "I'm sure of that now."

He bent his head, almost reverently, to kiss each of her firm, opulent breasts. "The first of many, I hope," he relied.

Elisabeth drew in a quick breath as she felt his mouth close over her nipple. "I missed you so much, Jon," she managed after a moment, tilting her head back and closing her eyes in blissful surrender as he enjoyed her. "I was terrified I would never see you again."

He suckled for a long, leisurely time before drawing back long enough to answer, "I was scared, too, wondering if you escaped the fire." He turned to her other breast, and Elisabeth moaned and entwined her fingers in his rich, dark hair, holding him close as he drank from her. If she never had another day to laugh and breathe and love, she thought, this one would be sweet enough to cherish through the rest of eternity.

Presently, he laid her down on the edge of the bed, running his hands along her inner thighs, easing her quivering legs apart for an intimate plundering. She felt her hair come undone from its pins and spread it over the covers with her fingers in a gesture of relinquishment.

Her soul was open to Jonathan now; there was no part of it he was not free to explore.

He knelt, his hands gripping the tender undersides of her knees, and nuzzled the moist delta where her womanhood nestled. "I love pleasing you, Elisabeth," he said. "I love making you give yourself up to me, totally, without reservation of any kind."

Elisabeth's breath was quick and shallow, and she could barely speak. "I need you," she whimpered.

Jonathan burrowed through and took her fiercely, and Elisabeth cried out, her body making a graceful arch on the mattress, her hands clutching and pounding at the blankets.

He consumed her until she was writhing wildly on the bed, until she was uttering low cries, until her skin was wet with perspiration and her muscles were aching with the effort of thrusting her toward him. He drove her straight out of herself and made her soar, and brought her back to earth with patient caresses and muttered reassurances.

She found him beside her on the lumpy hotel bed, after she'd returned to herself and could think and see clearly. Very gently, she touched his bandaged arm.

"Does it hurt much?"

He bent to scatter light kisses over her collarbone. "It hurts like hell, Mrs. Fortner. Just exactly how do you propose to comfort your husband in his time of need?"

She stretched like some contented cat, and he poised himself over her, one of his legs parting hers. "I intend to love him so thoroughly that he won't remember his name," she responded saucily, spreading her fingers in the coarse hair that covered his chest.

Jonathan groaned, touching his hardness to her softness, receiving warmth. Elisabeth guided him gently inside her, arching her back to take him deep within, and his magnificent gray eyes glazed with pleasure.

Slowly, slowly, she moved beneath him, tempting, teasing, taking and giving. With one hand thrust far into the mattress, the other resting against his middle in its sling and bandage, he met her thrusts, retreated, parried.

The release was sudden and ferocious, and it took Elisabeth completely by surprise because she'd thought she was finished, that all the responses from then on would be Jonathan's. But her body buckled in a seizure of satisfaction, and he lowered his mouth to hers, as much to muffle her cries as to kiss her.

When the last whimper of delight had been wrung from her, and only then, Jonathan gave up his formidable control and surrendered. He was like a magnificent savage as he lunged into her, drew back, and lunged again.

Finally, with a loud groan, he spilled himself inside her and then collapsed to lie trembling beside her on the mattress, his chest rising and falling with the effort to breathe. Elisabeth draped one leg across both of his and let her cheek rest against his chest.

For a long time, they were silent, and Elisabeth even slept for a while.

When she awakened, there were long shadows in the room and Jonathan's hand was running lightly up and down her back.

"I think you'll miss your world," he said sadly as she stirred against him and yawned. "Maybe you shouldn't stay, Elisabeth. Maybe you should take the necklace and go back and pretend that none of this ever happened."

She scrambled into a sitting position and stared down at him. "I'm not going anywhere, Jonathan Fortner. You're stuck with me and with our baby."

"But the medicine—the magic box…"

Elisabeth smiled and smoothed his hair, less anxious now. "In some ways the future is better," she conceded. "They've wiped out a lot of the diseases that are killing people now. And life is much easier, in terms of ordinary work, because there are so many labor-saving devices. But there are bad things, too, Jon—things I won't miss at all."

His forehead wrinkled as he frowned. "Like what?"

Elisabeth sighed. "Like nuclear bombs. Jonathan, my generation is capable of wiping out this *entire planet* with the push of a single button."

His frown deepened. "Would they actually be stupid enough to do that?"

"I don't know."

He sighed and settled deeper into the pillows. "Do you suppose all the rest of us would die, too, if they

did? I mean, the past and the present are obviously connected in ways we don't understand."

Elisabeth was saddened. "Let's hope and pray that
never happens."

Jonathan stroked her hair and held her close against
his chest. "What else can you tell me about the future?"

Entwining an index finger in a curl of hair on his
chest, she answered, "Around the turn of the century,
America will declare war on Spain. And then, about
1914 or so, the Germans will decide to take over the
world. France, England, Russia and eventually the
United States will take them on and beat them."

Jonathan stared pensively into her face, waiting for
more.

"Then, around 1929, the stock market will crash.
If we're still around then, we'll have to make sure we
invest the egg money carefully. After that—"

He laughed and held her close. "My little fortune-
teller. After that, what?"

"Another war, unfortunately," Elisabeth confessed
with a sigh. "Germany again, and Japan. As awful as
it was for everybody, I think most of the scientific and
medical advances made in the twentieth century happened because—well, necessity is the mother of inven-
tion, and nothing creates necessity like war."

Jonathan shuddered. "Tell me the good things."

Elisabeth talked about airplanes and microwave
ovens and Disneyland. She described movies, electric
Christmas-tree lights, corn dogs and Major League
Baseball games. Jonathan laughed when she swore that

a former actor had served two terms as President of the United States, and he absolutely refused to believe that men were having themselves changed into women and vice versa.

When Elisabeth was finished with her tales of the future, she and Jonathan made slow, sweet love.

Later, they ate a wedding supper brought to them by Big Lil's daughter. They consumed the food hungrily, greedily, never remembering after that exactly what they'd been served. Then they made love again.

Early the next morning they rose, and Elisabeth put on the dress she'd been married in, since she had nothing else to wear. Jonathan kissed her, said she was beautiful and promised to buy her as many gowns as she wanted once they reached Seattle.

Elisabeth was nervous and distracted. Finally she brought up the subject they'd both been avoiding. "Jon, the necklace—where is it?"

He paused in the act of rebandaging his arm and studied her for a long moment. "I left it at the house," he said. "Why?"

"There's something I have to do," she replied, her gaze skirting his, her hand already on the doorknob. "Please—tell me where to find the necklace."

The expression in his eyes was a bleak one, but he didn't ask the obvious question. "All right, Elisabeth," he said. "All right."

They drove out to Jonathan's house—their house— in his buggy. "The necklace is in my study," he said. "Under the ledger in the middle desk drawer."

As she hopped down from the rig, Elisabeth surveyed the ladder propped against the partially burned house. Apparently, the repair work had already begun.

She hummed as she went inside, found the necklace exactly where Jonathan had said it would be, and brought it out into the sunshine with her. Her husband stood beside the buggy, watching her pensively.

"I'm about to show you how much I love you, Jonathan Fortner," she said, and then she began climbing up the ladder.

"Lizzie!" Jonathan protested, bolting away from the buggy.

Elisabeth climbed until she reached the doorway that had once led from Trista's room into the main hallway. Holding her breath, she shut her eyes tightly, closed her fingers around the necklace and flung it over the threshold.

She was pleased when she opened her eyes and saw that the pendant had vanished. Holding her skirts aside with one hand, made her way quickly down the ladder.

Elisabeth Fortner had found the century where she belonged, and she meant to stay there.

* * * * *

Dear Reader,

One of the best things to happen to me as a writer is the sudden appearance of a character, fully formed and ready to go. Such was the case with Mike Gardner, the hero in *Marriage at Circle M*. I could see his face. I could see the way he walked. And best of all, I could hear his voice in my head. Whenever I wrote a piece of dialogue for Mike, I could hear him saying it in his husky but powerful voice. Mike is the kind of guy that might not speak loudly, but when he does, people listen.

Another great thing happened as I wrote this book. My heroine didn't want to go along with my plans for her. She had ideas of her own. I had to decide—my way or her way? The great thing about stories versus real life is that I knew if it didn't work, I could change it. So I let her have her way. It worked, and ever since, I've made it a point to really listen to what my characters tell me. Especially when they are about to do something that will complicate matters spectacularly!

It sounds as though I think of my characters as real people, and I do. It's the only way I can get inside their heads and think what they think, and more important, feel what they feel. And hopefully that translates into a wonderful romance with a sigh-worthy happy-ever-after for you, the reader.

I hope you enjoy the ride.

Love,

Donna

MARRIAGE AT CIRCLE M
Donna Alward

For my husband and children.

Chapter 1

When Mike Gardner came walking up the path in just *that way,* Grace knew she was in trouble.

And when he stopped at the foot of her stepladder, hooked his thumbs in his jeans pockets and squinted up at her, she gripped her paintbrush tighter so as not to drop it. Mike was all long, lazy strides and sexy smiles, and despite her best intentions, she'd never been able to remain immune to his charm. Not since she'd hit puberty, anyway.

"Mornin', Grace." The words weren't exactly drawled, but were drawn out just enough to give that impression.

Grace straightened her shoulders and did her best to look nonchalant as she swiped another stripe of white paint over the window trim. "Hello, Mike."

Great. Now why in the world did those two words come out all breathless, anyway?

She had to remember that it wasn't all that long ago that she'd made a fool of herself where Mike was concerned. It had been years since there had been anything between them. But she'd had a little too much punch, there'd been a little too much giggling and she'd blurted out one very ill-thought-out sentence. She still felt the heat of her embarrassment and every time they met now, she did everything she could to assure him—to assure herself, even, that Mike Gardner *was* completely resistible. Lord knew he didn't need her fawning over him the way the rest of the female population seemed to. Without thinking, she tucked an errant strand of blond hair back behind her ear, leaving it streaked with paint.

"You're up with the birds," he commented, a lazy smile creeping up his cheek as she chanced a look down at him.

"And you knew I would be, or you wouldn't be here so early." She pointedly checked her watch. "It's 7:46."

"It is?" His chin flattened ever so slightly. "I'm sorry, I thought it was later."

"You've likely been up and done chores already."

"Yes."

Darn him. She couldn't just stand up on the stepladder like an idiot, carrying on a conversation that was barely holding its own. Besides, she was all too aware that his height, paired with her distance up the ladder, put his line of vision right at her backside. She sighed, put her brush across the top of the paint-smeared can and took a step down—and her dew-slick sneaker slipped on the metal step.

His hands were there to catch her.

"Whoa, there."

She shrugged off his touch. It felt far too strong and too good. "I'm not one of your horses, Mike."

He laughed. "No, ma'am. You sure aren't."

It wasn't fair. She'd had a *thing* for Mike since she was fourteen, but he'd tended to treat her like a kid sister. An annoying one. For a brief time, when she'd been in high school, they'd been more. But that seemed a lifetime ago. For him to flirt now…weeks after she'd made a complete idiot of herself, it was too much. That one little slip of the lip was the only time she'd ever come close to telling him how she felt, and at the time he'd only laughed at her.

She was older…and far wiser now at twenty-seven. There was no room in her life for schoolgirl crushes. She planted her hands on her hips and stared him down. "Look, you obviously didn't come around for idle chit-chat. Tell me what's on your mind so I can get back to work."

Mike had to turn away to hide his smile. She was good and irritated, he could tell. And besides that, she looked wonderful this morning. Her blond hair was tucked into some sort of strange clip, and little pieces tangled around her ears. Her eyes flashed at him now, icy blue with annoyance. Looking up that stepladder at her slim, tanned legs had almost made him forget why he was here. And steadying her with his arms as she'd slipped had wiped his brain clean of any other thoughts whatsoever. He liked the feel of his hands on her skin.

He stepped back, ignoring her jab, instead turning to survey the small yellow bungalow she called home.

It had seen better days, but Grace had a way of making it welcoming. A caragana hedge flanked the west side of her paved drive—a driveway that was in need of some serious patchwork. He recognized the bleeding heart shrubs, next to some sort of bushes with tiny white flowers. Everything was dressed up by circles of lilies and stalks of purply blue flowers he remembered from one of his foster homes. The peeling trim on the eaves would soon be gleaming and white like the sections she'd already painted. Somehow she'd taken a plain, aging bungalow and made it home.

"You're painting."

She kept her eyes front as if refusing to look at him. "Your powers of deduction astound me. What tipped you off?"

He ignored that bit of sarcasm, too. She had to be tired, after all. The drips down the side of her paint can were fresh; she'd obviously been at it a while before he showed up. And he knew for a fact that she'd been up late last night, because her lights had been on when he'd been on his way back from town at nearly one o'clock. He wished… He wished she didn't have to work so hard for everything. But he was the last person who could make things better for her. At least for *right now* he was.

"How do you find time to do everything, Grace? Whenever I see you you're busy at something."

By getting up at 5:00 a.m., she thought. Instead she shoved her hands in the pockets of her shorts. "It keeps me out of trouble."

"Then I sure hate to ask what I'm about to."

Mike was serious, she realized, pushing away the urge to use sarcasm as a shield against him. Normally he said nothing at all or what he did say was disarming and funny. But Grace had known him long enough to know when he was troubled. And the tone of his voice right now told her something was definitely going on. When he merely stared at her house longer, she wrinkled her brow and went to him, gently placing a paint-splattered hand on his forearm.

"What's wrong?"

"Connor took Alex to the hospital yesterday afternoon."

Grace's eyes clouded with worry, a strange twisting in her belly at the news. Mike and Connor were like brothers, so much more than business partners. When Connor had to slaughter his beef herd, he and Mike had become partners in Circle M Quarterhorses.

"Is it the baby? Are they okay?" Alex had a baby due in a few months.

Mike didn't seem to be able to look at her, but she could feel the worry emanating from him. His arm was tense beneath her fingers and his jaw clamped tight. "She went into early labor, so they're keeping her in for a while. Doc says she'll be on bed rest from here on out. That's all I know for now."

"What about Maren?" Grace looked up at his profile. Maren was the couple's toddler, a princess with raven curls and sky-blue eyes like her mother's. "Is that why you're here? Do they need someone to watch her for a while?"

"No, no." Mike turned to her then, his lips relaxing just a little. "Connor's grandmother is looking after her. But…it's not fair of me to ask, but I was wondering, I mean *we* were wondering, if you'd consider coming back and doing the books for the farm for a while."

If it had been a less serious topic, Grace would have made a quip about that being a regular speech for Mike. Instead she just nodded. "Of course I will. I don't mind at all."

"I know you're already busy, and…"

"Mike, it's fine. Alex and Connor are my friends, too. I'm happy to help."

His relief was clear. "Thank you, Grace."

It was her own fancy that made his words sound like an endearment. But Mike didn't think of her in *that* way anymore. He only looked on her as a friend, she knew that. He'd made it abundantly clear long ago.

She'd already let girlish fantasy rule once in her life and look where that had gotten her. A few troubled years, a whole lot of hurt and then back here in small-town Alberta with a tiny yellow bungalow and a double bed with one pillow.

"You're welcome. I'll try to stop by tomorrow and get things up to speed."

The morning sun grew warmer as they stood on her front lawn, the dew evaporating off in the heat. This was just what she needed. To torture herself further by seeing Mike day in and day out at Circle M, a reminder of wanting what she couldn't have. But the truth was, she needed to do some repairs to the house and money was scarce. What she made by doing the odd book work and cleaning jobs didn't leave her with a lot extra at the end of the month. Besides, Mike wouldn't be there all the time now, would he?

"I guess I should be going," he remarked quietly. "I have a few errands and then, well, we're a man short at the ranch. And the building crew comes at nine."

Grace's head swiveled back to him. "Building crew?"

For the first time, Mike really smiled. The effect was devastating, making her heart thump ridiculously. Darn him for being able to cause such a reaction simply by smiling. His grayish-blue eyes lit up as he ran a rough hand through disobedient, coppery hair. "Yeah. We're breaking ground for my new house today."

How did I miss that bit of information? Grace wondered. Mike Gardner, with his own business and now a home. Was the eternal drifter really settling down? Wonders never ceased, it seemed.

"Anyway, if you need anything, just call Windover." Mike called the house by its rightful name, even though the now defunct beef ranch was home of Circle

M Quarterhorses. "I'm staying there while the house is going up."

Not only at the ranch, but living in the house, too. So much for not seeing him, then. And for wanting what she couldn't have. Surely she could stay immune to him for the short term, though, couldn't she?

Grace's hands were devoid of the white paint now, but bits of it still colored her hair. She pulled it back from her face, anchoring the twist blindly with pins at the back of her head. The heat lately had been cloying, and the only way to keep the tender skin of her neck from breaking out was to keep her heavy hair up.

She sighed, turning from the mirror and picking up the light cotton skirt from the foot of the bed.

The reason she kept busy...the real reason she kept taking odd jobs wasn't really for the money, no matter how much it came in handy.

It was, simply, to keep occupied. To have idle hands meant admitting how empty her life was. How empty it would likely always be. She only had herself to worry about, and that wasn't about to change. And so rather than sit at home, frittering away the time, she worked. Keeping her hands busy helped her forget about the disasters of the past. It gave her less time to sit and think about how everything could go wrong in the blink of an eye. Doing bookwork for the ranch again would fill even more hours.

And she absolutely wasn't putting on a skirt today because she was going out to Circle M, she told herself.

The light cotton print was simply cooler than anything else she had in her closet.

As she rolled down the windows of her car, she admitted that extra money wasn't something to scoff at. The vehicle was past its prime and had only been a base model in its newer days. As a result, she had no air-conditioning and nothing more than an AM/FM radio with inconsistent reception. She pulled out, heading west out of town toward the ranch. The brakes squeaked as she stopped at the intersection to the highway. One of these days she knew the car was going to up and die without any apology.

The drive to Circle M was a pretty one. Now, in late August, there was a hint of gold on the cottonwoods, and hay lay in giant green rolls in the fields. Depending on the turn of the road or the elevation, she caught glimpses of the Rocky Mountains, snow-capped and the unforgiving color of steel. It was, to Grace's mind, an almost perfect time of year. Another few weeks and the temperatures would mellow, the leaves would start to fall and everything would change from the dry, frantic heat of summer to the mellow, filling warmth of prairie autumn.

Turning north, she smiled at the pastures that had once held Black Angus and now held quarter horses, their hides gleaming in the sun, tails flickering at the flies hovering. Ahead, the main house at Circle M—Windover—stood tall against the azure sky.

It didn't look any different from the outside. But everything else at the ranch had changed.

The barns that had once housed beef cattle now held livestock of the equine variety. Windover Farm, as it had existed for over a hundred years, was no more, and in its place was Circle M. The disease crisis of a few years back had meant the destruction of Connor's Black Angus herd, which was almost as surprising as the fact that Mike finally stopped rodeoing and settled down to a full-time, lucrative business.

Seeing Mike on a more regular basis had inspired more than a few dreams on Grace's part. As she pulled up in front of the house, she pressed a hand to her stomach. It had been easier when he hadn't been in town that often. She'd been able to forget about their brief relationship…if it even could have been called a relationship. She'd been seventeen and he'd been twenty-one. For a few weeks they had been more than friends. For a few weeks she'd been blissfully happy.

But when the rodeo season started up again, he went with hardly a word. She'd been okay about it for a long time, or so she thought. They'd gone back to being the friends they were before, the few times their paths had crossed. Now that he was back to stay, seeing him so often brought back longings she thought were dead and buried. She got tongue-tied and bashful. Fiddled with her hair.

No one man should have the power to cause a girl to get so fluttery, and, well, girly. She was supposed to be past that by now. She left girly behind when she and Steve had signed the divorce papers. When she realized that happily ever after didn't really exist.

The house was quiet when she knocked, so she wandered around to the side of the house in case someone was outside.

She was in luck. Johanna, Connor's grandmother, was kneeling at a small flower garden with the curly-topped Maren babbling happily at her side.

"Good morning, Mrs. Madsen."

Johanna's head turned, a smile lighting up her face. "Grace, dear. It's so good to see you." Rising, she brushed off the knees of her slacks and held a hand out to the toddling baby beside her. "Maren, you remember Grace, don't you?"

Maren suddenly fell silent and popped a thumb into her mouth, and Grace laughed.

"She probably doesn't remember me. I haven't been around much."

"That's about to change, isn't it?"

Grace nodded at Johanna, the two exchanging a solemn look. "I thought I'd stop in today and get up to speed."

"Connor and Mike are both out, but you're no stranger to the setup. I know they're both happy you're here."

"How is Alex, then?"

"Being monitored." Johanna picked up the baby and climbed the steps to the deck. "So far she's doing okay, but at thirty-two weeks…"

"They want to buy her—and the baby—some more time." Grace followed Johanna inside, standing back as Maren was placed in her high chair.

"Exactly. The doctor said that even another couple of weeks can make a big difference with the baby's lungs. Of course Connor's worried sick."

Johanna put a sippy cup in front of Maren. "Connor's spending almost all his time at the hospital, and Mike isn't meant for bookwork, so I'm glad you're here to help."

"I'd do anything for...to help," she finished, coloring at her almost mistake. Even if she knew she'd do anything for Mike, she didn't need the rest of the world to know it. Thankfully Johanna seemed oblivious as she busied herself making iced tea.

The front door slammed and Grace jumped. When Mike strode into the kitchen, she took a step back, her gaze drawn undeniably toward his.

God, he looked fabulous. All coiled strength in his faded jeans and corded muscles beneath a blue T-shirt. His hat, the cream-colored Stetson he never worked without, was on his head, but when he saw her standing there he automatically reached up to remove it.

His hair clung to his scalp in dark curls and Grace watched as one solitary bead of sweat trickled from one temple down his jaw.

Maren smacked her cup on the tray of her chair while Johanna watched, clearly intrigued with the silent interplay between the couple.

"Grace."

"Mike." His name sounded strangled to her as it came out of her mouth. And she knew she was glad she'd chosen a skirt and pretty blouse after all.

"I, uh, just came to get something to drink."

"I think Johanna's making some iced tea."

Still their gazes clung and she remembered the feel of his hands on her arms yesterday morning. He swallowed, his Adam's apple bobbing. Goodness, they were staring at each other like idiots.

He broke away first. "Iced tea sounds perfect, but you're not here to look after me, Mrs. Madsen."

Johanna poured three glasses without batting an eye. "I'd like to know where all this Mrs. Madsen nonsense came from all of a sudden. I've known both of you so long I used to wipe your runny noses, so call me Johanna or Gram like everyone else."

Mike's lips quivered as he struggled not to smile. The Madsens were as close to family as he had, not counting his cousin Maggie.

Johanna took one look at Maren and plucked the girl up from her chair. "I'll just go change the baby," she suggested blandly. "Grace, I'm sure you remember your way to the office."

"Of course I do. I'll sort things out, not to worry."

"I'm sure Mike will help you. Won't you, Mike?"

His lips pursed together and he let his eyes twinkle at the older woman. "Indeed I will…Gram."

Her rusty laugh disappeared with the baby and he was left with Grace.

She looked beautiful today. As usual. But he thought he saw hints of purple beneath her eyes. Lord only knew what work she'd taken on now. She was always working. And now he'd helped her exhaustion along by asking for a favor. He should have found another way.

But another way would have meant that he wouldn't have an excuse to see her. And after she'd let the cat out of the bag, so to speak, at the Rileys's anniversary party, he thought about seeing her more and more. He'd been shocked to say the least, but not unpleasantly. Knowing Grace still felt some attraction for him seemed to legitimize his own for her. He'd let her get away once before, and had always been sorry. But knowing she still thought of him in *that* way changed everything. Heck, not that he'd admit it to her, but he'd made the excuse for a midmorning drink just because he'd seen her car pull into the yard.

Her hair was sneaking out of the twist, curling around her temples in damp tendrils. The warmth of the morning gave a glow to her skin. To him, she was a picture of femininity, of innocence, purity. Certainly too fine of a woman for a man like him to tangle with.

"You're looking tired. I hope this extra work won't put unnecessary strain on you."

That was it? Grace tried to keep her lips from falling open but failed. All those long stares and all he came up with was "you're looking tired"? Her elation at seeing him flew out the window.

"Your compliments make a girl all warm and fuzzy."

He at least had the decency to look chagrined. "I didn't mean to say you looked bad."

"Even better. You know, I can't imagine what the women around here see in you."

It was out before she could think better of it and she instantly flushed. They both knew it was a lie. He knew very well that she *was* one of those women. She'd said it herself as they'd danced. She covered the slip with more offensive:

"But I can assure you I can handle a little *unnecessary strain,* as you put it. I'm not made of china, Michael." She used his full name and watched his lip curl a little. She knew how much he hated being called Michael.

Mike had put his hat back on, the brim shading his eyes and making him look even larger than his six-foot-two frame.

"Is there anything I can do to help you then?"

Grace looked up and saw his eyes were earnest even though his tone was cold, and she nearly backed down. She acknowledged the attraction, but that was where it stopped. Mike didn't feel anything for her, that much was clear. Men who were interested told you how nice you looked, gave you compliments instead of remarking on the presence of bags beneath your eyes or asking you to balance the books. She'd done the longing gaze thing for far too many years, and it had gotten her nowhere. It hadn't been enough before. And it wouldn't get her anywhere in the future, either. Men didn't want women like her, not once they realized that she was more than the quiet, girl-next-door that they thought she was.

"Yes, Mike, there is something you can do for me. You can get out of the way and let me do my job."

Chapter 2

Grace shut the checkbook and sighed. Alex had done a good job with the books, but she *was* behind by a month or two. Not much wonder, Grace thought, taking a brain break. She leaned back in the desk chair and took a sip from her pop can. Alex was pregnant, chasing after a toddler and summer was the busiest time on a farm. Now it was up to Grace to straighten things out and keep things up-to-date. Even if Alex did get home soon, she was under orders for bed rest, and then after the baby came she'd be too exhausted to worry about payables and receivables. Grace wasn't sure if being close to Mike so often was going to be a blessing or a curse.

But she was all too happy to fill in. She loved accounting. It was gratifying to see all those numbers line up just right and have things balance out at the end of the day. It was neat and orderly, and every time she finished printing a report or balancing an account, she got this great sense of accomplishment. With so much of her life feeling arbitrary and out of sync, balancing those columns was like *something* in her life was where it was supposed to be.

The downside was, in order to put food on the table, she had to do other jobs just to make ends meet. It was a small town, and without her C.P.A., she didn't make enough to pay the bills with the few accounting jobs she had. She hired herself out as a cleaning lady as well. It supplemented her income and, to be honest, kept her from being too lonely. Yesterday she'd spent the entire day cleaning for Mrs. Darrin. When the cleaning was finished, she'd planned to go back home and finish painting the trim on her house. But Mrs. Darrin was feeling poorly and had asked Grace to tend to her garden as well, so Grace stayed and cut the grass and weeded the feeble bed in front of the house. After that, she'd stayed for tea. She appreciated the social contact almost as much as the paycheck. But because she'd put in a longer day, she'd been up since five this morning, finishing up the painting so she could spend the day at Windover.

"How's it going?"

She swiveled hard in her chair, her hand swinging out so that some of the liquid splashed out of the pop can and landed on her white capris. She scowled up at him, her heart pounding from the sight of him standing in the doorway. He was so tall in his boots that it seemed that his head almost grazed the top of the door frame.

"God, Mike, how on earth do you manage to sneak up on someone like that?"

"I made enough noise to wake the dead. You were in the zone."

Zoned out, more like it, but she wouldn't admit that.

Her eyes lit on a rivulet of sweat beaded at the hollow of his throat. There was something so elementally attractive about a hardworking man. Something that didn't come with expensive toiletries and business suits. It was that little bit of dirt, the little bit of scruff and the dedication and muscle it took to do what he did. When she didn't say anything back to him, he raised one eyebrow in question.

"You...you don't have your hat on," she stammered, immediately feeling stupid at such an inane comment.

His other eyebrow lifted. "It's around here somewhere."

Oh, this was crazy. Every time he was out of the way she swore she wouldn't be so affected the next time they met. Promised herself she'd forget about the past. Then she'd see him and she'd become a babbling idiot. She turned away from him deliberately, picking up her red pen and twisting it in her fingers.

"I still have work to do, so unless there's something you needed..."

Even without his customary hat, he towered above her until he lowered himself by her chair. His knees cracked as he squatted, balancing on the heels of his boots. He put a hand on the arm of her chair and swung it a little so she was semifacing him.

"I came to ask another favor. I'd ask Johanna, but…"

"But a woman her age…chasing after a nearly two-year-old is taking its toll on her. I know. What's up?"

He lifted his gray eyes to her. It was like magnets of opposite poles when she met his eyes with her own, pulling them together. As if nearly ten years hadn't elapsed and they were back in Lloyd Andersen's meadow on a cool Sunday morning. She was unable to turn away, instead drawn into the earnest depths.

"Alex is coming home tonight, and I wondered, that is…I know she's supposed to be on bed rest and all, but…"

His words drew her out of her reverie. "You want to do something nice?"

"Yeah." He smiled a little sheepishly and her heart warmed. It was one of the things she liked about him. He came across as all male and tough, then at the most unexpected times showed a thoughtful side.

"And you want me to help."

"It's not like I know much about this kind of thing. And Connor's with Alex and not here to see to it."

"I can make a special dinner," she replied. "Dress Maren up in something pretty, make it a low-key welcome home with just the family."

"Thank you, Grace. That's perfect."

She had a dirty house of her own, but it didn't matter very much right now. She sighed. It wasn't like anyone was going to see it besides herself. Spending the evening with the Madsens was just what the doctor ordered.

Mike heard the sigh and misinterpreted it. "I'm sorry, I probably shouldn't have asked." He straightened his knees, looming above her once more. "You're already busy and tired. I can just order something in."

"No, it's not that. I'm happy to…"

His mood changed so quickly her head spun. His lips thinned and his jaw hardened at her words. He almost seemed like he was angry at *her,* and she didn't have an idea why.

"You always are, Grace. *Happy to.* Every time someone asks for a favor, there you are. You're working yourself to death, and for what? You're clearly exhausted. Ordering in might be better—that way you get a break. Get some rest. I should have thought of it sooner."

Here he was again, telling her how *tired* she looked. Her temper fired. What did Mike know about anything? And who was he to tell her what to do? He'd never asked for her input before, not even when they'd been dating. He'd just been…gone. That certainly hadn't earned him the right to start dictating things now. "You know what, Mike? I'm a big girl. I think I know my own limits."

"I don't think you do." His voice was sharp and her eyebrows lifted at the tone. "You'd work yourself into the ground if I let you. Don't worry about dinner. Forget I mentioned it."

"You know, you're really starting to make me angry," she answered, the words low. It might have sounded threatening to someone other than Mike, but there wasn't much that got under his skin, and it was another thing about him that was making her mad right at that moment. "If you *let* me? I don't recall requiring your permission, Mike Gardner. If I didn't have time to do it, I'd say so. Whenever has it been a hardship spending time with Connor and Alex? It just so happens my evening is free, so there."

Great. Now, in her anger, she'd made it sound like she had no social life whatsoever.

"And you could spend it sleeping, from the looks of it," he continued, undeterred by her sharp tone. "I see how hard you work, Grace. You clean half the town, and do books for the other half. You're on just about everyone's 'fill-in' list and if there's something going on, you're in the thick of it! One of these days you're going to make yourself sick!"

She stood from her chair, tears of absolute anger threatening. "Who in the world do you think you are, to criticize me?" She was gratified when he took a step back. "Who died and made you my sole protector and guardian?"

"Well someone clearly has to, if you're not going to look after yourself!" His voice thundered through the room as they argued.

"I'm a grown woman, in case you hadn't noticed!"

"Oh, I noticed all right!" He blurted it out, then everything fell silent.

He noticed, her heart rejoiced. *Stop it, you ninny,*

she chided herself on the back of the thought. She was supposed to be infuriated with him right now. She *was* angry. She was in no mood to be played with. Not by Mike, not by anyone.

She cleared her throat, letting her hands drop to her sides. "Good, then. I'm glad we straightened that out. Now get out of my way so I can get started. If I'm making dinner, I need to finish this up." She sent him a withering look. "*Without* your interference."

Mike turned on a heel. Get out of her way? No problem! Not when she attacked him like that. She could just forget about him showing any concern for her welfare again!

He stalked out of the house, heading toward the east section where the concrete foundation for his house was being poured. Grace didn't understand anything.

He'd always thought of her as a kid sister. When he'd finally settled here in eighth grade, she'd been in fourth. When he'd graduated high school, she'd just finished middle school.

Then she had grown up, and he'd taken notice. She'd been a picture of innocent beauty, and for a while he'd let himself care about her. He'd let her care about him. For a brief time, he'd let his heart dictate his actions instead of his head. He'd held her, kissed her. Cherished her like she deserved. But he'd fallen too fast and he knew once she saw him for who he really was, she'd cut and run. So he'd made sure he'd done the running first. As soon as the rodeo season started up that year, he'd hit the road and hadn't looked back.

When she'd moved back after her divorce he'd been in town for a few weeks and was floored the first time he saw her. He kicked at the dry path with a leather toe, sending up a puff of dust. The years had made full the promise of the woman he'd thought she'd become. She was more than beautiful. She was exactly what a woman should be. Her beauty was natural, pure. It shone out from her, lit up by her generous heart and kind manner. The fact that her husband had seen fit to break her heart...he'd stewed about that one for a good long time, even partially blamed himself. It was a good thing the jerk didn't live close by. Mike didn't tend to let people get away with treating his friends like dirt beneath their shoes.

Because she was his friend, first and foremost, and he was torn between the girl she'd been and the woman she'd become. Stupid thing was, he had this uncanny urge to protect them both.

He wandered through the jobsite, joking with the men, grabbing a shovel and helping out. Still, she remained on his mind. Earlier in the summer, at the anniversary party for the Rileys, Grace had indulged in a few too many vodka coolers and he'd laughingly danced with her. Old friends. Only she'd smiled up at him widely and said, "Mike, you're so pretty."

He'd made a joke of it but she'd been undaunted. "I bet you're good in the sack, too. We've been ssspeculating." She swept an arm to encompass a group of young women, all giggling behind their hands and watching Mike and Grace dance. "All that...mmm," she'd finished, her eyelids drifting closed as she swayed her hips to the music.

He'd been shocked, to put it mildly, and more than a little embarrassed. Grace had come on to him and he hadn't had a clue how to answer. He'd thought she'd put their fling in the past, especially when she'd moved to Edmonton and married. Heck, he'd only been back in town permanently since spring, setting up business with Connor. As they moved to the music, her curves felt soft and sexy in his arms and he'd asked plainly, "You think about that?"

She'd suddenly seemed to realize what she'd said, because her posture straightened and she'd colored to the hue of fireweed. "Shut up," she'd snapped, trying to cover. "Don't let it go to your head."

Her quick change of tone had relaxed him, giving him the upper hand again and he'd managed to tease her about it.

But the problem was, it *had* gone to his head. He'd done nothing but think of it since. Wondering how they'd be together. Wanting to kiss her, wondering if it would be the same as he remembered. Wanting to hold her—all night long. In his mind he could see what being with Grace would be like.

But Grace deserved more than an ex-saddle bronc rider with a spotted past, and he knew it. And somehow, he was going to show her that he was more than that. He just needed more time.

Mike halted before the screen door, taking a deep breath. He'd been too hard on her, he'd realized. He hated seeing her working so much, but somehow all his well-intentioned concern had come out wrong and now she had gotten angry with him. Hopefully she wasn't still, but just in case, he'd cut across the field and come home along the ditch after leaving the building site.

He resisted the strange urge to knock. Instead he swung the door open and stepped inside.

He left his boots on the mat and made his way to the kitchen. He stopped in the doorway, watching Grace as she moved about the room.

As she carried plates to the table, the scent of frying chicken filled the air.

"Your table's missing something."

Her head snapped up. "When did you come in?"

"Just a minute ago. Supper smells great."

She resumed setting the table. "It's only chicken and salads. Something we can eat whenever they arrive. I dressed Maren and Johanna took her in. They're all coming back together."

"I thought you could use some decoration." He stepped inside the room, holding out his hand.

"Flowers. You picked flowers?" Her fingers put down the cutlery as she stared at him.

"I thought they might make things a little more special." He handed them to her, a mass of daisies and greenery he couldn't name but knew by sight. He hadn't picked weeds for a woman since he was in primary school and he'd tried to impress one of his foster moms.

Grace took the blooms from his hand, and he suddenly realized that he hadn't exactly given them to *her*.

He'd made it sound like they were for a centerpiece, that was all.

"I also thought they might soften you up for my apology."

Her hands stilled over the vase she'd taken from the top of a pine buffet in the corner. "Apology?"

"I'm sorry we fought earlier." He couldn't bring himself to say he was sorry for everything. He found he wasn't sorry for being concerned about her welfare. But he was sorry for upsetting her.

She turned to look at him, the vase of flowers in her hands. "I am, too."

Their gazes met across the room. Lord, she had a way of looking at a man that made him want to do all sorts of things for her. Her lips were open just a hint, ripe for kissing, and her eyes were soft and wide. For a fleeting moment he wondered what she'd do if he simply closed the distance between them and kissed her like he'd wanted to for weeks. But the timing was wrong and the moment passed. Grace looked away.

"I was just worried, that's all. I've known you a long time, Grace. I just want you to look after yourself."

She put the flowers in the middle of the table and stood back. "Thanks for your concern, Mike, but it's not necessary. I've been looking after myself for a while now." She moved back to the stove, taking the lid off the electric frying pan and capably turning the chicken with metal tongs.

Of course she had, he acknowledged silently. She'd been back in town for what, five or six years? Living on her own all that time. Without him. But that didn't stop the protective streak that seemed to rear its head every time she was around.

The screen door opened and voices filtered through the hall to the kitchen. "I think they've arrived," Grace remarked, grabbing a platter. "Timing's good, too. Chicken's done."

When Alex and Connor entered, Maren on Connor's arm, Mike forced a smile. "Welcome home."

Alex's eyes filled with tears. "Oh, you guys, you shouldn't have." She walked carefully, like she was afraid of breaking something. She looked over her shoulder at Johanna, then to the stove and Grace who was standing with the platter of chicken in her hands.

"You did this?"

"It was Mike's idea. Be thankful I did the cooking and not him."

Everyone laughed, including Mike who agreed. "I'll make the coffee. Everything else I'll trust to Grace."

"Wise move," Grace countered, but he was gratified to see her treat him to a genuine smile.

Alex's smile widened and she leaned up to give Mike a quick hug. "You softie," she whispered in his ear.

"Be quiet. That's a secret," he whispered back. Straightening, he chided her. "No work. We're going to look after everything so you can just look after that bundle in there." He pointed at her belly.

"That's what I've been telling her," Connor said, putting Maren in her high chair and handing her a cracker. "Nothing's more important than looking after our baby."

Mike looked at Grace. Her face carried a strange expression as she looked at Alex. He'd almost swear she looked...*wounded,* he supposed. Her eyes were luminous, wide with hurt. He'd never quite seen that look before and didn't know what to make of it. There was concern, he was sure, but there was something else. A deep, lingering sadness. But why would seeing Alex make her sad?

She caught him watching her and pasted on a smile, the expression disappearing as if it had never been. "Put the chicken on, will you, Mike? I'll get the rest of the food out of the fridge."

They all sat down to a celebratory dinner, but Mike couldn't forget that haunted look on Grace's face.

Connor and Alex were putting Maren to bed; Johanna was cleaning up the kitchen. Grace had tried to help but Johanna had shooed her away, saying the cooks didn't need to wash dishes. Grace knew she should just get in her car and go home, but instead she wandered out to the garden in the twilight, smelling the fragrant sweet peas that climbed the white latticed pergola.

The moon started its ascent. Frogs chirped from the pond down behind the barn. Grace sighed. If she went home now she'd end up feeling sorry for herself and spending the evening with a bowl of ice cream and a box of tissues. Despite the worry of the present, the Madsens were a happy family. Strong and bonded.

She'd thought she'd have that, once, but now knew it would never happen. Most times she was okay with it. But times like this…times like this it hit her hard, made her mourn what she'd lost and what she'd never have.

She'd never have her own family.

"Beautiful night, isn't it."

Mike's voice interrupted the quiet sounds of dusk and Grace swallowed the ball of emotion that had gathered in her throat. "Sure is."

"You going to tell me what's making you so blue?"

He was standing a little behind her and she kept her back to him. If she looked at him she wasn't sure she wouldn't lose it, and what an awkward mess that would be.

"I'm fine. Just enjoying the evening."

"Grace Lundquist, you're a bad liar."

She sighed, willing him to stay behind her. Her eyes closed. "Just leave it be, Mike."

He was quiet for a moment and Grace wondered if he'd gone. Then his voice came back, low and rumbly.

"I can't."

Oh, why did he have to be so concerned and caring all of a sudden? Mike didn't think of her in any way besides a friend, and even if he did, it wouldn't make sense to pursue anything, no matter how long she'd had a crush on him. He didn't stay anywhere for long, or with anyone. In all the years she'd known him, he'd only had brief, fun relationships. Nothing serious. And Grace didn't do brief and fun.

She had, once. And she'd thought Mike had really

cared about her. She supposed in his own way, he had. But not enough. He hadn't even broken up with her. He'd just *gone*.

She cared about him, yes. She admitted that much to herself. But she couldn't let herself get too close. She didn't trust him not to leave her again, and she wasn't into making the same mistake twice.

No, they'd get along much better if they stuck to friends only.

His hand rested on her shoulder and she leaned into the reassuring contact. "I'm okay. I promise."

"You didn't look fine at dinner. You looked like your whole world was crashing in around you."

Grace forced a smile and finally turned to meet his gaze. His eyes were dark with concern as his hand slid from her shoulder down to grip her fingers.

She pulled her hand away, attempting a laugh. "When did you get so dramatic, Mike? Worlds crashing around. As if."

"If you weren't upset, then what are you doing out here in the dark?"

"I didn't want to intrude. I should just head home."

A horse whickered softly in the moonshine. Mike turned his head toward the sound, smiling a little. "You shouldn't worry about intruding. I'm living here. You can't get much more in the way than that."

"It's only temporary."

"Yes, it is. I'm looking forward to having my own place."

Grace studied him, glad that the topic of conversation had been diverted away from her. He'd spent so many years without roots. Other than Maggie, his cousin-turned-foster parent, he'd never had a home. It just hadn't been his way. A home had always seemed to represent a commitment he didn't want to make.

"It seems funny, thinking of you with your own house, tied to a business. You've never been that type of guy."

His gray eyes penetrated hers. "I wasn't. Not for a long time. Things change."

"What things?" She tilted her head curiously.

"It didn't make sense to roam around without a purpose, looking for something yet not knowing what *it* was. I found myself wanting to settle, find a place for me. Build a business. Make a home, maybe even have a family."

And just like that, her world dropped out from under her. It was like her bones had suddenly turned to jelly and everything got too heavy to move. He watched her quietly, his strong body between her and the house.

She had to escape.

Mike and a house and a family. Words she never thought she'd ever hear from his lips.

Why had it taken him so long to figure it out? If only he hadn't taken a decade, things might have been different after all. A whole can of "what if's" was opened, the contents spilled out.

After the long, emotional day she'd had it was too much. Her eyes burned with tears she tried desperately to hold inside and her mouth twisted. She chewed on her lip to keep it from quivering.

"I've gotta go," she choked out, pushing past him and making a run for her car. She wrenched open the door and got in, turned the key to the ignition.

Just her luck. The one thing Mike was looking for now was the very thing she'd never be able to give him.

Chapter 3

Grace dragged herself out of bed. With a stroke of impeccable timing, she'd caught an early fall cold and it had completely knocked her out. Her head felt like a giant boulder sitting atop her neck, which might have been all right if only she could have breathed. But no, her nose was plugged, her throat was sore, and the only thing she wanted was to stay in bed and hide under the covers. Which was a crying shame, because outside everything was gilded and warm. The leaves were changing, her asters were blooming and bees hummed lazily in the mellow autumn sunshine.

With the teakettle on, she suddenly realized that tomorrow was payday at Circle M. Alex was confined to bed; it was up to Grace to make sure the checks got written. She sat at the table, resting her plugged head on her hands. No way was she heading out to the ranch. The last thing Alex—or Maren—needed was for her to pass on her cold.

Maybe someone from Circle M could drop off the paperwork and checkbook, she thought, getting up to pour the boiling water in her mug. Inspired, she picked up the phone and made the necessary call. After hanging up, she took the bag from her cup and added a squirt of lemon juice and a teaspoon of honey. Perhaps after her cup of tea she'd run a hot bath and try to steam away the congestion. And then maybe, just maybe, she'd feel human again.

Mike pulled into the driveway, grabbed the files from the passenger seat and hopped out of the truck. He skirted around the hood, heading for the back door, where there was a porch filled with natural light and plants and where he knew she liked to sit with a book, letting the breeze blow through the windows. He'd just drop off the ledger and checkbook, make sure she was okay and be on his way. Lord knew there was no shortage of work at Circle M lately. At least Connor was back, now that Alex was out of hospital.

It seemed to take Grace a long time to answer his knock, and when she did it took all he had not to gape.

She was dressed in snug jeans and a silky blue top that made his mouth water. He swallowed. The soft fabric dipped to a vee in the front, triangling the shape of her breasts, then flowing in folds to her waist. The sleeves clung to her upper arms, draping away gracefully past her elbows. It was a combination of innocent and sexy and for a brief moment he envisioned himself sliding his fingers over her soft shoulders while he kissed the daylights out of her.

The towel wrapped turban-style around her head might have made that difficult, however.

"I'm interrupting."

"It's okay." The words came out "it-th okay;" the steamy bath hadn't relieved all of her congestion. She sniffled, tried again. "Come on in."

Mike followed her in, still holding the materials she'd need to do payroll, his customary hat still shielding his eyes.

"Thank you, Mike, for delivering the books."

"Your cold sounds bad." When Johanna had told him that Grace was sick, his first thought hadn't been about working with the horses, or helping with the construction of his house. Instead he'd volunteered to be a delivery boy. He'd thought he could make sure she was all right after her outburst the other night. He wanted to take care of her. There was something about Grace that inspired that urge to protect, even though he knew she deserved better.

"I tried tea and honey and I took a decongestant, but it hasn't kicked in yet," she explained, leaning back against the kitchen counter.

"Yes, well, you can drop off the checks when they're done then. Payday is tomorrow, but the guys'll understand if you're a little late. You deserve a day in bed."

Grace looked up into Mike's eyes and he noticed

how flushed and pretty she looked. The thought of her *in bed* didn't help his current mental state, either.

"I'll have them there on time, you know that."

"It's okay. You need to rest," he insisted.

"Someone make you a doctor all of a sudden?" She drew away from the counter, crossing her arms in front of her.

His chin drew back at the sharp edge of her tone. "You're sick. It happens to everyone."

"Exactly. And the world doesn't stop just because someone has the sniffles. I said I'd have them done and I will. Besides, I have other work besides Circle M. I don't want to get behind."

"Work, work. That's all you ever do!" The words burst out of his mouth before he could stop them. Why was she being so stubborn? All he was trying to do was cut her some slack, and she wouldn't have any of it.

Grace put her hands on her hips as the towel slipped sideways on her head. *Here we go again,* she thought. Yes, she worked a lot, but it wasn't as though she had a family at home to look after. It was just her, and more than that, it was her time to do with what she wished. She'd bought this house all on her own after the divorce, and without a regular nine-to-five job, sometimes making the mortgage payment was difficult. Not to mention repairs and the fact that she tried to make it look like a home... And all that cost money. Instead she had to deal with Mike today, coming in and bossing her around. Why he felt it was his right to treat her like the girl who used to tag after him, she had no idea.

"Yes, I work a lot. In case you haven't noticed, I don't have an overflowing social calendar and like the rest of the world I have bills to pay!"

She spun away, angry with herself for letting Mike provoke her. The towel slipped all the way off and she caught it while strands of dark blond hair straggled down her back. With her free hand she pushed them back out of her face.

He studied her for a long moment before speaking.

"You having money troubles, Grace?" He said it quietly. Not criticizing. The way Mike, her old friend would have. His obvious caring was comforting in a way.

But seeing Mike lately was only making her more confused. She cared about him; always had. Yet he'd broken a bit of that trust, and she couldn't forget it.

"No...I'm not," she sighed. "But my cup doesn't runneth over, either."

"Let me help."

She looked up into his eyes, faltering for a moment at the genuine concern she saw there. But no, it wasn't Mike's problem, and she'd learned long ago that she could only depend on herself. She squared her shoulders.

"Thanks, but I'm fine. I *like* working, Mike."

"Aren't I allowed to be concerned about you?"

She sniffled once more and tucked her untidy hair behind her ears. "I'm not twelve anymore, Mike, and you don't need to keep the playground bullies in line." She swallowed, struggling to keep her voice cool and even.

He laughed, lightening the mood a little. "Seems to me there was a time that *you* kept the bullies in line for *me*."

She flushed, wishing he'd just forget about that. Even as a child, she'd stood up for him when others didn't. She knew now how silly it must have looked, a little squirt of a thing taking up for a boy much older than she'd been.

"Thanks for your concern, but I'm fine. You must have work to do today. I'll bring the checks over when they're done."

She didn't wait for him to leave, but took the books from the table and went into the living room. When the back screen clicked quietly, she let out a long breath.

Mike gave Thunder's chestnut hide a final, affectionate slap and left the stall, shutting the half door behind him. He'd bought Thunder and Lightning together as colts, the first horses he'd owned. They'd been named by the previous owner's young son, and while Mike thought of changing their names to something less cliquéd, one look at the boy's crestfallen face had sealed the deal. When he'd loaded them into the trailer, he'd promised that he'd keep the names that the youngster had given them. And he'd kept that promise.

Lightning was out in the corral. Thunder was inside today, waiting for the farrier. The last thing Mike needed now was a lame animal.

Over the years his path had crossed with Grace's, and during those times he'd always looked out for her, whether she knew it or not. He'd been off on the circuit when she'd met her husband, and when he'd come back she was already gone...married at nineteen and living in Edmonton. He couldn't change that. He had been the one to leave, after all.

Over the years he'd passed through town occasionally and it struck him that she'd been so *sad* when she'd moved into the tiny bungalow all alone. He saw glimpses of that sadness still. It made him want to bundle her in his arms and make it better. He wanted Grace for himself. In every way, no matter how much she deserved better. For a long time he'd despaired of it ever happening, thinking he'd squandered his chance. But now...now he was back for good and he knew if he bided his time, did things right...there was hope.

He strode down the length of the barn, his boots echoing on the concrete floor. Reaching the door, he saw her car come creeping up the driveway. She was true to her word no matter how sick she was. The paychecks would be handed out on time. His face darkened with a scowl.

He should walk away, let her deliver her things to the office and leave again. Instead he left the barn door open and strode toward the house.

This time Grace heard him open the front door. She'd been listening for it, to be honest, and had chosen to stay in the kitchen rather than the intimate, closed space of the study. She didn't plan to be there long; she didn't want to spread her germs to either Alex or Maren. Mike had been such a hardheaded idiot at the house earlier, she frowned. She had to keep her cool. The last thing she wanted was yet another spat with him. It seemed to be all they did lately, and she didn't quite understand why.

She made her hands busy, stuffing checks in envelopes and writing names on the front. She didn't look up from her work but knew when he was at the threshold. The air simply changed.

"Hello, Mike. Got your checks done."

He stepped in. "That's great. I'm glad you could fit it into your busy schedule."

When she looked up, it was work to keep her mouth from dropping open. Mike looked…formidable, standing squarely in the doorway, his hat still on his head and his jaw so tensed it almost made a right angle.

She took a deep breath, willing herself to stay calm. Funny how by just standing there, he could provoke her. His whole manner told her he was angry about something, although she didn't have a blessed idea what it was this time. Still, she attempted a light smile as she responded.

"I took some meds and had a nap." The words were slightly thick; the congestion hadn't quite cleared, although she was feeling much better. The tip of her nose wasn't even showing that much redness anymore. "It was no trouble getting them drawn up."

She didn't look up, but turned her attention back

to the envelopes. "I wanted to get them here. I have a couple of jobs lined up for tomorrow."

"While you're sick?"

"I'm much better, thank you, and for your information my plan was to go home, make some soup and watch a movie with a blanket before falling blissfully into sleep and waking up completely cured." She didn't even attempt to keep the sarcasm out of her tone.

Mike waited several seconds before speaking again.

"It didn't occur to you to maybe rest for a few days? Do you have a hard time telling people the word *no?*" he bit out.

She goggled at his sharp tone. So much for keeping her cool and not letting him get to her. "As a matter of fact, I don't. How's this? Do I want to discuss this with you *again? No!*" She spun away, fiddling with papers on the table without really seeing.

Why, oh why, was everything an argument with Mike these days? He'd always had this protective streak when it came to people he cared about. People like herself, like Connor. But lately, it was different. He acted almost like he was entitled to have a say in how she lived her life, and he absolutely did not.

"You couldn't have heard me this morning." She tried to muster her iciest tone, but failed when her plugged nose interfered. "I'm not discussing my schedule or health with you."

"Well, that's just fine." Mike swept an arm wide. "That's just great, Grace!"

The checks were forgotten behind her as she squared

off. "You know, Mike, I'm not fond of this proprietary attitude you seem to have lately. What gives you the right to dictate to me how I live my life?"

"The right?" He took two steps forward until she had to tilt her chin to meet his gaze. "The fact that you obviously need someone to, instead of letting you make disastrous decisions!" His voice thundered throughout the room.

"Keep your voice down," she warned. "There are other people in this house who are probably trying to rest."

He shoved his hands into his pockets, but didn't move.

"This is my life, Mike," she whispered harshly. "My decisions to make. My mistakes. Nobody—and that definitely includes you—is going to tell me what I can or can't do. Frankly going to work when one has a cold can hardly be called a 'disastrous' decision."

"I hate it that you look out for everyone else but yourself. Someday, Grace, that's going to catch up with you, and then where will you be?"

With a sigh, he dropped his shoulders from their offensive stance.

Surprise had her rooted to the spot when his hand lifted and his fingers grazed the soft skin of her cheek.

"I just want to look out for you."

The resistance drained from her body as her eyes fluttered closed against his touch, so suddenly tender and gentle. "I can take care of myself."

"Maybe." His other hand lifted so that now both his thumbs gently rubbed the crests of her cheekbones.

Her breath caught in her throat as she opened her eyes to find Mike's staring down at her. Staring through her, right into her core, it seemed, his gray eyes shadowed by the brim of his hat.

"Why does it matter to you?"

"It matters." His gaze dipped to her lips and clung there. "You matter."

She swallowed. She mattered? To Mike? And he wasn't looking at her now like he usually did. For the most part it was like they had never been more, like it was a blip on the road to where they were now. But now…friends didn't stare at lips the way he was looking at hers, or let their fingers caress cheeks.

Still cupping her jaw, he leaned in, his mouth only a breath away as he whispered, "I just can't let you get hurt, Grace…"

She reached up, circled his wrists with her hands and pulled them away from her face. She stepped back, putting distance between them. Longing still curled through her, a *wanting* that was almost too strong. She could feel his arms around her even though it had never happened. And it would be wrong, she realized.

"You can't let me?" Her words were soft in the confused silence. She chanced a look at Mike. He was rooted to the spot, his brows pulled together. He didn't understand. It was even more reason for her to pull away.

"You don't get it, Mike. You say *you* can't let me get

hurt. And I can't let you make decisions for me." *Not again,* she almost added.

"Even when you make mistakes?"

"Then they'll be my mistakes, not yours. Thank you for your concern, but it's unwarranted."

"You almost kissed me a moment ago."

Her tummy flopped over. Yes, she had. And her body still hummed, yearning to know if kissing Mike would be the same. Or different. Or better. She'd been *that* close.

"I think you almost kissed me." She tried to joke but it fell flat.

"Don't do that. Don't change the subject. There's more going on here than you'll admit."

Memory hummed between them, drawing out the silence. What if things were changing between them? What then? Would he back off, leave her when it suited him? Would she give him the chance to do that again? Could her heart take it?

She'd said enough while they were dancing, and had no desire to humiliate herself again, or set herself up for heartbreak.

"That's right, there is more going on," she averred. "There's you being very heavy-handed with me, don't you think?"

"I don't know what to think right now."

"That makes two of us."

He rubbed a hand over his face. "Dammit, Grace, I'm just trying to protect you."

"And I'm telling you I don't want or need your protection."

"Fine. Then there's nothing left for us to say."

He spun from the room and seconds later the front door slammed. A few seconds after that, she heard Maren's cry; the noise had awakened her from her nap. Johanna's muffled voice filtered down from the upstairs. In a few moments they'd both be up and about and Grace wanted to be gone before that happened. The last thing she needed was more questions.

Hastily she shoved the final check in an envelope and scribbled a quick note, putting it all in the center of the table. When she went out to her car, Mike had left.

Men, she thought irrationally, slamming into the car and shoving it into gear. She was two miles down the road when something felt wrong. Grace pushed on the gas pedal, her eyes widening with alarm at the sudden loud clunk that shook the car. Everything seized…she cranked the wheel and her foot instantly hit the brake. Her head snapped forward, hitting the wheel just above her right eye.

She was finally stopped dead, square in the middle of the road. Her heart pounded so loudly she could hear it in her ears.

She couldn't just sit here. She shifted into Park and then into Drive again. Nothing. She could not move.

"No, no, no," she chanted, shifting again, desperate to get off the road. "Do not quit on me, baby."

Unfortunately the vehicle wasn't listening, because it stubbornly stayed in the middle of the dirt road.

She turned off the engine, unbuckled her seat belt and got out.

Something smelled hot. She got down on her hands and knees and looked underneath. Reddish-pink fluid dripped on to the ground.

Grace got up, dusting off her pants and taking several deep breaths. She was fine. This wasn't like the other time. The car was stopped but she was unhurt. She left the driver's side door opened, grabbed the wheel with one hand and managed to push the hunk of metal a few feet closer to the shoulder of the road.

She hadn't gone off the road, hadn't hit anything. It could be worse, she reminded herself, knowing exactly how much worse it might have been. Panting from the exertion of pushing the car, she took a few moments to sit on the front bumper and catch her breath. Her hair was askew around her face, so she let it down all the way, letting it cascade over her shoulders.

Of all the things to happen today. First the cold, then fighting with Mike, twice even. Their arguing had to stop, and she had to come up with a way to get it through his thick head once and for all that she was running her own life. It had been much easier when he'd kept his distance, going about his business and just being the regular friend he'd always been.

Tears threatened. "Stop it," she chided herself. Just because she was tired and still a bit sick was no reason to get all emotional. And neither was Mike a reason. She got back up and lifted the hood, as if magically looking beneath it she'd figure out exactly what had gone wrong. Now that he seemed to be paying her more attention it was driving her crazy. But she'd asked for it, hadn't she? Asked for Mike to look at her differently.

She put the hood back down and sighed, remembering the feel of his fingers on her face, how close his lips had been to hers this afternoon. He was right. There was something between them.

But Mike was changing. He was settling down. He had his own business now, and was building a house... looking to the future, and probably a family. All the things she'd wanted back then.

For that very reason, there shouldn't be anything between them. Not if she were to be fair.

She grabbed her purse from the car and squinted up at the sun. At least there was no chance of rain. That would have been the icing on the cake. Her thin-soled sandals slapped on the light asphalt of the road as she started back toward the ranch. She'd have to go back and call for someone to tow the car. And who knew how much that would cost to fix. Her budget was already stretched too thin.

She was about a half mile from the vehicle when she saw a figure on horseback cutting through the pasture on her left. She kept walking. It could be any number of hands; she knew exactly how many because she'd written their checks that very afternoon.

The rider grew closer, astride a magnificent animal. She recognized the hat first, the horse second. It was Mike. And he was riding Lightning, his black gelding

with the distinctive crooked blaze running from forelock to nose. He trotted up, then slowed to a walk on
the other side of the fence. She stared straight ahead,
ignoring him.

"Trouble, Grace?" His smooth voice goaded her from
across the fence.

"I'm out for my afternoon stroll," she replied dryly.

"I see. Car die?" He sat back in the saddle, resting
one hand on a hard thigh.

Oh, duh, she thought. He knew darn well it had or
she wouldn't be walking.

"I'm just going back to call the garage and get it
towed."

"It's nearly two miles. And you're going to have blis-
ters in those cute little things."

She stopped, gave him a withering glare, then
reached down and slipped off the sandals, looping
the straps jauntily around her index finger and started
walking again, barefoot.

Lightning followed, Mike's laughter echoing with
that of a red-winged blackbird.

"I know you hate men coming to your rescue, and
telling you what to do," he began.

She should be spitting mad after their arguments.
She should be shaken by the close call she'd just had.
She should not be feeling the corners of her mouth
twitch, but a teasing Mike was horribly difficult to
resist. Always had been.

"That would assume one needed rescuing," she
countered, keeping her eyes on the road. If she looked

him in the eyes now he'd know he'd got to her, and she wasn't ready to give in. He'd get all proprietary again.

"But if you would allow me to offer you my assistance…"

Her lips quivered at his formal tone. He was incorrigible!

"Lightning and I would be happy to give you a lift back to the ranch."

She turned her head then, looking at him for the first time since he'd come up beside her.

She would always have a soft spot for Mike Gardner. Just looking at him, a little dusty, a whole lot man, astride his favourite horse…gray eyes crinkled around the edges with teasing while a smile flirted with the corners of his mouth…she couldn't resist.

Just this once.

"All right," she gave in. She slipped the sandals back on her feet and picked her way through the scratchy grass to the fence. Mike leaned over and lifted the top wire, making more space for her to crawl through. Once she was in the pasture she walked around Lightning's head, giving his forelock a little scratch as she went by.

"What happened to you?"

Suddenly Mike's voice changed and Grace looked up, confused. She was even more mystified when he leaped from the saddle, standing before her. "Are you all right?"

"Of course I am. Why wouldn't I be?"

Mike reached into his back pocket and pulled out a

hankie. A hankie? she thought irrationally. Mike Gardner carried hankies?

He pushed her hair back with a commanding hand and touched the white cotton to her forehead. She winced with surprise at the pain.

"You didn't know?" His voice was low, soothing.

"I must have bumped my head."

"It's bleeding." He dabbed at the cut. "Mostly in your hair. What happened?"

"She died. Just a big clunk and she seized up right there."

Grace tried not to think of how gentle his hands were as he tended to her wound.

"A clunk? You must have lost your transmission." His fingers parted her hair, dabbing softly at the blood and enlarging bump.

"Maybe. It won't go anywhere. I tried putting it in gear, but nothing." She pushed his hands away, having had enough fussing and probing. "There was some red fluid underneath, if that tells you anything."

"Sure sounds like transmission fluid." Mike bent at the knees, peering into her face. "Can you ride? I'll help you up."

"I wasn't really hurt," she protested, putting her foot in the stirrup. She really didn't feel much of anything at all. She grabbed the saddle horn, Mike's hands strong at her waist as she took a hop and slid into the saddle. Once astride, she realized the stirrups were too long for her legs.

She thought maybe he'd lead Lightning back to the

barn, which was far enough away now that it looked like a tiny shed dotting the prairie. But Mike put his boot in one stirrup, hoisted himself up and sat behind her.

The saddle was big, but regardless it wasn't made for two people. Her backside was cushioned intimately in the vee of his thighs as she gave him back both the stirrups, the length set for his much longer legs. His right arm came around her, gripping the reins; his left wrapped around her waist, holding her firmly against him.

It was the closest she'd ever been to being in Mike's arms in several years, and feeling him pressed against her sent memories flooding back. He was so close she could feel his heart beat against her shoulder, the way the muscles in his legs cradled hers. As angry as she was with him, being tucked securely against his body did things to her. Arousing things. She'd been only seventeen when they'd dated, and her stomach had quivered then every time he'd touched her. Now was no different. Her heart beat a little faster, her body became aware of every inch of contact.

"Hang on," he murmured in her ear, and the hair on the back of her neck prickled from the warmth of his breath.

He spurred Lightning and her breath caught in her chest as they took off at a rolling canter.

Her hair ruffled back from her face as she gripped the saddle horn, surprised by the jolt of the gait. And feeling more in danger than she had in a long time. A danger that had nothing to do with horses or cars but everything to do with a cowboy named Mike Gardner.

Chapter 4

Mike guided Lightning into the barn, the horse's hooves clopping steadily on the concrete floor. He dismounted, and Grace immediately felt the loss of his body pressed against hers. Wordlessly he dropped the reins, reached up and helped her out of the saddle.

In that moment, had he leaned the slightest bit forward, she would have forgotten about all the reasons why he infuriated her and she would have kissed him. Put her lips against his just to see how it would feel. Whether or not he still tasted the same as she remembered. It was the second time the urge had struck her that afternoon. His arms held her firmly as her feet touched the ground, but then he was gone, grabbing the reins again and leading Lightning down the corridor.

It was just as well. Grace took a restorative breath.

She had to get up to the house anyway and call the garage. A heaviness filled her chest at the thought that the car couldn't be fixed. What would she do then? She couldn't afford a new one, not now. And repairs were sure to stretch her budget far out of capacity.

She'd probably been stupid to buy the house. She could have come back and rented a small one-bedroom apartment. It really was all she needed. Then there wouldn't be upkeep costs, insurance, property taxes…but after leaving Edmonton, she'd been fierce about living independently. She hadn't come through the divorce with much, but there had been enough for a down payment. Her little yellow bungalow was her defiant way of saying she could make it on her own.

She left Mike with the horse and went back out in the sunshine, heading toward the house with long strides. It didn't matter now. She *had* bought the house, and the car, and had brought her share of legal fees with her when she'd come back. Now she'd just have to find a way to make ends meet like she always did. The only one who could take care of her was *her*. She'd learned that the hard way.

Phil answered the phone at Bob's Automotive when she called. Phil was Bob's son, but she still couldn't help but laugh every time she called and heard, "Bob's Automotive, Phil speaking." He promised he'd have someone pick up her car within the next hour.

She was hanging up when Mike came inside. "You get a tow?"

"I did. Phil's sending someone out."

"Great."

She moved past him and went outside on the narrow veranda. "Yeah, well, it's going to suck being without wheels. God knows how long it'll take to fix it."

He followed her back out the door. "If it's your tranny, and it sounds like it is, it could be a while."

Wonderful. Her shoulders drooped. How in the world was she supposed to pay for a whole new transmission?

Mike stepped forward, raising his hand and tenderly probing the bump on her forehead. "Seat belts. Honestly, Grace. Are you sure you're okay?"

She shrugged off his touch and his criticism. "You, 'Mr. Concussion From Too Many Saddlebroncs,' you're going to lecture me about seat belts? For your limited information, it was buckled. Knowing that old junker, it probably didn't function right. You don't need to beat it into me."

"Someone has to. You could have really been hurt if you'd actually gone off the road."

She turned to walk away but he reached out and caught her arm, pulling her back. "What if you have a concussion? Do you have a headache? Dizziness?"

His hand was still firm on her wrist and she fought against the excitement thrumming through her. Her laugh was tight and strained as she countered.

"You're familiar with concussion symptoms, but I guess you should be after what, four? Five?" She tilted her chin. "The only thing giving me a headache today is *you*."

The last thing she should have expected was for him

to smile. But he did. A slow, make-your-heart-burn smile that crawled up his cheek.

"Grace, I don't ever remember it being this much fun to argue with you."

She pulled away and put her hands on her hips, because she knew if she didn't she'd wipe that smirk off his face with her lips. She simply had to stop thinking about kissing him! "Maybe because you didn't stay around long enough to find out."

His grin faded. It was the desired outcome but it made her feel small for using it.

"Don't mind me. I have bigger concerns at the moment, thank you." She didn't intend for it to come out as coolly as it did.

Mike's chin flattened and he stared over her shoulder. "Don't worry about your car, I'll take care of it."

He'd what? Grace stiffened.

Second verse, third, fourth and fifth, same as the first. The man was unbelievable. When was he going to realize she didn't want to be taken care of?

"I'm perfectly capable, thank you just the same." She said the words through gritted teeth.

"Hey, you were out here working for Circle M. The least I can do is take care of fixing your car. Come to think of it, if you're without transportation, you can borrow one of the farm trucks."

"Here's a newsflash." She tossed her head. Darn it, it *was* starting to ache after all. The fact that he was right about her head only made her more annoyed. "I don't want, nor do I need your help." For a moment she swayed. In a flash, the adrenaline from the near miss drained from her and she started to shake. She could have been hurt again, and the realization slammed into her. She knew that fear, that shock of an eternity happening in a split second. Grace put her hands on the railing and tried deep breaths to gain control over her trembling.

She heard an engine approaching, wondering if it was Phil with the tow truck. Instead Connor's truck was coming up the driveway, swirling up dust.

"Look at you, you're shaking like a leaf." He came up behind her, rested a large palm on her back. His voice gentled. "Why are you so set on never letting anyone help you? Why do you have to do everything yourself?"

Mike wouldn't understand. He'd always done exactly what he wanted, when he wanted to do it. And that included leaving her behind. She'd hated being in town so much after he was gone that she'd rashly decided to go to Red Deer to college.

It had been a big mistake, and one she tried to forget so she didn't waste her energy with regret. Mike hadn't had choices taken away from him in the blink of an eye. The reason her heart had pounded so heavily when her car had skidded to a stop was from sheer fright. In that split second that she lost control, she relived her accident all over again.

Even now, with her delayed reaction happening long minutes after it was over, she relived the pain, the fear of being in the hospital, the devastation of waking up from surgery to the horrific news.

She knew why she was so independent. She'd trusted Mike, and when he wasn't there anymore, she'd relied on a substitute to make things right, and it had only gone wrong. She had acknowledged long ago that she'd been young and had tried to replace Mike by finding someone else. She wouldn't make the same mistakes again.

But he didn't know about her earlier accident. And she wasn't going to be the one to tell him and make herself even more pathetic in his eyes. She pulled away from his touch.

"Stop being such a Neanderthal and wake up to the fact that we're in the twenty-first century. Women are fully capable of looking after themselves. I don't need you, Mike."

His face changed, blanked completely. "How do you intend on getting home, then? Fly?"

Oh Lord, she hadn't thought of that. It seemed she did need him after all.

Connor's truck door slammed. Before Mike could blink, she turned and leaned over the rail, smiling sweetly.

"Connor? I've had some car trouble. Would you mind driving me home?"

She saw Connor's glance flicker to Mike and hold for a moment. She didn't need to turn around to know Mike was staring stonily ahead. She didn't hold the franchise on being stubborn.

"Mike could…"

"Oh, I don't want to trouble Mike. He already brought me back and made sure I was all right." She turned on the charm. "I just need a lift back to my house, and I can see to getting everything set right."

"Well, okay." He looked up again at Mike. "Tell Alex I'll be back in half an hour, will you?"

Mike didn't answer, just turned on a booted heel and went inside, slamming the screen door behind him. Grace climbed into the cab of the truck, shut the door and fastened her seat belt. Connor stood in the middle between the house and the truck for a moment, before getting in the vehicle and starting the engine.

Grace hesitated outside the glass and metal door of Bob's Automotive. Through the window she could see her poor sedan up on the hoist. She was scared half to death to hear what Phil had to say. She couldn't afford to replace her car even though she knew she should. At least Phil would let her take her car when it was done and let her pay a little each week until her bill was settled. It was one of the benefits of living in the town where she grew up.

She opened the glass and metal door and went inside. Instantly she was greeted by the grinding screech of air tools and coarse shouts of mechanics.

Phil caught sight of her standing by the front counter and approached, wiping his hands on a rag. "Morning, Grace," he greeted.

"Hey, Phil." She nodded towards the car. "It's not good, is it."

"You lost your transmission."

Her heart sank. Transmissions were bad. Very, very bad. She'd had a feeling, and remembered Mike commenting on the possibility, but she'd hoped it was something easier like a cracked hose.

"Is it worth fixing?"

"Well, you could buy another older model, but then there wouldn't be any guarantee it wouldn't do the same thing. Best thing I can do is replace it for you. I can have a look around for a cheaper, used one. But you've still got labor on top of that."

Naturally. She took a breath and held it. "Total damage?"

"A couple of thousand. Should be able to do it all up for under twenty-five hundred."

Twenty-five hundred dollars. Right now it might as well be twenty-five thousand. Her breath came out in a rush. Would she never catch a break?

"And how long?"

"Next Wednesday? Take me a few days to get a new tranny in, and we're swamped."

"Okay. Thanks, Phil."

She turned to walk back out the door when his voice stopped her. "Hey, Grace?"

"Yeah?" She looked over her shoulder. Phil looked genuinely sorry. He was ten years older than Grace, but his little sister had gone to school with her.

"Mike called in yesterday. We've already had a look

at your seat belt, and it's fixed. And if it's money that's got you panicked, don't worry. He said Circle M is going to cover it, since it happened while you were on the job."

Every nerve ending in her body stood up. How dare he go around her, go to Phil and just announce that he was paying for everything! After their conversation! She felt heat rise up her chest and neck, settling in her cheeks.

Her fingers tightened on the metal bar of the door, gripping until her knuckles turned white.

"Phil, the last I checked, the registration for that hunk of junk is in my name. Which means I pay for repairs. Under no circumstances do you talk to Mike Gardner, you hear? Circle M is *not* paying for a new transmission or any other maintenance. Period."

"Yes, ma'am." Phil paused for a moment, then cleared his throat. "If money's an issue anyway, we can work something out. We'll just put it on an account and you can pay a little every month. I know you're good for it."

Tears stung her eyes and she blinked them back. For a while she'd considered staying in Edmonton, living in the city and going back to school. But at moments like this, she knew she'd done the right thing coming back.

"Thanks, Phil," she answered. She went back outside into the fall sunshine, burning with humiliation. What in the world was Mike trying to do, anyway? He had to know she'd never agree to such a plan.

As much as she hated to do it, she was going to have

to find another job. And pray that somehow there ended up being a few extra hours in the day so she could get some sleep.

Grace covered her mouth, stifling a yawn. At least the bookwork had gone smoothly. It hadn't taken long to catch up. The checks were written according to the invoices and the envelopes made up and just waited for signatures. Connor and Mike were both out in the fields, thankfully. Johanna was on her way out for groceries, and Maren was sleeping. She heard the faint sound of the television from upstairs: Alex was watching.

The bed rest had to be driving Alex crazy. Grace looked at her watch. She'd make them both a cup of tea and have a visit. Lately there'd been lots of times she'd wished she could just lay in bed, but she knew without a doubt that if she had to be there, like Alex was now, she'd be climbing the walls. When she finally shut the computer down, she could hear giggles coming from upstairs. Maren was awake.

Grace made tea, grabbed a juice box from the fridge and went upstairs.

Maren snuggled Alex on the bed, her head resting against the growing mound of Alex's tummy. Absently Alex played with Maren's dark curls, twirling them around her index finger as a children's show flickered on the TV screen, holding Maren's attention.

It was a scene that Grace knew she'd never have,

and she swallowed against the bittersweet lump in her throat.

Alex turned and caught her standing in the doorway. "Grace! Come on in!"

Grace stepped inside. "I brought tea."

"Here, honey, slide down here. Mama's going to have something hot."

"Hotttt," Maren repeated the word.

"She's really starting to talk." Grace handed Alex a mug.

"Don't I know it. Babbles all day."

She put her tea on the bedside table and then inserted the straw into the juice box for Maren. Once the toddler was settled, Grace perched on the edge of the bed.

"So, how're you doing?"

Alex sighed. "I'm sick and tired of being in bed, sick and tired of being pregnant, sick and tired of not being able to do anything. I'm not even supposed to pick up my own daughter."

When Grace met Alex's eyes, she was dismayed to see tears glimmering in the corners.

"I'm sorry," she offered. "You just need to get out of this room."

Alex's frustration was clear, and understandable, Grace thought as she sipped her tea. She looked at Alex, dressed in maternity yoga pants and a baggy sweatshirt. What the woman needed was to feel like a *woman* again. Maybe she could help with that. First of all had to be getting her dressed. In something nicer than an old sweatshirt of Connor's.

"You need a girlie day."

Alex snorted. "Yeah, right. I'm not allowed to go anywhere."

"So what? I'll bring it to you."

She went to the bathroom and got out a brush, a makeup bag, nail polish and a bag of hair accessories.

While Maren watched, wide-eyed, Grace gently got Alex changed into a pair of maternity jeans and a cute red jersey top with long, slender sleeves. Once she was reclined on the bed once more, Grace picked up the brush and starting brushing out Alex's long, black hair. She and Alex had become friends since Alex had moved to Windover, but the intimate gesture of brushing her hair seemed to solidify their growing affection more than anything previous.

"So, what's happening between you and Mike?"

Grace could feel the blush in her cheeks, knew it was truly bad when the outsides of her ears burned. "Nothing."

Alex laughed, pointing to Grace's face. "Girls don't blush like that over nothing. You've been fighting like cats and dogs."

"He's just gotten overprotective lately." Grace dismissed the comment, focusing on Alex's hair. She gathered it up and began plaiting it into a loose French braid.

"There's something. I can feel it, even being up here away from everyone."

Grace met Alex's eyes in the mirror, her hands still plaiting blindly as she grabbed the opportunity to change the subject. Alex had to know she and Mike had been an item once, and she didn't want it to come up. "It's been horrid for you, hasn't it."

"I just keep reminding myself what the payoff will be. That's what really matters."

Hair finished, Grace took out polish and went to work on Alex's feet. Alex smiled, wiggling her red toes. "Thank you, Grace. I needed this today."

"Nonsense. Connor leaves you up here all day while he gets to go off and do all his *stuff.* Men," she muttered.

Alex laughed. "So he *is* getting to you."

"Hah. Mike Gardner is way too big for his britches, running around thinking he can tell everyone what to do. What is it about men that make them think they can just park us somewhere and we'll do exactly what we're told?"

Alex's lips twitched and she patted the mound of her belly. "They do come in handy sometimes."

Grace ran a hand through her hair. "Yeah. Handy. Look at this gorgeous fall day. It's fifteen degrees and it smells like fall and you're stuck here in bed. You've got a balcony out there, for Pete's sake!"

Abruptly she stood up. "You know what? You sit here. I have an idea."

She reached into the bag of hair accessories and pulled out an elastic and a scrunchie. "Today you're going to enjoy the outdoors, and we don't need a man to do it."

Grace stomped down the stairs, putting her hair in a

ponytail as she went. At the bottom she paused, twisting the tail around and around and anchoring it to the back of her head with the scrunchie—a cheater bun. *Stupid men. Poor Alex up there day in and day out on bed rest.*

She went out on to the back deck. The swing was too big; she'd never be able to move it alone. And regular patio chairs weren't that comfortable at the best of times, and she couldn't imagine how they'd feel to a heavily pregnant woman. But the other chair—she could manage that. She took the cushions off first and marched them upstairs.

"What are you doing?" Alex called after her as she hit the stairs again.

"You'll see," she shouted back.

Getting the furniture upstairs was another matter. It was a light metal frame, about the length of a love seat with a back on it. Alex could stretch out if she wanted, or simply tuck herself into the corner and enjoy the fresh air. It was big enough she could share it with Maren, or with Connor.

She got the contraption into the kitchen and through the wide doorway to the hall. Getting it around the corner of the stairs was nearly impossible, and Grace was terrified she'd slip and take a piece out of the woodwork. Panting, she took it one step at a time, cringing every time she heard the metal legs bang against the stair risers ahead. She was almost at the top when it slipped. She scrambled to catch it, saving it just in time from hitting the solid wood banister, but catching the side of her hand on a screw. She bit down on her lip to keep from cursing.

Getting it through the bedroom meant lifting the frame over the bed, then dragging it through the sliding doors that led to the balcony.

Once the seat was in place, Grace wiped her glistening brow and arranged the cushions. "Don't go out yet," she cautioned. "There's more."

She went back downstairs and retrieved a small table that Alex could use to set a drink on, or a book. The next trip revealed the huge snake plant from the study, which Grace placed in a corner, and a soft chenille blanket for when she might get a chill now that fall had settled in for good.

When it was done, she was red and sweating, pieces of hair dangling messily along the sides of her face, but with a triumphant smile.

"There. Now you can come out."

Alex moved gingerly, as she always did these days, settling herself in the seat and sighing.

"Connor should have seen to this long ago."

Alex smiled wistfully. "Don't blame Connor. He's been so preoccupied."

Grace sighed. "I know. But honestly, men just don't see the little things."

"But you did. Thank you so much, Grace." Maren scrambled up beside her mother, carrying a stuffed cat and a book. "Oh, dear, you're bleeding!" Alex pointed at Grace's hand.

Sure enough, she was. She must have done it when

the frame slipped. She hoped she hadn't got any blood on the cushions. "It's just a scratch."

"There's first-aid stuff in the bathroom downstairs. Oh, Grace."

Grace fluttered her other hand. "Don't worry about it. A Band-Aid and it'll be fine. You just enjoy what's left of the morning."

Grace was downstairs in the bathroom washing her hand when she heard the front door open. Booted feet paused, then went upstairs. Moments later they clattered back down.

Please, let it be Connor.

No such luck.

"What in the world were you thinking?"

She grabbed a Band-Aid from the box and turned to face Mike, regarding him blandly. "Good morning, Mike."

"You carried that stuff up there all by yourself?"

"I did. I'm not helpless, as you seem to think." She peeled the wrapping off the bandage and stuck the first tab on her hand.

"Helpless? You? Never. You have the temper of a snake."

She laughed. Finally. Maybe, just maybe she was finally getting through to him. He'd changed clothes, she realized. He looked far too neat and tidy for a man who'd been out working for hours already. His T-shirt was brown and hugged his shoulders, and his jeans were unblemished.

"Going somewhere?"

"What?" He furrowed his brow at her.

"Clean jeans, tidy shirt. I know you didn't do that just for me, Mike." She let her lips curve on one side and she raised an eyebrow in his direction.

For a moment he didn't say anything, and Grace got the giddy feeling she might have actually managed to embarrass him a little.

"I got thrown."

She couldn't help it, she snorted. "I see."

"Stupid colt. Scared of his own shadow." Mike shoved his hands in his pockets.

Grace laughed. "Kind of makes you realize why you stopped the circuit, huh. Saddlebronc riders that get thrown by colts don't really hit pay dirt. Just the *dirt*."

"I'm glad you find it funny."

She finished sticking the Band-Aid to her hand, giving it an extra pat. "I do, actually. Since you're still in one piece and all."

"So are you going to tell me why, exactly, you're bleeding?"

"Alex was stuck in that room day in and day out. She wanted to get some fresh air and sunshine. What's she doing now?"

Mike lowered his voice. "She's snuggled up with Maren, the two of them under the blanket, reading stories."

Grace smiled. "Oh, that's lovely."

Mike came forward and took her wrist in his hand. "You cut yourself. If you'd waited, I would have helped you take that seat upstairs."

"I didn't know when anyone would be coming back in, and I knew I could do it myself."

He took a second bandage and applied it to the rest of the cut on her hand. Having Mike doctor her so tenderly did things to her insides. If he'd stop being so bossy, maybe he'd see what was right in front of him. She frowned. That idea had complications of its own.

"You don't have to do everything by yourself," he countered. "I talked to Phil today. He said you refused to let me pay anything on your account."

"Of course I did."

"Why?"

She pulled her hand away. "Because I pay my own way. I live my own life. I make my own decisions. I...I don't rely on other people."

She didn't, not anymore. Mike had left her. Steve had let her down. It was far better to look after yourself and deal with those consequences.

"I know something about that," he answered.

"Yes, you do. And why do you make *your* own choices?"

His eyes met hers squarely. "Because relying on other people means eventually you'll be disappointed."

"That's right." She took a breath, finally challenging him. "People let other people down. *You* won't let anyone dictate your life. So why do you try to do it to me?"

"Because...because... Oh damn." He scowled. "Because you constantly seem to need it!"

Grace stepped back. That was what he thought of her then. Still the girl who couldn't look after herself.

She pressed her fingers to her eyes, worn-out. Tears threatened but she held them back. For weeks she'd been working long hours, and fighting with Mike so much lately drained her more than she'd cared to admit. Seeing Alex pregnant, her family around her, caused Grace so much hurt it actually pained her physically. All the things she wanted…security, love, a family of her own…never had they seemed so far away. She wanted to lift her chin and say something scathing, but for once it wasn't in her.

"You gave up the right to that a long time ago," she murmured. "And I'm tired of fighting." She tried to swallow the tears that clogged her throat. "I can't do it anymore, Mike. Just leave me alone."

Chapter 5

Mike took a step closer, putting his large hand on Grace's shoulder. "I'm sorry," he murmured. "I didn't mean to make you cry."

She sniffled, gaining control. "You didn't. I'm not crying. It's just everything has been piling up. I'm fine, really."

"You're not fine. You just said so."

She didn't have an answer to that. He was right. She'd asked to be left alone because she couldn't take the constant pressure from him anymore.

"I just need to take a break. That's all."

What she really wanted to do was rest against his solid strength. As infuriating as his overprotectiveness had been lately, the one thing she'd always known in her heart was that she could count on him. Even after he had left her, she knew if she were in trouble she could call and he'd be there. There weren't many people she could say that about. She sighed and leaned back into his hand. Just that much was a comfort. A feeling that for a few moments she wasn't alone.

Her back was still to him and she closed her eyes as he squeezed her shoulder. "There's more to this than just being tired, isn't there."

Grace swallowed against the lump in her throat. Mike's hand left her shoulder and his arms came around her, pulling her back against his chest. He said nothing else, just held her for a few minutes. She wished she could give him more. She wasn't the only one who needed a break. She knew he'd been working too hard himself, running the bulk of the ranch now as well as overseeing the building of his house. Like her, he didn't have family close by to rely on. He was carrying his own weight and a lot of Connor's, as well. She knew he didn't mind it in the least, but it didn't mean he wasn't tired or stressed out.

Reluctantly she pulled out of his arms and turned to face him. "Thank you," she murmured softly. "I needed that. I'm sorry, too. I've jumped down your throat lately when all you've been doing is trying to help."

"Let's get out of here," he suggested. "Let's forget about the arguments. Come with me and I'll show you how the house is coming along."

She had work waiting for her at home and a shift at the tavern that night, but it couldn't hurt to take a half hour and go with him. She wanted to spend time with him, she admitted to herself. It had been a long time since they'd spent time together that had no purpose other than to escape everyday pressures. And she *was* curious about the house. Every time she came out to the ranch, she saw changes. First the basement, then the frame. Now the roof was on and there were holes for windows and doors. She'd thought he'd build a regular two-story house, something like Windover. Instead the building that was forming was a low ranch style that turned a corner. She wondered what it would be like inside.

"That sounds nice. I'd love to see it."

The house sat northeast of Connor's, a rough gravel driveway leading to it off of the main ranch road. As they started past the barns, Grace saw two white pick-ups driving away toward the main road.

"Lunchtime, I guess," Mike commented as they walked side by side. Grace looked up at the house, admiring. It sat on top of a small knoll, and she had a feeling the view of the mountains from the west windows would be spectacular.

The late morning remained cool, and Grace tucked her arms around her even though she wore a thick sweater. Mike had thrown a jacket over his T-shirt, a rich brown that set off the coppery tones in his hair. He'd always had a way about him, long strides that covered ground without being hurried, a quiet assurance that he always knew exactly what he was doing. As they approached the house, he took her hand to lead her over the uneven spots. Grace hesitated a moment, captivated by the feel of her smaller hand in Mike's. Then he tugged, helping her over the mounds of uneven dirt to the front entrance.

Even without paint, or windows, or furniture, she was enthralled. It had a feeling about it. It was large, but the design was intimate. She wandered from room to room, shuffling against the wood and dust inside, side-stepping occasionally around tools left by the workmen. She went down a wide hall, and discovered bedrooms on the east side. At the very end was a huge room with a smaller one off it. It was the frame for the master bedroom and what she could only assume would be a private en suite.

She went back down the hall and found Mike standing in front of a vast opening, facing the mountains. They were visible in the clear autumn air, their white-tipped peaks a sharp contrast to the brilliant blue of the September sky.

"You're going to love it here."

Without looking at her, he answered, "My first home. Can you believe that? Over thirty, and I've never had my own place."

"It's going to be beautiful," she answered, her eyes on the same view as his. "You picked a great spot. Far enough away from Windover to be private, yet still on ranch land. And I can tell the house is going to be great. I can see the design and everything already." She could picture low tables, cozy couches and warm lamps in the living room. Maybe a television in the corner, and a comfortable chair where Mike would kick back with a beer at the end of a long day.

"I never thought I'd want to be tied down. But somehow…I guess I grew up."

She laughed lightly. Goodness, Mike wasn't getting sentimental, was he? All philosophical? These lapses really made it quite difficult for her to stay angry with him. Yet at the same time, she remembered wanting to give him this type of security long ago and how he'd run from it. She couldn't help but resent it just a bit.

"It happens to all of us sometime. Just takes longer for others, I guess."

She'd done her growing up long ago. Out of necessity.

He stepped away from the window, wandered to the next large room, which she assumed was the kitchen. She pictured him sitting at a table all by himself with a setting for one, eating dinner in the winter dark. It was a lonely image.

"Do you even know how to cook?" she teased from where she stood, her voice echoing through the open space.

He laughed. "Not really. Unless bacon and eggs counts."

She knew what was in store for him. She lived alone, and had for several years. No one to fight for the remote, or who ate something you'd set aside for later, or leaving their wet towels on the bathroom floor.

No one to talk to, to share a meal with, to watch a

movie with a bowl of popcorn between you. Living alone was a horribly solitary existence.

But it wasn't like she'd ever be living with Mike, either. Even without the complications she would bring to a relationship, she already knew how he felt about her. They'd been friends too long. He cared about her, she knew that. He always had. But if Connor weren't so concerned for Alex right now, he would have acted the same way toward Grace. Like an older brother. All other *atmosphere* between them was only a product of her own imaginings and a case of dwelling on sweet memories best forgotten.

"Where'd you go?"

Her head snapped up. He was standing close, too close. Her body warmed just from having him there, only an arm's length away. He was big and hulking in his heavy jacket, his cheeks ruddy from the brisk air. It wasn't fair for him to look so gorgeous when she was already fantasizing about him.

"Just thinking."

She turned away, but his hand on her arm stopped her from moving. "Don't run away."

"I'm not."

"Grace, you've been running away for years."

He sure picked a great time to finally get observant, she noted with irritation. "I don't know what you mean."

"Sure you do." His face told her he knew better. "What I don't get is why. Why do you work so hard to keep people at arm's length, when you obviously care very much about them? Everyone knows you, loves you. You're the town sweetheart. You do so much for people, yet I don't think any of them can say they know what makes you tick."

He didn't know the secrets she held so closely guarded, either. And if he did, she knew he'd look at her differently. She didn't want to see the look in his eyes when he realized what a disappointment she was. Even as she craved to be touched, to be loved by him again, she knew he wouldn't see her in the same way if he knew the truth. And she knew he'd run, just as he had before. She couldn't face that kind of hurt again.

But her secret was a burden she carried every day, and the more they argued, the more he showed his protective nature, the more she longed to finally let it out and be free of it.

"And you're gone again."

She shook her head, staring up into his eyes. There was no censure there, not this time. Instead there was just concern, and an edge of something else. It almost looked like desire. But no, that would be her fancies carrying her away again. He didn't think of her that way, she reminded herself.

"Mike..."

He was so close the zipper of his jacket was pressing against her sweater. Gently he placed a rough finger beneath her chin, tilting it up until her eyes met his. Automatically her gaze dropped to his lips and she was mesmerized as they pursed slightly as he whispered, "Shh."

Her breath caught, her heart stopped for an ethereal moment. Then he put his lips on hers and everything coursed through her in a rush.

At last. Every pore in her body seemed to breathe those two words as her eyes drifted closed. Mike let go of her chin and instead put his hands on her arms, just above her elbows, pulling her closer. His lips teased, coaxed with the lightest of touches. He wasn't pushing, she suddenly realized. He was being careful with her. Knowing it touched her heart, but she didn't need him to be careful. She just needed *him*.

She opened her lips a little wider in invitation. Carefully he deepened the kiss, like he was testing to see how she'd respond. She finally did what she'd wanted to do since the night they'd danced. She lifted her arms and threaded her fingers through his hair, pulling his head down and putting everything she could offer into the kiss. She wanted him, wanted to know she could make him lose control, wanted to know she made him want her as much as she wanted him.

Once she made it clear what she was asking, everything changed.

He broke off the kiss, took command. His gaze burned into hers and excitement raced to her every extremity like an electric current. He was suddenly bigger, stronger. Forceful, which she didn't fear but welcomed. Demanding. His wide hand cupped the back of her neck even as his body pushed her backward until her movement was stopped by the two-by-six stud of the living room wall.

Mike's legs spread wide and he pinned her there, taking her mouth completely.

He moaned, the sound vibrating in his throat, filling her with wonder. It had been nearly a decade since she'd last kissed him, but the taste of him was as familiar as if it had been yesterday. She was fortunate that he had her pressed so firmly against the wood because she knew that otherwise she'd be melted in one delicious puddle of ecstasy. Instead, she wilted, letting her body twine around him, filling all the lees between them.

When it seemed they couldn't possibly go on any longer in that position, Mike drew away. "Grace," he murmured. His hand slid from behind her head to her face, his wide fingers delicately brushing the pale skin of her cheekbone. Disbelief assaulted her as that gentle hand left her face and caressed the soft skin of her neck, slowly inching downward, tracing a line through the middle of her chest. She watched, holding her breath, as his eyes seductively followed the path of his fingers. In a moment she knew he'd be touching her in all the places she longed to be touched by him. And she knew in that same suspended moment that it wouldn't be fair. To either of them.

She closed her eyes. "Stop," she said huskily in the quiet of the empty house.

"You don't mean that."

When she looked up he still wasn't looking at her, but watching his own fingers as they moved on her body, a small smile playing on his lips. She swallowed, yearning for him to continue but desperate to stop before things went too far to turn back.

"Please, Mike, you need to stop."

"I don't want to stop."

Oh, he was making this difficult. She inhaled and squared her shoulders. "We can't do this. We don't want the same things."

Mike's jaw hardened as he felt her pull away. Didn't want the same things? He knew they wanted each other; that much was perfectly plain.

But neither did he want to rush things and ruin it. Grace had been right about one thing today, she was getting worn-out from spreading herself too thin. He didn't need to add to the stresses. He wanted to help her, look out for her. He wanted all sorts of things for her and he couldn't rush them.

"I'm sorry."

"Don't be. It just can't go any further, that's all."

She was avoiding looking at him and he wondered if he'd been wrong after all. She'd flirted with him that night at the party, but she'd had a few drinks and had been goaded on by her friends. That didn't mean she was crazy about him. In fact, they'd been fighting most of the time lately. Maybe he'd misread her feelings after all. For a moment he felt exactly like he had every time the social worker told him he was moving again. Expendable. Not exactly what people had in mind as a "keeper." He knew what happened when he let himself love. He always got hurt. When they'd been seeing each other, he'd been the one to go so that she wouldn't be the one doing the leaving.

He backed away. "I don't want to pressure you into anything." He sensed her relief and couldn't resist adding, "But I'm not sorry, either."

The look she gave him was so complicated he didn't even try to interpret it. What conclusion could he possibly reach when her face was such a contradiction of arousal, hope, fear and resignation? Nothing made sense. It should have been easy. Either she wanted him or she didn't.

"We don't want the same things," she repeated.

"What does that mean?" Looking down into her eyes, he sensed she meant something far deeper than the raw need he was feeling right now.

She straightened her sweater and put on a regular smile. "I have to get back," she evaded. "Thank you for showing me your house."

He reached out and grabbed her arm. "Wait."

She looked up at him, silently begging him to let her go. He could see it in her eyes. But he persisted because after all this time it needed saying.

"I left you before without a word. And, Grace, for that I'm truly sorry."

He saw her swallow, and her gaze dropped to between her feet.

"Forget it."

"Grace. I can't forget it after what just happened. Because if we're in danger of starting something again, we need to clear the air. You need to know that I was scared then and unfair to you. I wouldn't do that to you again."

He thought his words would reassure her, but instead her lips thinned almost as if in pain.

"Thank you for the apology," she replied, her voice soft, as if she didn't trust it. "But it doesn't matter now, because we aren't starting anything. I need to get back."

It made him inexplicably angry, but he let her walk away rather than drag her into another fight. His body was still humming with the energy of their kiss. Not starting anything? Hah!

He'd see about that.

Mike pocketed the truck keys and ran his fingers through his hair before putting his hat back on. Even from outside, he heard the rough beat of country music coming from the hotel tavern.

She was in there. *Working.*

He'd come across that tidbit of information quite by accident. Connor had stopped for some takeout as a treat for Alex one evening, and Grace had come in for her shift. It had taken two days for the topic to come up in conversation and it had been Alex who'd finally brought it up. He was sitting down with a couple of Johanna's cookies when she'd remarked on his foul mood and suggested a night out might put him in a better frame of mind.

He put his hand on the door handle. It had been a setup, pure and simple. He'd seen it on Alex's face as she casually dropped the hint that he could see Grace while he was there.

This, then, was how she was paying for the repairs on her car. It bugged him knowing she'd rather be a barmaid than take his assistance. And the tavern was so rough.

He lowered his hat, shadowing his eyes, and walked in.

The light was dim, the noise nearly deafening as he made his way to the bar. She hadn't seen him come in, he realized, taking a stool. She was at the end of the bar, pouring a glass of whatever was on tap, laughing at something a customer said. They traded glass for money, and she turned.

When she saw him, her face soured. He met the look squarely as she came to take his order.

"Beer, Mike?"

The question was carefully casual but Mike felt the coolness. He remembered all too well how she'd felt in his arms, how she'd tasted in his mouth. All it took was seeing her again to bring it all back. The way she looked tonight didn't help, either. Her low-slung jeans were worn in all the right places and sat on her hips, while her T-shirt clung to her ribs like a second skin.

"Yeah. In the bottle."

She raised one eyebrow in his direction; in his nasty mood he hadn't even said please. And he'd be damned if he'd backtrack now.

When he said nothing, she turned away and leaned over to retrieve his brand from the cooler. As she did, the hem of her T-shirt slid up, the waistband of her jeans down, and he saw the delectable hollow of her back.

He wet his lips, but before he could contemplate it further, she brought his bottle, placed it on a plain white cocktail napkin in front of him. "You starting a tab?"

"I'll pay as I go," he responded, standing to dig his wallet out of his pocket while she waited. He handed her a five and said, "Keep it."

She tucked it into her apron. "You hungry? Jack's running the kitchen tonight so it's edible."

"Not right now."

She turned to leave.

"What are you doing here, anyway?"

She smiled at him, but he could tell it wasn't sincere. "I'm working, what does it look like?"

"But why here?"

She came closer so they wouldn't have to shout over the voices and music, and to keep their conversation private from other patrons. "Because the tips are good, and the schedule works with my other jobs, that's why."

"Surely you could have found something better than this."

He'd gone and offended her again, he could tell by the way her eyes narrowed slightly. "It's temporary. One of the waitresses is on holiday for a few weeks. The timing was right and it was too good to pass up."

"But you wouldn't have to do it at all if you'd let me help."

"Hey, Grace! I'm dyin' of thirst over here!"

The call came from a local and Mike's eyes narrowed as she laughed good-naturedly in response. "Keep your shirt on, Joe. I'm coming."

She was better than this, Mike thought as he nursed his beer, watching her work the room. She didn't need to be working day and night and negotiating such a tough crowd. Lord, this was the roughest establishment in town. He should know. He'd spent many an evening here over the years.

He couldn't take his eyes off her. He noticed she always had a smile for everyone. Everyone but him, it seemed. She delivered platters of fries and burgers and baskets of chicken wings, carted countless trays of beer and the other local staple, rye and Coke. As the evening drew on he ordered another beer, threatened by her admonishment of "order something or give your stool to a paying customer." The noise grew louder, the crowd more raucous. At the table behind him, he picked up bits and pieces of the conversation, and he didn't like it. It was all innuendoes and testosterone mixed with alcohol. As long as they were there, Mike decided, he wasn't leaving Grace here alone.

"Hey, Grace, come to think of it, maybe I will have a steak sandwich."

She put the order in without saying anything. Both she and the other waitress, Pam, were hustling around trying to keep everyone fed and watered. She took the order of the table behind him, and when she went to the kitchen to place it he heard one of the men say, "Man, she's hot. The things I could do with a little filly like that."

Like hell. Mike scowled, growing angrier by the minute. This is what she put up with? The idiot that had spoken was no more than a randy kid who thought far too much of himself.

Grace delivered Mike's sandwich and smiled tightly. "I had Jack add hot sauce."

For the first time, he genuinely smiled back, surprised she'd remembered such a tiny detail about him after all their years apart. "Thanks for remembering."

"I've known you a long time, Mike. Have you forgotten that?"

Of course he hadn't. Grace, even as a teenager, had always been kind and giving. She'd never thought less of him because of his upbringing. In a world where he'd constantly been someone's add-on, she'd always taken him exactly as he was. She'd been there for him and he'd cared more about her than he ever had anyone. Which was why he'd run in the first place. Caring that much had scared the living hell out of him.

He caught her hand before she could leave again. "You know I haven't forgotten. I can always count on you, Grace."

Her smile faltered and he wondered what he'd said wrong.

"I'll be back," she promised, pulling her hand away.

He cut into his steak; all the while his radar was tuned to the men sitting behind him. Grace delivered a tray of drinks. "Here, honey, you keep the change."

A couple of snickers. "And how's about you let me buy you breakfast tomorrow?"

Mike put down his steak knife and spun a hundred and eighty degrees on his stool, lowering his head and staring down at the loudmouth. The man who had spoken was maybe twenty-two, twenty-three, with dusty boots and a belt buckle the size of a hubcap.

When Grace simply pocketed the cash, saying nothing, the laughter died down. Mike turned back to his sandwich as Grace walked back to the bar.

"Hey, I meant it about breakfast, baby," the guy called. "There's an extra twenty in it for you."

That was going too far. Even the innuendo of exchanging money for favors had Mike seeing red. Not his Grace. She wasn't that kind of woman and never would be. Mike stepped off his stool, walked over to the table and, calm-as-you-please, gripped the collar of the offender's shirt and lifted him clean out of his chair. "You just don't know when to shut up," he cautioned calmly.

Conversations halted. The music kept blaring but it sounded out of place in the room now devoid of laughter and chatter. It couldn't be any more clear that this group was passing through. Anyone in town knew better than to provoke Mike. His temper had a long fuse, but when it blew it was like fireworks. And right now everyone was watching to see the show.

Mike simply held the man up so that his toes barely touched the floor and stared him down.

"Hey, sorry, bud," he said. "Didn't mean to poach."

Mike waited a few seconds, then let him down by slow inches. He felt Grace's eyes on him but didn't care. Grace wasn't a buckle bunny out for an eight-second ride, whatever this piece of scum thought. If they weren't in a room full of people it would be a different story, but Mike held a thin rein on his temper.

When he turned he saw Grace staring at him, her face pale and eyes wide with something like fear and gratitude. He felt like he always did the moment he got bucked off, suspended and waiting to hit the ground of the rodeo infield. Good Lord, when had he fallen for her so hard? Right now, in this moment, he knew he'd do whatever it took to protect her. Knew if nothing else he wanted her to be *his*. Her words, "We don't want the same things…" rushed through his brain and he finally was certain of what he'd suspected all along. He did want those things. To settle down, make a home. To finish his house, living in it with her. The thing he'd never had going from foster home to foster home. And the staggering realization that it didn't scare him anymore. Well, he'd be damned.

Behind him more words reached his ears.

"Hey, I can't blame the guy. If I had a piece of tail that sweet, I wouldn't give it up, either."

He sent Grace a brief look of apology before spinning and delivering a single, punishing punch.

Chapter 6

The chair behind the man crashed to the floor as he backflipped over it from the force of Mike's punch. Mike followed, reaching down and lifting him up by his shirt collar as though he weighed nothing at all. In front of his face, Mike gritted his teeth and gave him a shake. The man's eyes bulged. "Apologize. Now. Or the only thing you'll be eating tonight is your teeth."

A thin line of blood trickled from the man's mouth where Mike's punch had split his lip open. "Sorry," he offered weakly.

Mike gave him a shake. "Not good enough. Not nearly."

"I beg your pardon, ma'am. No insult intended."

Mike put him down, curved his lips up in a cold smile. "Better. Now I suggest you collect your friends and find somewhere else to buy your beer. Red Deer's a few miles that way." He thumbed toward the door.

The three men with him didn't look like they took too kindly to that suggestion. Red Deer was more than a few miles down the road. But a quick survey of the room showed several locals standing at the ready. Vastly outnumbered, they thought better of it and cleared out.

Mike went back to his stool where Grace was waiting. Conversations struck up again.

"You need ice for that hand?" She asked it quietly.

"I'm good." He flexed his knuckles, wincing. Ice would have come in handy but there was no way he'd admit to wanting it.

"Okay then." She started to walk away.

Mike called after her. "You're welcome."

She came back then, and she didn't look happy, speaking in an undertone. "We'll discuss it later."

"Fine. You finish your shift and I'm taking you home."

"Don't you ever get tired of bossing people around?"

He chuckled. "I don't boss people around."

"Well, just me then."

"Something like that."

Grace made a frustrated sound in her throat. The man was so exasperating! He wasn't even flustered about causing a bar fight. When this got out...

"Fine." She slammed a glass down on the bar and glared.

Who did he think he was anyway? He waltzed in

here on a Friday night acting like he owned the place.
Acting like he owned *her*. There was nothing disgrace-
ful about making an honest living and paying her way.
Even if it meant she had to handle obnoxious men with
a little liquor in their system. She wasn't helpless. She
knew how to handle herself…either by joking around or
ignoring them altogether. And it wasn't like she didn't
have other guys around if things got rowdy. It *was* a
small town after all. But he just had to take it upon
himself to cause a huge scene. To look after everything.
He'd been doing that far too much lately. She'd thought
the other day they'd finally got past it. They seemed to
be friends again, equals. They'd met in the middle the
day he'd kissed her. She'd told him it could go nowhere.
But nothing she said seemed to get through his thick
head.

He'd picked that man up as if he'd weighed nothing
at all. He'd done it to defend her honor. She was spitting mad…and even angrier at herself because despite
it all, the very memory of it excited her.

As things started to wind down, she escaped to the
kitchen for a few minutes. Jack was starting to shut
things down and worked silently as she loaded the dishwasher. She and Mike had never been closer, despite
all the arguments. She'd sensed apology in his eyes
just before he'd thrown his punch, almost as if to say,
Sorry, honey, but I can't let that one slide. He'd kissed
her—not a brotherly kiss, but an all-consuming toe-
curling kiss. When they'd done that at his house, she
finally understood that he didn't look at her in a broth-

erly way. He saw her as a woman. As *his* woman. And he'd apologized of all things. Mike never said he was sorry to *anyone*.

She wanted to trust him again. But trusting her heart to someone came hard.

Nothing was making sense anymore. The closer they got to each other, the more muddled things became. She shouldn't have started any of this. If she could take back that single dance at the Riley's, she thought maybe she would. That had kicked it all off, and now she was going to have to put on the brakes.

Tears stung the backs of her eyes as she placed plates in neat rows on the bottom rack of the dishwasher. All that she wanted was within her reach. And to be fair to him, she was going to have to stop it now, before someone really got hurt. Before *she* really got hurt.

He was waiting for her when she came out again, his hat still sitting low across his forehead.

"You ready? I'll walk you home."

She should resist, tell him she'd go alone. But he'd only insist anyway. If she were going to set things straight and they were to be just friends after tonight, then she was going to enjoy one last walk home with him.

"I'm ready."

The air outside was fresh and crisp, a respite from the stale air inside the bar. "Frost tonight," she commented as they headed down Main Avenue.

"Feels like it."

Her stomach curled into itself when he took her palm

in his and they walked hand in hand. It was a simple gesture, but one so unlike the Mike she knew, her heart wept for what she knew she must do. Things couldn't go any further. She had to pass on any chance with him.

Their steps slowed, lingering, as their breaths made white puffs in the air before them. It seemed only seconds and they were before her bungalow. Too short. She wanted all the time she could have with him before sending him away.

"Here we are."

"Thanks for walking me home."

They wandered in as far as her back steps. She was two steps up when she turned. Mike removed his hat, holding it in his right hand as he gazed up at her.

"Can I come in?"

"I don't think so."

He paused, then followed her up the steps. She backed up until she was pressed against the door.

"Then I'll have to kiss you good-night at the door."

Her body shook, and it wasn't because of the chill. His hips pressed against hers, pinning her in place.

"Don't…"

She may as well have spoken to the air. He was already there, his body covering hers, warm and firm. His hat dropped to the doormat and he took her mouth completely.

One kiss, just one. Grace sighed into his mouth. The girls had been right. That night when they'd speculated about him. General consensus was that Mike would be a fantastic lover. If he did that as well as he kissed,

Grace knew she'd be a very satisfied woman. And as he pulled her against him, she was tempted to find out this once.

Except he'd be disappointed. The thought cooled her considerably. He thought she was something she wasn't…and now that he was obviously looking to start his own family… No, she couldn't face that. This time it would be her doing the leaving, and she regretted it deeply.

She broke the kiss and stepped away, digging into her pockets for her keys.

"Good night, Mike."

He put his hand on her screen door, preventing her from opening it. "That's it? After a kiss like that? Do I get to at least know why?"

Perhaps she should just come out with it and reveal all. A great uncomfortable silence would ensue and she wouldn't have to worry about Mike coming back. He'd be gone for good. Just like Steve, her ex-husband.

But she'd never told a living soul about the consequences of her accident. She wasn't ready. She didn't know if she'd ever be ready.

"I'm sorry. I'm tired. It was a long night."

He seemed to accept her excuse. "And I'm sorry about those idiots. Does that happen a lot?"

"Enough. I could have handled it."

He let go of the door. "Of course you could. You're doing such a bang-up job of handling your life so far."

He was baiting her and she knew it, but it gave her the opportunity she needed to push him away. "Considering it's my life to handle, I don't know why you keep pressing the issue, and why I must keep repeating myself. Your help was not required this evening."

"You're mad I hit him." He stated the obvious, his chin flattening with displeasure.

Heat expanded her chest. Never in her life had a man stood up for her that way, and even as she criticized him for it she knew it was one of those moments she'd cherish forever. For all his faults, Mike knew how to treat a woman. No man would insult her honor when he was around. After years of only having herself to rely on, it was a heady feeling, knowing he was there for her. She wished, somehow, she could be there for him the same way. But Mike never seemed to need anything.

"You would have had the backing of every man there, Mike. They all know you. The tavern's full of locals. If you'd asked those men to leave, they would have."

"And let him call you the equivalent of a tramp? I don't think so."

"He was being a jerk! It doesn't mean you have to turn into one!"

"Now *I'm* a jerk? Wow. So much for a little gratitude!"

"No one invited you to come in tonight, and no one asked for your assistance," she retorted coldly, wrapping her arms around her waist.

"Yeah, because you didn't even bother to tell me this was how you were paying for the new transmission. I had to hear from Alex!"

And Alex had seen fit to tell all and try her hand at matchmaking. It was all starting to make sense now. She uncrossed her arms and took a step, going toe to toe with him.

"And you came in and started a spitting match because someone had a bigger belt buckle than you!"

His gray eyes burned into hers in the dark. "You have to know why I did it."

"It doesn't matter." She swallowed. *Please don't say any more,* she silently begged.

His voice was a husky whisper as he came even closer, their bodies only a shiver away. "I think it does matter. You have to know my feelings for you. Grace, I…"

"Stop, Mike, please." The words came out thick with pent-up emotion. "Don't say any more. We can only be friends. Like we used to be."

"I don't believe you. I know how you feel in my arms, how you kiss me…not like old friends. You have to see I've started to settle down. I'm not on the road anymore. I have a business, and a house. Grace—I haven't been able to stop thinking about you since the night we danced. I want a second chance. To do it right this time."

That dance was going to haunt her for the rest of her life, she was sure of it. She should have kept her mouth shut instead of taking the dare. But she couldn't forget the memory of how it felt to be in his arms at last, the smell of him, the way their feet shuffled across the floor as he smiled his crooked, enigmatic smile down at her.

"That night was a mistake on my part." She wanted to get away, he was so close, but there was nowhere to go. Oh Lord, he was trying to make her see that he was worthy of her and it was breaking her heart. She wanted to be able to offer him what he was asking, but it was impossible. He deserved a woman who could give him what he wanted. A family of his own. One he'd never had before. And she couldn't do that. He said he wouldn't leave her, but she knew deep down that was exactly what would happen in the end.

"I had too much to drink and flirted where I had no right to flirt." She cleared her throat and strengthened her tone. "I'm sorry for giving you the impression there was more there. That's my fault. I did it on a dare."

His face hardened and she felt him close himself off to her. Grace fought back the horrible urge to cry. *Just go,* she pleaded. If he'd leave she could at least go inside and cry in private.

"I see. Then I guess I'll leave you here."

"I guess so." She knew she shouldn't ask anything of him now, but she couldn't resist. She didn't want to lose his friendship altogether. "Will you do me a favor?"

He picked up his hat and placed it on his head so she couldn't see his eyes. He was shutting her out, just like she wanted. She already missed him.

"Depends."

"Will you tell Johanna to let me know if anything happens with Alex? She's getting closer to her due date, and I'm still worried about her. Let her know if there's anything I can do…"

"I'll tell her."

He didn't say anything more, but went down the steps and up the driveway. Grace fumbled with her keys, going into the house and straight through to the front veranda. She watched him walk down the street until he was out of sight.

Then she gave in and let the tears come; hot, stinging ones full of regret for what might have been and what could never be.

Grace pocketed her tips and laid her folded apron on top of the bar. Three weeks had passed in a blur. Between her hourly wage and her tips, she'd paid for nearly two-thirds of the repairs on her car. The rest she'd make up with the extra she was making doing books for Circle M. She was tired and happy to be finished, and grateful for the brief, but profitable opportunity.

Keeping busy had kept her mind off of Mike, too, she thought as she walked home in the early evening dusk. Mike had taken a risk and shown his feelings and she'd done nothing but shut him down. Knowing him as she did, she knew it had to have been a hard thing for him to do. He deserved so much more. For Mike to ask for love…well, it was unheard of. She couldn't return it, no matter how much she wanted to. She'd told him it was a dare, flirting with him. It wasn't strictly true, but it had gotten the job done.

She reached home and entered, turning on lights as she went through. She sighed, grabbing a can of pop from the fridge and going out to her veranda to enjoy the quiet. Mike hadn't noticed her as a girl much, but he'd been a friend despite their age difference back then. If he thought someone was picking on her, he took care of it. When she got her driver's license, he and Connor had taken her out and taught her how to drive a stick shift in Connor's beaten-up pickup. After she'd broken up with her high-school boyfriend, he'd found her at her favorite spot, up on top of a hill west of town, looking over the Rockies. She'd been crying, but he'd admitted he'd come there, too, to think. Sitting in the tall grass, chewing on hay, they'd talked a lot, and it was there that he'd first leaned over and kissed her. She could still feel the wonder of that moment. For a few short weeks, they had grown closer. He'd been twenty-one, but their relationship had been tenuous and sweet. They'd held hands. Kissed. Had gone to a movie with Connor and his girlfriend at the time.

Their last date, Grace had made a picnic and they'd gone back to Andersen's field. A few days later she heard from Connor that Mike was gone.

Andersen's field was still her go-to spot when life got to be too much to handle. But they'd never met there again.

He'd been gone a lot, working, traveling to rodeos. She finished her senior year of high school and went to community college in Red Deer. Her first year she'd met Steve, her software applications instructor, and no one had been there to warn her of moving too fast. She'd married that summer, Steve got a new job in Edmonton and she went with him without finishing her certificate.

Grace put down the pop can as her stomach churned. She tried not to think about her failed marriage, but sometimes it was hard not to when she was alone on a Saturday night with only the hum of the refrigerator keeping her company. She'd rushed into it, partly out of hurt and partly out of defiance. And what a colossal mistake.

She stared out the window as full nighttime overcame the sky. It had been a night similar to this, and she'd been driving home from a night class. She hadn't seen the deer by the side of the road, and when it leaped in front of her she'd hit the brakes and wrenched the wheel.

That was all she remembered. When she woke up, she was in the hospital.

Consistent knocking on her back door brought her to her senses. She shook her head and hurried to see what the matter was. When she turned on the outside light, Mike was standing beneath it.

"What's wrong?" She opened the door without pausing, forgetting all about her earlier mental meanderings. She could tell by the worried lines on his face that something had happened. He hadn't even changed out of his work clothes, despite the hour, and his ever-present hat was missing.

"Connor took Alex to the hospital."

"But her due date is in a few days. There's no cause for worry."

Mike lifted his eyes to hers, and she clearly saw pain there. "She's bleeding. He didn't wait for the ambulance, just put her in the truck and went."

"Oh God. Come in."

"I'm following him in. If anything happens to her...I don't want him to be alone. She's his entire world."

Grace's lip quivered. Sometimes Mike was so guarded she forgot he had a sensitive heart. Every woman wanted to be loved the way Connor so obviously loved his wife. And of course Mike wanted to be there for his best friend. All their issues were forgotten as she looked into his worried eyes. "I'll go with you."

"I was hoping you'd say that."

She hurried to get her purse, fighting against the sense of doom that tingled down her spine.

When she came back Mike was waiting, holding the door for her. "Thank you for coming, Grace," he murmured as she locked the door. "I didn't want to do this alone."

She was touched that finally she could do something for him, after all the times he'd looked out for her. Any anger she'd felt about him being too protective evaporated when she saw the concern on his face. He was the same way with all the people that meant so much to him. "I wouldn't have it any other way," she replied, opening the door to his truck and climbing into the passenger side. "Alex and Connor are...well, we've all been linked for a long time, Mike."

Mike spun out the driveway and headed toward Main Avenue and the road east out of town. "Connor's the closest thing to a brother I've ever had, and Alex has made me a part of their family. If anything happens to her or the baby…"

Grace reached over and put a hand on his arm. "Don't think like that. Look at all they've been through already. She's tough and strong-willed. We're all going to come through this.…"

Her voice trailed off. It was so hard to focus on Alex right now when the very situation brought everything back to her so vividly. She looked over at Mike's tight profile. He was so worried over Alex and the baby. And all she could offer him was friendship. She missed the easy way they used to have with each other before she'd complicated things, and more than ever was convinced that they couldn't be both friends *and* lovers. If nothing else, she'd sit with him tonight in his worry. She'd be there for him in the only way she could.

It seemed to take forever to finally reach the hospital. Together they strode through the emergency doors to the triage desk. The nurse there said that Alex had already been taken to obstetrics and gave them directions.

The waiting room in labor and delivery was strangely empty and a television played to a nonexistent audience. Magazines were scattered on a table and a vending machine stood in a corner. Grace dug in her wallet for coins.

"Mike, I'm going to ask about Alex. Will you get us

some coffee?" She pressed the change into his hand, hoping giving him something to do would help.

He nodded.

When she came back, he was sitting on the love seat, holding both cups and staring at the television screen without seeing anything. It was tuned to the news, the anchor woman's muffled voice providing the only sound in the room.

"All they'd tell me is that the doctors are in with her. But I asked her to let Connor know we're here if she sees him."

They waited in silence. There was nothing to say.

Grace wondered if Steve had waited this way for word about her. Even now, the antiseptic smell, the hushed tones, brought back memories she'd rather forget. By the time she'd awakened it was all over, and all that was left to do was heal, or at least try to. And Steve would never speak of the accident afterward. Once, during an argument, she'd pried it out of him that he'd seen her with tubes and wires coming out of everywhere and that from his perspective, she hadn't been the wife he knew when she'd been like that. For a long time she'd wondered how to make him see she was still his wife, and not the prone patient hooked up to machines. She'd tried right up until the end.

She was surprised to find tears in her eyes. She'd cried about it lots in the beginning, but it was all in the past now. Had been since she moved back only a little more than two years after leaving in the first place. As far as the town knew, her marriage hadn't worked out, plain and simple. Some had said she married too young. She knew the truth. She hadn't stepped foot in a hospital since. Not until right now, and being here now left her raw and aching.

Mike's hand slid over and covered hers. "You okay?"

"I'm all right." She carefully kept her gaze away from his. He had an uncanny ability to see too much. "Wish we'd hear something."

Connor came around the corner, wearing a disposable gown and stripping off latex gloves. "The nurse said you were here."

Mike and Grace stood together. "And?"

Connor made it brief. "She's getting an epidural right now. Then I'm going into the O.R. with her. This baby's coming by C-section."

"Alex is okay?"

The night seemed to have put ten years on Connor's face. "She's hanging in there, but she's weak and they said the baby's in distress." His voice broke a little and he cleared his throat. "She's a trouper. Refuses to go under, insists on being awake for the whole thing. I've got to get back. But I'm glad you came. I'll let you know as soon as I have news."

"Connor?"

Grace's voice interrupted his departure and he turned back.

"Give Alex our love and let her know we're waiting to meet the newest Madsen."

"I will."

He strode back down the hall.

"I hate waiting."

Mike's responding laugh was a dry huff. "I don't think anyone really enjoys it." They walked back over to the love seat, consumed with worry for Alex and the baby, needing a distraction.

"If you could be doing anything right now, what would it be?"

He sat down. "Come here, and I'll show you." He patted the cushion beside him.

When she sat, he put his arm along the top of the back and curved it around her, pulling her close. She shifted, angling herself slightly sideways and leaning into his body, pulling his arm around her securely. Even knowing it was wrong, nothing felt better than being held in his arms.

"Connor's worried." His voice rumbled softly against her hair.

"Of course he is."

"They lost one already, you know."

She cranked her head to the side, trying to look up at him. "They did?"

"She had a miscarriage before this pregnancy. Connor told me when she went into early labor the first time."

"I didn't know that." Now all the caution and worry made sense.

"Alex is in there fighting for their baby."

Her throat closed against the ball of emotion that settled there.

"Right now, Grace, holding you is the only thing that makes sense."

Grace gave up the struggle. Nothing else mattered than the right outcome for the people that had come to mean so much to them both. She wrapped her arms around his strong one, turning her head into his shoulder and dropping a kiss against the muscle there.

"Then hold on to me, Mike."

Chapter 7

Connor didn't return with the news, but a nurse on silent shoes did, at two in the morning.

"Mr. Gardner?"

Mike shook Grace gently, never taking his eyes off of the sight of her sleeping. Strands of her pale hair fell over her cheek, lending a look of innocence. Her face was peaceful, even more beautiful than usual with the lines of stress gone.

"Grace, wake up."

She sighed and he felt her burrow deeper into his arms. It was so right, having her there. At times he was sure she felt it, too. When she stopped fighting him, the connection between them was undeniable. Strong and pure.

But there was news and as much as he wished he

could hold her all night, he reluctantly said her name again.

"Grace."

Her eyelids fluttered open, staring up into his and his breath caught. Her lips were slightly open and her gaze was as blue as a September sky. In that one unguarded moment, he knew she'd lied about the only-friends part. Something was holding her back, but he knew there was more when she looked at him that way. They had a connection. She was as tangled up in him as he was in her.

"The nurse is here."

She sat up, fully awake now, and Mike immediately missed the feeling of her warm body curled against his. Grace tucked the errant strands of hair behind her ears and straightened her clothing, looking up at the nurse.

"Alex? And the baby?"

The nurse smiled. "Both fine. Mr. and Mrs. Madsen are resting, and the baby is a strapping boy. Mr. Madsen asked me to tell you that his name is James Michael Madsen."

Mike grinned, a flash of brightness that sucked the stress out of the room and filled it with brilliance. "Son of a gun."

"He also sent this message." She pulled out a small piece of paper. "Tell Grace to get Mike home and make him sleep, because I'm taking a few days off."

Grace laughed. "If they're resting, we'll just go. We can come back another time and see them. Thank you for letting us know."

"You're entirely welcome." With a parting smile, she was gone again on quiet shoes.

Now that the heavy feeling was gone, Mike's grin was wide and relaxed. "James Michael. I can't believe he did that. I had a feeling he'd name it after Jim if it was a boy, but not me."

He leaned back in his chair, remembering the day Connor's family had died and the guilt that Connor had carried around for years. "I was with him when he got the news, you know," he told Grace softly, as if saying it louder would be disrespectful. "A bunch of us had gone to Sylvan Lake for the day. We swam, took out a boat, had a cooler of beer…just the guys out for a day of R and R."

Grace was turned and watching him now. "I didn't know that."

"I'll never forget the look on his face as long as I live," Mike continued. "He insisted on driving down to the accident scene alone. And he's never talked about it since. I know I'm not James, but he's the closest thing to a brother I've ever had."

The very idea that someone thought enough of him to bestow any part of his name on their child just seemed too huge to comprehend.

Grace smiled up at him. "You're touched."

"Of course I am." He looked down at her, confused at her obvious surprise, still reeling from the news and the feel of her body against his.

"You don't think you're special enough for someone to name a kid after you?"

"Something like that."

"Don't underestimate yourself, Mike. You've got a family already, whether you like it or not. Just because they're not blood, doesn't matter."

He gripped her fingers in his. "I'm beginning to see that."

He let his eyes gaze warmly on hers. For a moment he considered kissing her as their gazes clung, but then he straightened as if nothing had passed between them. It wasn't the time. But he wanted to come up with some way to keep her with him longer. If he kept trying, perhaps he could break down the barriers she kept erecting between them.

"I'm not going to be able to sleep now. How about I buy you breakfast?"

"At two-thirty in the morning?"

"Why not? There's got to be something open twenty-four hours."

"I don't know, I…"

He tugged on her hand, leading her to the elevators. "There's blueberry pancakes in it for you."

"Now you're playing dirty. You *know* those are my favorite."

When she pulled back on his hand he paused. Of course, just because he was pumped didn't mean she was. He'd almost forgotten how hard she'd been working. She'd want to get home and rest. She probably had a busy day tomorrow.

"I didn't think," he apologized, slowing down and

pressing the down button on the elevator. "You must be tired. And with your schedule…"

"I do have a demanding boss."

He wrinkled his brow. "Someone giving you a hard time?"

"He's expecting me to show up in the morning and if I stay out all night with you, I'm not going to be much good."

"He won't understand about Alex? Which job are we talking about here?" If it came to it, he'd explain to this person himself. He stood taller, squaring his shoulders.

"I guess I could talk to him." Her eyes twinkled up at him.

Mike stared down at her as a pretty smile curved across her face.

"So, how about it, boss? You gonna be mad if I don't show up in the morning?"

He grinned, realizing she was teasing him and he teased back. "I can guarantee that all it'll cost you is a bite of pancake and a smile."

"Then let's go. I don't think I could sleep now, either."

Mike killed the engine and Grace pressed a hand to her belly.

Her house waited, dark and lonely, and she didn't want to go inside. She was still too fragile. At the hospital she'd fallen asleep, but even in her slumber she could hear the beep of machines and hushed voices. When Mike had awakened her, she'd been so glad to see his face above hers. She felt safe there. For a moment, as she'd looked into his eyes, there'd been nothing but the two of them in the universe. And then she'd awakened fully, getting the good news about Alex and the baby.

On the heels of that was a keen sadness of knowing what had brought her to this point in her life. She'd painted on a smile, happy for the good news and pleased for Mike. She'd teased Mike, thinking that diversion was as good a plan as any. But even breakfast at the twenty-four-hour restaurant hadn't helped. She'd thought by staying away, giving herself some time to acclimatize, she'd be fine, but exactly the opposite had happened. It had given her feelings time to build until they were nearly overwhelming. She was a mess.

"Well, we're here." Mike's voice interrupted her thoughts and she jumped.

"Hey, are you okay?" He shifted in the seat, looking over at her. "You're white as a sheet."

"I'm just tired," she managed to get out. It was a lie.

Over pancakes and coffee she'd fought the feeling that she was losing complete control of her life. She'd tried to enjoy Mike's company, share in his joy about baby James. But seeing him that way was a stark reminder of all he wanted now and all she couldn't give him. Of all that she wanted to give him, even knowing there was no possible way she could. And the heartbreak of losing chance after chance.

Every day for six years she'd thought she'd dealt with the changes fate had brought to her life, but now she knew she really hadn't succeeded. Being in the hospital had been difficult, and had brought back memories of the last time she'd been there. But she and Mike had been focused on Alex and the baby and somehow even that had delayed her reaction. But now, knowing everyone was safe and happy and healthy, it drained every bit of strength from her. If she went inside now, alone, she wasn't sure she could make it through five minutes without completely losing it. And that thought scared the hell out of her. She knew how long it had taken her to function again after the last meltdown. She'd spent several months numb to everything, protecting herself in a shell of not feeling anything at all. She'd do *anything* to keep that from happening again.

"You want to come in?"

"You need your sleep. I've kept you out late enough, don't you think?"

She regarded him in the dim glow of the dash lights. He was so strong, so sure of himself. All legs and boots and lean muscle, always ready to do what needed to be done. A man to count on. Could she count on him now?

"I…" She swallowed. "I don't want to be alone."

"You want me to sit with you?"

Her breaths came shallow and quick. "I want…" She looked into his eyes. His were earnest and open, inviting her to explain. He waited patiently, one wrist slung over the steering wheel.

She needed him, and it frightened her to admit it out loud. She glanced back at the house. The other alternative was to go in there alone and finally face the fact that she could never be what she wanted to be. Dealing with that right now was far more scary than facing this attraction, or whatever it was they'd been doing lately. Once he knew the truth, he'd run for sure. What if this was her only chance? Could she let it get away?

Taking a breath, she blurted it out. "I want to be with you, Mike."

"Be with me," he echoed. He didn't sound sure of what that meant, and his eyebrows furrowed in the middle.

She faced him squarely. Yes, being with Mike was what she wanted, so much more than facing what was waiting for her inside. For a second, images flashed through her head like the rapid shutter of a camera: the red lights of the ambulance, the drip of her IV, the sound of the doctor's voice and the kind look in his eyes, Steve's telling her he was leaving, Connor's face tonight. She couldn't breathe, couldn't feel. And she needed to feel right now, something other than pain and failure. She needed life and hope.

He was waiting.

"I want you." She said the words with her heart in her throat and saw his eyes widen. "I've always wanted you, Mike."

"Grace, I…" He paused. Then blindly reached for the keys and shut off the engine, leaving the truck still and silent.

"Maybe we should talk about this."

Grace's responding laugh was dry and humorless. The very idea of the reticent Mike wanting to "talk" about things was out of character. He was putting her off, she could feel it. Humiliation stung at the back of her eyelids and she grabbed her purse with one hand while struggling to open her door with the other. "Never mind," she stammered, fighting with the strap of her purse which got entangled on the seat belt. "Forget I mentioned it."

She ripped the strap free and slammed the door, trotting to the house before she lost it completely.

His door slammed and he called her name.

Her keys were buried in her purse and she tore open the zipper, frantically searching. What had she been thinking, propositioning him? This time she didn't have alcohol as an excuse.

"Wait."

He put his hand around her wrist and her fingers stilled.

"Grace, don't run away from me. You've been running all fall. I can feel it. Even though we were getting closer, you kept holding something back. I just want to know why that changed tonight."

She turned slowly. His gray eyes were asking hers for an honest answer. The yellow glow from her porch light danced off the copper tints of his hair. Maybe this would be her only chance, and if that were the case, did she really want to spoil it by admitting to him she could never give him the family, the kind of home life he wanted? Wouldn't it be better to go away with one beautiful memory of what loving him was like? It certainly beat the alternative of sending him away and having to face all her shortcomings alone as the sun came up.

"I've wanted you for nearly half my life. And tonight I realized I was tired of fighting it. Of thinking too much, doubting every move. Of doubting you. I want to feel. And I want it to be with you. Is that wrong?"

"No, baby, it's not wrong." His voice was husky with relief and he pulled her close, tucking her within his arms.

She felt his lips press against her hair. One large, gentle hand slid up her back and beneath her hair, taking command of her neck.

"I want you, too, Grace. I've thought about it ever since the night we danced. Since long before then."

"You have?"

He tipped her neck up. "You don't believe me?"

Her breath came quicker at his burning gaze. "It's hard to believe."

He didn't answer. Instead he bent his head and kissed her, taking her mouth completely. His lips commanded hers to open and his arms pulled her close against his body.

He pressed his forehead to hers as the kiss broke off. "Do you believe me now?"

Grace slid her hand up his arm, marveling at the feel of the muscles corded beneath his shirt. "But you never said anything before."

"I was waiting for you to be ready. I was waiting for me to be ready. It took a long time for me to get to a place where I was ready to stop running. Even after I moved back for good…I didn't think you'd give me a second glance. I left you before… I didn't want to be unfair to you." He paused, then commanded, "Look at me."

She did, captured by the honesty in his eyes.

"I'm not running now, Grace."

She lifted his hand and pressed a kiss to the palm. Releasing it, she reached into her purse and got out her house keys. With shaking hands she fed the key into the lock and opened the door.

She left the foyer light off, instead walking straight through to the kitchen. The outside door shut with a click, and she heard Mike turning the lock again. The simple sound was filled with such intimacy—the closing out of another world, keeping them in their own cocoon of each other.

She stood in the middle of the kitchen floor, suddenly unsure of what to do. It seemed everything was firsts today. First visit to the hospital since the accident. The first time with Mike. The first time she was going to make love since her divorce. She shuddered as his hands fell on to her shoulders and his body warmed the skin of her back through her sweater. Her eyes slid closed, her body heavy with languor. Six long years. It seemed an eternity since she'd been twenty-one.

"I'm not sure what to do," she whispered softly.

He chuckled, the vibration of his chest causing rippling reactions through her stomach. "You *were* married, Grace. It's like riding a bike."

"Yes, but…" Her voice dropped off. This was weird.

This was the problem with falling for someone who was also your friend, she realized. She wanted him to see her as brand-new, as his lover, yet at the same time longed to reveal things to him, things that were safe because of their long friendship. For a moment she wanted to believe that he meant what he said. That he wouldn't leave her.

"But?" He turned her to face him. "You keep looking away from me. Are you scared?"

"Not of you," she admitted. Still she couldn't look in his eyes.

He bent at the knees so their eyes were level. "Are you telling me this is your first time since your divorce?"

She turned her head away, but not before she felt heat creep up her cheeks. "You must think I'm... Oh, I'm not sure what you think."

"I'll tell you what I think." His hands skimmed down her ribs and settled at her waist. "I think I'm glad. I find I'm very relieved that there hasn't been anyone since."

"Why?" His thumbs toyed with the waist of her jeans and she couldn't help but meet his eyes, colorlessly dark in the dim light.

"Because I hate the thought of any man's hands on you but mine."

Her breath caught as his fingers played with the hem of her sweater. His lips touched the side of her ear, down the lobe. "Right now I'd kill any man who dared to lay a hand on you."

For weeks she'd fought his possessiveness, but now,

in his arms, she reveled in it. Gloried in it. Right now, in this moment, she was his. There was nothing she'd ever wanted more.

Her fingers trembling with anticipation, she undid the bottom button of his shirt, then the next, and the next, until finally the cotton gaped open, revealing a slice of strong chest. He cupped her jaws with his hands and pulled her against him, dropping his mouth to hers. The man knew how to kiss. She moaned deep in her throat and his arms tightened around her, so close now that her back arched a little. Her hand slipped beneath his shirt, touching the warm skin along his ribs. The tips of her fingers traced a scar, the skin smoother and tighter along the line of the wound. He lifted his mouth long enough to say against her lips, "When I was eighteen and still green."

She'd be lying if she said his rough rodeo past didn't add a little excitement to the puzzle that was Mike. But now she knew that this side, the side that he was giving to her, was more than she'd ever imagined she'd have. It was strong and beautiful and she wished he would look at her forever the way he was looking at her now.

She reached for the hem of her sweater and pulled it over her head, standing before him now in only her low-slung jeans and plain black bra.

Without saying one more word, she took him by the hand and led him to the bedroom.

Chapter 8

Grace rolled over at the sound of raindrops hitting the glass of her bedroom window. She looked at her clock radio: 1:42. She'd slept through the morning. A deep, dark, satisfied sleep.

She rose, grabbing her robe from behind the door and shoving her arms through the sleeves. Memories of what had happened in the early hours still caused tingles to spiral through her body. Now things were even more complicated, if that were possible. Just when she decided that she and Mike had to remain friends, she'd done something so insane she needed her head examined. Sleeping with him was avoidance of her own hurts, pure and simple, and worse, he'd started showing her a new side of him. One that made him even more irresistible. Now she knew he was tender, caring and completely consuming as a lover. More than she'd ever imagined in her dreams. It wasn't supposed to happen like this!

She wandered to the kitchen, thinking a cup of tea might soothe her. She'd make some toast, and have a think about what to do next.

Entering the kitchen she saw the folded paper on top of the kitchen table, propped up against one of the pewter candlesticks. Opening it she saw his scrawl, legible only because she was so familiar with it. *Hope you slept well. I'll pick you up at five-thirty so we can visit Alex and the baby. Love, M.*

Love, M? Grace stared at the writing, her heart sinking. Oh, what had she done? She should have known Mike wasn't a typical guy. He was the kind of guy who never wrote notes or said the word *love* unless he absolutely had to. He was a man who'd grown up with little affection in his life. One who took every bit of it to heart but rarely gave it out. He thought she didn't understand, but she did. And he was suddenly turning the tables and giving it to her. A woman who desperately wanted it but didn't deserve it. Didn't know what to do with it.

At some point he'd awakened and left. That didn't hurt her feelings; she knew he had a ranch to run, especially in Connor's absence.

What frightened her to death was what in the world she'd say to him when she saw him again.

Schoolgirl fantasies were gone. She was crazy about him. Had fought it, told herself it was wrong for him, picked arguments against their developing intimacy. But she'd awakened in the solitude of her room, with the warm feel of him still in the sheets. She admitted to herself that it had always been Mike for her, even after he'd abandoned her. Her feelings for him had dictated so many choices in her life, good and bad. It would be the albatross around her neck for as long as she lived.

She had actually taken advantage of him. Used his feelings to her own purpose and she was deeply sorry for it. Sorry that she hadn't been able to be completely honest with him because she was terrified of losing her one chance to know what it was like to be loved by him.

Somehow she had to get through the visit to the hospital. Then she was going to have to talk to Mike. She had to tell him the truth. It was the only thing that was fair to him.

He picked her up at five-thirty as promised. Mike ran a hand through his hair before opening the door, expecting to do the old-fashioned thing and go in to get her, usher her to the truck and out of the light rain. But before he could do it, she met him coming around the hood of the truck instead of giving him time to come in, the hood of her raincoat protecting her hair and making her blue eyes stand out like beacons.

"Hey," he offered as a greeting and accompanying it with a smile.

She was so beautiful, he realized, even more so after what had transpired last night. Now he knew the sweet taste of her; the feel of her soft skin beneath his fingertips. The way she arched her neck and whispered his name in the shadows of dawn. Now he knew what it was like to be hers, and he knew more than ever that he wanted to be with her for more than just a single night. He imagined her in his bed at the new house; drinking coffee with him at the kitchen table in the dew-kissed mornings. He wanted to make up for the past. Show her she could trust him to stay.

He leaned in and dropped a light kiss on her surprised lips, the strawberry taste of her gloss clinging to his mouth. He pulled away, smiling down into her eyes before going to open her door. Silently she climbed up into the cab, settling herself while he slammed the door behind her.

"You're quiet." He put the truck in Reverse and slung his arm over the back of the seat, negotiating his way out on to the street.

"Just tired."

His head swiveled back and he was charmed to see a blush infuse her cheeks. He didn't need to say anything. They both knew the sun had already been up by the time they'd fallen asleep, and it had changed to rain by the time he'd awakened. She'd been naked and in his arms, and when he quietly left, she was still curled up in the bedding, warm and well loved. If he could, he'd forget all about the hospital and go back there again. But Connor was expecting them and he had no idea how to suggest such a thing to Grace.

He turned his attention to driving, gesturing with a

thumb toward a plastic container on her lap. "What's in there?"

"Cookies. Chocolate chocolate chip."

"Chocolate overload?"

"Alex's favorite, I've learned. She's going to be in there a few days, and eating hospital food." Grace grimaced with disgust. "She can do with some treats, trust me."

The change of subject relaxed the atmosphere in the truck. They let the radio fill the comfortable silence as they drove to the hospital. Once there, they made their way directly to the maternity wing and from there to Alex's room, just down the hall from the nursery. Mike looked in at all the babies lined up in their clear plastic bassinets, but didn't see any with the name Madsen on the card. He wondered how many of these tiny parcels were wanted and loved and how many had been surprises and complications, like he'd been. He watched as one baby—a girl—waved a tiny mittened fist in the air as she cried, and he wondered if anyone had come to see him when he was born. It was a question he didn't dwell on long, for he knew he would never know the answer now.

There was at least one baby in this hospital that he knew had been wanted. Baby James was lucky. He'd been planned and loved long before he'd ever been born. And that was how it would be for his own children someday. To shower them with love and to let them know how wanted they had been.

Alex was sitting up in bed, finishing her supper

when Mike and Grace walked in. Connor sat in a vinyl chair beside her, and the rolling bassinet was by the window. Mike caught a glimpse of white and blue blanket.

"I see our timing's right. I brought dessert," Grace announced. She held out the container, smiling when Alex beamed up at her. Mike went over to the window next to Connor's chair.

"Connor told me you guys stayed last night. I appreciate it."

"We were worried," Mike chimed in. "But you did great, Alex."

"I did, didn't I? And what do you think of our little Jamie?"

Connor lifted the tiny blue bundle out of the bed, cradling him in his arms. "He's got excellent lungs already," he joked. "When he's hungry, you know it."

"Like his daddy," Alex added. She shifted tenderly in the bed.

"You must be sore," Grace remarked, but her voice lacked its usual vigor. She went to Alex and helped adjust her pillow. "C-section isn't easy, huh."

Mike tilted his head and watched Grace. Normally she was easy and welcoming, but for some reason she seemed tense and awkward. There seemed to be some strain around her lips, and her eyes seemed to evade rather than invite.

"I thought labor with Maren was bad, but right now I'm just so drained, you know?"

Grace stepped back but Alex reached out for her

hand. "But that doesn't mean I'm not glad to see you. I am. Profoundly. Especially if that's chocolate in that dish."

"Would I bring you anything else?" She opened the lid on the dish, holding it out for Alex to pick a cookie.

Mike took off his coat and laid it over the back of the second chair. "Hey, you wanna hold him?" Connor's voice came quietly from beside him.

He pushed back his hat a little. Hold the baby? It wasn't something he'd ever done before. With Maren he'd played, but not when she was this young. He'd always let someone else do the holding. But times were changing, by the minute it seemed. He looked over at Grace, perched on the edge of the bed with Alex and chatting over cookies. He could easily picture her with a baby in her arms, one with white-blond hair and big blue eyes. And the thought of Grace having anyone else's babies...

Now that was a picture he couldn't reconcile. No way.

"Go ahead. You'll be fine."

Mike made a vee with his arms and Connor shifted the blue and white bundle. "Make sure you support his head and it's all good."

Mike shifted his arm so that the tiny head was cushioned against his bicep. He looked down at the little face, the nearly transparent eyelids and the way Jamie's lips sucked in and out as he slept. Mike crossed one ankle over the other, leaning back against the windowsill and making himself comfortable.

A complete little person. Warm and trusting. And he was surprised to discover that holding him was the most natural thing in the world.

His eyes met Grace's and held, burning with the remembrance of making love only hours before. Her soft sighs in the gray darkness. The silken touch of her skin against his.

"It's about time."

Connor's voice interrupted. Grace ripped her gaze away from Mike's and turned her attention to Connor, confused. "About time?"

"That you two finally came to your senses." He grinned widely at his wife. "You owe me ten bucks. I *said* it would be before Thanksgiving."

"Sneaky," Alex grumbled at her husband. "That's only a few days away."

Mike's smile only widened. Why shouldn't he be happy? He'd thought about being with Grace for months, and things were finally moving forward with them. Their friendship had deepened. And last night… last night had been indescribable. He felt a connection with her that he'd never felt before.

"I think we're busted, Grace." He adjusted the baby and winked at Alex. "Seems you had it figured out before we did. Better late than never, though."

He looked at Grace. She was sitting stiffly on the bed, and the thin smile she pasted on her face wasn't real. Dread curled through his belly. Was she regretting last night, then?

"So, what happened between you two? No sense keeping secrets now."

Mike could clearly see that Grace was uncomfortable and kept to his habit of few words. "I don't know what you're talking about," he answered cryptically.

Alex nudged Grace with a hand. "And look at that. Holding Jamie as if he did it every day."

Grace dutifully looked up at him. And what he saw in her eyes shocked him.

Sadness. Deep-in-the-soul sorrow. And for some reason she looked almost apologetic. Why in the world would there be tears fluttering on her lashes?

Alex didn't even seem to notice how quiet Grace had gotten. Baby James started to fuss and Mike started moving his arms in a soothing motion, his eyes never leaving Grace's wounded ones.

"Just think, Mike, what kind of babies you two could have."

Babies. His and Grace's. Instantly his face warmed. What if... Oh God. They'd been so tired, so keyed up he hadn't even given protection a second thought. What if Grace ended up pregnant after last night? He felt none of the dread he thought he'd expect in such a situation. Instead the idea of having babies with Grace was distinctly alluring. His gaze darted to her belly and back up.

Apparently she was having the same thought, because all the color had drained from her face. He saw her visibly exhale, and then gasp for air.

Without a word, she jumped off the bed and darted from the room.

"What in the world?" Alex looked to Connor and Mike. "Did I say something?"

"I don't know," Mike answered. He handed Jamie back to Connor. "But I'm going after her."

He jogged out of the room. If she was worried about getting pregnant, he could reassure her on that score. He certainly wouldn't abandon her. Exactly the opposite. At the end of the hall he saw the staircase door slide shut. When he got there, she was halfway down the first flight, sitting on the cold metal risers and crying so hard each sob was a gulp for air.

"My God, Grace! What's wrong?"

"Just leave me alone!"

"Not likely. Not when you're like this." He lifted her off the steps and folded her into his arms.

She sagged against him for a few minutes until she regained some sense of control. But when he took her by the shoulders, he felt the tremors there. Her face was pale and her eyes haunted with misery.

"Grace, if this is about us forgetting to use a condom last night…"

"A condom?" The words came out coated with disbelief. "You think…"

"It's my fault, but I just want you to know that if you get pregnant, it'll be okay." He dropped light kisses on her bruised eyelids. "More than okay, in fact. You have to know I wouldn't leave you. Not again. Please believe me."

It seemed to be the exact *wrong* thing to say. Her breath started jerking again, holding in sobs that were fighting to get out.

He cursed, clearly afraid for her now. She was as close to breaking as he'd ever seen her. "We need to get you out of here."

"I want to believe… I can't… I mean we need to… I have to tell you something, Mike, and I…" The words just kept stammering out, making no sense.

"Not here."

She nodded, her breath coming in short spurts. "I hate hospitals, did you know that?"

It explained a lot about his sense of something holding her back the last few days. Now that he thought about it, each time they'd come through the hospital doors she'd donned some sort of invisible armor. "I'll go back and get our coats and take you home. We can talk there."

"Thank…you."

When he was gone, she sat back down on the steps, trembling. It had been Alex's words that set her off. Between the hospital and the baby and her exploding feelings for Mike, she'd been a bomb ready to go off.

What kind of babies you two could have…could have…could have…

Those words echoed in her head over and over. This was supposed to be a happy day. No beeps or hushed, worried voices. No sickness, just joy at a healthy baby boy being brought into the world. But that wasn't what it meant to her. It meant nothing less than complete devastation and she was strangled by her own despair. Now Mike was worried about not using protection and that she might be pregnant. If it weren't so heartbreaking, the irony would be hilarious.

Mike came back with their things, gently helping her with her coat before donning his own.

"What did they say?"

"They're just worried about you. Alex is sure she said something wrong, but I assured her you'd be fine." He zipped up his jacket.

"Thank you."

"Except you're not fine."

He took her elbow and they went down the rest of the steps to the first floor, then out through the lobby and to the parking lot. Once in the truck, he turned to her. "Where do you want to go?"

She didn't want to go home, that much she knew. She'd hidden away in her house far too much already. Besides, right now it was a place full of memories of Mike, and she was going to find it difficult enough to get through this without remembering how he'd kissed her in the kitchen or how they'd made love in her bed less than twenty-four hours ago.

"I want to go to the ranch," she said.

It was full dark by the time they got there. The only light on was the living room. The rain of the day had soaked into the grass, heightening the musty smell of fall leaves. "Do you want to go inside?"

She shook her head. "No. I need to be out here, where I can breathe."

He led her around the house to the pergola that Connor had built. The rosebush that had bloomed around the bottom of it this year was now brown and brittle. Wood and iron benches flanked it, surrounded by small perennial beds—Alex's handiwork.

Grace went over to the latticed arch and ran her fingers down the painted wood.

"Connor built this for Alex, did you know that?"

"He built it for their wedding." Mike's voice was low and strong in the silence of the evening.

A husband and babies. Things that Grace had always wanted. But she'd lost one and couldn't have the other.

The loss of it overwhelmed her and tears came again. She went over to the bench and sat down, crying quietly, the drops falling hot and painful on her hands.

Without a word, Mike sat beside her, took her in his arms and let her sob it out.

When it seemed that she was quieting, he rubbed her back gently. "You going to tell me what happened in there? What's causing all this pain? Because it's clear to me this has been building up for a long time."

Grace leaned against the hard wall of his chest, too exhausted to move. Right now it felt as though the whole universe was conspiring against her. She'd been the one to start the ball rolling. She'd wanted to be with Mike, but it had never been like this. Fantasizing about him as a lover wasn't remotely the same as falling for him as a man. Mike himself seemed happy about how things had developed between them.

That in itself was a complete turnaround. For years

he'd been Mike Gardner, bronc rider, self-proclaimed bachelor and all-round tough guy. But not now, and not with her. Now he was Mike, businessman, friend, lover and potential family man. The one person she could count on. And he needed to know she was not who he thought she was. Even if it meant she lost him.

He ran a warm hand over her back. "I'm sorry, Grace. I screwed things up between us and I'm trying to make up for it now."

"What?"

She lifted her head. He thought this was about him. And she supposed in a way it was. When he'd treated her like she was disposable, she'd retaliated by moving away, marrying Steve. It didn't make sense now, but at eighteen it sure had. His leaving had precipitated her making the biggest mistake of her life.

But it was her mistake to own, not his. He was not to blame.

He didn't look away but faced her straight on, the very picture of honesty. "I need to tell you why I disappeared. I need you to understand."

He drew back a little and took her hands in his larger ones. "I'd gone my whole life without love. I knew how to deal with that. But I didn't know how to deal with the feelings I had for you. And suddenly you had feelings for me. Being with you was...beautiful. It was all I had imagined and for that reason I was terrified that it wasn't real and it wouldn't last.

"I knew I couldn't bear it if you broke up with me. I had come to care for you that much. You have to understand that every time I thought I'd found a family, I'd been shipped off somewhere else. Maggie was the only one who put up with me and I didn't make it easy, even for her."

He sighed. "Don't you get it Grace? I was falling in love with you and too scared to admit it. So I did what was easy. I left."

Oh God, he was laying his heart bare and she didn't think she could take much more.

"It wasn't easy for me."

"I know. When I came back, you'd married and divorced and were living in your little bungalow. I told myself you'd moved on and that I deserved that. I knew that I had blown my chance with you and that it would be wrong for me to ask for a second one. I didn't want to lose what friendship we had left. But then at the Riley's, you gave me hope. I knew if I just had time, you would…"

"Stop."

Grace lifted her hand, closing her eyes and willing him to stop talking. He couldn't know what his protests of constancy were doing to her.

"You need to stop, Mike. You broke my trust when you walked away. Not only walked away but did it without saying a word. No call, no letter, no nothing. How do I know that you won't leave again when something gets to be too much for you?"

"Because I grew up, Grace. And I learned from my mistake. That's how you know."

"What do you want, Mike? What are your dreams, your hopes? What's your vision of the future?"

She held her breath, fearful of how he'd answer yet needing to know.

He lifted his hand, gently covering her cheek with his palm. "I see you, Grace. I see you and me and Circle M. I see our children. For the first time, I *see* a future."

Tears gathered in her eyes. "And what if one of those things doesn't work out? Will you cut and run if it gets too much?"

His brow furrowed. "I don't understand. What are you asking?"

"I'm sorry," she murmured, grasping the hand on her cheek and drawing it down into her lap. "It must seem like I'm talking in riddles. And I'll explain, but you have to let me or I won't get through it."

The cool of the evening seeped through her coat and into her bones. This, then, was the moment of truth. This was the test of his devotion and she'd give anything to be able to avoid it. But it had to be done. Sooner rather than later. To let things go on was only asking for greater hurt.

"I just couldn't handle it...the hospital...the baby... the look on your face when you held him..."

His wide hand squeezed her knee. Regret flooded through her. He deserved so much more. He'd done nothing except drive her crazy with his constant meddling—his way of showing his support and caring. He'd made amends for the past. She'd put the wheels of all this in motion and now it was her job to stop it.

She pulled away from his touch and looked up into his face. The moon tried hard to peek through the clouds now that the rain had passed. His eyes were soft with concern for her, a tenderness that broke her heart.

"I should have told you long ago. But...but I've never told anyone what I'm about to tell you. It was just too hard."

"Whatever it is, just tell me." He tried a reassuring smile. "I know you, Grace. It can't possibly be that bad. You're too good a person."

She wasn't, and that was what he didn't understand. He'd somehow put her on a pedestal, thinking she was something she was not, thinking it was his job to protect her. But the damage had already been done.

She leaned back against his arm. "When I left Sundre for school, you were still drifting. I was angry with you for what you had done to me and in a way, I suppose I was determined to show you that someone cared about me the way you didn't. The logic was flawed but I was thinking with my feelings. I was only eighteen. I met Steve and everything happened very quickly. By the time you were back working in town, we were married and moving to Edmonton. And you were gone again. When I came back a few years later, you were still gone. Riding the circuit. Working at ranches. Whatever suited you at the time. You were always...temporary. And I kept to myself, telling myself that I wanted to preserve the friendship we'd had before. Mom and Dad had retired and gone to Edson. But I didn't know where else to go but home."

Mike's hand stroked her thigh, warm little trails of sensation down the back of her leg. His touch was so comforting, and she hated what she had to do next.

"But you know all that." She focused on the memories of what had come during those "gone" years that Mike didn't know about, so that she could get through it without breaking down again. She relayed it as a reporter would: emotionless and matter-of-factly. It was the only way she'd manage without falling to pieces.

"Steve wanted children, but not right away. He wanted us both to work for a while longer. Wait until we could afford it better. I was driving the highway one night on my way home from a night class and a deer jumped on to the road in front of me. I swerved, but there was traffic and I had to snap the wheel back. I hit the deer and put the car off the road, hitting a tree."

His hand stopped moving. Her heart beat a little faster, knowing what was coming and fearing his reaction, wondering if it would be dismay, disappointment, repulsion. None of those were things she wanted him to feel about her.

"When I woke up, I was in the hospital, in intensive care. I'd ruptured my spleen, had internal injuries. It wasn't for a few days that I finally heard what they'd done to me in the O.R. I'd had a perforated uterus. They…" Her voice broke a little but she summoned her strength and carried on until the end. "They did a hysterectomy."

Now that it was out, she swallowed against the hard lump of tears lodged solidly in her throat. She'd done it. She'd said the words, but it didn't make her feel better. All it did was make it more real than it had been in a long, long time. It was the death of hope.

With dread she looked up at him.

Mike's hand had left her leg and was covering his mouth. He was clearly shocked, staring at her with a mix of dismay and disbelief.

His fingers scraped down over his jaw and chin. "You never told anyone? Not ever?"

"Steve stayed with me through recovery, but nothing was the same. We just…fell apart. He wanted things I couldn't give him." *Like you want things I can't give you,* she thought. She'd never wanted to have that feeling again—the encompassing, true feeling of utter failure. Of feeling like less of a woman than her husband wanted. It had eaten her up after the accident and now it threatened to do so again. She made herself go on, to finish it and get it over with.

"Steve filed for divorce. He didn't want a wife who was damaged. Nothing fit into his plans anymore, you see. He'd had it all worked out, and suddenly nothing made sense, and he saw it as my fault. I came home. And I've tried to…" She stopped. Two tears dropped from her lashes onto her lap as she stared at the material there, willing herself to hold it together.

"The bottom line is, I can't have children, Mike. Those babies you're picturing? I'll never be able to give them to you."

Moments of heavy silence followed, until Mike stood up. He paused. "I don't know what to say."

But what he didn't say said everything for him. She could feel his withdrawal in the cool night air. He was pulling away from her, just like she knew he would. He could say all he wanted about being sorry for leaving her in the past, but this moment was the truth she had always known.

"I know this is a shock to you."

His face was flat, devoid of any expression at all. "I saw the scar last night, but I thought it had been from when you had your appendix out."

"No. It's all from my internal injuries. I didn't even have a say…I just woke up and it was gone."

"I'm sorry," he got out, then abruptly turned, walking away toward the barns, his steps quickening the farther away he got.

He was doing what she'd expected. Leaving. Just like before. Without a word of ending. But it didn't stop how much it hurt to watch him go.

Everything in her wanted to go after him.

But she couldn't. She knew she didn't have the right.

Chapter 9

She'd put it off long enough.

Day after tomorrow was Thanksgiving, and Grace hadn't been to Circle M since the night she'd told Mike about her accident. Nor had he called. Alex was home from the hospital now and the last of the leaves were struggling to stay on the trees in the early October chill.

She took her purse from the hook and grabbed her car keys. It was no less than she'd expected, after all. He didn't need to say the words for her to know. She'd already been made to feel like less of a woman. And she cared about Mike too much to pretend to be something she was not. She needed to get back to building her life again. Only this time she'd make the right decisions.

Before she lost her courage again, she locked the house and hopped into her car. It was high time she got back to work. She owed the garage another two hundred dollars and change, and then she'd be free and clear. But financially it didn't spell the end of demands. Impending winter meant higher heating bills. Now that the baby was born, Alex would be itching to take the books back over within a few months. And then Grace wouldn't have to worry about running into Mike so much. It was bad enough that he was stuck in her thoughts night and day.

She turned the key in the ignition. Only to be rewarded by a constant clicking sound.

"You've got to be kidding me," she growled at the car. "Start, dammit!"

She tried again, but nothing.

The last time she'd had car trouble Mike had literally ridden to her rescue, but he wasn't there to save her anymore. He'd run, the way she knew he would. His silence said everything. She was back to relying on herself. And that was just what she was going to do.

She went back inside and called the garage. Thirty long minutes later Phil was there to give her a boost. With Mike in the passenger seat of the truck.

What in the world was he doing here?

Phil popped the hood while Mike hung back a bit. Grace put her hands in her pockets. Of all the ways she'd thought they'd meet next, it wasn't this way.

"Hey, Mike," Phil called. "Turn it over, will you?"

Mike sent her a long, complicated look and then moved to get in the driver's side of the car, dutifully turning the key.

"Again?"

Still, there was nothing but a recurring clicking sound from under the hood.

"She's dead, all right."

Mike got back out of the car. "I'll get the spare from the truck, then."

Grace followed him. He wore the usual jeans and boots but had eschewed his cowboy hat, leaving his head bare. "What are you doing here?"

Mike's gaze fell on her. "I was at the garage picking up a part for Connor when you called. Phil was coming out alone—I thought he could use a hand."

That was all, then. Grace looked away as Mike took a new battery to Phil and their two deep voices blended as they spoke. Mike had been there anyway and was being helpful. The way he always was. The closeness she'd felt between them before was gone.

It was a new beginning, and she should have been happy that he wasn't avoiding her any longer. They could perhaps start rebuilding their friendship. She knew it was what she *should* want. But she could still feel what it had been like to have him surround her, skin to skin. Forgetting wasn't going to be easy.

The engine roared to life this time, and Mike got out, leaving it running and the door open.

"You're all set now, Grace." Phil wiped his hands on a rag from his pocket. "You can catch up with me later."

"Thanks, Phil." She tried to sound grateful, but instead felt only frustration.

He probably wouldn't charge her for coming out to

the house. But there was still the cost of the battery that would be added to her bill. Something else on the never ending list of not getting ahead.

Mike went back to Phil's truck and Grace's eyes followed him. He was cold, so cold. So distant. And she'd done that. With Phil here, there was no way they could talk. And he obviously wasn't seeking her out to put things right. She squared her shoulders. There was no sense weeping about it. What was done was done.

She went up to the driver's side window. "Thanks, guys. I appreciate you both coming out to help." She said the words to them both but her eyes clung to Mike's.

"You're welcome," Phil answered. Mike lifted a finger carelessly, only to realize his hat wasn't there. Normally she'd have teased him, but not now. It was almost as if there was too much between them, weighing them down, making smiles and light comments impossible.

With a wave, Phil was gone.

She got into her running car and headed toward the ranch. At least she knew Mike wouldn't be there since he was running errands in town.

From the outside, Windover looked exactly the same, but inside, it was a changed place. Grace could feel it as soon as she walked in the house. Alex was home again, and there was newborn evidence everywhere. In the kitchen it was a bouncy seat on the top of the counter. She passed the laundry room and saw a basket of tiny blue clothes next to a small bottle of baby laundry detergent. All reminders of a life she wouldn't have. She went into the study and shut the door.

Get in, get it done and get out, she thought, settling into the chair and booting up the computer. If she could get this finished, she wouldn't have to come back for a few weeks. She dreaded seeing Mike now, knowing he was going to look at her differently. She didn't want to see that look of disappointment. Perhaps space and a little time would make it easier, instead of the raw wound it was now.

A knock on the door startled her away from her spreadsheet and her head swiveled to the doorway.

"Alex! Shouldn't you be resting?"

Alex stepped inside. "Are you kidding? I've spent weeks in bed. It's a relief to be up and about and thirty pounds lighter." She smiled at Grace. "I really just wanted to come in and ask if you would stay for a cup of tea with me after you finished. Gram's taken Maren to Millie's to make pies for the church sale and Connor's out with Mike."

At the mention of Mike's name, Grace averted her eyes. "I should finish up in another few minutes."

A thin cry echoed from upstairs and Alex smiled. "Oops, take your time. The boss is awake." She slipped from the room and Grace heard her go upstairs, her soft voice soothing the baby.

When Grace finished she packed up the things and left everything on the desk. The way Alex was bouncing back, she might want to take over again anytime. She'd miss the money, but maybe it would be easier for them both to simply move on if she wasn't around anymore.

She went into the kitchen. It was empty, but she moved to the patio doors anyway, looking out over the vast, brown landscape that dipped to the foot of the mountains. They'd had snow at the higher elevations, and the peaks were pristine white against the piercing blue of the sky. Two figures moved off to the left. Connor and Mike on horseback, she realized. She knew her car was visible from the barns, and even knowing they were leaving things unspoken, Mike hadn't sought her out. It hurt, even though she knew she had no right to be mad. She'd slept with him without telling him the truth; he'd responded by baring his heart to her. She couldn't blame him for being angry about it.

She turned from the window and went looking for Alex, finding her in the living room. She halted at the door, instantly embarrassed to find Alex nursing Jamie in the rocking chair. "Oh, I'm sorry."

Alex looked up. "Don't be. Come on in." She smiled at Grace.

Grace took a seat in the chair to Alex's left. She wasn't accustomed to seeing someone breast-feed, let alone be so relaxed and casual about it. Even though she could see very little between the baby's head and the flannel receiving blanket tucked around him.

"Are you okay, Grace?"

Grace looked up, but didn't know what to say. Her eyes met Alex's. She'd gone so long without trusting anyone with the secrets of her heart, but her emotions had been so up and down this fall that suddenly they were all so overwhelming. And her relationship with Alex had grown over the last months. She'd let the secret out once, and felt the undeniable urge to unburden herself to someone who might not run away. She knew she could trust Alex.

Alex misinterpreted her silence, withdrawing. "I'm sorry if I'm overstepping."

"No, no, of course not," Grace assured her. "I'm just not used to talking about it, that's all."

"I thought you could use a female perspective on whatever's going on between you. Neither one of you is happy."

Grace tensed, unsure of what to say. "My relationship with Mike isn't like yours with Connor."

"But the other night, he went after you and brought you home. I know you two have gotten closer lately."

"Not anymore. I sort of fixed that the other night."

"You argued?"

"Not exactly…but we talked. I think it's safe to say Mike isn't interested in who I turned out to be."

Jamie's head drooped slightly and Alex looked down, an affectionate chuckle escaping her lips. "He fell asleep." With a finger she wiped a dribble of milk from the corner of his mouth.

Deftly she put everything back in place and wrapped him up in his blanket, rocking the chair gently. "Mike is crazy about you, Grace. We weren't wrong at the hospital, were we? Something happened."

Grace nodded as the words came spilling out. "Yes,

something happened. The night you had Jamie. But I did it for the wrong reasons, and now he knows, and he walked away from me and it's just all gone wrong."

"I don't understand."

Grace trusted Alex, as a woman and as a friend. She took a breath. "When I was twenty, I had an accident and they had to do a hysterectomy. You know what that means. It spelled the end of my marriage. The night Connor rushed you to the hospital and you had Jamie…that was the first time I've been in a hospital since the accident. I was feeling vulnerable and fragile and didn't want to be alone…so I…I wasn't."

"But Mike would understand that," Alex said.

"He didn't know."

"About the hospital?"

"About the accident, about me not being able to have children, none of it."

Understanding dawned in Alex's eyes. "Until we opened our big mouths when you came to visit. Oh, we prattled on about having babies and teasing the two of you, and all the time you were hurting. I'm so sorry."

"No! Don't be! It's not your fault. You couldn't have known, and you were right. Things were happening. But I was feeling raw and I knew I had to tell Mike and then someone mentioned babies and I just couldn't take it anymore. I should have told him sooner. Oh, Alex, he was so caring, thinking I was upset about maybe getting pregnant. But you have to understand." She met Alex's eyes evenly. "Until that night, I hadn't told anyone. Not even my parents."

"And what happened?"

"We came back here and I told him everything. He just walked away from me. Didn't say a word. Just turned and walked into the barns and left me sitting there all alone."

"Connor mentioned he drove you home and that you'd been crying. But he's not like me. I meddle. I think it's a requirement of motherhood."

"Mike is really mad at me."

"He's surprised, that's all," Alex countered.

"No, not surprised. Well, maybe he is, but he's more disappointed. I know that. I've known Mike a long time. We dated once, and he hurt me badly. He's apologized for all of it, and instead of things working out I've thrown a whole monkey wrench into the works."

She ran a hand through her hair. "He pictures himself having the family he never had before. He's told me so. And I can't give it to him. I let things go on between us all the while knowing how he'd react. So he's not to blame in this. I am."

"And that had better be the last time I hear you blaming yourself for anything. It was an accident, Grace."

"I don't know when I would have told him. We seemed to argue so often, and then things started happening and is there ever a right time to spring news like that on someone? Oh, I've messed things up big-time."

Alex adjusted the baby. "Have you spoken to Mike since?"

Grace shook her head. "No." She sighed. "My battery died this morning, and he was at the garage when

I called. He came out with Phil and they put in a new one, but he was like a stranger."

Alex muttered something about stupid men under her breath. "We're having dinner here on Monday. I want you to come."

"You should enjoy your holiday. You don't need our *atmosphere* getting in your way. Right now it might be better for us to keep our distance from each other and move on. So we don't hurt each other further."

"Nonsense. The longer you leave things without even seeing each other, the worse it's going to get. We're eating at one. Where else are you going to go, hmm?"

Grace started to speak but Alex cut her off. "If you say home alone, I'm going to come over and shake some sense into you."

Grace's stomach fluttered at the thought of being in the same room as Mike. What in the world would they say to each other? Would he say anything at all?

But then…losing Mike's friendship was a difficult pill to swallow. Perhaps Alex was right. If they got this first meeting over with, perhaps they could start putting back together the friendship they'd had over the years. Maybe that was more important than anything else.

"Oh, all right. Only if Johanna's making cranberry stuffing."

At Alex's raised eyebrows, Grace laughed. "*Everyone* knows about Mrs. Madsen's famous stuffing."

"I'm putting Jamie to bed now, and we'll have that cup of tea." She rose from the rocker and gave Grace's arm a squeeze on the way by. "Thank you for telling me, Grace," she said softly. "I know it wasn't easy. But take it from one who knows. Finally trusting someone with your secrets is the real way to start healing. Things are going to get better. You just remember that."

It sure didn't feel like anything was healing. Grace stood on the front porch of Windover, holding a scalloped glass bowl of coleslaw and too scared to ring the bell.

What would he say? How would he look?

How would he look at her? Happy to see her? She doubted it. Uncomfortable, surely.

"You waiting for the butler?"

Connor's voice came from behind her and she jumped. "Just being chicken."

"Today's a day for turkey, not chicken. Besides, it's just dinner. There's nothing that's been done that can't be fixed."

Oh, but there was. She couldn't take back time; the accident, the operation or how she'd slept with Mike before telling him the truth. She couldn't repair the damage done by those things. But she smiled weakly. Connor was only trying to help. She wondered how much Mike had told him. Being men, probably very little.

"I can smell it out here," she admitted, smiling at him.

"Then let's eat," he said, rubbing his hands together with anticipation.

Grace laughed as he opened the door.

"It's about time you came in," Alex scolded, wagging a finger at her husband before bustling around the kitchen once more. "You need to wash up and the turkey is going to come out any minute for you to carve."

"Yes, dear," he answered cheekily, heading for the bathroom and soap and water. Grace put her bowl of salad on the counter as Johanna put Maren in her booster seat. She hung her coat on the row of hooks by the front door and was just turning back to ask Alex if she could help with anything when Mike turned the corner into the kitchen.

They both halted and stared across the table at each other. Grace swallowed as they stood there like idiots. He'd obviously come in and showered. His hair lay thickly against his head, a couple of curls springing forward as they dried. His face was smooth and freshly shaved, the red shirt he wore neat and pressed. Grace realized suddenly that red was his favorite color. He wore it more than any other.

Finally Mike spoke first. "Happy Thanksgiving, Grace."

She tugged at the hem of her sweater. She wanted to say *I'm sorry* and a million other things to him, but instead merely answered, "Happy Thanksgiving."

"Mike, will you light the candles? Grace, if you could put the rolls on, we're ready to eat." Alex issued last-minute instructions.

When the table was loaded everyone sat down, baby

Jamie snoozing contentedly in a Moses basket on the counter.

Alex asked Connor to say the blessing. Belatedly Grace realized that Alex was playing matchmaker even with seating arrangements. Alex and Connor sat at the head and foot. Johanna sat on one side, supposedly to help Maren with her dinner, which left Mike and Grace to fill out the other side. To make matters worse, everyone was joining hands. She gripped Alex's on her right and after a prolonged second, Mike took her left hand in his.

Just that much…that simple touch…told her that no matter how she'd blown things apart the other night, they were far from over—at least on her part. Mike meant more to her. As his hand covered hers firmly, she realized that Mike was *everything*. She had to try to find a way to rebuild their friendship. It was all she could have now, she knew that. But he was too important to let their connection go completely.

The blessing was over and the kitchen was filled once more with chatter and the clattering of silverware against china. Grace dutifully filled her plate with the traditional dinner: turkey, stuffing, snowy mashed potatoes with a puddle of rich gravy, bright orange carrots. There was her coleslaw and cranberry sauce, and a traditional Scandinavian turnip casserole.

She realized her folly when she attempted to swallow the first bite. She had a plate loaded with food and no inclination to actually eat it. Beside her, Mike bumped her elbow as he buttered a fresh roll. She shivered. She wanted to forget the food and touch him. Put a hand on his warm thigh, strong beneath the stiff denim, and feel the reassurance of his body close to hers. When had he become her comfort? She wasn't sure, but it was true. She'd come to lean on him. And she felt the absence of that closeness acutely, especially now when she felt like everything was falling apart.

She managed to get through the meal, and got up to help Johanna with dessert. Without asking, she put a slice of warm apple pie with ice cream on a plate, and then squeezed another piece of pumpkin beside it. Johanna started with the coffeepot while Grace served the pie.

Mike's face split into a wide smile when she placed the plate in front of him. He looked up, for the first time his expression unguarded. "How did you know?"

She smiled back. "I've known you for nearly twenty years. Of course I knew."

His gray-blue eyes warmed and for the second time she longed to apologize. For a minute it seemed he wanted to say something. The moment drew out and Grace realized no one else had pie yet. She turned back to the counter, but felt sure his eyes lingered on her.

The coffeepot was drained and a second put on; Jamie woke up and Alex disappeared to change and feed him. While she was gone, Grace and Johanna started on the massive cleanup. For Alex to host such a dinner so soon after delivering was ambitious, even with Johanna's help. Grace was determined Alex be spared the dishes.

Connor took Maren upstairs for her afternoon nap while Grace loaded the dishwasher and Johanna ran water in the sink for what wouldn't fit in the dishwasher racks. Mike, the odd man out, looked after clearing the table linens and taking the leaf out of the pine table.

When the dishwasher was humming happily and the last of the things were tucked away, the afternoon was waning. Grace peeked in the living room to say her goodbyes, but the scene before her wrenched her heart completely.

Connor sat in the corner of the sofa, one foot on the floor and the other along the cushions. Alex sat in the lee of his legs, resting against him, her head turned to his shoulder. And Jamie lay on her chest, his tiny head facing Grace so that she could see the perfectly formed lips and the eyelashes lying against his cheeks. All three were sleeping. Connor's right arm covered Alex and his hand rested on the tiny foot of his son.

It was so perfect that Grace stared at them with a heavy heart. It was something she and Mike would never have, and never had she felt the absolute desolation of the knowledge as acutely. Finally, feeling like she was intruding, she backed out of the room and went to get her purse. There was nothing more for her here. With her emotions in so fragile a place, she really wanted to avoid having to deal with Mike and all the feelings she was having trouble holding inside.

"Heading out already?"

Mike's warm voice stopped her and she turned to see him in the hall behind her. Why now, when she was feeling as low as she possibly could? It took great fortitude for her to try to smile normally and reply, "Everyone is resting. I thought it was as good a time as any to sneak away."

"Would you be sneaking away from me, then?"

He wasn't smiling, wasn't teasing. His eyes probed hers, asking for time and for the briefest of seconds, she wanted to lift her hand and smooth it along his jaw.

It was an honest question and deserved an honest answer. She held his eyes with hers as she answered truthfully.

"Yes, I probably would be."

"I'm sorry about that."

He was apologizing to her? She didn't expect it and she knew they had to talk it out, even if the very idea frightened her, simply by acknowledging what needed to be faced. He had nothing to be sorry for.

"I'm the one who's sorry."

Still he didn't move.

"I should get going," she continued.

"Why don't you take a walk with me first?"

Oh, how she wanted to. But there was a dangerous thing called hope and no matter how much she wanted to preserve their friendship, she knew that allowing herself to hope was a mistake. Dragging out all those feelings again was just opening a wound.

"Mike, I..."

"When do I ever take no for an answer?" He finally smiled. "Just a walk. It's a beautiful fall day, and we might not have many more this nice before winter's here for good. Cold front's coming in and we're in for some damp, chilly weather."

She paused again and his casual smile faded. "Please, Grace. I want us to talk."

She put down her purse. "All right. I'll go."

He took her coat and held it while she threaded her arms through the sleeves. His hands lingered just a moment on her shoulders, then he reached past her to open the door.

Chapter 10

Mike led her south of the barns through the pasture. Ever since she'd told him she couldn't have children, he couldn't figure out how he should react. He felt all sorts of things about it: hurt, anger, disappointment. For them both. But that wasn't her fault. It was his. He'd walked away, then hadn't attempted to make contact. He'd done exactly what he'd said he wouldn't. She'd been so cold to him today he knew she was angry and hurt. Even now, her mouth was set in a remote line and her eyes evaded looking at him at all. And hurting her further was the last thing he wanted to do.

He let the silence settle things for a while as their footsteps crunched through dead grass and dried leaves. He stopped and plucked a daisy, amazed that it still survived after the frosts they'd had. He stared at the white petals, then handed it to her silently. She took it, twisted the stem in her fingers, a small smile finally playing on her lips. It felt right, like she was more receptive to him and ready to talk, and he took her hand, guiding her to a huge boulder. She climbed up and sat on its flat top, pulling her knees up to her chest. Mike hopped up beside her.

"I'm sorry," he began as they both stared off at the valley that dipped to the southwest. He'd never apologized to a woman since he'd begged for Mrs. Hawkins to keep him when he was nine, but he needed to say it a lot lately to Grace. The jagged line of the Rockies spread before them and Mike breathed deeply, searching for the words. "I shouldn't have walked away like that, and I'm sorry."

She didn't look at him. "I was wrong in not telling you before."

He turned slightly. God, she was strong, he realized. She'd dealt with her personal tragedy on her own, had come out still standing tall. Her hair blew back from her face in the westerly wind, her cheeks prettily pink in the cool fall air. The last thing she should be doing is blaming herself.

"Is that why you think I'm mad?"

"It's something you should have known before we slept together."

"And you think that's a deal breaker." He prodded her, trying to discover how she really felt about all of it. It was true. He was angry that she hadn't told him before, but not because they'd slept together first. With

Grace, for the first time ever, it wasn't about sex. There
had been women before and after her, but they hadn't
been in his heart the way she was. It was about her and
he felt cheated that she hadn't trusted him with it.

"Isn't it? Can you say that you would have taken
things that far if you'd already known?"

He hesitated. What if she was right? If he'd known in
advance, would he have pursued her? Kissed her? Made
love to her? He wanted to say yes, that it didn't matter,
but he honestly couldn't. If he'd known she couldn't
have children, he might have stepped back and thought
about it long and hard before letting things develop.

"It doesn't matter if I would have or not. We did, and
it's that we have to deal with," he evaded.

"You want things I can't give you, so what we did is
really irrelevant. I don't blame you for walking away
the other night. I expected it. That's why I put off telling you."

He turned away. She thought he was angry because
she hadn't told him about her condition before they'd
had sex. She couldn't be more wrong.

"I didn't walk away from you in anger, Grace," he
answered. "I was shocked. It was not what I'd expected
and I wasn't clear how to handle it. But I wasn't mad,
I promise you that." On the contrary. He'd ached for
her. Her pain had been raw, fresh and debilitating and
he hadn't known what to do to help her. He knew he
should have had the right things to say, but that had
never been a strong point of character with him. He'd

always been a man of plain words, not one that always had the right thing to say at the appropriate time.

He should have done something but at the time he couldn't escape the horrifying image of her lying in a hospital bed.

Or the red anger of knowing the man she'd married had used it as an excuse to end their marriage. He hadn't known what to do with those feelings churned up inside, but he knew one thing…he didn't want her to have to deal with them. He'd walked away.

Grace held back the tears but couldn't keep her chin from wobbling. "Disappointed, then."

"Grace." He took her cold hand in his, couched it between his palms. His skin warmed hers and she clung to the sound of his voice, even and strong.

"I am not disappointed in you. What happened wasn't your fault and nobody blames you. You have to know that."

She finally looked up at him, her eyes bright with anguish at his kind tone. How could he not be disappointed with her when she was with herself? It was so clear to her that Mike wanted things she couldn't give him. She used her pain like armor to keep him away, save herself from further hurt.

"Steve blamed me. Enough that he moved on to a whole woman."

"He said that? A whole woman?" Grace watched Mike's fingers flex and bunch by his sides. "Forget Steve." Mike scowled. "Steve doesn't warrant your consideration. You are no less of a woman. Believe me."

A hint of a sad smile tipped her lips. "Thank you for that. But Steve isn't the point, either. I've seen your house. I know that you built it with a family in mind. And I also know how much that means to you." She lifted her face to the mountains. "I know how you grew up, Mike, and I took advantage of that."

He turned his head away, but not before she saw his expression change. For a moment he almost looked guilty.

"You think you took advantage of me." He snorted out a chuckle.

"I slept with you knowing it was temporary. There can't be anything long-term between us. You know that." Her heart cracked a little even as she said the words. It was true, but saying it made it seem more permanent.

Mike stepped off the rock and walked away, shaking his head. He spun back. She watched him evenly, gathering all the strength she had to keep from crying. She knew things about Mike that very few people knew, and one was that he'd had his share of people casting him aside. She didn't want him to think she was doing that. She was setting him free to find the life he really wanted.

She longed to throw herself in his arms but knew it would ultimately be unfair. Turning him away now would be less hurtful than what would happen if they ignored the facts. So she watched him, trying to accept the inevitable. Hoping he would, too, so she could hold her head high and lick her wounds in private.

"Sleeping together was my fault. I knew you were upset and I did it because I wanted you. If anyone took advantage, it was me. I should never have expected you to give me more."

Just when she thought she couldn't hurt any more. He thought she didn't want him? Was he crazy? He was all she'd dreamed of for such a long time she wasn't sure she could forget *how*. Wasn't sure she even wanted to.

All the resentment she'd harbored over the years bubbled over. But she held her temper. If it had to end now, she didn't want it to be with a drawn-out argument. They'd done their share of that this fall.

"I mean, I'm not that guy," he continued. His voice held an edge of "I don't care" attitude. "I'm not the kind of man a woman loves, I know that. I made the mistake of thinking there was something more between us. But I was wrong."

She stared at him, watching him withdraw into himself. He was shrugging this off as if it was nothing, but she knew better. That was what he thought this was about? Not being lovable?

God, would he never get it?

"This isn't about you!" Her knees dropped down and she braced her hands on the gray stone. "This is about both of us needing things that we can't give each other, don't you see that? I know how you grew up. I know you think you don't deserve love, and that's wrong. I get it, Mike. But your past doesn't matter to me. It never has! That isn't why, so don't brush this off as some fatal flaw you have!"

She knew he'd been tossed from one foster home to another. Always passed off to be someone else's problem until his cousin Maggie stepped in. Maggie had tried, everyone knew that, but she'd been young herself, and unprepared for a boy on the edge of manhood invading her space. Grace remembered his face years ago when he'd casually tossed away the comments made about his childhood. He'd worn the same devil-may-care expression then, too. The one she knew hid a whole lot of pain. The one that told her he'd die before admitting she'd hurt his feelings.

The closest he'd ever come was when he'd found her crying in a field. To make her feel better, he'd revealed a few paltry slivers about what his young life had been like. And then he'd kissed her, and she'd dared to hope. She'd only dated the other boy to try to get Mike's attention.

She was now very well acquainted with what he'd felt back then—loneliness and utter inadequacy.

He couldn't know how much what he'd been through mirrored exactly how she felt about her marriage to Steve. She'd never measured up. How she'd tried to please him, live up to an ideal that didn't exist. And how could she possibly do that again? If it hurt leaving Mike now, how much would it kill her when he finally realized she'd never be what he truly wanted?

She gentled her voice. "You don't think I saw how

lonely you were, or how much you longed for a real family?"

"Is that what you think this is about?" He backed away from her kindness, putting more distance between them. "I don't want your pity!"

His voice echoed down over the hill and to the valley, the words ringing in her ears. Indignation burned through her.

Nor did she want his. She hopped down from the boulder, squaring off against him. "And that's what I'm saying! We want different things! It's not wrong for you to want a family, and the home you never had! But don't you see? I can't give them to you!"

"I'm not asking you to carry my burdens for me!"

They were shouting at each other now, and she let the anger and frustration carry her. "That's pretty funny, considering you've tried running my life for the last two months!"

"We're back to that again?"

"Why are we arguing again?" She exploded with frustration.

"Because I care about you, dammit!"

Her chest heaved with invigorated breathing, and she struggled to regain control. He cared, yes. But he hadn't once said he loved her. And that was probably for the best after all. Especially if things were ending here.

"Then care enough about me to be my friend. That's all we can be."

His gaze met hers, long and complicated. Her heart

pounded, wanting him to say the words, even though she knew it would be a mistake. Wanting him to say he would fight for her, even though she kept pushing him away. That he would fight for them.

She watched as the anger drained away from him. His face relaxed. But now, with his frustration gone, he simply looked sad and empty.

Mike's voice was soft as he answered. "I'll always be your friend, Grace, you know that."

Her breath hitched. Why, after everything, those words made her want to cry, she didn't know. She held on to the thin thread of control, swallowing several times and trying to exhale slowly.

The whole discussion had been a roller coaster of ups and downs, understanding and anger, and Grace wanted off. When he held out his hand, she took it, let him pull her in and rested her head against his wide chest. His heart beat there against her ear, strong and fast. His arms circled her, protecting, soothing.

After several minutes, she finally spoke. "I was afraid we'd lost this."

His heart leaped.

"Lost what?" He tilted his chin down, gazing at the top of her head and the tip of her nose.

"The other morning…you were so cold. I don't think I could stand it if I lost your friendship, Mike. It means a lot, knowing you're here when I need you. I've always known it. Always."

"I couldn't say anything to you then, not in front of

Phil. I wasn't sure how you'd react, but I had to know you were okay."

She pulled out of his arms, looking up. He looked so much shorter, so much more approachable without his hat, she realized. Although the cowboy hat lent another sort of allure to him. "I thought you were done with me for good. I thought I'd lost a friend as well as…" She paused.

"As well as a lover?"

"Y-yes."

His gaze seared into hers, but his words belayed what his eyes were saying.

"It's getting dark. You should get back."

"You're not coming?"

"No, you go ahead. I'm going to check the west pasture."

He was avoiding her already, she realized, and despite their agreement to be friends, she knew he was distancing himself. It was what was right, she supposed. Only it hurt more than she'd ever imagined. She didn't want to go, but there wasn't anything left to say. At least this time they'd ended it with words.

"All right. Happy Thanksgiving, Mike."

"You, too."

She turned on a heel and walked away. She didn't look back, couldn't. She didn't want to know if he'd walked away, too, or if he was still standing there watching her go.

When he couldn't hear her footsteps anymore, he turned back around. She was already at the gate. With a sigh, he dropped down on the boulder, resting his elbows on his knees.

Damn.

Now that she was gone, he could think about what had just happened, because in the thick of it emotions had gotten in the way. In his mind he went over and over what had been said...and what hadn't.

Her anger had only masked her pain, he realized that now. And he'd played right along with it. As much as the spunky, independent Grace had driven him crazy, he would have given anything to have her back in place of the wounded spirit he knew she was trying to hide.

He wasn't angry that she didn't tell him, and he wasn't disappointed in her. That much, at least, was clear. It was equally clear to him that she *was* angry, and disappointed in how things turned out. And she had every right to be.

The sun dipped lower in the autumn sky, and a chill settled, seeping through the fabric of his shirt. He chafed his hands together, keeping them warm. There were some things he hadn't been able to say. It was obvious she was hurting and he didn't need to add to her burden. But the truth of it was, knowing how much pain she was in, knowing why, he felt completely and utterly helpless.

She had no uterus. That was the plain, ugly truth. There would be no babies for her, not ever. It had cost her not only children but her husband, and now she thought it had cost her him. She was blaming herself and he could do nothing to fix it. And that was what he knew how to do. Fix things. But nothing he could do could change what had happened to her. He could not make this go away for her and it was the one thing he hated the most.

He'd wanted to say "Let me help you," but he didn't know how. How in the world could he make that right for her? What was done was done. He realized she was taking their relationship down from where it had gone and leaving it as friends only, and he resented it even as he understood why she was doing it. She was giving him an out and trying to preserve their long-time friendship. She was turning him away.

His jaw clenched against the pain of it. Just friends. Was that all he was good for, then? And yet, he didn't have the heart to be angry with her for it.

He had been cold, but only because he'd felt incredibly awkward and guilty for leaving her when she'd needed him. In hindsight he should have stayed, tried to help her through it, made sure she got home all right. Instead he'd left it up to Connor. Like a coward, Mike had hidden with his horses until Connor got home. The next morning, Connor had eyed him speculatively over the breakfast table, but Mike had remained stonily silent. He didn't like that about himself.

He hadn't put all this in motion to just walk away now. She had healing to do, and he didn't want to press the issue right at this moment. But she wouldn't get rid of him that easily.

He stood up, suddenly seeing the daisy he'd picked sitting wilted on the stone beside him. He picked it up,

the head of the flower flat on the palm of his hand.
The daisy was strong and resilient. Just like Grace. He
tucked it in his shirt pocket.

She needed to be convinced.

What she needed was wooing.

Daisies appeared everywhere she went.

On the dash of her car when she left Mrs. Cooper's
after cleaning her house. Tucked in the handle of her
screen door. On the desk at Windover when she went
to do payroll. One every day, until she began looking
for it. Wondering where it would show up next. Wondering why.

She had no doubt as to the who, however. She knew
it was Mike. He'd given her the first blossom on
Thanksgiving and there'd been one every day since.
What she didn't understand was why he was doing it.

He wanted children, had said the words to her. And
knowing what he knew, why was he still pursuing her?
It was ridiculous. He had to know it was over between
them. She wanted him to stop this nonsense so they
could keep the good memories of what had been.

She stopped at the grocery store, and then paid a visit
to Phil. When she left the garage, it was with a sense of
relief and freedom. Her repair bill was finally paid. It
was one less thing for her to worry about, a small detail
in the overall scheme of things but something positive
to cling to. And she'd done it on her own.

It was nearly dinnertime, and she realized there had
not been a daisy today. She quelled the disappointment

stirring in her heart. When had she started expecting them? She wasn't sure, but as she drove home she knew that at some point she'd started looking for them to show up. And as much as she wanted him to stop it, she couldn't help but wonder where the next one would turn up.

Perhaps her lack of communication had finally got through to him and he was done. It was what she wanted, right?

Twilight was settling in early these days and the afternoon was starting to dim when she pulled into her yard. She grabbed her bag of groceries and went up the back steps, pausing at the mailbox to pick up the day's mail.

And there was her daisy.

She didn't know where he was getting them. It was too cold for them to be blooming wild anymore; they had to come from a florist. The stem of it was taped to a tiny envelope. She slid her finger underneath the flap and pulled out a plain card. It was adorned only by Mike's rough handwriting, and like the man, it was of few words.

Saturday night, 7:00 p.m. Housewarming at Mike's, Circle M Ranch. BYOB. Music and food provided.

Not a request for a personal assignation, then. She wasn't sure if she was relieved or not. And for a moment she considered not going. But then she lifted the flap on the card and he'd scrawled two words. *Please come.*

She knew she couldn't ignore the personal request. And she also knew she was incredibly curious about how his house had turned out.

She probably would regret it, but as she went inside she was already planning what she was going to wear.

Chapter 11

The lights were blazing from Mike's windows, the drive filled with cars and trucks of various sizes when Grace pulled up and killed the engine.

Even from the distance down the lane, she could hear the steady thump of a bass drum coming from the garage. The huge double door was up, and she could tell by the sound erupting that the band was set up there with the flat, concrete floor acting as a dance floor for those so inclined. Normally she'd be excited about this type of party, so common among the community. But tonight she felt alone, outside the festivities. The fact that it was carefree, no-one-can-tie-me-down Mike that was celebrating a new house made everything seem more odd.

Grace made her way past the garage, lifting a hand

to wave at a few people, offering a smile as she balanced a plastic container on her palm. Normally she was upbeat and relaxed at this sort of function, but not tonight. When she got to the door, she pulled her hand away from the knob. She had the feeling she should turn back and go home. She shouldn't be here. There was no point. The last time she'd been at a similar gathering, she'd made a complete fool of herself with Mike and had set this whole thing in motion. Now look where that had gotten her. Hurt and confused.

She was about to turn away when the door flew open and Alex stood there with baby Jamie in her arms.

"Finally!" Alex's grin was from ear to ear. "We were wondering when you'd show up!"

There was no turning back now.

She stepped inside and followed Alex to the kitchen. Because the other woman carried the baby, people moved aside for her to pass, and before Grace could protest, she was standing before Mike, who was dumping potato chips into a bowl.

He smiled, and her heart caught.

"Hey, Grace. Glad you could make it." He picked up the snacks, still grinning easily in her direction.

She'd steeled herself, prepared herself for seeing him again. Had given herself a stern talking-to about it being over and them being friends. She'd thrown away every single daisy that had been delivered to her, after a suitable period of admiration. And she'd been so sure that they could go back to their old relationship.

Then he said her name and smiled and it was all out

the window. She cared for him as much as she ever had. Her heart fluttered and her hands ached to reach out and touch him, to lose herself in his arms.

Alex was watching her strangely so she pasted on a smile and held out the container. "No potted plant from me, you'd kill it in a week," she joked weakly. "But I brought something else instead."

He put down the bowl in his hands and reached for the white plastic. "What is it?"

"Open it."

He lifted the lid and sighed appreciatively. "Caramel apple pie."

"I didn't think you'd do much baking for yourself, and I know what your appetite is like."

His eyes met hers and she felt the blush creep up her cheeks. Appetites indeed. A memory flashed through her mind, one of soft skin and sighs in the dark light of predawn. Her pulse jumped. Oh, this was silly! She had to at least try to keep things normal.

"Your party is hoppin'." Grace made her voice sound jaunty, keeping the strain from it. "Live band and everything."

"We've got a good turnout. Not just for me but for Circle M, too."

"Work in everything," Alex pretended to gripe. "Can't just have a party for party's sake. He and Connor have angles working you can't even imagine." She lifted Jamie up so he was face-to-face with her. "Speaking of, let's find your daddy and get you home, little man."

Alex put a hand on Grace's arm. "We're going to take the kids home with Johanna, but we'll be back."

Grace looked up at Mike. "They are obscenely happy."

"Yes, they are." His pale eyes searched hers and again wishes snuck in, ones she knew she had no right to have.

"Excuse me for a few minutes, okay?" He put his fingers on her arm. "I've got a few things to look after. But I'll be back."

He disappeared. Grace took the opportunity to grab a can of pop from a cooler sitting in the corner of the large kitchen. She wandered over to the bay window. Now, in the dark, the view was black, with only the hulking shadows of trucks and cars viewable.

The house was crowded, stifling. She grabbed a handful of pretzels from a low table and wandered out to the garage.

The band was playing something fast and couples were moving and turning in an East Coast Swing. Grace laughed as she saw Connor swirling Alex under his arm. On the sidelines, Johanna held the baby and Mike held Maren in his arms, the black-haired tot clapping her chubby hands along to the rousing music. Mike caught her watching, smiled and shrugged as if to say, "What could I do?" Seeing him holding the little girl only reinforced the knowledge that they'd done the right thing, breaking it off. He'd always want children of his own, and she'd hate to look into his eyes down the road and see resentment there for the babies she'd never be able to give him.

When the song ended, Connor took Maren from Mike's arms and the family left the concrete floor for the crisp fall air outside. Mike threaded his way through the crowd until he was at Grace's side.

"They were all set to leave, and then Connor decided he wanted to dance first."

"Connor's changed so much since Alex came into his life." Grace gazed at their departing figures. Connor held Maren in one arm, but his free hand was clasped in Alex's.

"Love will do that to a man," Mike answered.

Grace's gaze darted to his. But before she could think, he grabbed her hand and tugged. "Come on. It's time we danced."

The band struck up an old Vince Gill tune, and Mike pulled her into his arms for a waltz. Grace's breath grew shallow and she struggled to relax, her feet finding the three-count rhythm with his lead. The last time she'd danced with Mike she'd been drinking and that was how this whole thing had started. It had seemed harmless at the time, flirting and innuendoes. But Mike wasn't harmless. He was devastating.

His feet shuffled with the other couples, guiding her across the cold concrete floor. His hand was wide and firm along the hollow of her back as the words of the old song touched her, struck by their poignancy. She didn't have to wait for love to find her; she already knew. Knew because suddenly, in the space of a moment, love was being held in Mike's arms. Strong and secure, a shoulder to lean on when life got to be too much. It wasn't a random thing that Mike was the first person she'd ever shared her burden with, even if by doing so she'd killed her chances to be with him. Tears stung the back of her eyes as she wished yet again that she could give him everything he wanted. What he deserved. Most of the time she'd been able to forget feeling so inadequate. It was only when faced with her growing feelings, of wanting things, that she felt more of a disappointment than ever before.

As the guitarist played a solo, his arms pulled her closer and his steps shortened, making their turns more intimate. His hand slid beneath the hem of her sweater, resting sweetly on the tender skin of her back.

Her body came alive where his fingers touched, where their bodies grazed and met through the movements of the dance. One night with Mike wouldn't be enough. She'd known it then and had denied it. If she'd known how this would have all transpired months ago when she'd propositioned him, would she still have said what she had? About him being a tiger in bed? There was so much more to him, and as much as it hurt her to know they had no future, she couldn't bring herself to be sorry that they'd had something that had burned so brightly before dying out.

She could always hold in her heart the memory of what it was like to once have been loved by Mike Gardner. It would have to be enough.

The song's final notes drifted out and voices started

chattering again. Mike looked up at the singer, then back down at Grace.

"One more," he demanded, his hand still firm on her back. The music started, and for a moment Grace didn't recognize the old-fashioned-sounding tune. Then it struck her, and she smiled wistfully.

It was a deliberate ploy, but it touched her heart in ways she hadn't imagined.

It was the one-two-three rhythm of "I'll Give You a Daisy a Day, Dear." The sweetness of it filled her, the surprise of discovering Mike could be so sentimental. As they swirled around the makeshift floor, she rested her head in the hollow of his shoulder and let her body follow his like a shadow.

The band switched to an upbeat tempo and she heard Mike's voice, husky in her ear, "Come with me. I want to show you something."

He kept her hand in his, threading them through the other dancers and to the door of the house. The crowd inside had thinned, most now in the garage with the music or outside on the deck.

"You haven't seen the house since it was finished." They passed another couple in the foyer. "The decorating's still a bit sparse, but you'll get the idea."

Now that the throng had moved outside, Grace realized that there was very little in the living room. There was a coffee table and a single sofa, but no chairs, no knickknacks or pictures on the walls that made a house a home. In the kitchen was a drop leaf table with two chairs; the dining area was completely empty except for a temporary card table holding munchies and plastic bottles of pop for mixing drinks. Grace smiled to herself. Here was clearly a bachelor's pad, functional yet without the little touches. Yet the space was so well designed, she couldn't help but love it anyway. She felt guilty walking over the fine hardwood in her sneakers. As they passed through the kitchen to the hallway, she ran her fingers over the glossy woodwork. Everything was so new, so fresh.

The bathroom door was open, the light on for guests, but he guided her past it, and past the other doors leading to the spare bedrooms. "They aren't decorated yet," he explained softly. "I wanted to get the other rooms done first."

At the end of the hall he led her into his bedroom. A lamp burned in the corner, throwing a little circle of warm light into the space. It, too, was large and mostly empty except for a queen-size bed and a plain maple dresser. A navy comforter was pulled up over the bed, slightly askew and a pillow crooked on the top.

It was lonely, Grace realized. She left him at the door and went to the en suite, marveling at the white tile, the veined marble around the sink and the deep jetted tub. It was stunning, but somehow sterile. Like it hadn't been used. Waiting.

She went back out, turning off the light. "Your house is great, Mike. You must be so proud."

He shut the bedroom door, closing them in. "It's very plain, but there's a reason for that."

"There is?" He was walking closer and she tensed,

sensing something unpleasant was coming, which had to be ridiculous. Not after the way he'd touched her as they'd danced. There was nothing unpleasant in the whole evening. They'd been mending fences.

He stopped before her, and taking his hand from behind his back, held out a single daisy.

"I'm no good at decorating."

She laughed, a nervous giggle, belatedly reaching out to take the daisy. "Mike, you don't have to keep giving me flowers. Even a daisy a day." He had to have a standing order at the florist by now. "I'm not mad at you."

"Is that why you think I'm doing it?"

"Isn't it? Things haven't really been that great between us since…"

"Since the night we visited Alex at the hospital."

"Yes."

"It took me a while, and I know I've been, well, absent, I suppose. But I've figured out how to fix it."

"Oh, Mike," she sighed, turning away. "I don't know how we'd even begin to really fix things."

He reached out and his hand gripped her forearm. He tugged, pulling her close, then tipping her chin up with a finger.

"This is a good place to start," he murmured. His eyes closed, the lashes fluttering on his skin as he placed his lips gently on hers.

"Like this," he whispered, kissing the corners of her mouth, each one like a warm drop of candle wax, soft, marking her, making her ache in every sensitive part of her body.

She wound her hands up and around his shoulders, her fingertips touching the coarse hair on the back of his neck as the daisy fell to the floor. Loving Mike could be so easy, so natural. Her lips opened, responding as he covered her mouth fully and drew her up against the tall, hard length of his body. He was what she wanted. What she craved. What she needed. He always had been.

His hands ran down her arms, finally gripping her fingers in his as he dragged his mouth away. "Don't you see, Grace?"

Her breath came in short, aroused gasps. "See what?"

Oh goodness. When he turned those gray eyes on her that way she lost all her bearings. It had always been that way. His gaze plumbed hers earnestly, as if he was waiting for an answer to an unasked question.

"Don't you see I built this for you? That it's waiting for you? For you and me?"

The room tipped, then righted itself as she stared at him.

"Built this for me?" she echoed it stupidly. "But… you started building it before we ever even… You broke ground the day you told me Alex was in hospital."

"And designed it before then."

"I don't understand."

He lifted one of her hands and pressed a kiss to it. "Did you think I hadn't noticed you before then?

And the night we danced, and you said those things...
I couldn't stop thinking about you. For the first time,
I could see myself really settling. Not just with the
ranch...the business was already going...but person-
ally. I wanted to deserve you. I thought—after I'd made
such a mess of things the first time—that it was over.
And then you said those things and everything changed.
I made *plans.*"

But Mike doesn't plan, she thought in a daze. "You
planned this. The dating. The house. Everything."

It came out flatly and she saw the corners of his
lips turn down in a frown. "I didn't orchestrate every
movement, if that's what you mean," he replied tightly.
"I just... I wanted... Oh, dammit, I wanted you to have
this. To have *me.*"

Panic left her cold. "Did it ever occur to you to ask
me what I wanted?"

When he remained speechless, she backed away.
This wasn't right. When she'd married Steve, he'd had
their life planned out. He'd suggested the new job and
the move to Edmonton. He'd found the perfect house.
He'd been the one to want to wait to have children. And
when he'd decided their marriage wasn't going to work
anymore he'd been the one to file for divorce.

And the moment she'd signed her name to the papers, she'd decided right then and there that no man
would ever plan her life out for her again.

Yet that was exactly what she'd allowed Mike to do.
He'd controlled the reins all along, she realized. And it

had to stop here before they got even more hurt, if that were possible.

"Ask you?"

She gathered all the strength she had inside and wrapped herself in it for protection. "Did you expect me to be flattered, Mike? To fall at your feet and thank you for your devotion?"

From the incredulous expression on his face, she could tell that was exactly what he'd expected, and it infuriated her further.

"And the daisies? Was that your brilliant lead-up? Soften me up and then hit me with a grand gesture?"

His jaw hardened. "You do understand what I'm trying to say here, don't you, Grace? And you're throwing it all back in my face."

"Ever since I started doing the books for Circle M you've thought it your *right* to run my life. To tell me where I can or can't work. Tried to pay my way. But not once did you think that you could have been insulting me!"

His head snapped up. "You feel insulted? Me wanting to be with you, building you a house, wanting to take care of you, that *insults* you?"

"Don't you respect me enough to let me make my own decisions?"

"This isn't about that!"

She began to pace, her sneakers making dull thuds against the bare floor. "It's exactly about that! I went through this once already, Mike, and I won't do it again! Steve had our whole life mapped out—house, cars, kids when it was time…and when things didn't go according to plan he left. I made up my mind then and there that I would never give anyone that control again! I make my own decisions. I run my own life. I don't need you to take care of me! I can't believe you thought this would be okay!"

"What should I have done then, Grace? Come to you months ago and told you I was designing a house? And that I wanted you in it, so could you please give me your input? That's ludicrous!"

He really didn't see that he'd done anything wrong, she realized. He still thought it was okay that he'd done all this without a word to her. "I already have a house. You might have considered that. And you might have considered telling me your feelings and asking mine before doing such a stupid thing as building a house for me."

His voice dripped ice. "And what would you have said to me, Grace? If I'd come to you and told you that I thought I was falling for you and I wanted to build us a house and have babies?"

Those last words were like cold steel slicing into her body, a low blow she hadn't thought he was capable of. "That's unfair. Knowing what you know…I can't believe you'd use that against me."

"I didn't know then, remember? For all I knew, until a few weeks ago, you could have, and probably wanted, children!"

"Because it was my business to tell!"

"And isn't it interesting, that when you finally did

tell me, it was after we'd made love and you were scared to death!"

The room went deathly silent.

"What are you saying, Mike? That I used what happened to me?" The words were low and carefully enunciated.

"Maybe that's exactly what I'm saying. You used it to hide from me. You take your injury and wear it like armor to keep anyone from getting too close. And look what happened the one time you let your guard down. We made love. We were as close as two human beings could be and that scared the life out of you. And you're back to hiding behind it again! Using it to hide what your real problem is!"

"Oh, please," she replied, the words ripe with contempt. "Please, tell me what my *problem* is."

Mike hooked his thumbs into his pockets. "Your problem, Grace, is that you're terrified. You're scared I can't love you enough. That eventually I'm going to leave. Like I did before. You don't believe me when I say I'm in this for the long run. You think that someday I'll turn around and realize you aren't what I wanted after all. And so you hide behind what you think is real so that you don't have to deal with that."

When it was out he inhaled sharply, surprised he'd been callous—and courageous—enough to say all that. All the color drained from her face and tears streaked down her cheeks, although her eyes never blinked. He watched the pain etch itself on her features as all he'd said sunk in, saw flickers of hatred burn in her eyes.

But this time he wouldn't turn away. She could hate him, hit him, cry, whatever. But he wasn't backing down. This was too important. If nothing else, they had to take this back down to the basics, start over.

Her mouth opened and closed a few times, but no words came out. Finally, after several seconds, she pushed past him, wrenched open the door and flew down the hall.

He followed her with long strides, ignoring the curious stares from his guests. She ran out the front door and down the driveway to her car. He paused on the front steps, his hands braced on the railing.

When he turned his head, he saw Alex and Connor staring up from the bottom of the stairs.

"Mike?"

He swallowed against the lump in his throat. He'd been too hard on her. He'd thought he'd been doing the right thing by telling her about the house.

He'd been very wrong.

He was sure of one thing, though. With his brutal honesty, he'd done enough damage for one night. For a lifetime.

"Go after her," Alex urged.

Connor said nothing. But when Mike looked in his friend's eyes he knew Connor understood.

"Let her go," Mike said hoarsely, looking out over the road where her headlights flashed out of sight. "Nothing's going to fix this now."

Chapter 12

Mike gritted his teeth as Alex put her hands on her hips and said, "She's distraught. You should at least go after her."

"And say what, Alex? I can't fix this. She needs time. Time to figure out what she truly wants."

"Men!" Alex exploded. Connor gave her a warning glance but she kept at Mike anyway.

He let her. It momentarily distracted him from remembering the crushed look on Grace's face. He hadn't meant to be cruel.

"She doesn't need *time*. She needs *you*, only you're too stupid to see it!"

Mike met Alex's eyes evenly. "I don't know how to help her. Lord knows I've tried. I don't know what else to do. All we end up doing is hurting each other more."

He knew everything he'd said tonight had been excruciatingly painful and to say more would be to break their bond completely. That was the last thing he wanted.

Alex sighed, her face softening. She came up the steps to the landing and lifted a hand to his face, touching his cheek gently. "Love her, Mike. Just love her and everything else will fall into place."

With that she was gone.

Could it really be that easy?

Mike looked at Alex and Connor as they walked home through the shadows, the porch light from Windover guiding their way. He shook his head in wonderment. Connor had proposed to Alex on the same day he'd met her, and acknowledging that they'd grown to love each other had been a huge risk. But so obviously worth it. He ran his fingers through his hair. It was easier to build houses and make plans than to talk about emotions. But maybe that was what Grace needed. Maybe that was what they both needed in order to move past this.

Grace pulled her knees closer to her chest, wrapping her arms around them. Very few people knew of this place, and she liked it that way. From the top of this hill she could see straight west to the mountains, the sky opened up before her. The only way here was on the dirt service road. It was where she came to think, to be alone. To heal.

The trees that bordered the meadow were completely naked now, and the afternoon light that filtered through the light cloud cover had lost its fall richness and seemed watery and thin. She shivered once in her heavy jacket, then took gloves out of the pockets and slid them on. Winter was coming. The warm wooing of fall was over and the cold seemed here to stay.

It had been four days since Mike's housewarming and there'd been no word from him after all. No phone calls, no daisies. It had been silly of her to hope he'd come back and say he was sorry, but after their harsh words, it was probably time she accepted it was truly over. There was nothing left to work out.

A magpie pecked at the ground, its long blue tail bobbing awkwardly. She'd discovered this spot as a teen, had first truly fallen for Mike in its spring grasses, had come here before she left for college, had returned after she and Steve had split up, and a few times since when life seemed to get to be too much. She hadn't been here in a long time. But now…she'd come back because never, not even after her divorce, had she felt as empty as she did right at this moment.

She rocked gently, the dry grass crackling beneath her bottom. She missed Mike, more than she'd thought she could. At first she'd been angry, righteous and convinced he was wrong. She'd cried what felt like buckets, but eventually all that had burned out and she started to wonder if he was right.

What if it wasn't about the babies but about her? Was she really hiding behind her infertility, so that she wouldn't get left again? And what did that mean? She'd never have a relationship again?

Now it was her birthday, she was twenty-eight years old, alone and more screwed up than she'd ever been in her life.

Did she really believe Mike would leave her eventually? That she wouldn't measure up?

She didn't like the answer that came back. Didn't like what it said about who she'd become.

She turned at the sound of a vehicle approaching along the road. His truck turned the corner and pulled up next to her car. Nerves skittered along her arms and legs. Mike was the only person who knew how she felt about this place. He hadn't forgotten, then. That he'd thought to find her here told her how close they really had become.

And how far apart they were, for her to seek it out.

When he stepped out of the truck, bundled against the cold in his brown jacket and his hat shadowing his face, her breath quickened. Just when she thought everything was over, he appeared. And she couldn't stop the reaction that rippled through her body at seeing him again.

But it could mean nothing, she reminded herself. It could simply be about the accounts for Circle M. Or tying up their loose ends, getting some closure. She pushed herself to her feet, tucking her hair behind her ears nervously.

He slammed the truck door and approached with his long, lazy strides. Seeing him felt so good she wanted to cry with relief. But knowing all that had gone wrong between them kept her rooted to her spot, waiting.

When he reached her, he held out his hand. In it was not one daisy, but a whole bouquet. At least forty stems, all blinking up cheerily at her. The fresh white petals and yellow centers were a touch of spring in an otherwise decidedly Novemberish day. "Happy birthday, Grace," he said softly.

His hand was holding out the flowers and he looked at her expectantly. She reached out to take the stems from his hand, their gloved fingers brushing. The current sang through her skin, even through the fabric covering her hands. "Thank you," she whispered softly, lifting them to her nose and giving them a long sniff. They smelled like summer.

"Today's not a one-daisy day."

She swallowed, gathering up her courage and meeting his gaze directly. "There haven't been any one-daisy days lately."

He took her left hand in his, his thumbs resting possessively on the top of her knuckles. "I know," he said, "And I'm sorry."

His eyes were earnest in his apology. As much as she wanted to stay mad at him for all he'd done, she didn't have the energy. Her lips rubbed together as emotions piled one on top of each other. She struggled to respond, but the words wouldn't come. He was here. He'd not only remembered her birthday, but knew her well enough to know where to find her when she was troubled. In her heart, she knew that no matter how things were fractured, nothing was over between them.

He squeezed her hands and kept going, his breath making white clouds in the air between them.

"I went about things all wrong. I shouldn't have sprung the house on you like I did. I won't apologize for picturing you in it when I planned it. But I will say I'm sorry for expecting you to conform to what I wanted. And I'm very sorry for hurting you. The last thing I ever wanted to do was hurt you, Grace. You must know that."

Oh, his eyes were pleading with her, and the sincerity in the gray-blue depths touched her. Mike wasn't a man of many words, especially not the sentimental kind. For him to express his regret so earnestly told her how badly he was feeling, too.

"I know you wouldn't, not on purpose. But you did hurt me, Mike, and I don't bounce back as well as a lot of people think."

"I know that now. I never understood it until...well, until you were gone and I had a chance to think. I was..."

He stopped.

He couldn't make the words come out. She tried to help. "You were..."

He cleared his throat gruffly. "I was scared. I was afraid you would say no. So I tried to control the situation."

"And you tried to control where I worked and how I fixed my car and how much sleep I got." She tucked away a strand of hair that ruffled across her lips in the cold breeze.

"You know why."

She turned away. Yes, she knew why, but it was no good unless he could bring himself to say it, and she knew Mike well enough to know he couldn't say the words. And she couldn't go further without hearing them.

She'd thought that their final goodbye had been with a resounding crash last Saturday night, but now realized that it would happen with barely a whisper as they finished closing all their doors.

He didn't love her like she needed him to. And he'd been right; she'd always wonder when he'd realize it and decide it was time to move on. What she wanted was more than he was capable of. And anything less wouldn't cut it.

"It doesn't matter now, Mike. I'm just glad we're not ending things with animosity between us."

He hadn't come all this way only to fail. Maybe he'd gone about it the wrong way—planning their lives out without consulting her had been a serious error in judgment on his part—but he couldn't let her walk away now. Not after all they'd shared. He knew what he'd overcome to get to this point. To a point where being with her mattered more than admitting his own fears and shortcomings. If he failed, he'd be back to where he started, and he was too afraid to go back there again. For once in his life, he was more scared to lose someone than to love them.

"But it does matter. It's the most important thing, don't you see? I know I was heavy-handed and it looked like I didn't trust you to run your own life. But I did it because I loved you so much it scared the hell out of me."

Her knees went watery and she wished she could sit down so he wouldn't see her tremble. He loved her. He'd actually brought himself to say the words, words she never thought she'd ever hear from his lips. It should have made things easier. She'd thought that if he said it, and meant it, she'd be free. But she wasn't. Because now she absolutely knew they'd both come out of this hurt sooner or later. Maybe he loved her now, but down the road, when he wanted the family they couldn't have, things would change. She didn't know which was worse…letting go now, or letting things go on and have him resent her as she knew he would.

And right now she hated herself for all that she was, and wasn't. She hated the accident that meant that she could never have children. The longing to have his babies was so strong, but there had never been a possibility of that. Had she been hiding behind it to avoid feeling too much? To deny the fact that the idea of loving him and losing him was so painful she didn't know if she could bear it?

Because she'd never loved Steve the way she loved Mike, and it was tearing her apart, being so close and yet with such a gulf between them.

"Grace." He stood before her, his large hands resting on her shoulders, reassuring her. Now that he'd said it, let out how he felt, it was like he'd been set free. "Baby, you've got to say it. You've got to tell me how you're feeling. It's the only way we can move past it, don't you see?"

His eyes searched hers as more emotions than he could fathom ran across her face. She'd been suffering so much for so long, without telling anyone. And when she finally trusted him with it, he'd turned it against her. He wouldn't do that again.

"You trusted me before," he coaxed. "Trust me again, Grace. Just say it, and stop letting it control you."

"I can't."

With a growl of frustration Mike turned and started to walk away. The world dropped out from underneath her as she realized that if he walked away now it would be her fault. She would be the one to drive the permanent wedge between them and that was something she couldn't bear. He wasn't more than a dozen steps before she called out.

"Mike! Wait..."

He stopped and a sick feeling revolved in her stomach as the fears fought to be given voice. Her breath came in short gasps.

"I feel...I feel..." Oh God, she couldn't do it. It was too much pain. She took a breath and set it free on a trail of tears. "I feel *broken*."

In an instant, he closed the distance between them and she was in his arms, cradled against him, wrapped in his strong embrace as it all came out in one giant release. The bouquet of daisies dropped. He held her as they sank into the cold grass, holding her close on his lap. His hat fell to the ground as she said it again, her voice rife with despair.

"Mike, I'm broken."

"Oh, baby, you are not broken. I promise."

"Then why does nothing make sense anymore?"

"I don't know. Maybe because you're letting yourself *feel* for the first time in a long time. We both are. Being without you is suddenly the scariest thing I've ever known."

His voice was thick with his own emotions, she realized as she sobbed against his chest. All the hurt…it all came spilling out finally. It was more than revealing her secret, more than making love to avoid facing the truth. It was laying herself bare with the one person she trusted enough to see it.

"I'm never enough, don't you see that? I always feel like there's something lacking." Her breath hitched between the words as she tried unsuccessfully to control the sobs. "Like if I just did *better* it would be okay. I'm…I'm doing the best I can and it's not good enough. It's never good enough."

"And if you're not perfect, then the people you love will let you go and look for someone they want more. And you'll be back where you started, only a little more hurt and a little more guarded. And it gets harder and harder for someone to crack the layers."

She sighed and shifted so that she could look up in his face. He looked so tortured himself she knew he understood, and she forgot her own pain for a moment and wondered how much he'd been suffering, too.

"Like you."

He nodded. "Don't you know how hard it was for me to tell you how I feel? The moment you put your heart out there, it's asking to be stomped on."

"And you thought I would, after the other night." He'd offered her everything he had, and she'd thrown it back in his face. No matter what her reasons, she knew that had hurt him deeply.

He nodded. "It just got to a point where *not* saying it got harder than telling you how I felt." He wrapped his arms tighter around her. "I'm glad you trusted me, Grace."

"I feel safe with you." She said it and knew it was completely true. "You were right, I did trust you before. And what made everything ten times harder was knowing that even though I felt safe and secure, I still felt like eventually you'd realize we'd made a mistake. I couldn't admit how much my feelings for you had grown."

Mike tucked her head beneath his chin. "Growing up like I did...I couldn't say those things. Sooner or later I got moved around to another house, another set of parents. If I didn't get close, then I didn't get hurt. I was so busy protecting myself that I didn't have time to think about how badly I wanted someone to want me. To love me. But then...then there was you. And you were different."

"How was I different?"

He smiled, lifting a finger and running it over where her hairline met her left ear. "You were always so gentle. Beautiful and kind and sweet. Strong and loyal. Four years younger and a pain in the neck. Remember that time when you were in fifth grade and Billy Perkins was making fun of me for being a foster kid? You let him have a piece of your mind. And while it was embarrassing for a kid my age to have a little girl stand up for him, you never knew how much it meant to me. And then…for a while I let you in. You'll never know how those few weeks we were together affected me. I felt love for the first time in a long time. And it scared me and I pushed you away.

"But even after you went away and came back, I always looked out for you, because I knew you'd do the same for me. And then one night you danced with me and said some wildly inappropriate things. I couldn't help but imagine what it would be like to be with you again."

He pressed his forehead to hers.

"Grace, you said before you trusted me because I made you feel safe. Don't you see it? I've never in my life told a woman I loved her. And despite everything, I did it today because you're my safe place, too. In some way, you always have been."

For long moments they sat just that way, eyes closed, absorbing strength from each other. Grace didn't know whether to cry or laugh. She was brimming over with every emotion she could imagine.

"I wish…" She paused, sighed. "I don't know how to fix me."

"Honey, trust me. You do not need to be fixed. I promise."

"I love you, Mike. I always have."

She didn't realize how much he'd been waiting for her to say it until she did and all the air in his lungs came out in a grand rush. He slid her off his legs and stood up abruptly, striding away with his back to her, halting just as quickly and dropping his head toward the ground.

"I'm sorry," she whispered, rising and moving to stand slightly behind him, her hand gentle on his upper arm. "I didn't know."

He didn't look at her, but she saw a tear drop onto his hand and her heart broke all over again, this time for the man who'd gone without love his whole life, who would rather die than admit how much he needed it.

"No one's ever said it to you before, have they?"

He shook his head and her own tears threatened yet again.

Mike brushed a hand over his face and let out a small laugh. "God, what a pair we make."

Her fingers trailed down to grasp his. "It's okay to cry, you know. There was a lifetime of hurt building up in both of us." She smiled to herself. "I went a long time without crying, but the last few months I've more than made up for it."

After one brief, bracing breath, he faced her again. The lines on his face were gone, the strain absent.

"We both let fear get in the way. But I'm not scared of this, Grace. I'm not afraid of *us*."

He cupped her face in his hands and captured her lips in a kiss that took her breath away. The first one with the words shared between them, and it felt different. Freer, more honest. She opened to him fully; this was no time for holding back. His arms came around her, cinching her ribs and lifting her until her toes dangled off the ground as he assaulted her with his mouth.

When the kiss broke off, she dropped her gaze. There was more, much more they had to talk about. Because despite everything, she still wasn't convinced that anything was going to work. It physically hurt her to pull her hand away. He was giving her everything she'd ever wanted…laying his heart on the line…but…

"Stop that." His command had her head snapping up sharply.

"Stop what?"

"Don't pull away. I can feel you doing it, putting that distance between us again. Don't. Not after all we've done to get this far."

"Don't do this," she whispered. He was going to pursue it, she could tell. And they still had one very large problem.

"Don't do what? I don't understand. I told you I loved you, and you said you loved me. What more is there?"

She faced him, trying to keep her expression neutral to hide the pain she felt at saying the words. "Don't give me hope where there isn't any, Mike. We both know there's still the issue of the family I'll never be able to give you."

"You mean that we'll never have babies together."

She winced when he put it so plainly. "Yes, that's exactly what I mean. You know you want kids. Maren adores you, and I know it's mutual. I've seen how you look at Jamie. It's not fair for you to be tied down to someone who can't give you that."

"Don't you think that's my decision?"

"Maybe...but it's me that'll be hurt when you decide to walk away. When you realize you want more than I can give you."

"When I said I love you, I meant it to be forever. Don't you get that I love you as you are?" His large hands were firm on her forearms. "You look at me, Grace Lundquist. Maybe in the beginning you were this ideal I had. Sweet and caring and beautiful. Cherished. And you still are those things...but you're so much more than that. I want *you,* not some ideal woman I've constructed in my head."

She persisted. "You say that now, but you know you want children."

"It so happens, I've been doing some thinking about that."

She stared at the buttons of his shirt. How easy it would be to reach out and touch him, run her fingers over those buttons, open them, feel the smooth skin of his chest. Forget that issues even existed between them. But she couldn't afford to ignore it.

"We have some options, you know." He dipped his head to look down on her. "There are too many kids out there in foster care that need someone to love and care for them. Someone who won't send them back when things don't go quite right. Someone who will let them know that they're worth the trouble. When Jamie was born, I looked in the nursery and wondered how many of those babies weren't wanted. Trust me, Grace. Blood doesn't matter as much as love."

Her head swam. Mike would consider adopting? A glimpse of hope for the future flashed through her mind, of her, and Mike, and a row of children in all shapes and sizes. Her heart thumped heavily. "You'd be happy, even though they wouldn't be yours?"

He lifted a hand and tenderly cradled her cheek in his warmth. "Happy? Are you kidding? They'd be ours. Yours and mine and our family. Do you think Connor loves Maren any less because she's not his flesh and blood?"

When he pulled away, he took a step and reached into the pocket of his jacket. He took out a small box wrapped in silver foil paper and tied with white ribbon.

"A birthday requires more of a present than just flowers, don't you think?" He held it out in his hand, offering it to her.

She took the box, her heart beating erratically. Surely not. It was the right size, but it could be earrings or a brooch. After all that had happened today, there couldn't possibly be a proposal, too. It was all too much.

Tentatively she untied the ribbon, letting it slip off the shiny paper. She removed the paper neatly, finding a square jeweler's box inside. She lifted the top and took out the velvet box.

With a faint creak she opened the lid, her hand trembling as she beheld the diamond-studded band inside.

"Oh, Mike."

Mike, rodeo rider, tough guy and all-round cowboy was getting down on one knee in an Alberta meadow and she didn't know what to do. Speechless, she let him take her free hand in his as he looked up at her.

"Marry me, Grace. I know I was pushy and inconsiderate before. I'm sorry that I tried to control everything. Where we live…that's something we can decide together. I want to see you in a white dress, beneath that arch that Connor built for Alex. I want to hear the minister call us husband and wife and know that it's real."

She opened her lips to respond but he kept going, to her increasing delight. All her hopes, all her dreams, were being filled; all her fears allayed as the words from his heart healed her in ways that time never could.

"Don't you see, Grace? I love you. And it's not the kind of love that gets bored or that has expectations. It just *is*. It's a part of me, like breathing."

Her fingers covered her mouth. She knew. Knew in her heart that she had nothing to fear with Mike. He would safeguard her with everything he was. He was offering her all of himself—she only had to be strong enough to take it.

He rose, standing before her. She looked up into his eyes, wanting him to look at her in just *this way* for the rest of her life.

"Love me, Mike. Marry me."

She slid off her glove as he took the ring from the box. Her hand trembled as he slid it over her finger.

"Thank God," he whispered, pulling her close in his arms.

* * * * *

*Meet two diamonds in the rough in the poignant
new* CADENCE CREEK COWBOYS *duet
from acclaimed author Donna Alward!*

Enjoy this sneak peek from book 1,
THE LAST REAL COWBOY, *available May 2012
from Harlequin® Romance.*

"YOUR CAT BIT ME!"

Heat rushed to Angela's face as Sam's words moved her
to action. She scrambled after Morris and picked him up.
Cursed animal, he snuggled into her arms sweet as honey.
"He has a thing about strangers. Particularly men." She
rushed to the half bath and locked Morris inside. "I think he
was abused as a kitten," she continued, wondering if there
was anything more she could do to make Sam Diamond
more aggravated. "The vet said his tail was broken in three
places. That's why it's crooked. But he really isn't a bad
cat—he just has a protective streak. He…"

Her voice trailed off. Sam was staring at her as if she was
crazy. "I'll shut up now," she murmured.

"Really," Sam said drily, as if she'd stated the impossible.

Morris meowed in protest, the howl only barely muffled
through the door.

"You're a real bleeding heart, aren't you, Ms. Beck?"
He glowered at her. "Maybe I need to come up with a better
sob story, eh? Maybe that'll get you off my back."

That did it. "Since when did helping others become a
flaw, Diamond?" She took a step forward, feeling her temper get the better of her. "Maybe if you took your head out
of your charmed, privileged life for two seconds you'd see
someone other than yourself. And as far as Morris goes,
maybe I am a bleeding heart because I can't stand to see

another creature abused. And if he's a little leery of men, he has good reason. I consider him a fine judge of character!"

Sam's dark eyes flared. "A fine judge of…" He made a sound like air whistling out of a tube. Morris howled again. "You know nothing about me. Nothing."

"I know you're a big bully who thinks I'll dance to his tune because I need his money. But I won't pander to you like Charles Spring and the others on the board. You can threaten, you can take funding away. Go for it. Because I would rather that than me betray all Butterfly House stands for by letting myself be pushed around by the likes of you."

Will the sparks flying between Sam and Angela ignite into romance?

Find out in THE LAST REAL COWBOY by Donna Alward, available in May 2012. And stay tuned for THE REBEL RANCHER, book 2 in the CADENCE CREEK COWBOYS *duet, coming in June 2012!*

Harlequin *Romance*

Save $1.00 on the purchase of
THE LAST REAL COWBOY
by award-winning author
Donna Alward,

Available in May 2012,
or on any other Harlequin® Romance book.

Available wherever books are sold, including most bookstores,
supermarkets, drugstores and discount stores.

- ✂

Save $1.00

**on the purchase of
THE LAST REAL COWBOY by
award-winning author Donna Alward,**
available in May 2012,
or on any other Harlequin® Romance book.

Coupon valid until August 31, 2012. Redeemable at participating retail outlets
in the U.S. and Canada only. Limit one coupon per customer.

52610341

Canadian Retailers: Harlequin Enterprises Limited will pay the face value
of this coupon plus 10.25¢ if submitted by customer for this product only. Any
other use constitutes fraud. Coupon is nonassignable. Void if taxed, prohibited
or restricted by law. Consumer must pay any government taxes. Void if copied.
Nielsen Clearing House ("NCH") customers submit coupons and proof of sales to
Harlequin Enterprises Limited, P.O. Box 3000, Saint John, NB E2L 4L3, Canada.
Non-NCH retailer—for reimbursement submit coupons and proof of sales directly
to Harlequin Enterprises Limited, Retail Marketing Department, 225 Duncan Mill
Rd., Don Mills, ON M3B 3K9, Canada.

5 65373 00076 2   (8100)0 11792

U.S. Retailers: Harlequin Enterprises
Limited will pay the face value of this coupon
plus 8¢ if submitted by customer for this
product only. Any other use constitutes fraud.
Coupon is nonassignable. Void if taxed,
prohibited or restricted by law. Consumer must
pay any government taxes. Void if copied. For
reimbursement submit coupons and proof of
sales directly to Harlequin Enterprises Limited,
P.O. Box 880478, El Paso, TX 88588-0478,
U.S.A. Cash value 1/100 cents.

® and TM are trademarks owned and used by the trademark owner and/or its licensee.
© 2012 Harlequin Enterprises Limited

NYTCOUP0412

REQUEST YOUR FREE BOOKS!

2 FREE NOVELS
FROM THE ROMANCE COLLECTION
PLUS 2 FREE GIFTS!

YES! Please send me 2 FREE novels from the Romance Collection and my 2 FREE gifts (gifts are worth about $10). After receiving them, if I don't wish to receive any more books, I can return the shipping statement marked "cancel." If I don't cancel, I will receive 4 brand-new novels every month and be billed just $5.99 per book in the U.S. or $6.49 per book in Canada. That's a saving of at least 25% off the cover price. It's quite a bargain! Shipping and handling is just 50¢ per book in the U.S. and 75¢ per book in Canada.* I understand that accepting the 2 free books and gifts places me under no obligation to buy anything. I can always return a shipment and cancel at any time. Even if I never buy another book, the two free books and gifts are mine to keep forever.

194/394 MDN FELQ

Name	(PLEASE PRINT)	
Address		Apt. #
City	State/Prov.	Zip/Postal Code

Signature (if under 18, a parent or guardian must sign)

Mail to the **Reader Service:**
IN U.S.A.: P.O. Box 1867, Buffalo, NY 14240-1867
IN CANADA: P.O. Box 609, Fort Erie, Ontario L2A 5X3

Not valid for current subscribers to the Romance Collection
or the Romance/Suspense Collection.

Want to try two free books from another line?
Call 1-800-873-8635 or visit www.ReaderService.com.

* Terms and prices subject to change without notice. Prices do not include applicable taxes. Sales tax applicable in N.Y. Canadian residents will be charged applicable taxes. Offer not valid in Quebec. This offer is limited to one order per household. All orders subject to credit approval. Credit or debit balances in a customer's account(s) may be offset by any other outstanding balance owed by or to the customer. Please allow 4 to 6 weeks for delivery. Offer available while quantities last.

Your Privacy—The Reader Service is committed to protecting your privacy. Our Privacy Policy is available online at www.ReaderService.com or upon request from the Reader Service.

We make a portion of our mailing list available to reputable third parties that offer products we believe may interest you. If you prefer that we not exchange your name with third parties, or if you wish to clarify or modify your communication preferences, please visit us at www.ReaderService.com/consumerschoice or write to us at Reader Service Preference Service, P.O. Box 9062, Buffalo, NY 14269. Include your complete name and address.

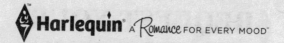

CLASSICS

Quintessential, modern love stories
that are romance at its finest.

Harlequin Presents®
Glamorous international settings…
unforgettable men…passionate
romances—Harlequin Presents
promises you the world!

Harlequin Presents® Extra
Meet more of your favorite Presents
heroes and travel to glamorous
international locations in our regular
monthly themed collections.

Harlequin® Romance
The anticipation, the thrill of the chase
and the sheer rush of falling in love!

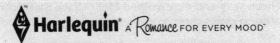

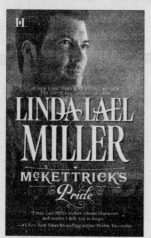